THE
GENOME

THE GENOME

A NOVEL

SERGEI LUKYANENKO

OPEN ROAD

INTEGRATED MEDIA

NEW YORK

Copyright © 2014 by Sergei Lukyanenko

Translated by Liv Bliss

Cover design by Mauricio Díaz

978-1-4976-4396-3

Published in 2014 by Open Road Integrated Media, Inc.
345 Hudson Street
New York, NY 10014
www.openroadmedia.com

The author is fully aware that many will deem this novel cynical and immoral. And yet, with humble respect, he dedicates the book to people capable of Love, Friendship, and Hard Work.

THE
GENOME

OPERON I, RECESSIVE.

THE SPESHES.

CHAPTER 1.

Alex gazed into the sky.

Its appearance was strange. Irregular. Unprecedented.

The kind that happens over worlds still unspoiled by civilization. The kind of sky that might happen over Earth, humanity's home planet, a world trashed and flushed clean three times over.

But over Quicksilver Pit, the industrial center of the sector, a planet of three shipyards with all the necessary infrastructure, this kind of sky simply should not be.

Alex gazed up.

Clear, iridescent blue. Scattered threads of clouds. Pink glow of the setting sun. A glider gamboling as playfully as a puppy in a snowdrift. Never before, not through the hospital window, not on the planetary news programs, had he seen such a sky over Quicksilver Pit.

There was something odd about the whole city today. The setting sun splashed a warm pink over the walls of the buildings. The last remnants of dirty snow clung to the support columns of the old monorail, spaced out along the highway. Once in a very long while, a car would rush by, as if afraid to tear the silence, slipping away so fast it seemed in a hurry to escape this suddenly unfamiliar, pink world.

Or maybe this was the way the world should look to a person just emerging from five months' confinement to a hospital ward.

"No one meeting you?"

Alex turned to the guard. Whiling away his time, bored in his plexiglass booth, the guard cut a strapping figure. Ruddy cheeks, shoulders three feet wide, a stun gun on his belt, and a bulletproof vest over his uniform—as though someone planned to storm the hospital.

"I don't have anybody."

"You from far away?"

"Uh-huh." Alex reached for his cigarettes. Drew the smoke of the strong local tobacco deep into his lungs.

"Need a taxi? You're dressed kind of light for this weather, friend . . ."

The guard was evidently eager to help.

"No, thanks. I'll take the rail."

"Comes once an hour," warned the guard. "It's free public transport, for the naturals . . ."

To be honest, he looked like a natural himself. Not that you could tell anything by looks.

"That's why I'm taking the rail, 'cos it's free."

The guard gave Alex a once-over, then glanced at the hospital buildings behind him.

"No, no, I am a spesh," explained Alex. "I'm just broke, that's all.

Work insurance plan. I couldn't have paid for the treatment myself. They could have brought me here in a basket . . . well, maybe they did. I don't remember."

He slashed a hand across his own waist, indicating the invisible line that, five months ago, had divided his body and his life in two. He felt an overwhelming need to share, to talk to someone who hadn't seen his medical charts, someone who would listen, appreciate, click his tongue . . .

"Rotten luck," sighed the guard. "Well, now you're all right? Main parts back to normal?"

Alex stepped on the cigarette butt and nodded in response to the guard's conspiratorial smirk.

"Like new . . . Well, thanks."

"For what?" replied the guard in surprise.

But Alex was already on his way to the road. He walked fast, not looking back. They had really done a splendid job of patching him up. He couldn't have wished for better treatment . . . especially in his situation. But now, since having signed the last insurance document half an hour ago, affirming that he had no complaints against the medical personnel and proclaiming his condition "identical to pre-trauma state," nothing connected him to the hospital anymore. Absolutely nothing.

Or to this planet, for that matter. But leaving Quicksilver Pit would be much harder.

On the side of the highway, he waited for a speeding car to pass, a luxurious, sporty, bright-red *Cayman*. Crossed over to the monorail support column, and walked up the spiral staircase—the elevator, of course, was out of order.

"Well, we're on our own again, just you and me. Right, Demon?" he said into the air. Then glanced sideways at his shoulder.

Alex's clothes really were all wrong for the weather, even this unexpected thaw which had burst upon the city on the eve of Independence Day. His jeans and shoes, bought for pennies donated by a local charity fund, were more or less all right. But the leather vest over a sleeveless jersey looked weird.

At least his Demon seemed to be having a good time.

It lived on his left shoulder: a color tattoo some four inches tall, a small demon with a pitchfork in its hands, who stared into space with a gloomy and disapproving air. Its long tail was wrapped around its waist, probably to keep the Demon's legs from getting tangled up in it. The Demon's short gray fur looked like a set of fuzzy clinging overalls.

For a while Alex stared suspiciously at the Demon's little face. It wore an inquisitive, calm expression. Self-assured.

"We're gonna make it, bro," said Alex. He leaned over the guardrail of the train stop, looked down below, spat onto the shiny steel rail.

There was nobody else around. Maybe the free municipal transport was unpopular, or maybe it was just that kind of day. A day of a blue sky, a pink sunset, the end of a holiday. Yesterday the whole hospital had celebrated . . . Even Alex, formally still a patient, was given some alcohol, mixed with glucose and vitamins.

Here at the height of some thirty-two feet, gusty wind reigned supreme. Alex even considered going back down and taking shelter behind the column while he waited for the train. But, after all, it was more interesting up here. There was a panoramic view of the city, its even rows of skyscrapers, its grid of straight roads already showing bright flashes of ads. It was a very geometrical city. On the other side, beyond the empty, long-derelict fields, he could make out the dim outlines of the spaceport. The port was too close to the city, Alex thought . . . Well, maybe that was what had saved his life. His surgeon had let it slip that the life-support IC unit to which Alex had been connected spent its back-up battery power and clicked off just as he was put onto the operating table.

Who could have ever guessed he would actually need his comprehensive insurance policy one day? Someone in the office of the Third Freight-and-Passenger station would gnash his teeth signing off on the medical bills. Well, they didn't really have a choice.

"We'll make it," he promised his Demon again. Spat once more onto the rail. Felt a slight tremor. The monorail car was drawing near.

It moved at a very leisurely pace. Alex estimated its speed at thirty point two miles per hour. It was completely covered with spirited graffiti, as though the car was trying to compensate for its lack of speed by the intricate brightness of its decoration. It was almost dusk, and some of the signs and drawings gave off a dim phosphorescence; others sparkled, flowed, changed colors.

"Don't you dare not stop . . ." murmured Alex anxiously, but the monorail car was already slowing down. With a hissing sound, it opened its wide door, decorated with a fairly talented caricature of Quicksilver Pit's president, Mr. San Li. Alex smiled at the thought of how much better this would have looked in the hospital than the obligatory copies of the president's portrait in every ward. He entered the monorail car.

The inside didn't look any better than the outside. Hard plastic seats, a derelict TV screen on the dead-bolted partition separating the passengers from the driver.

The passengers fit right in.

A dozen young hoodlums, sprawling in their seats in the back corner of the car. Typical naturals of the type that make do with dirty work. All were drunk. All were dopers. All were staring at Alex with the same torpid curiosity. Just a few paces away, dozing off in her window seat, sat a girl of about fifteen, as dingy and scruffy as the rest of them, dark circles under her eyes.

Alex sat down at the head of the car. With a jolt, it started up again.

"What do we think of the locals, Demon?" he asked, glancing at the tattoo. The Demon's little face twisted into a grimace of disgust.

"I'm with you," whispered Alex. Tried to make himself a little more comfortable, fully realizing the futility of the attempt.

Well . . . At least it was warmer inside . . . He thought he might even nod off for a bit, while the monorail was crawling through the suburbs.

"Get away from me!"

Alex turned around.

Great. Just what he needed. A chance to be heroic. Right out of the hospital.

One of the guys had moved next to the girl. He was slowly, unhurriedly unbuttoning her coat.

"I said, shove off!" said the girl harshly.

The other naturals just watched. Both their pal and Alex. Hell, would they have had the guts to try this if he were wearing his master-pilot uniform?

Not likely.

But who would think him a spesh now?

The girl glanced at Alex. The expression in her eyes was nice. Incongruous with the rest of her appearance.

"Tell me, Demon, do we need this?" asked Alex.

The tattoo on his shoulder didn't say anything. It couldn't talk. The Demon's lips were tight, and its fists opened slightly, letting out its claws. Its squinting eyes filled with fiery red.

"You sure?" asked Alex with a sigh. Got up and walked toward the girl. The guy next to her immediately turned, tensed. He wasn't as drunk as he let on. The whole group got quiet.

"She isn't interested," said Alex.

The guy licked his lips, got up. Alex saw rough, bulging muscles rolling under his coarse sweater. Looked like an altered body. Probably modified for physical strength. Really bad news . . . Guess this wasn't just public transport for the naturals.

"She's interested," the guy informed him. "Just playing hard to get. The way we do it 'round here. You got that? Two's fun, three's a crowd, get it?"

A harsh slurring accent made his speech barely intelligible. Seemed like in pursuit of physical strength, all other functions had been minimized.

Alex looked at the girl.

"It's okay," she said. "I'm all right, thanks."

The Demon on his shoulder looked perplexed.

"Yeah!" said the fellow triumphantly, bending towards his newly subdued prey.

"I said shove off, you jerk!" said the girl sharply. "You stupid, or what?!"

Alex leaned on an empty seat. The situation was getting interesting.

The guy let out a low growl—his small mind just could not process the need to retreat. He stretched out his hand, casually sinking it into the girl's open coat.

"I warned you," she said.

Her first blow doubled up the pseudo-natural. Her second, with spread-out fingers, broke through his sweater, where a bloodstain instantly appeared. The third blow smashed his head into the window. It crunched, covered with a web of cracks, but held together.

A moment later the girl was standing next to Alex. The hoodlums, stunned, sat speechless.

"Any of you move, and you'll catch hell," said the girl quietly.

The fellow slowly sank to the floor. Groaned, holding his head in his hands.

Alex glanced sideways at the Demon.

The creature smirked, crouched, as if ready to leap off his shoulder to join the fray with relish.

"I liked it, too," said Alex. The car slowed down, the door hissed, opening.

"We'd better get off," Alex told the girl.

"I'll manage," she answered curtly.

"I almost believe you. But how'll you manage the police? Let's go."

12

Somewhat cautiously, he took hold of her arm. The girl obeyed.

They jumped out onto the platform, and the monorail door closed behind them. Could the driver have stopped just for them? The naturals had already come back to their senses. Some of them were helping the altered fellow get to his feet. His head wobbled slightly as he tried to walk. Others were shaking their fists at the window.

"I wasn't bothering them!" exclaimed the girl.

She raised her hand, shaking off a few droplets of blood.

"That kind doesn't need any bothering."

Alex watched the monorail depart. It had already sped up to about forty miles an hour, probably the best it could do. As if the driver had decided to get the brawlers as far apart from each other as possible.

"Did you notice—that guy was also a spesh?"

"A spesh?" she said with a note of curiosity, omitting the "also." Maybe she didn't want to deny the obvious, or maybe she just hadn't noticed. She sniffed, got out a crumpled handkerchief, wiped off her hand.

"Yeah, maybe. He recovered too fast."

Alex watched the girl with growing curiosity. She really couldn't have been more than fifteen . . . and considering the obvious alteration of the body . . .

"What's your name?" he said. The girl glanced at him as though he was asking about her banking code. "I'm Alex, spesh."

"Kim . . ." and after a short pause, she added, "spesh."

"And this is Demon," Alex turned slightly, showing her the tattoo on his shoulder. "Just Demon."

The Demon smiled an ingratiating smile, crossing its legs, hiding its tail behind its back, and leaning on the pitchfork as though it were an elegant walking stick. Kim's face promptly grew serious.

"It . . . He wasn't like that before. I saw . . ."

"Of course. Demon can change."

A look of distrust came into her dark eyes. Well . . . Quicksilver Pit was, after all, a backwater place, despite its status as an industrial center.

"Don't be afraid," said Alex. "It's just an emotion scanner. See?"

Kim didn't pretend to understand and just shook her head.

"It's not much, really. A liquid-crystal screen inserted right under the skin. Look at my Demon, and you know what I'm feeling. Afraid or angry, thinking or daydreaming . . . it's all right here."

"Wow! Neat . . ." The girl stretched out her hand, threw a questioning glance at Alex, then cautiously touched his shoulder.

The Demon smiled very slightly.

"I like that," said Kim. "And you don't mind being all exposed like that?"

"When I mind, I turn off the lights." At this, the Demon's smile grew a bit wider.

"I see," the girl nodded. "Thanks for your help, spesh Alex. Best of luck to you!"

She ran down the stairs, lightly, easily, not a hint of fear at the shaky railing and more than a thirty-foot drop below her. Alex leaned over, watching her descend, barely visible in the dusk. They were somewhere at the very edge of town; all around stretched row upon row of dark and seemingly abandoned buildings. Maybe these were warehouses, maybe long-closed factories, or tenements so ugly that no one could bear to live there.

"Hey, friend-spesh!" shouted Alex, as the girl reached the ground below. "You hungry?"

"Very." Kim answered simply. "But I'm broke."

"Wait up!"

Alex glanced at the Demon. It shrugged.

"Yup, we're out of the habit . . ." agreed Alex, and jumped over the railing. Thirty-two feet. Free-fall acceleration on Quicksilver Pit was twenty-seven point two feet per second. He turned in the air, assuming the right position, bending his knees at impact, and then squatting slightly to counteract inertia. A leap like this would cost a natural a broken spine. Alex's body reacted precisely as it was designed to.

A soft, muted wave of pain rolled through him, while the reconstructed tissues absorbed the impact. Alex straightened, looked at the girl.

Kim stood in a fighting pose, a strange one impossible for any natural, a stance from the yu-dao martial art. Legs forward, as though they had been broken and twisted at the knee, torso leaning backward, left hand, palm open toward Alex, at her face, and right arm thrust forward.

A sixth-level defensive stance.

"I'm not attacking," said Alex quickly. "Friend-spesh, this is not an attack. I was simply trying out my body."

Kim straightened up smoothly. It seemed to Alex that he could hear the light rustle of her joints coming out of fighting mode.

"Who are you, spesh Alex?"

"A master-pilot."

With a glance, the girl assessed the height of his recent jump.

"Thirty-two point two feet. My impact velocity was . . ."

"You've been modified for gravity overloads?"

"Exactly. I retain mobility at six Gs and consciousness at twelve."

"And measure distances like a radar."

"Both distance and velocity."

Alex stretched his hand toward her.

"Friend-spesh, I have the money to buy dinner for two. Would you accept my offer, no strings attached, no payback expected?"

At this, the girl relaxed. Alex only hoped she would not catch a glimpse of the Demon, would not notice its mischievous smirk. He had addressed Kim with deliberate courtesy, according to all the rules of etiquette, as if addressing a lady and not the girl that she was, despite all her abilities as a spesh, after all.

"I accept your offer, friend-spesh," she said quickly. "I don't see any harm in it."

Dinner for two was quite a bit of an exaggeration. A light snack for two would be more like it, and at one of the cheapest fast-food joints at that. But Alex had not wasted his last opportunity for a square meal, back when he was still in the full care of the hospital.

And Kim, it seemed, had long been enduring financial difficulties.

The menu choices at McRobbins were few and well known to every child. Still, Alex handed the girl a menu.

Kim ordered heavy whipped cream, a protein shake, some vita-minized ice cream, and two glasses of mineral water. Without a second's hesitation over her choices, she traced her finger along the menu, touched the picture of the "enter" button. Threw Alex a questioning glance.

"Coffee for me," he said. "Just coffee."

"I spent all your money?" Kim asked bluntly.

"Yes. But that isn't a problem. I am fully formed, and you . . ." Alex lowered his voice, "are a nymph." The girl's face blazed red.

"Take it easy," continued Alex quietly, "please relax. Everyone goes through this. There's nothing to be embarrassed about."

"How did you know?"

"The food. You ordered a very typical meal. Fat, protein, carbohydrates, vitamins, minerals, water. Nothing else. How long do you have till pupation?"

"I don't know."

"Kim, I'm not your enemy."

"I have no idea!" she shouted. A family at a nearby table—two naturals and their son, a boy-spesh—stared at them. The boy's eyes, narrow and too wide-set, were unnaturally bright. It occurred to Alex in passing that he could not even begin to guess the direction of the boy's transformation.

"Kim . . ."

"I really don't know," the girl said a little more calmly. "My metamorphosis is off track. According to the schedule, the chrysalis stage should have happened a month ago."

Alex shook his head. Awful. Really awful. An off-track metamorphosis was no joke. He ought to keep away from the girl, but . . . he might have already made one step too close.

"You have medical insurance?"

"No."

"I won't even ask about money, but parents? Friends?"

Kim was silent, her lips tight. Mad, it seemed, at the stupid questions.

"I see."

Alex reached for his cigarettes, lit up. Glanced sideways at the Demon.

The little devil held its head in its hands, its little face looking lost and scared.

"I'll be going," Kim said quietly. "Sorry."

"Stay where you are," said Alex curtly. "Your order is on its way." A young fellow in bright orange shorts, a white T-shirt with the McRobbins logo, and a smile on his face, unloaded all the cups and glasses one by one upon the table. Obviously a natural, he took the girl for a sweet tooth, and the strange selection of food told him nothing.

"Where is the nearest place to stay, friend? Something cheap?" Alex stretched out his arm, holding a credit card by its activation center. The waiter moved his wrist over the card, and his electronic bracelet beeped softly, reading off the payment.

"Hilton, of course," he answered. "The closest is a five-minute walk down the boulevard toward the center."

No surprise, no contempt. McRobbins did not get any other kind of customer. Only those who stayed in the cheapest chain hotels and preferred municipal transport.

"Thanks, friend."

The fellow left, obviously not hoping for a tip. And he was right. They simply had no money for it.

Alex took a sip of coffee—surprisingly tolerable—and watched the girl.

Kim was eating.

She started off with ice cream, and that was bad. Everything was bad, of course, but especially the carbohydrate craving. It was a sign that pupation was close; otherwise, the nymph would have picked the protein shake first. Time was running out.

At this point, Alex did not even want to look at the Demon.

Kim shook her head, as though the soft, slightly melted ice cream was hard to swallow. Her dark hair spilled over her shoulders. She gulped down half a glass of water, scraped out the ice cream cup, and without a pause, with the same spoon, moved on to the whipped cream.

Really awful. Her body had already stored up enough protein for the metamorphosis. Well, actually, it only seemed like there was enough. Skin and bones . . . Breasts were barely noticeable under the sweater. What was going on here? The creation of a fighter-spesh was one of the most expensive genetic procedures, affecting the whole body. To disrupt this kind of metamorphosis with bad nutrition, sleep deprivation, and stress was like having an unusually large diamond and then failing to cut it properly.

"Thanks very much, Alex." Kim was finally done with the food. She had looked as if she was forcing herself to finish the protein shake. Her eyes were now glazed over, drowsy. "I guess I . . . needed that . . ."

Alex nodded. He had not decided anything yet, or maybe was afraid to admit to himself what he had decided.

"Why is your Demon looking away?"

The tattoo on his shoulder had changed dramatically. The Demon was crouching and looking away, the tip of its ear twitching nervously.

"It's like a cartoon," said Kim, not waiting for an answer. "Was it a part of your transformation, or can it be added afterwards?"

"Afterwards."

"I'll also . . . get one . . . just like it." She was getting really sleepy.

"Let's go." Alex got up. Grabbed her by the arm. A fighter-spesh should have reacted to the sudden movement, but Kim did not even twitch. "Let's go. Quickly now."

The girl followed him as if hypnotized. The transparent doors of the eatery opened, letting both of them out into the street, where the cold wind revived the girl a little.

"Not so cozy out here, is it?" she said with a laugh. "Why are you holding me like that?"

"We're going to a hotel," answered Alex without stopping. "You need to sleep."

"Yes, I do," agreed the girl. She seemed drunk or drugged. And in some sense, she was—her body had already begun to release endorphins into her bloodstream. "It's so uncomfortable out here."

Alex knew all too well what she meant. The chrysalis stage was the most dangerous time in a spesh's life. As its onset approached, a person suffered intense agoraphobia. To remain out in the open was not just uncomfortable, but insanely frightening.

"We'll walk really fast," Alex told her. "We'll get to the Hilton and get a tiny, cozy room, nice and quiet. I'll put you to bed, cover you up with a blanket, turn off the light, and you'll get some sleep. When you wake up, everything will be fine."

"All right," said Kim. "Let's walk really fast."

She let out a light, faltering giggle, familiar to any man whose girlfriend had ever had too many drinks. A second later, the tone of her voice changed completely.

"You won't harm me? Will you?"

The girl put her hand on Alex's shoulder. She was not quite tall enough to hug a grown man, but Alex fully realized that even these slender fingers, now barely touching his neck, were capable of breaking his spine in an instant.

Suspiciousness, at times completely unreasonable, was also a sign of approaching pupation. And the two of them were, after all, practically strangers.

"I won't harm you," replied Alex. "Let's hurry up. It's cold."

"All right."

The boulevard was deserted. There were few people on Quicksilver Pit who enjoyed walking at night, so it was empty and completely dark. Walking fast along the street, Alex felt the girl's hand tremble a little on his shoulder. It trembled, getting dryer and more and more feverish.

Damn! What was he doing?

The waiter had not lied. The Hilton really was close. Alex knew that a long, long time ago, before the space era, the hotel chain had been considered posh and expensive. But at the beginning of the galactic expansion, its owners made a bet on cheap mass lodgings. As it turned out, their bet paid off.

The outside of the hotel, a squat three-story structure, did look rather decent. Its walls, covered by plastic-crumb panels, retained their juicy orange color for decades, and the laser ad hovering in the air above it was as truthful as it could be. It promised "maximum comfort at minimal price."

With Kim hanging onto him, barely able to shuffle along, Alex pushed his way into the hotel lobby.

The night clerk, a natural of about forty, threw an appraising glance at them. Gave a friendly smile. To him, of course, it all looked very simple—a spesh out for a good time had picked up a young natural for the night. Alex had no intention of arguing with him.

"A room with minimal parameters . . . for three hours," said Alex, catching a glimpse of the price list. That completely cleaned out his account.

"Second floor, number twenty-six," said the clerk, reaching out with his cash scanner. Alex took out his credit card, approved the transaction. "Hey, you're with him, kiddo?"

"Yes," said Kim, almost inaudibly. "I'll get to bed, get a blanket, and we'll turn off the light." At this, the clerk discretely winked at Alex.

"Let's go." Alex had a feeling that the girl might collapse any second now. "Let's go where it's dark and quiet . . ."

This seemed to have the desired effect. Hanging on to him, Kim moved towards the elevator.

Alex had kept his promise about the silence. The Hilton management knew how irritating noise could be to the customers of their hotels, be it street noise or the sounds coming from the adjacent rooms. It wasn't sound-suppressors they had installed, of course—the thin walls had been filled with cheap vacuum foam.

The lights in the tiny room came on mercilessly bright, showing its squalid interior—a double but rather narrow bed with unimaginably bright-colored bedding of synthetic fibers, two plastic chairs, a plastic table, a cheap screen on the wall, and a half-open bathroom door with a sticker above the knob, proudly proclaiming that it was "Sterile."

Kim whimpered feebly, covering her eyes with her right hand. Her left was still clutching Alex.

"Dim the lights!" ordered Alex, forgetting for a second where he was. Cursed. Touching his finger to the sensor, he lowered the brightness of the lights. The ceiling lamps dimmed, turned a pallid blue for a second, and began flickering in a happy disco mode. After a few more attempts, he managed to achieve a dimmer pinkish tone—cloying, but easy on the eyes.

"It hurts," complained Kim weakly. Her receptors surely had a higher pain threshold, and now she was also in a state of pre-metamorphosis self-anesthetization. But pain was still breaking through all the barriers.

"Hang in there, give me a second," said Alex, scooping her up into his arms. "You do understand what is happening to you, right? You've entered your chrysalis stage."

She said nothing, giving only a limp nod. Alex put her on the bed, started unbuttoning her coat.

"But you promised . . . not to hurt me . . ." said Kim.

"Don't worry. I only want to help."

He peeled off her coat, her jeans, and her sweater. All she had on now were thin panties, freshly soaked with blood. She must have felt herself bleeding—she made a weak attempt to cover herself with her hand.

"You've got your period?" asked Alex.

"No . . . Too early."

"I see."

Hesitating no longer, Alex took off her soiled underwear, flipped the blanket open, and arranged her body more comfortably on the bed. Kim did not help him in any way, but offered no resistance, either. All better now. She must have postponed the metamorphosis as long as she could. Not consciously—the mind had no control over the process—but just by realizing how vulnerable she had been. Alex's presence had broken the delicate balance between the genetic program and the pupation-inhibiting hormones. The girl had put her trust in him, and the tightly wound spring had started to unravel.

"Does the light bother you?" he asked.

"No . . ."

Her voice was changing. The larynx was being transformed.

"Kim, try to understand what I am saying. It's very important, okay?"

"Okay."

"You are entering a transformational trance. Soon you'll start seeing things . . . all kinds of things. Your body will be changing according to the prescribed program. Everything will be fine, I'm sure. But it will hurt a little. You think you can handle it?"

The girl nodded weakly. A few drops of blood slid down from her nostrils.

"Thirsty?"

"No . . . Not yet."

Alex sighed. What he knew of the chrysalis stage was no more than any other spesh with a basic education and personal experience of the process. The main thing was that the transformation should take place under a specialist's care. And in case of a disrupted metamorphosis—in the hospital.

Damn it . . .

His pockets were empty.

And he knew nobody here.

A strange planet, a strange town, and a strange girl, entering the chrysalis stage . . .

He slid his hands under her little, trembling body, lifted her up.

Eighty-five, maybe eighty-six pounds. Unforgivably little for a metamorphosis. And . . . there was something else alarming, irregular. A body-mass imbalance uncharacteristic of humans.

"Kim!"

The girl opened her eyes.

"Are you cyborged?"

"No . . ."

"No artificial organs? Pacemakers, transplants, built-in weapons?"

"No."

"Is your body biologically clean? Completely? No foreign objects?" He could be mistaken. His sense of balance was enhanced for the rare occasions when a master-pilot had to use a really tiny craft, such as a glider or even a rocket pack.

But Kim was silent, looking at him in fear.

"You can't enter chrysalis if you have implants, kid! Your body won't be able to handle it!"

This was a complete disaster. If for some reason the girl had been slipped an artificial organ, she was doomed.

"Swear on your life . . ."

"What?"

"Swear that you'll keep . . ."

Her hand crawled down her stomach, stopping somewhere above the right kidney. For a second, her fingers weakly pressed and stretched the skin. Then a shiver ran down her body, and the skin beneath her fingers came open, revealing a small pocket.

It was not an artificial organ, after all. Not even a built-in gun. Just a hiding place, a practically undetectable cavity.

"Here . . ."

Alex lowered Kim onto the bed and carefully took a heavy crystal out of her hand.

A truncated cone with a one-point-nine-five-inch base. Clear as a diamond. And as expensive as a diamond of its size.

Alex lifted the crystal up, looked through it at the light. The ceiling lamp's pink glow turned white. He squeezed the crystal and felt a tough resilience.

Exactly. A gel-crystal.

"Where did you get this?" was all that he managed to say.

"Keep it safe . . ." Kim's fingers squeezed his wrist with such force that Alex gave a slight gasp from the pain. "Swear to keep it safe!"

"I swear."

How absurd. A homeless, starving child was carrying around a huge fortune. Crystals of this size were used on star cruisers, in planetary computer centers, in virtual reality bases, and in navigational centers of the largest spaceports. There were probably not more than five or six such crystals on the whole planet of Quicksilver Pit.

"You promise me?"

"I promise."

Alex leaned over and touched his lips to her forehead.

"Sleep. I know how to care for gel-crystals. Don't worry."

She believed him. She simply had no other choice. After a few seconds, the girl's eyes closed, but it was not sleep. Obeying the program, her consciousness faded.

Alex threw the blanket over her.

A short respite, an hour, an hour and a half at the most. Now her body would begin to prepare for the metamorphosis.

Still, she probably wouldn't make it.

Clutching the crystal—though it was almost impossible to break, he did not wish to take any chances—Alex walked over to the table. Put the crystal into a glass, then poured in some water from a decanter. That was good for gel-crystals.

Glanced sideways at Kim. The girl's breathing was slow and deep. Her nose had stopped bleeding . . . for now.

"Computer," said Alex forcefully, inwardly ready for the terminal not to work.

To Alex's relief, the screen flooded with a dim white light. The management of Hilton didn't exactly have to make information services available in a unit of "minimal parameters."

"This is the basic service mode," announced the computer courteously. "Your connection is limited to the local city area. Only free information services will be provided."

Alex hissed through clenched teeth. Wanted to look at the Demon, but changed his mind. Most likely, the Demon would be sitting with its back to him. Perhaps it had even left altogether, offended by its master's stupidity.

"Information on gel-crystals," said Alex.

"Completed. Limited mode."

Great . . .

"Gel-crystals with base diameter larger than one point nine inches."

"Completed. Limited mode."

"Crimes connected to this group of crystals."

"Completed. Limited mode."

"Theft of crystals with base diameter larger than one point nine inches."

"Completed."

Alex smiled.

Of course, he wouldn't be able to access any secret police archives. Well, this would have to do.

"List the last five cases."

"Unable to comply. Gel-crystals of specified size were objects of theft three times. Shall I list data?"

"Yes. Brief descriptions only."

"Year 2131. Base crystal of space liner *Sri Lanka*. Stolen during mutiny on board ship, supposedly by master-pilot Andreas Wolf, spesh. Recovered and returned to the Lunar Express corporation after the mutiny had been suppressed. Currently used on space liner *Sri Lanka*. Further details not available."

Alex scowled. He already knew this case, but it hadn't immediately come to mind. He hadn't connected the shameful story of the spesh who led a mutiny and the theft of the crystal.

"Year 2164. Gel-crystal of amusement complex Andalusia, planet Athena. Stolen by technician Dyeri Doneskou, natural.

Recovered during an attempted resale. Recycled upon loss of function resulting from improper storage conditions. Details?"

"No. Next."

"Year 2173. Base crystal of space cruiser *Tron*. Stolen by an unknown person. Never recovered. Further details unavailable."

Alex looked at Kim in considerable doubt. She was a spesh, certainly. But to believe that ten years ago, as a child, she could have stolen the gel-crystal from a military ship . . .

"Is the gel-crystal from the *Tron* still being searched for?"

"No information available."

Made sense. The military gave no rewards for the return of stolen articles. And they seldom asked for police assistance with any internal problems. Remarkable that these details had leaked into the open infonet at all.

So then, could it have been the space cruiser *Tron*?

Alex squatted in front of the table. Looked at the glass, where the now-invisible crystal lay.

It was not just its intrinsic value. If this was the crystal, and if it still contained all of the data from the military fleet's flagship . . . even ten years old . . .

"How come I always get myself into shit, and when I do, it's always up to my ears . . .?" Alex asked rhetorically.

The crystal could not answer him, the girl was asleep, and the computer did not consider it an appropriate question. Alex sighed. Well, there was no proof, after all. It could very well have been a completely different crystal.

"Computer. Access the employment vacancy pages."

"Completed."

At least this service was available.

"Vacancies on the planet Quicksilver Pit for a master-pilot, spesh, thirty-four years of age, six years of experience, first-class qualifications, no restrictions, confirmed loyalty, misdemeanor record clean . . . um . . . no restrictions, full medical clearance as of today. Display text only."

There were vacancies. Five of them, to be exact.

Alex moved up to the screen.

The first announcement made him smirk. Orbital and sub-orbital freight transit. A *Hamster*-class barge. To offer this job to a master-pilot . . . Someone had a real sense of humor. Thirty credits per week. No sign-up bonus. Free lodging at the Hilton.

"Delete the first entry."

The second and third opportunities were not much better. Two freight routes—Quicksilver Pit to and from the hyperterminal, and Quicksilver Pit to and from the asteroid belt. Two barges, one *Hamster*-class, the other a *Badger*. Sixty credits per week. Lodging at the Hilton or in a company-sponsored apartment.

"Delete the second and third entries."

Were master-pilots a dime a dozen in this place? Or . . . maybe there really was no demand for speshes of his skill level.

The fourth vacancy caught his attention. The space liner *Goethe*. Second master-pilot. The independent company Solar. One hundred credits. Full benefits. A sign-up bonus equal to one month's salary. All expenses paid. There were, however, some special conditions . . . a non-negotiable five-year contract.

"Delete."

The fifth vacancy was a military one. A fleet-supply vessel.

Seventy credits with full benefits. A one-year contract. A very attractive offer.

Except it would be a military thing . . .

"Delete."

The girl moaned weakly. Alex turned to her. Kim awkwardly rolled her head on the pillow. Her eyes were open.

"The crystal . . ."

"Everything's fine. It's safe."

"Uh-huh."

She lost consciousness again.

Well, she did realize how precious the crystal was, if she could interrupt her own trance for it.

"What am I going to do with you?" said Alex under his breath.

An off-track metamorphosis was no joke. She would be getting visions any second now. She might turn violent, and a fighter-spesh out of control—that would be a disaster. But even if she stayed quiet, she would still need food, she would need rest, and medicine. All that cost money, and he had none.

"A new entry just in," the computer informed him. Alex read over the new vacancy announcement that had appeared on the screen.

Spaceship *Mirror*. Unclassified vessel, assembled on Earth. Master-pilot, simultaneous appointment as the ship's captain. As the ship's captain!

Alex gave a start. Stared intensely at the dry lines of the announcement. No established routes. Two hundred credits per week. Sign-up bonus equal to two months' salary. All-expenses-paid lodging on board the ship and "rank-appropriate accommodations at all spaceports." The Sky Company. A two-year contract.

"This doesn't happen," said Alex firmly. "Ever."

Could not resist the urge to glance at his shoulder. The Demon really was sitting with its back to him, but had now turned its head and stared at Alex quizzically.

"Contracts like this don't come along, especially . . . at just the right moment," announced Alex. "Right?" The Demon was obviously in complete agreement.

"Delete entry?" queried the computer.

"Don't you dare . . . Details!"

"No further information available."

"Open data on the spaceship *Mirror* and the Sky Company."

"No information available."

A contract like this should be snapped up at once—that is, if you were stupid. Two hundred credits per week was too much, even for the combined position of captain and master-pilot. No information on the company, or on the ship, no further details of the contract . . . Before you enter into anything, you should always know how to exit. This was a rule Alex had learned after his first contract, which he signed thinking it was for one year, but which actually dragged on for three.

And the main thing—the rank of captain! This was more than a contract. It was a whole new destiny.

Kim moaned.

"It's a real bind, ain't it?" Alex asked the Demon. The tattoo frowned back at him.

"Go back to the contract for the space liner *Goethe*," said Alex.

"Access denied. That contract has been signed." Alex licked his lips. Took out his credit card. Stretched his arm toward the screen.

"Request to sign the contract with the Sky Company for the combined position of captain and master-pilot of the spaceship *Mirror*."

About ten seconds passed, and then came the computer's reply:

"Your application has been accepted."

From a slot below the screen a small sheet of paper slid out. Alex read over it quickly. It was an absolutely standard contract, approved by the union. With a tiny little quirk. Alex still had no information about the ship or the company . . .

"You have five minutes for deliberation."

"Inquiry on the date of departure from this planet," said Alex.

"No later than in three standard days."

"Information on all crewmembers."

"The choice of crewmembers is left to the captain's discretion."

"Such tasty cheese can only mean a mousetrap," Alex murmured.

He didn't know why the contract bothered him. He could not formulate his misgivings. Perhaps because it was simply way too good . . .

"Switch to contract-signing mode," Alex ordered the computer.

The text of the contract appeared on the screen.

"I, Alexander Romanov, master-pilot, spesh, citizen of Earth, agree to the standard labor contract, as it appears on the screen, with the Sky Company, and take upon myself the responsibilities of captain and master-pilot of the spaceship *Mirror* for two years."

"Accepted," reported the computer. "Your information has been submitted to the union of pilots and the Sky Company. Shall I transfer the money into your account?"

"Yes."

"Completed. Shall I provide the documentation on the spacecraft?"

"Yes. In hard copy."

Alex felt the mousetrap snap closed somewhere behind him. But at the moment, he had more important things to worry about.

"Switch to shopping mode."

"Unable to comply. Your room is configured to minimal parameters."

"Pay for this room for the duration of twenty-four hours at maximum parameters."

"Accepted."

"The nearest pharmacy with emergency delivery services. Switch to video mode."

Somewhere in the downstairs lobby, the night clerk probably smirked, seeing that Alex had purchased an extra twenty-four hours at maximum price. No surprise there—the spesh had decided to prolong his pleasure.

"Hope he has this much fun with his next date!" murmured Alex, catching a sidelong glimpse of the girl's motionless body. And the computer screen was already showing the face of a girl-natural, dressed in the pale-green uniform of a pharmacy clerk.

CHAPTER 2.

Pupation began exactly at midnight, as though Kim's body had been consulting a clock. The girl yelped, then stretched out, tossing off the blanket. She tensed up on the bed, slowly twisting into a rigid arch. Alex twirled an anesthetic ampoule in his fingers, but decided to wait. Metamorphosis was always a very unpleasant process, even if the expected transformation was minimal. And in the case of a fighter-spesh, especially when the normal schedule was disrupted . . . She vomited—nothing but bile. Alex brought her some water, helped her up to drink. It was unlikely that she understood what was happening, but she greedily put the glass to her lips.

Then the bleeding started. Pupation was always much harder on women than it was on men, for physiological reasons. According to Alex's estimations, she must have lost at least one point five pints of blood. He gave Kim two intravenous injections of blood substitute, three point five ounces each, but did not manage to give her the third injection. He had run out of time. Her veins started slipping away under his fingers. The girl's whole body quivered. Her pores oozed blood and sweat. Alex sat quiet near the bed, every now and then cleaning it up with anti-bacterial wipes. The used ones already formed a small dirty pile on the floor. The Demon on his shoulder scowled in disgust.

"Just deal with it, pal," Alex told it. "Someone had to wipe up my blood and shit, too."

Yes, but—the Demon could have pointed out—those were nurses, naturals, who were used to this kind of work and were getting paid to do it. But colloidal tattoos could not talk.

At two in the morning, the girl's body stiffened. Her pulse was barely discernible, and her heartbeat was very slow and labored. Alex accessed a medical database, read the recommendations, then lifted Kim out of the bed, took her to the bathroom, and put her into warm water. The bathroom had, of course, a kit for the handicapped, and Alex strapped Kim's body in, so she wouldn't drown.

He spent the next quarter of an hour, a short respite promised by the computer, airing out the room. He sealed the soiled clothes and wipes in a plastic bag. Went out into the hallway and got a cup of coffee from the vending machine.

When he got back, Kim had already ripped one of the straps and was trying to reach the warm cloudy bath water with her lips.

"Silly thing," said Alex, taking her out of the bath. "You're a mess, aren't you?" The girl said nothing. At this stage, she retained only basic animal instincts. But in his arms, she suddenly relaxed, let herself be lowered onto the mattress, greedily gulped down two glasses of mineral water, and then lay quiet.

Alex stood for a moment watching her, then shrugged his

shoulders in dismay. Apparently, the initial transformation of the body was finished—her inner organs had undergone modification. But outwardly, Kim did not in any way resemble a regular fighter-spesh, with their thick grayish skin, wider-set eyes, sculpted musculature, and enlarged fingers.

The next stage of the metamorphosis should have been the stabilization of the body. But here, the girl surprised him.

Her transformation started all over again. A second wave of body modification was possible, but such genetic programming was rare—extremely rare.

This time Kim began crying out from the pain. Her cries were very weak—she was too exhausted to cry—but so piteous that if anyone had heard her, the police would surely have stormed the room five minutes later.

Alex gave her two injections of a narcotic painkiller. A quarter of an hour later, unable to stand it, he gave her a shot of cardio-stimulant and added another dose of the narcotic.

The Demon on his shoulder indignantly twirled a finger near its temple.

"I know, I know. If she dies, I'll get blamed for it all," Alex agreed.

When he attempted to listen to her heart again, all he heard was silence.

But the girl's breathing was regular.

It took a couple of minutes, but finally it occurred to him to listen all over her rib cage.

Her heart had moved to the center of her chest.

"Holy shit, girl!" was all he could say, straightening his back. The girl, of course, could not have known in advance all that would happen to her. And she had not had the time to tell him all the details of her metamorphosis.

This could very well be a logical transformation for a fighter-spesh. It might save her life if someone shot straight at the heart.

Around four o'clock in the morning, Kim quieted down. Her breathing grew deeper, more even. Her heart, having settled in the middle of her chest, beat calmly and rhythmically. On the other hand, her cheeks looked hollow, and her ribs and pelvic bones stuck out as though she had been starved for a week. The pocket in her abdomen opened and the skin sucked in, crater-like, making apparent the muscle ring around the opening. This kind of thing in a fighter-spesh was not quite as useless as it was strange. It would be more likely to benefit a smuggler, but who would need a smuggler-spesh?

"Your parents sure had some funny ideas," said Alex, and wiped the sweat off the girl's face. It was hard to believe that only a few hours earlier she had knocked out a huge guy with just three blows.

But the stabilization process was proceeding smoothly, as if it was taking place exactly as planned, in a hospital ward, and under the watchful eye of experienced doctors. Alex ran out of wipes, so he patted the girl with a wet towel and sat down at the window for a smoke. It looked as though she had managed the physiological transformation just fine. But a spesh was not just a collection of muscles, nerves, and inner organs. There was also the mind. And that was, after all, the most important thing.

Kim moaned.

Alex put out his cigarette, sat down beside her, took her hand. A friend of his, a navigator-spesh from the Third

Freight-and-Passenger station, had been convinced that any spesh coming out of the chrysalis stage got a fixation on those who were around when it happened, undergoing a sort of imprinting. As an example, he had offered his own case. He later married the nurse who had taken care of him during the transformation. Alex did not contest the beauty of this theory, although he himself had never felt any special attraction to the doctors and nurses who had been with him during his metamorphosis. If any imprinting had left its mark on him, it must have been his liking for the strong sweet coffee he was given repeatedly during his pupation.

The girl started saying something. Clearly, but in a strange language. Not in Lingua, or English, or Chinese, or German, or Russian . . . Alex had almost decided to turn on the computer for a synchronous translation, but changed his mind. That would be like peeping through a keyhole.

"I don't want this!" Kim said all of a sudden. Her voice had not changed much, and Alex was happy about that. Wouldn't it be just dandy if she kept the same body but acquired a loud, commanding tone of voice!

"Like it or not—you're in," he said. "Hang in there."

"Don't . . . Please . . . don't . . ." Kim begged piteously. Alex stroked her cheek. The girl's mind was now lost in the realms of dream and fantasy. It was one thing to change the body. Another thing altogether to change the soul. This was the most delicate part of the metamorphosis. Now Kim was experiencing situations pre-programmed before she was born. She was adapting to them. Learning to love her future profession.

Alex remembered his own metamorphosis very clearly. The intoxicating feeling of flight. The depths of space. The scattered diamonds of stars. Piloting a craft through a stellar photosphere, through asteroid belts, through the violent atmospheres of giant planets, through space torn by attacking squadrons . . .

To be honest, he was not sure that he had even needed such a psychological crash course. He had always wanted to be a pilot anyway, since early childhood. And it was true happiness to know that your dream would inevitably come true.

But a fighter's dreams had to be different.

And the weak barrier between fantasy and reality could be breached at any second. A fighter-spesh could kill with one blow.

Wouldn't that be ironic—the girl would wake up in the morning to see the lifeless corpse of the guy who had struggled to pull her through all night long.

It occurred to Alex to tie her up. But that could only do harm. If her clouded mind took his actions for aggression, he would be done for.

"Hang in there, kid," he said. "Just a little bit longer. The worst is already over."

He was lying, but it was a necessary lie.

"You know . . ." Her voice was quiet, but . . . there was something about it. A kind of unimaginable, heartfelt honesty, a shy courage, frankness, gratitude.

"You know, when I first saw you, I realized, it was forever . . ."

Alex choked on his own breath. Kim's eyes were still closed. She was lost in her own fantasy world.

Alex glanced at his Demon, as if for reassurance. The Demon's jaw dropped.

"Yeah . . ." said Alex. "It would be nice to hear somebody say that to me. Kinda stupid of me, I know, but I'd like it."

Kim was smiling, her eyes closed. He wiped the sweat off her face again. Thought a while, and then said to the Demon, "Then again, maybe not. After that kind of thing, it's hard to be a jerk, but I'd have to, anyway." The Demon nodded its approval.

"Balmont," said the girl suddenly. Was quiet for a second. "Aivazovsky. Gauguin. Michelangelo."

Alex shrugged. Went to the window, turned up its transparency level. A murky sunrise was already on its way, dimly seen through clouds and smog—the way it was supposed to be on Quicksilver Pit. Yesterday was over, gone, past.

"Poe. Shelley. Shakespeare. Keats. Nabokov. Akutagawa . . ."

"Pushkin," suggested Alex, without turning.

"Pushkin. Lermontov. Fet . . ."

Kim was quiet for a moment and then started up again, talking faster.

"Verlaine. Rimbaud. Burns. Heine. Goethe. Schiller. Baudelaire. Whitman. Wilde."

"That's right, don't get stuck on the Russians," said Alex. "A solid classical education. I approve. Except—what good is it to a fighter?"

"Basho. Sappho."

"Which order do you recite them in, I wonder . . ."

"Chopin. Tchaikovsky."

"Are we done with the poets, then?" asked Alex.

"Dante . . ." said the girl with a hint of doubt. "Gumilev. Bykov. Robespierre."

"What's that?" asked Alex, suddenly interested. Looked back at Kim. She licked her lips and started talking very rapidly.

"Churchill. Lenin. Marx. Gandhi. Gates. Dan Lao Wang . . ."

Alex lowered himself into a chair, closed his eyes, stretched out his legs. He was very tired. And the girl kept talking and talking, zooming through Earth's history with the ease and precision of an artillery round. The list was slightly unbalanced in favor of music and poetry, but politics, art, architecture, and science were covered.

Seemed like Kim really was following the track of her metamorphosis. The facts loaded into her prenatally were now exploding in her mind like tiny bombs. Behind every name she recited was a whole image of the person, complete with dates of life and death, life events, paintings and poems, lines from speeches, rumors, maybe even films and archival videos.

All that was nice. But totally useless for a fighter-spesh.

Alex dozed off.

Several times he was awakened by silence. Kim would get quiet, and then start speaking in German, which Alex barely knew, then switch to Japanese, English, Russian, Chinese. She was long done with the names. Now she was simply holding conversations with nonexistent people. Conversations about nothing.

"Your offer is very flattering, monsieur . . ."

Then Alex would again sink into sleep. He was trained to rest sporadically, dropping off for a few minutes, waking up instantaneously to evaluate the situation, then going back to sleep. It was a very useful skill in his line of work. But no one had ever instructed him in World History. No spesh had any need for that.

"Yes, Your Highness . . ."

The pilot slept.

"Alex . . ."

He opened his eyes.

The girl was sitting on the edge of the bed, with a sheet wrapped around her. Her cheeks were hollowed, and her eyes shone feverishly. But she was fully conscious.

And not at all different.

"Where's the crystal?"

Alex threw an indicative glance at the table. Kim jumped up, holding the sheet to her chest, walked toward the table, and took up the glass.

"In here?"

The pilot gave a silent nod.

Kim's fingers slid into the water. Felt the invisible facets of the crystal, and her face immediately relaxed.

"Turn around . . . please."

He turned around. When he looked back at her again, the glass was half empty and no longer contained the crystal.

"I went through my metamorphosis?" asked the girl.

Alex nodded.

"Really?"

"Yes."

Kim laughed softly.

"I . . . I was so scared. An off-track metamorphosis can kill you, right?"

"It tried to. I didn't consent."

"Alex . . ." She immediately became serious. "Friend-spesh, I am grateful for your help. I will pay you back in kind."

"I believe you." Reluctantly, he got up from the chair. Last night's impressions had already faded a bit. Only fatigue remained.

"Take a shower, and I'll get us some breakfast, room service. You hungry?"

"Famished."

"All is well, then."

He searched her face for any traces of change. If only her eyes now had vertical pupils, or she had pointy ears . . . or there was any change in her skin tone and texture . . .

Alex reached over and patted Kim on the cheek. She smiled, accepting this display of affection without any embarrassment.

Her skin was just skin.

"Why does your Demon look so puzzled?"

Alex gloomily glanced at the tattoo.

"Because he's stupid. Kinda like me. Go wash up."

"Thanks." She leaned toward him slightly, getting on her tip-toes, and kissed his cheek. Then, giggling, vanished behind the bathroom door.

"I just don't get it!" said Alex bluntly. Was it possible that the metamorphosis did get off track after all? The psychological phase went fine, but the body remained unchanged? But her heart did move. And then there was that pocket under her ribs . . . Well, the pocket had been there before.

He went up to the computer screen and ordered a hearty breakfast for three from the hotel cafe. He had no doubt that Kim could handle enough food for two.

When she came out, looking refreshed in her cheap hotel bathrobe, the breakfast had already arrived. Scrambled eggs with mushrooms, boiled veal, tons of toast and juice, plus coffee—Alex had his own ideas about breakfast for a young spesh girl.

"Oh, I can't eat all that," protested Kim, catching a glimpse of the table.

"It only seems like a lot. Come here." He unwrapped her robe, and the girl tensed up a little. Alex did not pay any attention to that. Touched her chest.

Okay, fine. Her heart was in the middle. Her lungs had probably equalized in size. Where her esophagus and trachea had moved was anybody's guess.

"Kim, what were you supposed to transform into?"

"Something wrong?" she asked quickly.

"I'd have to know what's right before I could tell you if anything is wrong. What were you supposed to become?"

"A fighter-spesh . . . I think."

"You think?"

"No one ever told me much about it." Kim kept looking down at his hand. "I think I was meant to be a fighter-spesh . . . I have . . . I mean, I had a friend . . . He was programmed to become a fighter . . . and . . . we had the same training . . ."

"Weapons, hand-to-hand combat, tactics and strategy?" Alex moved his hand away.

"Yes . . ."

45

"Weird. You know that a fighter's skin, for example, changes in texture and takes on a grayish tint?"

Kim frowned. "I actually think that's beautiful . . ."

"I won't argue with you. But it didn't happen to your skin. And you have no other signs of change."

"Something went wrong, then? I'm not done with my metamorphosis?"

She was really scared.

"Maybe, maybe not. Every specialization has its own subcategories. I am not an expert on fighter transformations . . . You'll have to see a doctor. Sit down and eat."

Kim ate fast, and that was not at all surprising. What was surprising was that she nevertheless managed to eat gracefully, even beautifully.

Alex finished his eggs, drank his coffee, and went over to the computer screen. His ship's documentation was waiting there in the printer tray.

He started to read, fully expecting to be unpleasantly surprised.

But as he read, he grew more and more confused.

Mirror was an interstellar-class vessel built for versatility. Something between a pleasure craft and a passenger ship, it had a biodome, good rigging, very decent weapons, and a great set of engines. A dream of a ship. An up-to-six-member crew, and space for twice that number of passengers. All in all, not a contract Alex would have turned down even if he had a lot of time to really think it over. The rank of captain, and the right to pick his own crew . . .

"No one is this lucky . . ." he murmured.

"Alex, where did you get the money? Yesterday you were broke."

"I found a job." Alex folded the sheet, stuck it in his coat pocket. "Kim, where are you from?"

"Far away."

"Okay. Do you have anywhere to go in this city? A place to live, a way to make some money?" Her eyes looked a little frightened.

"No. I mean, yes . . . but I'd rather not."

"I see," said Alex. "I have to leave for now. You can stay here. You can wait for me or just rest up and disappear."

"I'll . . . wait for you." The girl lowered her eyes.

"Okay. Get your card, I'll transfer some money over. You'll need to change."

"I don't have a card."

"An ID? Even a child card?"

"I have no documents."

Another nuisance. Alex walked to the computer screen, opened an account, and transferred some money to a hotel credit line.

"Anyway, order some clothes. Try to eat often. Not a lot, but often."

"I know that."

Alex nodded and said nothing more. Nothing of the necessity to avoid too much physical activity in the first few days after the metamorphosis, nothing of the possible dizziness and fainting spells, nothing of the benefits of a sauna—the hotel had one.

"Block the door behind me," he told her.

Quicksilver Pit had been colonized about two hundred years before, probably after the completion of the very first hyper-channel station on the Moon in the middle of the twenty-first century. Alex probably could have found out the exact history on the information net, but he wasn't all that interested. What difference did it make which of the stations, searching blindly through the vast ocean of hyperspace, had plotted a channel from Earth to Quicksilver Pit?

In any case, the planet had not escaped the common fate of all the early Earth colonies. It was an outpost, and amid its boundless jungle, the first villages, garrisons, and factories had been founded. The first steps had been careful, but later, once it became apparent that the local biosphere was defenseless in the face of humanity, development grew more and more active. An emigration wave from the overpopulated Earth, mass cloning of infants, which increased the population growth rate dozens of times above normal—all that was commonplace.

Except that this colony still seemed incapable of getting rid of the yoke of an industrial giant—it had too many minerals and fossil fuels, and an infrastructure that was too well developed. The planet was suffocating in industrial waste, but human greed still had the upper hand. In Alex's opinion, the situation would probably remain unchanged for another twenty or thirty years.

He left the Hilton and managed to avoid any inquisitive glances from the clerk—the shift had already changed. In a little side street nearby, a few bored cab drivers were whiling away the time in their old clunkers.

"To the port," said Alex, sitting down next to a cab driver.

"Spaceport?" asked the guy for some reason. He was a pleasant-looking middle-aged natural.

"You have some other kind?"

"The airport . . . and the river port to the north . . ." came the upbeat reply, while the driver was steering onto the street. "And we have three different spaceports 'round town."

"Central civilian."

"Uh-huh." The driver whipped the car into the sparse traffic flow, ran through the sensors of the route-finder, and took his hands off the steering wheel. To Alex, that seemed a little rash—the old navigation system didn't look reliable at all. But he chose not to say anything.

For a few minutes, they rode in silence. Against all expectations, the car moved smoothly, keeping its distances, without needlessly jerking around.

"You from far off?" inquired the driver.

"Yup. From Earth."

"I've been there," the driver reported, noticeably proud of the fact. "Nice place. Our old mother-planet and all . . . But ours is better."

"Home is always best," replied Alex tactfully. He was well aware of colonial attitudes. It was either complete self-abasement and adoration of Earth, or proudly protruding chins and careful avoidance of all the facts.

"I was in the army," said the cab driver. "For four years. Left as a sergeant . . . you know. We had exercises on Earth. For three weeks."

"Really?"

Alex couldn't have cared less about the driver's heroic military feats, which were most likely just a few peacekeeping assignments. And the details of the fellow's visit to Earth were also of no interest to him. But politeness prompted him to keep up the conversation.

"Yes, sir! For three whole weeks. We were in . . . whatchamacallit . . . America."

"North or South?"

"There's two of 'em?" The driver laughed, honestly accepting his ignorance. "Well, it was cold. Must've been the north one, then. We went to hunt the . . . um . . . penguins. It was close, just hop across the straits in a boat, and have all the fun you want. Don't get me wrong, it was all legal, with a license."

"I don't like hunting."

"Too bad. Most fun a man can have. War and hunting . . . But war . . . well, that's dangerous."

Alex barely suppressed a smile. A very heroic and manly approach.

"By the way . . . can I pay the fare in advance?"

The cab driver looked him over one more time, probably doubting his creditworthiness. Which was odd: if he had doubts, why take such a passenger?

Alex reached for his card and activated it. Caught a glance of the amount on the ticker. Very reasonable.

"Thanks." The driver seemed content. "And why are you off to the spaceport?"

"I'm a pilot."

"Oh . . . well then . . ." The driver laughed uneasily. "Thought naturals couldn't be pilots."

"I'm a spesh. We have practically no differences in appearance."

"They changed you a lot?"

"Enough. If, for instance, we ran into that truck head on . . ." As Alex said this, the driver hurriedly looked at the road and even touched the steering wheel. ". . . you would be smashed into paste. Too much inertia. And I would survive. And probably walk away from the accident."

"You're a funny guy." Saying this, the cab driver did, nevertheless, leave his hands upon the steering wheel. "But your clothes . . . they ain't pilot's."

"Yeah, well . . . I'll change 'em."

"And that tattoo of yours . . . Hey, take a look at what I got in the army!" Alex pensively looked at the driver's hand. Every finger was decorated by an image of a naked girl. The little finger had a flirtatious nymphet, the ring finger a curvy black girl, the middle one a long-legged model with blond curls, the index finger a stripper wrapped around a pole, and the thumb an Asian beauty crouching in a strange pose. On the hand itself reclined a cocky soldier wearing a suit of force field armor and also, for some reason, a dress-uniform beret. Even from the back, he looked sated and relaxed.

"Nice work," Alex agreed.

"I'll have to get rid of it, though," sighed the driver. "I mean, it's a good souvenir and all, but . . . my daughter's getting older now . . . it ain't decent. She'll look at Daddy's hand—and he's got a whole harem instead of fingers—"

"That's just your normal army thing," said Alex, "a whole harem instead of fingers." The driver looked at him guardedly, but the pilot's face remained impenetrable.

"That a joke?" he asked uncertainly.

"Of course not. Tell you what. Erase only the girls. Keep the soldier. That'll be your souvenir." At that, the driver's face lit up.

"Hey, yeah! Smart! Didn't even occur to me . . ."

"Yeah, well . . ."

The car was already passing the widely separated supports of the monorail, somewhere in the vicinity of the hospital. Alex was surprised at how light traffic was.

"For freight transit, there's the underground route," said the driver, having guessed the reason for Alex's surprise. "They run passenger capsules, too. Who the hell likes to be under there, though . . ."

This was apparently a sore spot—the subway must have been drawing away some of the better-tipping passengers. For a few minutes, the driver told Alex the history of the subway project. To listen to him, the subway was completely worthless to everyone except the corrupt bureaucrats from Town Hall.

Alex closed his eyes. He regretted having kept up the conversation, after all. He should have just paid the fare and taken a nap. Half an hour of sleep—that wouldn't have been half bad.

"Hey, I like that little tattoo you got," the driver complimented him. "I mean, it ain't all that much to look at, just a snot of a thing. But the little devil's face is well done! You can see how he's tired, and bored, and . . . er . . . maybe stuck-up, even. Like he doesn't give a damn about anyone."

"That's bad," murmured Alex. "I didn't order that."

"Come on, it came out good!" The driver seemed to have grown more comfortable with Alex. "You're a good guy, for a spesh. No, don't get me wrong . . . I personally have no problem with you guys. But the speshes, well . . . sort of look down on us naturals sometimes. Right?"

"It happens."

"I even wanted to get a specialty for my little daughter, when I found out my wife was expecting. Not too expensive here, you know. The government helps out, you can pay in installments for ten years. But guess what happened?"

"What?"

"We didn't agree. Know what I was thinking? It'd be best for the kid to be a good technician. Always in demand, good pay, and, like I said, it ain't too expensive. Back in the army, we had this independent plumbing contractor, a young lady-spesh. You should've seen her get those rusted bolts off barehanded! Caught leaks by ear sixty feet away! And, boy, could she blow out those sewer pipes! And a real looker, besides. Well, I tell my wife . . . but she's all in tears—says: 'I don't want my daughter to spend her whole life in sewers and basements!' What the hell? I mean, work is one thing, life is something else. So I ask her, what you want then? She says: 'Let the girl be a model.' Now you tell me, ain't that just loony?"

"Yup."

"Those specifications ain't subsidized by the government . . . they cost something terrible . . . And what kind of work is that, anyway—shaking your ass on a catwalk?! And you know what? One day they want 'em skinny as a rail—next day they only want the chubby ones. How do you know what they want next?"

Alex was quiet.

"Hey, spesh, you asleep?"

He did not answer, and the driver fell silent. Seemed even a bit offended. He stopped the car at the spaceport a little too abruptly, as though wishing that Alex would smash his face into the windshield.

"Thanks," said Alex, opening his eyes. He really had dozed off, but his body reacted quickly, readjusted to the inertia, and fixed itself firmly in the car seat, as soon as the car's brakes engaged. "Good luck to you."

He did not leave any more tip than had already been included in the fare.

The central civilian spaceport of Quicksilver Pit was not all that its name suggested. Sometime in the past, it had been the main loading dock for ships traveling into orbit. But about twenty years before, another civilian spaceport had been built, farther away from the capital and capable of receiving the larger, modern spaceships. The new spaceport did not receive the title of Central, though in reality that's what it was.

Alex smoked, standing near the automatic glass doors. There were lots of people around, but this spaceport seemed more crowded because the buildings themselves were small. Periodically, as each shuttle arrived, a crowd would spill out through the doors. The people all looked alike, as if they were clones. Each shift on the orbital factories and shipyards lasted three days and three nights, but there were a lot—a whole lot—of factories orbiting Quicksilver Pit.

Throwing away his cigarette, Alex entered the building. He had suddenly realized that he was simply putting off his last steps toward the ship as long as possible.

Port authority clerks scurried around. Menial workers in uniforms and civilian passengers crowded around registration desks. Security officers strolled back and forth, every one of them a spesh—of deceptively small stature, with narrow shoulders.

Alex walked through the crowd toward one of the entrances

leading to the service tiers of the spaceport. He noticed several security officers pause some distance away to keep an eye on him.

He said, looking at the camera panel, "Alexander Romanov, spesh, captain and master-pilot of the spaceship *Mirror*, the Sky Company, Earth-based."

His identity chip, implanted under the skin just below his collarbone some twenty years before, pulsed almost imperceptibly. A full-blown identity check, complete with an express genotype analysis, was in progress.

Alex waited patiently while the molecular detectors in his capillary net caught a brand-new lymphocyte, just entering the bloodstream, then split it apart to compare it with the one they had on file. It was impossible to fool the identity chip in maximum vigilance mode. Even if you surgically removed it from the body and placed it in a vial of the owner's freshly drawn blood, it would not give a false result. The identity check could take a few minutes, but security was more important than convenience.

"Identity established, access permitted," replied the computer terminal. It was a human voice, so it must have been an actual operator, rather than a machine, which had performed the screening. The force field blocking the entrance changed its polarity, allowing him to pass. "Do you require assistance?"

"Is the floor plan standard here? The spider room in the usual place?"

"The usual place," replied the operator. "Proceed." The rank of captain would have allowed Alex to use the transit platforms. But it was not a long walk, so he preferred to go to the spider room on foot. It was a subtle pleasure that was hard to explain—to walk through the wide, half-empty tunnels stretching under the buildings of the port, to nod to the passers-by. There were no passengers here, no tradesmen, no pickpockets, none of the scum that accumulated in any transit artery like cholesterol in human veins. All who remained here were his people. Even if not all were speshes.

The spider room was the spaceport name for the accounting and contract departments. The name reflected both the appearance of such departments and their functionaries, and the eternal antagonism between the technical workers and the paper-pushing bureaucrats. The spiders often retaliated with a vengeance. At times, Alex felt that if it were up to them, no ship would ever leave port.

"Are you here on business?" inquired the guard at the entrance to the bureaucratic realm. The question was almost a ritual one, and Alex had heard it in dozens of spaceports.

"No, I'm just a masochist," Alex retorted, as usual.

The guard smirked and touched a sensor, unblocking the entrance. He would probably have been happy to let a terrorist into the spider room, but for some reason no terrorist ever turned up to threaten the lives of accountants.

Alex walked in.

The spider room was utterly quiet. Many other departments preferred to have some background music. Not here. Well, maybe they did have music, but at each individual workstation.

Twenty spiders, or to be exact, she-spiders, turned their heads simultaneously and peered at Alex. Almost all of them used the simplest neuro-shunts, and delicate bundles of wires stretched down from their temples to the desktop computers. Only a few accountant-speshes went without these dubious ornaments. Neuro-terminals were built into the headrests of their chairs.

"Good morning," said Alex.

He always felt slightly uncomfortable entering a spider room. It wasn't fear or hostility . . . more like a nagging feeling of shame at bothering these people with his seemingly petty and useless business, while they were busy solving truly important problems.

The spiders were quiet, busy with their silent network dialog. Only one girl, the youngest and prettiest one, was moving her lips—she had not yet rid herself of this useless habit. Alex had no intention of taking advantage of her weakness, but her mouth moved so distinctly that he could not help reading her lips. "He's hot . . . girls, let me . . . come on . . ."

Oh, no! All that would mean was that she'd take three times longer than necessary to process his documents.

One of the accountant-speshes gestured to him to come up. That was good. He could hope that this spesh-woman, in her virtual detachment, would not take too long.

"Name?" said the spider. Her eyes were closed, and she did not even bother to take a look at the pilot for politeness's sake. The information from the computer receptors was enough for her. Well, at least she was nice enough to talk to him in person rather than using a computer speaker and a voice synthesizer. She had a pale, bluish face, thin lips, swollen eyelids covered with red traces of capillaries, and short, smoothly pulled-back hair.

"Alex Romanov, spesh, master-pilot . . ." he began, and the spider lifted her hand, indicating that he had provided enough information.

Alex stopped in mid-sentence. Stood there, looking at the spider's desktop computer. The screen was turned off, so he had no way of knowing what the spider was doing at the moment. Perhaps she was preparing someone's contract. Or looking for ways to evade taxes. Or sorting warehouse cargo. Or maybe she was making love to a partner on the other side of the galaxy. The little computer with a small sticker proudly proclaiming "Gel-Crystal inside" allowed her to do a whole lot. Even if the crystal was only the size of a matchhead . . .

"The spaceship *Mirror* of the Sky Company," said the spider.

She opened her eyes.

This was so unexpected that Alex started.

It was as though a mighty sorcerer had whispered a magic word, turning the computer's living appendage human again.

The spider turned out to be rather young. Even pretty. If only she would change the hair, visit a cosmetologist, and replace her work overalls with a dress . . .

"Your papers," she said.

Alex did not understand her. He reached into his pocket for his copy of the contract. But the she-spider was already handing him the freshly printed ship permit.

"Identity stamp."

Alex licked his finger, touched it to the stamp. A few rainbow waves ran through the thin plastic sheet.

"Good luck," said the spider.

"That's it?" asked Alex, utterly confused.

"Yes. That's it. Is there a problem?"

"Well . . ."

"The ship is launch-ready. You have your permit. Can I help you with anything else?"

He had nothing to say. The spiders had done their part. The way they were supposed to . . . in an ideal world. But for some reason, this time there were no long excursions into Alex's life story, no such questions as: Were you really an enuresis sufferer at the age of five? What were the reasons for your deep emotional attachment to your paralyzed grandmother? Did you drink a lot before the bar fight on Zasada?

"Thank you," said Alex. "Excuse me."

"Yes?"

"No . . . nothing."

He turned and started to walk toward the door, feeling the gaze of all the spiders on his back.

What in the world was going on?

Was this their customer appreciation day?

Were quality assurance inspectors watching every spider room employee?

Did Alex's face remind the spider of her high school sweetheart?

Too good to be true was also bad. The guard looked at Alex in surprise. Then asked, "That bad, eh?"

"Yeah . . . seems like it . . ."

"Early this morning, another spesh . . . the guy barely walks in, then rushes out all red in the face, hands shaking. Turns out he's missing some info about relatives on his mother's side. They told him to go get it. Three days' running around at least, he said. No one's ever been interested in these relatives, and now all of a sudden . . . For some insurance discount, can you believe that? For his own good. And the ship he's been hired on is leaving tonight."

The guard laughed without malice, with compassion, even. He himself must have had occasion to deal with the spiders.

"Insurance is a good thing," said Alex. Nodded to the guard and went on to the transit platform, left by someone nearby. Maybe it had even been left there by that other spesh, the unfortunate guy who was now fighting with the spiders of the imperial archives.

According to the papers, his ship was waiting not in the hangar but right out on the landing field. This probably meant it had not been on the planet for very long. Alex stood on the platform, lightly holding onto the handrail—a part of his specialization, imprinted through repetition, was the habit of always having at least three balance points when on a moving object. The platform glided out into the main tunnel and hurtled along at full speed underneath the landing field.

Alex suddenly realized what had been bothering him from the very beginning.

The right to choose his own crew.

Things like that just weren't done. Well, to be exact, they could be done, but only with the vessels built on this planet. But *Mirror* had been assembled on Earth.

Someone had to have been in charge of the ship on its way to Quicksilver Pit. Okay, so it may have not been a full crew; it could have been the bare minimum—a pilot, a navigator, and a power engineer. But to hire people for a one-way trip and then to start looking for a whole new crew on another planet—that was absurd.

Earth could offer a far better choice of specialists than a colony world, even a well-developed one.

And then there was the useful tradition of keeping at least one member of the previous crew aboard. Every ship had its own unique character, and an experienced person could often save not only time and money, but the very life of the vessel.

Weird . . .

The platform slowed down, stabilized under an exit shaft, and slowly started rising. Sixty-five feet up, through layers of rock and then the concrete pad of the landing field . . . Alex glanced at the Demon. It seemed thoughtful and wary.

Right. Something was odd, but what could it be . . .? It was like that old joke about speshes that had been making its rounds among naturals for the last hundred years—"I smell a rat, but where is it?"

"But we needed the money. We couldn't let the girl die, could we?" Alex asked the Demon.

Judging by the little devil's face, they very well could have. So what was up?

The ship was an experimental model? Something dangerous, still being tested—trick a crew into it, and watch what happens? Not likely. Judging by the papers, it was a very good ship, and it had no unexpected novelties. All the equipment was standard. A dangerous route, perhaps? Also bull. People got lured into danger by money, insurance, discounts . . . anything but lies. There would always be volunteers to stick their heads into a lion's jaws; why make people do it against their will?

Something barely legal? The same objections applied.

So it wasn't about the ship. Everything was always about people, not metal.

Alex shook his head and tried to toss his doubts away. Not for good . . . just to put them away into a far corner of his mind.

The platform slid out through the open aperture of a hatch, wobbled a little as it adjusted to the new bearing, and sailed on over the landing field. After a few seconds, Alex really did forget all his troubles.

He was home. . . .

Although it had lost its former prominence, the spaceport was still fully alive. Two shuttles were landing simultaneously. At a distance, Alex identified them as a couple of old *Manta Rays*, maybe the third or fourth model. He guessed what they were not so much by their shape as by the piloting trajectory and landing speed. In the middle of the field, spreading wide the three rings of its supports, stood a heavy *Cachalot* freighter, probably of the maximum tonnage allowable in this spaceport. From it crawled a line of autoloaders clutching tanks and containers in their grippers. Working on a delicate pleasure ship, *Otter*, were small repair-robots that crawled along the ship's surface, checking and repairing the skin.

Here was the only place worth living. Here and in flight.

Alex was smiling.

His mood was no longer affected by the dull grayness of the sky, where smog and rain clouds blended into a foul-smelling cocktail. Above this sky was another, clear and boundless, created for the freedom of flight . . . for him personally.

Then the platform skirted the *Otter*, and Alex saw his own ship. *Mirror* stood in the launch-ready position. It looked as though a giant discus hurled by a titan had stopped in midair and remained, hovering above the ground, in no hurry to soar into the sky. A bio-ceramic disc of ninety-eight point four feet in diameter, six supports, three main engines in a slightly unusual arrangement clustered in the stern . . . well, that might even be a good thing. The bulge of the bridge deck was slightly larger than average for a vessel of this size. It looked like co-piloting was possible.

Alex swallowed to get rid of a lump in his throat.

Mirror was blindingly beautiful. The perfect ship, with its enlarged bridge, its unusual engine configuration, the tender green of its armor . . .

It was love at first sight. Just the ship's appearance was enough.

The same feeling as when a person capable of love is shaken at the sight of a face in a crowd. There might be dozens, hundreds, or thousands of other faces around, but they all are no longer important.

Sometimes Alex regretted not being able to love other humans. But only till he fell in love with a ship.

"Hello . . ." he whispered, gazing at *Mirror*.

The platform slowed down. Alex jumped down onto the concrete and walked up to the ship. Reached over, touching the armor carefully with just his fingertips. The bio-ceramic surface was warm and resilient. Alive.

"You know who I am . . ." said Alex quietly. "Right? You can see me . . . Hello . . ."

He went around the ship, touching the armor with his hand as far up as he could reach. The ship was silent. It was studying him, too.

"Do you like me?"

Now he was glad that there was no one aboard. This was his moment. Or, rather, he shared this moment with the ship.

"Receive your captain."

The identity chip below his collarbone remained motionless. *Mirror* had not requested a full identity check. And that was nice. It was a sign of reciprocity. Of trust.

A hatch opened overhead, and down slid a ladder with a small platform on the bottom end. Alex stepped onto it and let the ship take him up inside.

The cargo bay turned out to be standard. Three high-speed spacesuit blocks, a strapped-in scooter. Alex waited for the skin plating to grow together beneath his feet, stepped off the platform, which had become part of the floor, and walked over to the central hall of the ship.

So far, everything was as usual. The configuration of the ship dictated the layout of the inner quarters, with only one alteration— the side engines had been moved aft and replaced by battle stations. The inspection should always start with them. Then he had to open the envelope with instructions in the captain's quarters, and only after that, proceed to the bridge. But now he did not give a damn about the prescribed procedure. He started walking toward the bridge. The ship ran a gentle wave of light in front of him along the hallway, adjusting to his speed rather than setting the pace.

"Captain's access," said Alex, stopping in front of a hatch.

This time, his identification chip pulsated. The ship could not give him complete control without a full identity check.

Then the hatch door drew itself into the wall.

The bridge was indeed constructed for two pilots. Alex stood for a moment, evaluating the small oval space—the screens in the walls shone with a matte whiteness, the pilot chairs were open, the reserve panels fully charged.

All was normal. He had been afraid that a two-person bridge on such a small ship might turn out to be uncomfortable. But so far he saw no such thing. The captain's pilot's chair was slightly in front of the other one—an appropriate symbol. Maybe two pilots would even be a good thing.

Although a lot depended on who became the co-pilot.

Alex walked over to the pilot's chair. Lay down, fastened himself in manually.

The ship waited patiently.

Alex closed his eyes.

Was it fear? No . . . not fear. More like excitement, the kind a teenager feels before his first kiss, when it is already sure to happen, lips nearing each other . . . but everything still undiscovered, wonderful, never experienced by anyone ever before . . .

Alex had been a master-pilot on ships far larger than *Mirror*, but had captain's access only on the old training-vessel, a *Heron*, one of three at the flight academy.

To continue the analogy—the *Heron* was a whore. An experienced, skillful, good-natured prostitute, each day instructing another young novice in the art of flying. Alex remembered his first ship, thought of it often with warmth and gratitude, but now everything was different.

Or would be . . .

"Contact . . ." he said, dropping back in his pilot's chair.

And felt a warm wave take root in the back of his head, and then, flaring up, rush through his body. The altered neurons of the occipital lobe of his brain entered into a resonance with the neuro-terminal.

The world vanished. It died away in a blinding flash, and then was reborn.

Alex turned into his ship.

He stretched. Every bit of his discus-shaped body quivered slightly on its supports. Felt the beat of the ship's gluon reactor. He turned on his sensors and took in the space around the port. The newly landed *Manta Rays*, a *Cayman* just entering the stratosphere, sharp needles of gliders, dipping and soaring over the city, beyond the no-fly zone . . .

But this was not yet the complete confluence. Somewhere very close, almost interwoven with his consciousness, the ship had its own life. It was lending him its body—it became an extension of his mind—and yet it was watching him from a distance. Alex turned off the sensors and remained in the dark silence of the inner space.

One-on-one with the rainbow-colored haze.

"Touch me . . ."

Iridescent fog, sun-illuminated clouds, swarming lights.

"Become one with me . . ."

The rainbow trembled and spilled into a rain of flares.

They became one being.

Spaceships, like supercomputers, fully automated factories, ocean liners, and other semianimate creatures, were not true individuals. Humans did not need competitors. Some people thought that the artificial minds of ships were limited to the intelligence level of dogs; others compared them to rats. Which comparison was most flattering was a matter of opinion.

But at this moment, none of that mattered.

They had formed a whole—the man, with all his memories, skills, and experience, and the ship, a collection of specialized programs—connected to each other by a single moral and ethical matrix. The ship could be sad, or happy; it knew fear and enmity, attraction and disgust. Sure, maybe only at the level of a dog or a rat, a cat or a pig. But he would let all those who had never experienced a confluence have their endless battles of wit.

Alex knew a simple, secret truth. Every ship had a soul.

And only those who became captains could fully know this soul.

"I won't hurt you . . ."

The ship could not reply. Words were used by the service programs, which were intricate, well trained, capable of keeping up a conversation, and utterly brainless.

But as for that which made up a ship's soul, there was only non-verbal communication, in the brief instant of unity with its captain.

"I love you . . ."

The ship had no face, no age, no gender, no voice.

Only a rainbow-colored web of emotions, forever frozen on the brink of self-awareness.

Loving a ship was as absurd as having sex with an animal. Officially, no one ever used the word "love" to describe the relationship between a ship and its captain. They called it "empathy" or "emotional contact."

Yet everyone knew the truth.

This was what made up the very attractiveness and the sharp bitterness of the captain's position. To leave your ship was like leaving your sweetheart. Sure, this relationship could diminish—its brightness could fade. A captain could even wish to leave his ship, and a ship, by the same token, could refuse to accept its captain. There were those who went from ship to ship with the flippancy of a Don Juan. And then there were ships that did not accept anyone, did not go for any "emotional contact."

Still, being a captain was nothing to be flippant about. Sooner or later, everyone who had ever said "contact" while in the captain's chair reached this realization.

Now this moment had arrived for Alex.

The rainbow-colored web touched him, shyly, tenderly, carefully . . .

Alex waited, now just as incorporeal, stretched out over black darkness, wide-open to everything.

"Love me . . ."

And a warm rainbow washed over him.

CHAPTER 3.

His legs were slightly shaky. Alex got up from the captain's chair as it softly pushed him up, just the way he liked it to.

Everything had changed.

The world had acquired meaning. A unique and all-important meaning.

He wondered if those who could love other humans ever felt this way. He doubted it.

"Thank you," he whispered.

Now the ship was all his. It could fly with another pilot and obey the orders of the flight control or a military patrol officer, but only if Alex did not cancel the orders. Although "order" was the wrong word. They were not orders or even requests; they were more like wishes.

"I'll be back tomorrow morning," he said. "Prepare my quarters. And quarters for two more people—no, make it three more, just in case."

"Your quarters are ready," reported the ship's service computer.

"Good. See you tomorrow."

This time, there was no reply. Alex's words had been addressed to that part of the ship that could not talk.

"Sushi, sir?"

A waitress stopped next to his table, a small aquarium cart hovering near her shoulder. Alex stretched his neck a bit to take a look at the cart.

"Yes, please."

"Traditional-style or roasted?"

"Roasted." Alex did not bother mentioning to her that it was not his mistrust of the local cuisine, but a habit, well established from his school days, of cooking, if only slightly, any protein that was not from Earth. "I'd like a large serving, please. From the right corner, at the very bottom."

"At the bottom, the krill's already asleep," said the girl uneasily. She lifted up a glass colander. The cart obligingly lowered itself and drew out little panels with cooking forms, an oven, and a small press. "I could make a few runs at the top . . ."

"No, no. Right from the very bottom," said Alex, looking at the iridescent dots inside the aquarium. "When krill is slightly drowsy, the flavor is better. Oh, and double the spices, please."

"All right." The waitress seemed to like the order. Alex watched her as she gingerly scooped out the slumbering krill from the bottom of the aquarium, skillfully poured it into a bowl, stirred in the seven-spice mixture, squeezed the krill mass with a small hand-press, then sliced it into thin strips and tossed it onto a burning-hot stone plate.

"Please don't fry it all the way through," hastily added Alex. "Just a little, to make the chitin a bit crunchy."

In a moment, he had a serving of sushi on his plate. It was wonderfully fresh, with a lot of spicy, fragrant steam rising from it. Amazingly enough, Quicksilver Pit's oceans remained practically unpolluted, and all the seafood was natural. Alex knew that artificial protein was much cheaper, more nutritious, and less dangerous than the natural stuff. But a marked preference for natural foods was a tradition among pilots.

Besides, Alex rather liked it. He was grateful to his parents for not including a modernized digestive system into the parameters of his specialization. Of course, it took up extra space, required extra time for eating, and extra energy was expended on digestion. But the alternative—forever eating artificial protein at McRobbins—no, thanks!

He poured some light soy sauce over his sushi and took a taste. Wonderful! The Maguro sushi had not been brought yet, but the spaceport's Japanese cafe was so good that Alex already expected all the food he ordered to be delicious. Although, judging by the price, the Maguro sushi would probably be made with cloned tuna tissue, growing in a bucket in the kitchen somewhere. Still, it wouldn't be pure synthetic protein with added artificial flavors.

By the time a waiter changed his plate, Alex was already full and quite content with life. He surprised the waiter by asking him for a telephone. He had changed out of his motley outfit and into a standard captain's uniform with master-pilot badges, but had simply forgotten to bring a communicator from the ship. Confluence did have its aftereffects. An odd mixture of exhilaration and languor still lingered within him.

He dialed the number of the hotel room computer. Kim

answered almost immediately. The display screen of the borrowed telephone was tiny, and the hotel equipment was also far from perfect. Still, he could tell that the girl's expression was calm.

"Everything's okay?"

"Uh-huh." She sniffed. "I'm practicing."

"What?"

"Trying out my muscles. Is it normal that I don't get tired?"

"Probably. But don't overdo it, okay?"

They were both silent for a few moments.

"You coming back?" she said at last.

"Yes. Will you be there?"

Her smile was barely discernible, or maybe Alex was just imagining it.

"We'll see. Probably."

"Get some rest. Don't wear yourself out," said Alex. Hung up and handed the phone back to the waiter, who had tactfully stepped aside to give Alex a bit of privacy.

Too bad the long sleeves of his new uniform hid the Demon. He toyed with the idea of cutting out a little window in the sleeve's deep-blue cloth and covering it with a piece of see-through plastic . . .

His crew would die laughing . . . that is, when he got a crew.

Actually, the crew was the very reason he was still at the spaceport. In the rare instances when the hiring was left to the captain's discretion, there were two ways to do it. You could consult the official search on the infonet. Hardly anyone ever did that. Or you could hold a series of personal interviews—the method preferred by anyone with any common sense. The spaceports' watering holes were the places to conduct such interviews.

Alex wondered how many people were already watching him from afar, curious, anxious, waiting for him to finish his lunch.

The Maguro sushi was good, but Alex had to force himself to finish it. He ordered some sake and an expensive Earth-made cigar. He liked sake, but didn't care for cigars. But it was a signal well understood by every astronaut, so he had to forget about cigarettes for now.

The waiter stood nearby with a tray, upon which was a box of cigars, a guillotine cigar cutter, and a massive crystal lighter. Alex took his time lighting up.

"Happy hiring, sir," said the waiter, and he left.

Everyone who had worked at a spaceport for at least a week would know exactly what it meant if a captain smoked a cigar.

"May I?"

Alex threw an appraising glance at the first candidate.

He was a young or recently rejuvenated man. Dark-haired, with features that revealed a predominantly Asian genetic heritage. He was dressed in civilian clothes. The outward traces of his specialization were very faint—his pupils were too narrow in the dim cafe light, his forehead was high, and his posture unnaturally straight, as though he was a well-drilled soldier. This was a pilot. A master-pilot.

"Please . . ." Alex gently pushed the bowl of hot water holding the bottle of sake towards him. This, too, was a sign.

They had a drink in silence, openly evaluating each other. At this point, the interview could be cut short. The pilot could simply get up, thank Alex for the sake, and leave. Or Alex could put down his cigar and look away. That would mean "no." They would not work together well.

"You're also a pilot." The man broke the silence first.

"Yes, I am."

"A master-pilot," he was thinking aloud, "and you're looking for another master-pilot? You must have a large ship."

"Does that bother you?"

"No."

"Good. But what I have is a small, multifunctional vessel."

The pilot winced. He asked with a hint of hope, "Are there a lot of duties besides piloting?"

"Not really."

"Then what you need is a regular pilot," said the man firmly. "Two master-pilots on the same ship is kind of odd."

"You're right. But I have orders from the ship's owner. The co-pilot has to be a master."

There was a spark of curiosity in the man's eyes. He hesitated for a second, but then shook his head.

"No . . . It won't do. Good luck to you, Captain."

"Not interested in the terms of the contract?" Alex asked him. He liked the stranger, and the man did not look as though he'd been riding high lately.

"No, thank you." The pilot smiled dryly. "Don't want to be tempted."

He gave a quick nod and got up. That was it. And everyone saw that it was he who had refused the offer, and not the captain who rejected his candidacy.

Alex drew in the cigar's thick, heavy smoke. No, cigars weren't his thing.

He understood the pilot's position perfectly. For a master to agree to co-pilot, he would have to be really desperate. He would rather drag a clumsy *Hamster* full of pig iron around the orbit than play second fiddle on the most interesting routes. But the owner's instructions were perfectly clear.

A six-member crew.

A captain with the specialization of master-pilot. Another master-pilot. A navigator. An engineer. A fighter. And a doctor.

No cargo specialist, no trade expert . . . Or, to be more precise, these positions were optional, in case they were an additional specialization for one of the crewmembers. So they were not being hired for trading missions. There would be no linguists or xeno-psychologists. That would mean no contact with the Others was expected. All the work would be taking place within the Human Empire.

And yet . . .

The requirement for two master-pilots could only mean lengthy and difficult routes.

A fighter on board meant possible visits to troubled planets.

A doctor meant very long trips.

All this was hard to reconcile. Even more disquieting were the possible reasons for giving Alex such easy access to the rank of captain and carte blanche in hiring the crew, when its odd composition could only mean highly unusual and difficult trips.

"May I?"

Alex looked up.

A very serious and intelligent face. A light-haired Europeoid of a rare, unmixed genotype. Judging by the badges on his uniform and the visible signs of specialization, he was an engineer. A Star of

Valor on his lapel meant he was a retired military man. And if an honor ever truly had to be earned, it was the Star of Valor. He was an ideal candidate . . . But . . . but Alex did not like him for some reason.

They studied each other for a few seconds.

"You are probably right, Captain," said his would-be engineer politely. "We won't get along. Too bad. I've been out of work for a while."

"Would you care for a drink?"

"No, thank you. You obviously have a long day ahead of you. I wouldn't want to waste your time." He walked away. Alex followed him with a gloomy stare.

A professional. A good spesh, and a good man. But they wouldn't work well together. When you spend half your life in a hermetically sealed tin can, you learn to see that at first glance.

His hiring spree had started out badly. And in some places, they believed that if a captain rejected the first three candidates right off the bat, you shouldn't bother approaching him. You wouldn't have any luck. Astronauts were the most superstitious people in the universe.

"Captain?"

The woman hadn't even observed the customary interval. Leaned on the table with both hands, inclining slightly towards Alex.

"Looking for a crew?"

She was not young. Tall, almost as tall as Alex. Black. Beautiful. But not a natural kind of beauty. It was the work of plastic surgeons who make a transformed body look more attractive. Her face had a kind of geometrically precise diamond shape. Her eyes were too large, almost like Kim's. Her hands and nails were oddly shaped . . . She had the pin of a cargo specialist on her blouse. The expression on his face had probably given something away.

"Don't need a cargo tech?" asked the woman bluntly.

"Unfortunately not. My ship is small. Not a freighter."

"Excuse my intrusion then, Captain . . ."

"Wait!"

"Yes?" The lady slightly raised her eyebrows.

"Your specialization is not cargo technician."

"You're right. But a small ship won't need a doctor, either."

"Actually, we do."

"Curious . . ." After a few seconds' hesitation, she sat down. "Will you offer me a drink?"

"Yes, of course."

Alex hastily filled up a small cup, handed it to the woman. They clinked their cups.

"What kind of ship do you have?"

"*Mirror* is an unclassified vessel assembled on Earth. Most parameters are of a modernized discus yacht of moderate tonnage. A six-member crew, myself included." Alex caught himself cajoling the woman. Almost trying to ingratiate himself to her.

"Curious," she said again. "Does it at least have a sick bay? Or is that combined with the galley?"

"A fully equipped sick bay. Must have been stripped from a destroyer."

"Hell." She laughed a bit uneasily. "Must have been? Have you been the captain for long?"

"A couple of hours."

"Right. Who else is in the crew?"

"Just me."

"Okay, I get it."

She twirled the sake cup in her fingers, still not in any hurry to drink.

"Details?"

"Union base pay for unclassified ships, plus a twenty percent bonus. A two-year contract."

"And where are we flying?"

"Don't know."

"Purpose?"

"Don't know that, either."

"Sounds marvelous, Captain . . ."

"I know how it sounds. But I have already accepted the offer."

"Perhaps you just didn't have a choice?"

She had guessed right, so Alex decided it would be better to say nothing.

"All right . . . I'm Janet Ruello, forty-six years of age, doctor-spesh, cargo technician . . ." She hesitated a split second and continued, ". . . gunner-spesh, linguist-spesh, junior pilot-spesh, ready to consider your offer."

Alex pushed away his sake cup. Looked hard at Ruello. She was absolutely serious.

"Four specializations?"

"Five. But the fifth one is irrelevant."

"I'd like to know what it is anyway."

An angry irony appeared in the woman's dark eyes.

"Executioner-spesh. Officially, it has another name, but that's what it is. Actually, that is my main specialization."

"You're from Eben!" exclaimed Alex, finally catching on. "Damn . . ."

"Yes, I am." The woman glared back at him. "The planet Eben is quarantined. I was born there. I served in the Mutual Understanding Corporation until the age of thirty. Was taken prisoner of war during the battle of Pokryvalo. Five years of psychotherapy. Temporary citizenship of the Empire, with a permit to work and reproduce."

Now it was clear to Alex why this woman with five—well, let it be four—specializations was wearing the pin of a cargo technician, a profession she had acquired on her own.

"What is your decision?" she asked dryly.

"May I ask you something, off the record?"

"Yes. I think that would be fine . . ." She looked suddenly embarrassed.

"Do you have any experience with determining specialization?"

Janet shrugged.

"Well, I'm not an expert, of course, but I have some experience. It's standard procedure in our fleet to determine which specialization will turn out to be the dominant one, and whether there are any physiological conflicts in the body. For example, the work of a doctor and a detective cannot be combined for psychological reasons, and the jobs of a navigator and a pilot because of physiology. Everybody knows that, but there are many situations which are much more complicated."

Janet, it seemed, was happy to talk. Alex nodded, satisfied with her answer, and then asked, "And why did you lose the war so quickly? Ten years ago, Eben's fleet almost matched the firepower of the Imperial forces. And you had all that training . . . each person had at least three specializations, right? I mean, what happened?"

"You really don't know?" A slight note of surprise flashed in Janet's voice. "We had not been trained to fight against humans! Quite the opposite . . . We believed that the human race had to rule the universe. Another six months, or a year, and nothing could have stopped us, believe me. Oh, Deus Irae! Our *Liturgy*-class space cruisers could have blasted off a star's photosphere, turning it into a supernova! The cleansing fire that would have burned away all the planets of the Others!"

"Good thing you didn't have the time to build those cruisers!" said Alex, closely watching Janet's reaction.

"Not so. Two cruisers were ready. They couldn't have broken through to the sectors of the Others, but to blow away the Sun or Sirius—child's play!" she laughed without mirth. "My dear Captain, we could not fight against humans! It was a shortcoming of our own propaganda. We could cajole, or beg, or explain . . . take prisoners and brainwash them . . . but to kill our own kind . . ."

"The Empire also suffered losses . . ."

"Mostly by accident. Sometimes as a result of nervous breakdowns. Some officers shot to kill and then sent a ray into their own heads as soon as they realized that they had killed their blood brothers. You didn't have such problems."

"Last question, Janet. Forgive me, but I have to ask."

"Go ahead. I understand."

"What is your present attitude toward Eben's ideology? Put

yourself in my shoes . . . to have a person aboard who was born to exterminate any non-human intelligence . . ."

"I still hold firm to my view that the human race is the ideal one in the universe. Chosen by the Creator." Janet was silent for a moment, and then added rather dryly, "Alex, you do understand that the consequences of a specialization are irreversible. Absolutely irreversible."

"But how do you manage to lead a normal life, if you still believe that so strongly?" Alex looked around to see if he could find at least one of the Others. Quicksilver Pit was far from the frontier, but some trading vessels of the Others did fly here. Too bad—there were no non-humans in the cafe. Not a single bulky, clumsy Fenhuan, wrapped into folds of pseudo-feathers, nor a small and agile Bronin, nor a Zzygou . . . not that those "fragrant" creatures would be allowed to come into a restaurant.

"Now I am convinced," said Janet very firmly, "that the xenocidal methods of our ruling church were a disastrous mistake. They are unacceptable for moral and ethical reasons, because by killing the Others without being threatened ourselves, we would be dropping down to their level. The human race must conquer the galaxy by peaceful methods, by perfecting our technology and biotechnology, expanding to other planets, creating beauty, and multiplying vigorously. That is the way to drive the defective races to extinction, clearing the galactic space for us humans. I am even inclined to think that we would then have a duty to preserve their cultural monuments, establish museums and memorials, and use every opportunity to keep the remnants of their worlds' biodiversity in zoos and on reservations."

"And you live your life based on these convictions?"

"Yes, of course. In the ten years since my liberation, I have given birth to four healthy and intelligent children, and specialized them in socially useful, peaceful professions." She thought for a moment, and then added, "Well, nominally peaceful . . . You don't have to worry, Captain. When I see one of the Others, I won't remember any methods to exterminate it. Unless there is imminent danger."

"All right, then. If the contract and the ship suit you . . ."

Janet nodded. A slight smile appeared on her face.

"I think they will suit me. I would prefer a job in cargo, but being a doctor won't be bad. All my other specializations are much more unpleasant. You need recommendations from previous employers?"

"Yes, please. I have no doubt that your qualifications are excellent, but that's the procedure."

Alex handed her one of the copies of the contract he had brought with him, and they had another drink to seal the preliminary agreement. Then Janet left.

Alex's cigar had long smoldered to ashes. In any case, he was supposed to order another one, and so he did.

A medical doctor from Eben . . . that was a great irony of fate. Well, fate was a master of irony.

He had absolutely no doubts about Janet's professional qualities. All of her other specializations were a definite plus, even if she never got to use them. She was practically incapable of aggression towards humans because of the shortcoming of Eben's propaganda machine, the shortcoming which had enabled the Empire to quarantine the planet, to seal it off from the rest of the galaxy.

But would Janet lose it at the sight of a non-human? Would she remember her specialization of executioner-spesh? No, that was hardly possible. She had, after all, been released by the military psychologists, free to interact with society, even have contact with the Others. The psychologists must have been sure of their tactics. Come to think of it, that was a very clever solution to the problem. They did not touch the main postulate of the Ebenian worldview—namely, the idea that humanity was the master race. All they did was convince the POWs of the necessity of using peaceful means to achieve galactic domination. So out of a hundred thousand raging prisoners who would never again see their unfortunate home world, they got a hundred thousand well-qualified speshes who were also fanatically loyal to humanity. The military was forbidden to recruit them, as far as Alex knew. In the military, their faith might acquire thousands of new believers, and the psychological blocks could be dashed to pieces.

"Captain?"

This fellow was very young, barely twenty. Obviously right out of the academy.

"Yes?"

"Do you have a vacancy for an engineer-spesh?"

People were all so impatient today for some reason! Alex had had occasion to witness a hiring ritual conducted by his former captain, Richard Klein—or Roaring Richard, as others used to call him behind his back. During the hiring, Richard seemed to be a completely different person—thorough, patient, even somewhat drowsy. And those who approached his table behaved the same way . . .

"Yes, I do."

"Will I suit you?"

The guy was also a typical Europeoid, and, of course, a spesh—otherwise he could not be an engineer. His skin was really pink, ruddy. He had a bit of a baby face, with sparkling, slightly bulging eyes. His long dark-gray hair lay heavy on his shoulders like a lead screen, which was its function, after all. Making a person resistant to radiation was no easy task. To give just one example—while at work, his testicles had to be retracted inside the pelvic cavity.

"Take a look at the contract," said Alex, handing the fellow a copy. "Gluon reactors, have you had any experience with them?"

"No real work experience," replied the youth absently, reading through the contract. "But I know them well. My last year of school, that's all we studied. And I got here on a ship with gluon engines."

"Did you get your training on Earth?"

"Yes, of course." He paused to think about one of the contract stipulations, and it occurred to Alex that the young fellow might not be as naive as he looked.

A sudden thought made Alex ask, "And what was the name of the ship that brought you here?"

"The *Intrepid*. It was a yacht, with a name like a military cruiser . . ." The fellow looked up from the contract, then nodded. "I like your offer. I don't really want to fly large ships just yet. If you agree to take an engineer with only two weeks' work experience, I'll be on my way to pack."

"Well, we'll risk it, son," said Alex, unsuccessfully trying to give his tone of voice a dash of Richard Klein's haughtiness. "We all had to start somewhere, right?"

Naturally, he wouldn't tell the youth that the post of engineer was the only one where a young recent graduate would actually be preferred. The reason was that any experience working with one type of reactor did nothing to prepare you to work with another type. The behavior of the gluon stream was not statistically predictable, and taking aboard a young novice who was not overloaded with habits would be better than working with an experienced veteran.

"Thank you," said the youngster candidly. "You won't regret it, sir! I, Paul Lourier, nineteen years of age, engineer-spesh, accept your contract."

Unlike all the others interviewed so far, he did not even ask to see the ship. He just signed the contract. Alex promised himself that he'd fight to get the fellow a bonus at the first opportunity. Such acts of trust should be rewarded.

"May I?"

The next candidate was wearing a plaid kilt and a loose-fitting bright blue shirt. He was sturdy and red-headed, but with his almond-shaped eyes, he looked positively Asian. He had an earring in his left ear, and a clip player in his right. His long hair was tightened into a braid. His cheeks bore iridescent spiral drawings—maybe tattoos, maybe just cosmetics. For a few seconds, Alex tried to determine the man's specialization, then gave it up and nodded. Poured a cup of sake.

This candidate also chose to take the bull by the horns.

"Do you need a navigator?"

"Yes."

"Then take a look at this."

He produced a pack of recommendation letters and put them down before Alex.

The collection was impressive. Five years of service in the Imperial Forces on a great variety of different types of vessels, from torpedo boats to battle cruisers. He had changed ships suspiciously often, but at the same time, his recommendations were stellar. "Energy conservation" … "Calculation of hyper-jump in a battle situation" … "During an instrument failure, accomplished ship orientation manually" … "Successfully repaired equipment . . . guided solely by intuition, despite a complete lack of experience in the area . . ."

"Puck Generalov, you've changed your place of employment rather frequently," noted Alex. And something else bothered him about the stellar recommendations. But what was it?

"That's just my personality." The navigator straightened a fold on his kilt, threw one leg over the other. Took a tiny sip of sake. "Just personality. But no one has ever had any complaints about me as a professional."

"Are you conflict-prone?"

"That would be reflected in the documents, Captain."

"That's right. Still . . . I have a small ship. Will a job as a navigator on a yacht suit you?"

"Absolutely. I like small and fast ships."

Generalov took out a crumpled pack of cigarettes, took one out, struck a match on the tabletop, and lit up. Then he inquired, "By the way, I'm gay. Does that bother you?"

"Should it?" said Alex, confused.

"Well, you know, there are many different approaches to ethics . . ."

"I'm from Earth. You don't have to worry about me being prejudiced," answered Alex dryly. Something was still bothering him, but what was it? "I guess you'd want to see the ship? I expect all the crewmembers to show up for a meeting tomorrow morning."

The navigator nodded again. And mentioned casually, "Oh, and by the way, I am also a natural. Would that be a problem?"

Alex was stunned, speechless.

Of course, not all astronauts were speshes. Only a few occupations absolutely required a modified body and mind—engineers, tactical commanders, linguists, and a few other rare professions. All the rest were theoretically open to the naturals. Alex knew some among ship doctors, among gunners . . . he had even met one natural who had been a pilot, though the guy was very old. But to become a navigator! To hold in your mind the five-dimensional picture of the universe, fifteen hundred main hyper-channels, a minimum of thirty thousand known routes, and at least three hundred thousand gravitational peaks . . .

A navigator did not just have to have increased intuition and a sense of space as good as a pilot's. First and foremost, he had to have a mind that worked like a computer, a transformed nervous system, with strengthened logical capacity and reduced emotional reactions. This was what had roused Alex's suspicions. In all the recommendations, however stellar and laudatory, there was no mention of the word "spesh."

"I don't have to worry about your being prejudiced, right?" asked Generalov politely. Alex forced himself to nod.

"No . . . You don't have to worry . . . I'm taking you aboard . . . that is, if the ship and the contract suit you."

The kilt-wearing man watched him, picking at his ear clip. Maybe he was trying to tune it to another station, or maybe he was simply nervous.

"There's the answer to your question," he said all of a sudden.

"What question?"

"Why I change ships so frequently. You fell into the usual trap. It's hard to admit to being prejudiced, but working alongside a natural is unpleasant. You'll take me aboard and then try to get rid of me at the first opportunity. With the best of references, of course, because pilots can't lie."

"Yes, we can."

"Don't make me laugh, Captain. We haven't signed the contract yet—I can ignore seniority for the moment. So let me just say . . ." Generalov puffed his cigarette, smiled. ". . . this would, by the way, be another chance for you to back out. Who needs a troublemaker for a navigator? And no, Captain, you are not capable of lying. The capacity for love is removed in all pilots, and that's very useful. Those who love are not inclined to take risks, except, of course, for the sake of those they love, and a pilot must be ready to die at any moment. But to balance it out, all your other moral qualities are enhanced—integrity, kindness, loyalty, generosity. I bet you're the kind of guy who would jump out on the road to save a lousy mutt, and rescue kittens from a tree, and contribute to charity funds, and give alms to every beggar you pass. So, for you, lying is an agonizing process, extremely unpleasant and almost impossible. Pilots prefer to keep things back, or to dodge the question, rather than lie. You do resent me, don't you?"

"No," Alex forced himself to say.

Respect lit up Generalov's eyes for a moment.

"You are a strong man, Captain. What's your sign?"

"Aries."

"And I'm a Virgo." Generalov smiled. "It's a good combination, you know. We'll get along. Give me that contract of yours!"

Alex silently handed him the form.

Puck looked through the standard lines, shrugged at the numbers.

"Not bad . . ."

He licked his finger and pressed it down to the identification point. Then he separated the sheet in half, gave one part of it back to Alex, and stuck the other into a pocket on his kilt.

"You are now a crew member of the spaceship *Mirror*," Alex told him.

At this, Generalov straightened up, as though he had been pierced through with a stiff pole, and his face lost the smirk he'd been wearing.

"Your orders, Captain."

Only his eyes still retained a tiny spark of irony.

"To change into a standard navigator uniform. Get rid of facial paint. Be at the ship tomorrow at nine a.m."

"Aye-aye, Captain."

"That will be all."

"Permission to spend the evening in the bar, Captain."

"That is your business," said Alex after a moment's contemplation. "But I need you to be in top working shape in the morning."

"Of course." Puck seemed to be waiting for other orders.

"Have you been job hunting a while?"

"A month."

"Okay. Are there any master-pilots here in the hall?"

Generalov did not even look around.

"Only one. The one who approached you first."

"All right . . . see you tomorrow."

After the navigator left, Alex threw back his sake in one gulp. Found the waiter with a glance, made a light gesture in the air, as if signing his check. That sly natural had really put one over on him! One should never underestimate the genetically unaltered, never! First that absurd question about his attitude toward gays, as if it were any of the captain's business who his crewmembers slept with. And then, after Alex had declared that he wasn't biased, came the real blow.

A navigator who was a natural . . . impossible!

And what would be the reaction of the other crewmembers? Janet, who had five specializations? The young engineer, just out of college?

Well, if any of them protested, that would be another reason to back out . . . no, unfortunately, Janet had not signed the contract yet. Unless Paul Lourier refused to trust his life to a natural . . .

For a second, a crazy thought flashed through Alex's mind—what if he were to ask, or even to order, the engineer to oppose Generalov's candidacy? Paul had signed the contract earlier, and from a formal point of view, Alex had a duty to consider his opinion.

The thought came and passed, leaving an unpleasant trace. On one point, Generalov was absolutely right. Lying was hard for pilots. This was part of the price they paid for the stars. Along with their inability to love other humans.

A waiter came. Alex paid his bill and quickly left the dining hall. Two vacancies remained unfilled, but he had an idea about one of them. It was a crazy idea, but it was worth a try.

The hotel front desk had yet another clerk behind it this time. This fellow did not pay any attention to Alex and beamed at the mere sight of the captain's uniform. Such important customers were rare at the Hilton.

Alex went up to his room and touched the doorbell sensor. Caught himself feeling intensely curious. Had Kim really waited for him, or had she preferred to disappear, having first cleaned out the room's credit line?

One always had to pay for believing in people's honesty. But Alex found a strange, perverse pleasure in it on those rare occasions when his faith was vindicated.

Kim opened the door.

She had waited!

Alex shook his head, though he was glad to see the unfeigned joy on the girl's face.

"Kim . . . I asked you to block the door. You didn't even look through the peephole."

"How do you know?"

"When the door camera is on, the lens turns on an infrared light. I can see it clearly."

"Oh . . ." Kim stepped back from the door to let him pass. "Well . . . I didn't have to look. I knew it was you." Now it was Alex's turn to be surprised.

"How did you know?"

"By the sound of your steps. You have a peculiar walk, as if you're trying not to lift your feet from the floor."

"Oh? I hadn't ever noticed . . ." Alex closed the door. Looked down at his feet. "Do I drag my feet?"

"You don't drag them, you just hurry to put them back down. And you never let both feet leave the ground at the same time!" Kim jumped up. "What are you so serious about? I am sorry I didn't look through the peephole. I'll get in the habit, I promise!"

"If both your feet leave the ground, that means you're running . . ." Alex bit his lip. Both your feet . . . and if your feet and legs and pelvis leave without your consent, that's called a work-related injury. "Kim, I get it. There's no artificial gravity on *Hamsters* and other system freighters. I trained on those for about six months. And got used to depending on Velcro. Or maybe it was a part of my specialization. To never lose my balance points."

Kim's interest in the subject seemed to be exhausted.

"That's great. Very useful precaution, friend-spesh. See how I've spent your money?"

She spread out her arms and whirled around, all the while trying to keep him in her field of vision.

"I see. You've changed."

Her worn-out jeans and sweater had been replaced by a black pantsuit. In it, Kim resembled a young professional. Her white blouse and a tiny black tie further enhanced this resemblance.

"Does it look good on me?" asked Kim.

"Yes, very good."

The girl smiled.

"And you look good in your uniform."

"You even look a little older," Alex continued. "You might pass for someone who's had her metamorphosis six months ago and been through some accelerated training courses already."

"Why? Is that important?"

"Probably. We have to talk, Kim."

She immediately got serious. Alex took her by the hand, led her into the room, and made her sit down in a chair. He sat down in front of her, then got out his cigarettes and lit up.

"Give me a cigarette."

Alex lit another cigarette and handed it to her.

"We have to talk" is a magic phrase. One of the few that instantly puts a person into a serious mode. No one ever says it in order to talk about the weather or to discuss weekend plans.

It is very instructive to watch the reaction of a person expecting a serious conversation. Some people get nervous, some withdraw into themselves, some prepare for a confrontation.

Kim simply braced herself.

"What is your name? Your full name?"

"Kim O'Hara."

"How old are you?"

"Fourteen. As of one month ago."

"Are you from Quicksilver Pit?"

"No." Kim shook her head.

"Then where are you from?"

"I won't answer that."

Alex sighed. He never expected this conversation to be easy, but the girl's tone of voice was really beginning to trouble him.

"Kim, I must know."

"Why?"

The girl switched to a counterattack.

"Kim, do you have friends or relatives on Quicksilver Pit?"

Silence.

"How long have you been on this planet?"

"What is it to you?"

Great. Why did it have to be this way? You try to help, and all you get is ingratitude!

"All right." Alex interrupted the silence that had stretched between them. "Let's figure out why I need to know this. Yesterday, I pulled you through an off-track metamorphosis. Right?"

Kim took a deep breath and exhaled audibly. Whispered:

"I am thankful, friend-spesh . . ."

"You don't have to thank me. I could not act otherwise, so I can take no credit for that. But for the same reason that I had to help you . . ."

Kim looked at him in surprise.

"For that very reason, I can't just walk away and leave you to your fate. Do you need help?"

The girl lowered her eyes.

"Do you or don't you?" asked Alex harshly. "I got hired onto a ship. Okay? In a couple of days I'm leaving Quicksilver Pit, and I may be gone for a very long time. Do you need help?"

"Yes. I do."

"That's better."

Well, no, it wasn't really better. But at least it was out in the open.

Kim got up, went over to the window, and stood still, gazing into the dim evening sky. She stuck her hands in her pockets and again stood still, having suddenly lost all her happy enthusiasm.

Alex bit his lip. Was this real, or was she just pretending? Either way, it was useless. Apparently the girl did not really understand the reason why he cared about her.

"Where are you from, Kim?"

"Edem."

"How in the world did you end up here?" Alex was feverishly trying to visualize the route. Damn . . . the opposite side of the human sector of space! No less than seven hyper-channel trips or a direct jump in a courier ship. But there were no direct flights from Edem to Quicksilver Pit. There was no demand for them at all. "You're very far away from home."

"I don't have a home anymore. I ran away from my family."

"Why? No, never mind. That's not important. How did you get over to Quicksilver Pit?"

"I'm gifted."

"I believe you, Kim. But before the metamorphosis, you were legally still a minor. To traverse two hundred light years without any documents, or any money . . ."

"Who said I had no money?"

Alex nodded. She was right.

"All right. But why Quicksilver Pit?"

"I had my reasons to head nowhere but here."

"Kim . . . if you won't trust me, like you trusted me yesterday, it won't work between us."

"And what is supposed to work?"

It seemed she was crying, after all. Quietly, inaudibly. To walk over to her now, to hug her, to console her, would be the most natural thing to do. And absolutely the wrong thing to do.

"Are you a fighter-spesh?"

"I guess so."

"What do you mean, you guess so? Kim, every child-spesh knows what he or she is going to be. If a geisha-girl and a boy-doctor play doctor together, they play differently. The girl will be interested in the erotic part of the game. She'll study the rudimentary sexual reactions. The boy will try to listen to her chest, get her pulse, feel her bone structure, and examine her tonsils. If an architect-child builds a sand castle, that castle will last for a week. How did you play as a kid? Did you like to fight?"

"Yes."

"Did you win?"

"Of course."

"What about playing with dolls?"

"I wouldn't mind a doll even now." Kim giggled suddenly. "When I ran away from home, I took Lucita with me. She's my favorite doll. But she was lost with my bag . . . on a ship."

Alex rubbed his forehead. He had had occasion to see girl-speshes who were honed to become fighters. Did they play with dolls? Maybe, but for some reason, he thought that the future fighters were more likely to use their dolls for practice, as punch dummies . . .

"I played doctor, too," said Kim suddenly. "But I don't know what was more interesting to me—the pulse rate, or the sexual reactions."

"Kim, my ship needs a fighter-spesh."

The girl turned to him.

"Really?"

"Yes. But you have no ID. And no fighter certificate, either. How about we go to the nearest clinic tomorrow, run a genetic analysis, and have your new documents issued?"

"No!"

"Why not?"

"They'll come looking for me, don't you see that?"

"You've had your metamorphosis. You're of age now. Even if, according to your specialization agreement, you owe your parents the reimbursement of its cost, that can't infringe on your individual rights . . ."

"No!"

Her voice had risen to a shout. To keep insisting would be pointless.

"But you have nothing against employment on a ship?"

"Nothing."

"I'll think of something, Kim. If you are really a fighter-spesh, then everything's all right."

The girl looked at him, frowning. Alex patiently waited.

"Why do you even bother helping me?"

He answered with a question. "How much do you know about pilot-speshes?"

"Nothing. Well, you told me you guys have strong bones and a good eye . . ."

"And we also have a heightened sense of responsibility. A pilot never forsakes his crew or his passengers."

"But . . . I'm not your crew . . ." The girl came closer to him, sat down on the floor beside his chair, looked deep into his eyes.

"Yesterday, I had no crew, Kim. I helped you out on the monorail, fed you . . . and things just kept going from there. So there's no point thanking me for my selfless kindness. That's just the way I'm made. See?"

"How strange . . ." All her recent tears had vanished without a trace. Kim stretched out her hand, touched Alex's face. "So you're . . . not free?"

"What makes you say that?"

Her hand was caressing his face, slowly, as though she were a blind girl, exploring his features.

"You are forced to be kind and caring . . ."

"Kim, we are all forced to do different things. A soldier has a duty to give his life for humanity, a doctor to save the life of a patient, a pilot to protect his crew. Even the naturals aren't any more free than we are. We speshes change at the moment of metamorphosis, when the nucleic bombs go off. The naturals are also coerced all their lives by their parents, school, society . . ."

"That's different."

"No, it's the same thing, Kim. I know that I have a heightened sense of responsibility towards others. So what? Is that a bad thing? If I were a cynical, heartless bastard . . . like a detective-spesh, for instance . . . then I'd have something to worry about."

"You wouldn't worry. You would think that was the right way to be."

"Kim . . ."

Alex gently pulled her up from the floor, sat her down onto his lap.

"You are right about some things, of course. But I'm not at all bothered by the details of my specialization. That would be like complaining about being beautiful, or healthy, or smart. If everyone were specialized in at least a few basic moral qualities, life would be better."

Kim nodded. But she still looked rather uncomfortable. Could it be the material basis for his actions that kept bothering her?

"Kim, don't worry about it. I'm glad I could help you out. I would have done it even without any kind of specialization. You are a very nice girl."

"You like me, then?" She looked into his eyes.

"Yes."

"Alex . . ." Her fingers slid up through the pilot's hair. "Don't misunderstand me, okay?"

"I'll try."

"Maybe you think I am sorry for you. It's not that. Or that I am trying to repay you for your kindness. It's not that, either . . ."

Alex put a gentle hand to her lips.

"Kim. Don't."

The girl shook her head.

"No! You don't understand! Alex . . . I know things never happen like that. You don't believe me!"

"Kim, I do believe you, but . . ."

"No, you don't! You think I'm a little horny bitch. And that I got over from Edem that way, too . . ."

Alex kept his silence. He did not exclude that possibility, but did not think it the only option, either.

"Maybe you think this is the way I want to repay my debt . . . but it's not that. Honest! Do you believe me?"

Alex gazed into her eyes for a second. Many people were skilled in the art of lying. But was it possible to lie like *this*?

"Kim, I do believe you. Are you sure you have to do this?" Instead of an answer, she leaned over and kissed his lips. Her kiss had none of the maddeningly alluring skill of a real geisha-spesh. It was the kiss of an ordinary girl with very little sexual experience. But at the same time . . .

Alex suddenly realized that he had absolutely no wish to change her mind.

For a few minutes they kissed, greedily, rapturously. Alex took off Kim's tightly fitted jacket, unbuttoned her blouse. Still kissing him, she swayed her shoulders, sliding out of her clothes. She kept clinging to Alex, as though shy of her nakedness, and that helped him chase away the pesky memories of the previous night, when her naked body held no erotic appeal, only fear and pain.

Damn . . .

Damn!

"Kim," said Alex, trying to move away, "Kim, Kim, wait . . ."

The girl sat still, looking at him a little fearfully. She had already managed to unzip her pants and half-take them off . . . a real scene from an erotic comedy . . .

"Kim . . . you just had your metamorphosis . . ."

"So what?"

Her voice shook a little. She was a lot more excited than Alex.

"Kim . . . you can't have sexual contact for at least a week. When I was done with my metamorphosis, my girlfriend came to visit, and the doctor warned us right away to wait at least a week. . . . That's the general rule."

"But why?"

"Kim . . ." The pilot hugged her tightly. "Let's not. Your development already got messed up once. Let's not rush things."

For a second she stared at him, shocked and speechless, as though she wasn't sure if the pilot was telling her the truth or just kidding, clumsily. Then her lips started trembling.

Alex held her back as she tried to free herself from his embrace. Hugged her, whispered in her ear:

"Kim, it's gonna be all right. Don't rush things. I'll make you a crewmember. Wait just a little while."

"You don't like me!" whispered Kim, sobbing.

"I do . . . Kim, honey, don't cry. I just don't want any harm to come to you."

"It's all your stupid sense of responsibility!" she yelled, lifting her wet face for a second. "It's all your specialization! And nothing would've happened! I feel just fine!"

There was no point in arguing, so Alex said nothing. They sat for a few minutes in the chair together. The girl sobbed quietly, clinging to Alex and no longer trying to wrench herself free. Then, fidgeting awkwardly on his lap, she pulled on her pants, leaned away slightly. Asked, in a probing tone of voice:

"You really are attracted to me?"

"You haven't noticed?"

Kim wiped her eyes with her hand.

"Friend-spesh, don't lie to me, okay? I had only two men in my life, so I don't know, maybe I'm ugly . . ."

"Oh, come on," said Alex with a sly grin. "You know you are a very pretty girl. Fighters' looks aren't programmed, so this is entirely your own achievement."

"Vladimir also said that."

"Vladimir?"

"My first guy. He was a good friend of my parents, and I liked him, too. My parents arranged for him to be my sex instructor. But we didn't meet for very long. Vladimir was a very busy man. An artist-spesh. His paintings are even exhibited on Earth. He did my portrait, too, by the way."

"You have interesting customs," said Alex.

"Why do you say that?"

"On Earth, where I come from, it isn't customary to have real sex instructors. We do have training at school, but only in virtual reality."

Kim shrugged.

"Earth is a rich planet. And technology-crazy. I . . . I had a virtual lover, too. But that's not really common. Everything ought to be natural, as my school sex teacher used to say."

Alex thought in passing of the crystal the girl was hiding in her altered body. Its capacity would have been enough to teach every last schoolgirl on Edem . . .

Why are other people's secrets always so tantalizing?

"Kim, you want to go out to eat?"

"At McRobbins?"

"Ugh." Alex scowled. "Today I took my post as captain. This calls for a celebration. I'll find out which restaurant in town specializes in Earthly cuisine, and we'll go there."

"Will you get me some ice cream?"

"Absolutely."

"Yeah!" Kim smiled and slipped off his lap. "Then give me a sec, I have to put myself together."

She disappeared behind the bathroom door, and there came the sound of running water. Alex got up and walked over to the window.

Was there any trace of yesterday's sky?

No, not even a tiny bit. A thick, ragged layer of dirty, gray clouds. Neither winter, nor spring; neither snow, nor rain. A cold, lead-colored drizzle filled the air. Faded, cheerless rainbows clung to the streetlights.

"It must feel great to be a ship's captain!" yelled Kim from the bathroom.

"It's awesome!" replied Alex.

And smiled.

The warmth of the captain's chair.

Darkness and the multicolored web.

The breath of another soul.

I love you.

Love me.

Be one with me.

How hard life must be for those unable to ever experience it . . .

CHAPTER 4.

They were all waiting at the ship.

Janet, feigning indifference, was looking over the blister of the battle station on the left side. Alex could tell immediately that she liked the vessel a lot.

Puck and Paul were discussing something. Judging by the embarrassed look on the engineer's face, he had just been hit with the news of the navigator's biological status. Although the young fellow looked only slightly shocked.

Upon seeing Alex, Paul straightened his back. Kim walked at Alex's side, trailing slightly as she gazed inquisitively around the landing field. Generalov turned around and also straightened. He had washed off the face paint, and Alex was pleased. Janet limited herself to just a nod—she was not yet a member of the crew. But a tightly packed bag, the kind suited for a minimum of personal belongings, was dangling from her shoulder, and that was encouraging.

"This is Kim O'Hara," Alex introduced the girl, "our . . . possibly, our fighter-spesh."

Paul looked surprised, but glad, too. Puck's face remained unreadable. Janet was silent.

"Paul Lourier, our engineer. Puck Generalov, our navigator. Janet Ruello . . . possibly, our doctor."

"Still having a problem finding a co-pilot?" inquired Janet politely.

Alex nodded. "Yes. I hope to solve the problem today. Do any crewmembers have any objections to the candidacy of Janet or Kim?"

Generalov coughed. Glanced sideways at Paul, as if hoping for his support, and then asked bluntly:

"Captain, as far as I know, having a fighter-spesh on board pre-supposes dangerous trips, right?"

"Possibly. Dangerous trips, or a paranoid boss." Alex gave a dry smile. It's always important to distance yourself from the company owners.

"And you're certain that Ms. O'Hara is adequately trained?"

"In the case of a fighter-spesh, the word 'training' doesn't really apply." Alex regretted these words as soon as they left his lips. Now it looked like he was pointing out the natural's deficiency. Puck could play all the games he wanted, flaunting his naturalness and professional mastery, pushing people's buttons . . . but he still couldn't help feeling deficient.

But Generalov kept his cool.

"I agree with you, Captain. But in case of real danger, I would prefer to have a male fighter aboard. And it's not in any way connected to my sexual preferences."

Alex looked around at Kim. The girl was fingering her white lace collar and smiling at the navigator—a sweet, happy smile.

"Puck, imagine a stranger approaching our group. Whom would he not see as dangerous?"

"All right. I see your point," nodded Generalov. He did not even glance at Kim. "But a fighter-spesh should not be so much a camouflaged killer, as a warning presence."

"I hold a different view. The fighter has to guarantee security."

"And she will be able to guarantee it?"

Alex looked at Kim, caught her questioning glance, and gave a slight nod.

The next split second, the girl was already standing next to Generalov. Her right hand was squeezing his throat, and her left gripped his genitals through the fabric of the uniform.

"Which do you prefer, pain or death?" asked Kim in ice-cold tones. "Choose now."

Puck tried to stir, but that proved to be a bad decision. A grimace of pain contorted his face, and he froze.

"Choose now," repeated Kim.

No one needed a more vivid proof of the fighter's capabilities. No natural could have covered the distance so fast—the movement was imperceptible to the naked eye. Moving in accelerated time was possible only after a total transformation of musculature and the nervous system. Alex said quietly:

"Let our navigator go, Kim." Another split second—this time Alex managed to see a faint shadow and feel a slight movement of the air. He tried to estimate the speed of Kim's movements, but couldn't do it very exactly. In the neighborhood of ninety miles an hour.

Of course, no spesh could keep that speed up for more than a minute. But there wasn't any need for that. They would all be dead by now, if Kim had wanted.

"Puck, do you still have any doubts about her training?"

What a fine beginning for their work together . . . a hateful quarrel between two crewmembers.

Puck cleared his throat, rubbing his neck.

"I take it back, Captain." He finally looked at Kim. Lowered his head slightly.

The girl returned his polite and rather ceremonious bow. Her cheeks were flushed, her hair awry. Those were the outward, the most innocuous, manifestations of what had just happened. Now she ought to have something sweet to drink. A full sugar bowl of coffee, for instance, followed by a piece of meat. Her cells needed to recuperate.

"Good going, kid!" said Janet unexpectedly. "Well, Captain, shall we take a look at the ship?"

The person most interested in the ship was Kim. She had probably never flown on a discus yacht. In the cargo bay, she stared at the transparent six-and-a-half-foot-tall plastic cylinders, then looked at Alex in bewilderment.

"Those are spacesuit units," he told her quietly. But not quietly enough. Generalov heard him and turned his head. A great opportunity to stick it to the captain—a fighter-spesh who had no knowledge of the most elementary features of a ship!

"Captain, permission to test out the wardrobe functions."

"Go ahead," said Alex. What was the natural up to this time . . . ?

Puck stepped over to one of the units, slapped his hand on

the sensor to make the cylinder come open. A thin split appeared in the plastic, then widened to make an opening. The navigator stepped in, and the two sides reattached.

"A full-blown test," Janet said, in a mildly mocking tone. "Show-off . . ."

The plastic clouded up a little as the spacesuit gel filled the inside of the hollow cylinder walls. Then tiny sprayers opened up, and a billowing gray mist filled the cylinder. Invisible force field needles stitched the mist into thick fabric, tightly wrapping Puck from head to toe. Only the navigator's face had a clear space in front of it.

The unit worked fast. When the air inside the cylinder cleared, Puck was fully enveloped in a silvery suit. The spacesuit bulged a little on his back, around his waist, and under his chin—that is, everywhere the gel molecules were forming not just a flexible armor, but also the life-support systems. The face shield of the helmet was the last to condense out of the mist.

The cylinder opened, and Puck stepped out into the cargo bay. He gave Kim a tiny wink, and Alex felt a slight twinge of concern. Was that a sign of respect on Generalov's part? Or was he flirting, despite his declared orientation?

"Captain, the cargo bay systems are functioning properly. Spacesuit assembly time—fifteen seconds."

"Thank you, Navigator. Will you be taking it off?"

Generalov looked at his new suit with obvious pleasure.

"With your permission, sir, not yet."

Alex shrugged. Narcissism was a flaw that could be lived with.

They left the cargo bay and entered the ship's main hall. Puck was the last to follow. His silvery armor crackled slightly, making its final adjustments to his body.

"Everything's standard," said Alex, stopping. "Six cabins are at our disposal."

"Will the quarters also be assigned the standard way?" inquired Janet.

Alex nodded. Although . . . which order would she consider standard? Their crew composition was a little odd.

"Starboard side—captain, fighter, navigator; spaceport side—co-pilot, doctor, engineer. Any objections?"

"Makes sense," confirmed Janet. "A direct hit to either side would still enable the crew to function. Your permission to occupy my quarters?"

"Should I consider this an indication of your joining the crew?"

"Yes."

Alex silently reached for a copy of the contract and handed it to Janet. The black woman threw a passing glance at the text, licked her finger, and forcefully pressed the identification point. Then she gave Alex his part of the copy.

"I'm glad," said Alex. He could have found more heartfelt words, but there was hardly any need for that. Janet was from Eben, so she would not be all that sentimental.

What she said next confirmed his opinion.

"Captain, where is the sick bay?"

"One second." Alex looked at Puck. Narcissistic and irritating as he may have been, he was still worried about only one thing at this moment. Only a navigator could feel almost the same level of attachment to the ship as a captain. "Puck, will you be able to find the navigation module?"

"Yes, of course. I am familiar with discus yachts."

Generalov looked straight down the hall. A door at the end led to the bridge, but there was another door next to it.

"You may go inspect your work station."

"Aye-aye, Captain . . ." The navigator quickly headed down the hall. His space suit had fully adjusted to its new owner, and now his movements were absolutely quiet.

"I envy him a little," remarked Janet suddenly.

"Why?" said Alex.

"Are you familiar with navigation, Captain?"

"Somewhat. The required academic minimum, plus two refresher courses."

"Then you would agree that those are very interesting sensations, Captain."

The hatch door of the navigation module opened in front of Generalov. He looked back at his fellow crewmembers, and then stepped in.

"Let's hope I didn't make a mistake," said Alex. All of Puck's recommendations may have been great, but Alex was still worried.

"If necessary, I will be able to set a course from any point in space," Janet promised him.

"I don't doubt it. But I'd rather not bring shame upon myself and disappoint the bosses . . ." Alex stopped himself. No need to share his concerns with the crew. A captain could be aloof, or close with his crew. In a small ship, the latter was even preferable. But a captain should never show any signs of weakness. He had no right.

"In any case, everyone should be given a chance," he concluded. "Paul?"

"Yes, Captain."

The young engineer was obviously not a chatty type. Or had been brought up in the spirit of strict subordination.

"Where is the reactor on this ship?"

"Aft, Captain."

Alex grinned.

"What about the engines? Are you sure that they and the gluon reactor all fit in the rear of *Mirror*?"

"The reactor module is located aft on this ship, Captain." Paul shyly returned the captain's smile. "In between the engines. We have a tandem gluon reactor called *Niagara*, the newest technology available to the civilian fleet. Radiation screening is done entirely by a force field, with no hard shield. It's really beautiful, Captain, even in the parts of the spectrum that can be seen by a non-specialist."

"Paul, you must have had great teachers!"

"Thank you, Captain. I am also grateful to my academy. But this isn't a typical ship. The thing is, I've already flown on it."

"Flown on it?"

"Then it was called the *Intrepid*. I don't know why anyone would change a ship's name. Granted, the original one didn't fit very well."

"Paul, are you sure?"

The engineer blushed.

"Captain, my quarters were second on the port side. There is this tradition, you see . . ."

Alex walked quickly to the quarters that Janet would be occupying. Put his hand on the lock.

"Open. Captain's orders."

The right for inviolable private space was recognized even on military ships. The identity chip under his collarbone pulsated, confirming Alex's special authority.

The door slid into the wall.

Alex entered the cabin—the usual furnishings, comfortable and functional, like a solitary prison cell. Well, maybe the info terminal was too large for a prison.

The bathroom unit was really tiny. Alex silently sat on the toilet lid, turned his face to the wall.

The small inscription, carved into the plastic with a pocket-knife, was not particularly original.

"Tested and approved. Paul Lourier, engineer-spesh."

Alex looked up. Janet, Kim, and Paul were in the room, staring at him. Paul looked embarrassed, and Janet smiled a barely perceptible smile. Kim didn't understand a thing. Had he now taken his pants down and started doing what people normally do on the toilet, she would probably have taken it for some kind of elaborate space ritual.

"There's a penalty for this kind of thing, Engineer."

"Yes, Captain. Already received it, Captain. Tradition, Captain."

Why were the greenhorns always such sticklers for tradition?

Alex got up, and the damned toilet behind him rumbled softly, starting the self-cleaning cycle, just in case. Damn those simple electronics!

Kim snickered.

"Janet, would you mind if Paul took these quarters, and you took the third on the port side? I suspect this is his only chance to avoid getting another penalty."

"As you wish, Captain."

Alex looked at the engineer next.

"Paul Lourier, I need to see you tonight in my quarters. I will have a few questions for you."

"Aye-aye, Captain."

"Now you may get settled in here . . . or go inspect your work station."

"Aye-aye, Captain. I'll check the reactor."

"Janet." Alex nodded to the doctor. "I have a special request for you. Do you know where the sick bay is?"

"No, I don't."

"Thank God. According to the schematics, it's right before the recreation lounge." He shifted his gaze to Kim. "You're coming with us."

While Janet was inspecting the sick bay facilities, Alex and Kim sat on an examination table. The doctor-spesh didn't need any assistance, although Alex had some idea about the equipment around them. A universal regeneration unit, a folding surgical table, anabiosis capsules attached lengthwise to the wall—after all, if you're dying, what do you care whether you sleep standing up or lying down? Sick bay was painted a range of soothing green-blue tones, and light—a calming yellow sunshine—was flowing down from the entire ceiling.

"Was I right to behave the way I did with the navigator?" asked Kim quietly.

"Yes." Alex nodded. "Strange as it seems, it was the right thing to do."

"What's so strange about it?"

"Well, you humiliated him. In front of the whole crew. After that, we could expect anything."

"But instead he . . ."

"Yes. Stopped doubting you, and that's great. Did you expect this reaction from the start?"

"Of course."

"Why of course?"

"He's used to flaunting his deficiency." Kim lifted her eyebrows. "He's even proud of it. And if a spesh demonstrates something that a natural simply can't do, Generalov doesn't get offended, not in the least. Quite the opposite, he'll find a chance to demonstrate his navigation mastery, and then he'll be proud of himself. That would make him our equal, you see?"

"Interesting." Alex shrugged his shoulders. "I can certainly see that happening. But you didn't have enough information for a conclusion like that. I hadn't told you anything about him, really . . ."

"For me, it was enough."

"Impressive," said Alex.

Janet finished inspecting the regeneration unit and walked up to them.

"Captain, I am more than happy. A good ship, and an excellent sick bay. This isn't the newest equipment, but all these models have been proved absolutely reliable."

She really did look happy—maybe she had still been worried about the "sick bay/galley" combination.

"I hope we won't have to use any of this equipment."

"Of course, Captain. Permission to look at the rest of the ship?"

"Wait a minute, Janet. I have a request for you . . . a personal favor to ask."

Janet looked thoughtfully at him, then at Kim.

"All right, Captain."

"Could you do a genetic test on Kim?"

"Depends on what kind of test . . ." A look of surprise appeared briefly on her face. "A test of your mutual compatibility?"

Kim snorted.

"No." Alex strained to keep his cool. The thought that he was planning to start reproducing with a fourteen-year-old girl was a bit much. But the favor he was about to ask her was just as strange. "Janet, I'd like to make sure that Kim really is a fighter-spesh."

"Captain?"

He sighed.

"The situation is rather strange, Janet . . ."

"I think I'm beginning to get the picture." Janet was talking to him, but all her attention was concentrated on Kim.

"Kim had her metamorphosis the night before last."

"Really . . ."

Janet leaned on the table next to Kim. Authoritatively took her by the chin, turned her face to take a closer look. Alex had no idea what she must have seen. But the look of slight mistrust left her eyes.

"It's not in the traditions of the Empire to take aboard speshes immediately after transformation."

"Of course," agreed Alex. "But there is no direct rule against it, either."

"I believe you. But what does genetic analysis have to do with it?" Kim herself had been silent, allowing them to discuss her fate. Alex suspected her silence wouldn't last much longer.

"She does not have a fighter-spesh certificate."

"I can issue that without any tests," said Janet calmly. "Her ID has all her medical information. Specialization type, altered genes, and the probable somatic profile."

"She doesn't have an ID. She's . . . lost it."

Janet was silent for a minute. Then she said firmly:

"Captain, any person, spesh or natural, who loses an ID can go to the nearest clinic. After a genotype analysis, the central databank will release the information on their identity."

"We cannot do that, Janet."

A brief glance from Kim was his reward for the "we."

"Why not?"

"Kim has severed all ties with her past. She doesn't want her family to know where she is. And if the databank receives an inquiry, they'll certainly notice it—then there will be no avoiding them."

"Why?" the doctor was genuinely surprised. "I'm pretty well acquainted with the laws of the Empire, Captain. After the metamorphosis, a spesh becomes an absolutely autonomous person. She has the right to work, to keep in touch with those she chooses, to enter into or cancel any kinship alliance, to live or commit suicide . . ."

Alex sighed, threw a questioning glance at Kim. He could not offer any objections at all—Janet was absolutely right.

"I'm from Edem," said the girl.

"A little patriarchal, but a nice planet." Janet gave an encouraging nod. "Kim, what are you afraid of? You are a fighter-spesh, so you are quite capable of protecting yourself from any unwanted attention. And the law is totally on your side. We can go to the spaceport's clinic together . . ."

"No!"

Kim jumped up, backing away from them. Janet and Alex exchanged glances.

"We're wasting our time," said Alex. "Janet, perhaps it might be better for you and Kim to talk alone."

"No," cried Kim. "I won't talk to her alone!"

"Why not?" Janet's voice was still warm and soothing. "Kim, I like you, let's not quarrel, okay?"

Kim relaxed a little.

"It's not you . . ."

"It's him, then?" Janet nodded toward Alex. "He's harmed you?"

Kim must have thought that was funny.

"It's hard to harm me."

"It is indeed. Let's discuss the problem and find some way to solve it, all right?" Janet stretched her hand toward the girl.

Kim hesitated a moment. Then she limply slapped the doctor's palm and sat back down between them. Janet was silent, looking at the girl.

"I'll be killed if they find me," said Kim shrilly.

"It's hard to kill a fighter-spesh," rejoined Janet, not really challenging the remark itself.

"It's hard, but possible. They'll send another spesh. Or two."

"Why? In that case, my dear, they would incur serious problems with the law. Especially since you are now under double protection—of the Empire itself, and of the space fleet union."

Kim gave a crooked grin.

"You know, you're older than I am, but I swear I know more about problems with the law!"

"Maybe you're from an influential, conservative family, and your clan is upset with your escape?"

Alex thought Janet's version of events was quite likely. But Kim shook her head.

"No. But I do know what I'm talking about. The moment I surface . . . I'm a goner. I'll be dead, and you guys will all be in a bind."

Alex expected a reproachful, or even an indignant, reaction from Janet. To bring aboard a girl-fighter who was more of a danger than she was a defense . . . But apparently, Janet really did like Kim.

"Well, you tell me. If that's the case, what can I do?" The doctor spread out her arms. "A spesh-certification is easy to issue. You are a fighter-spesh, I am sure of that. But I have a duty, dear, to establish your identity first. And you don't have an ID."

Kim was silent.

"We have one other option, Janet," said Alex hesitantly, with a slight quiver in his voice. He had entered a tricky realm of loopholes, something he had never liked to do.

"And what might that be, Captain?"

"You could issue Kim a fighter-spesh certificate. Then . . ." Janet frowned, shaking her head, but Alex continued, unabashed. ". . . then Kim and I go to the nearest registration center. And file a temporary marriage contract—based on the spesh-certificates. They're identification enough to do that."

"I understand that they're enough. But I refuse to issue a fake certificate."

"Janet, wait! After the marriage, Kim gets a new ID, with the name Kim Romanov . . . Kim, will you take my last name?"

Kim was staring at him wide-eyed, still not quite comprehending.

". . . and there are no inquiries to the databank. The information will be entered there, but so what? How many girls named Kim are in the galaxy?"

"But I can't break the law!" Even Janet's patience had its limits.

"And you won't be breaking any laws. We'll all come back to the ship right away, and you'll enter all the information from her new ID. Suppose I asked you to issue a temporary certificate and promised to show you the ID a little later. You could go for this tiny infringement, couldn't you?"

"Not a single computer in the world would let this through. How can I write that the spesh-certificate was issued based on a document that hadn't been received yet? Are you telling me you can travel back into the past, Captain?"

"Yes, I can."

Janet was silent.

"Ship time is determined by the captain. I could run the clock by Greenwich Time. Or by Great Beijing. The time at home port. The time of the planets we visit. You see? What time is indicated on your documents?"

"Ship time . . ."

"You see? If anyone checked, everything would look as

though . . ." Alex took a deep breath. ". . . the ship's captain had entered into a marriage union with a member of his crew, after which the bride had a genetic test that confirmed her status as a fighter-spesh . . ."

"Wait a second!" Janet waved her hand. "Are you serious, Captain? Are these just theoretical guesses or . . ."

"All captains use this trick. The union knows all about it, but they let it slide."

"They use this trick? To sneak aboard girls with no documents?" asked Janet quizzically.

"No. To give the crew additional bonuses, or get an extra contract on the side, to hide unauthorized shore leave . . . for many other small infringements. No one can track all of this down, Janet. Planets live according to their own time. And so do spaceships."

Janet looked at him darkly.

"I have long reconciled myself to the fact that the Empire is a crazy and anarchic world, Captain. But I didn't expect this kind of craziness."

"Will you help us, Janet?"

"But *I* would know that the law had been broken," she said wistfully.

"Yes. You would. But I do believe Kim. She has no other way to become legal and re-enter society. If you refuse, you would, in fact, be killing the girl. And you are a doctor."

Janet sighed. Looked at Kim, who sat motionless, tensely awaiting her answer.

"Take off your clothes. You can leave your underwear on."

"Thank you, Janet," said Alex.

"You're a madman, sir. And you're dragging me into your madness. Keep in mind that I am breaking the law not for you personally, and not even by your order!"

Alex nodded.

Kim had already taken off her suit and was standing there, waiting.

"Over here." Janet waved her hand. "You'll have to step into the white circle for a minute or two. It's a computer scan, nothing to be afraid of."

"Is this really necessary? The genetic analysis and . . ." began Alex. Janet glared at him.

"Listen, Captain! You've already dragged me into this shady business! So spare me your advice! I must do a tomography scan."

She turned and walked over to the main sick bay control panel. Kim cast a brief, stealthy glance at the doctor's back and then dipped her hand under her little camisole. Another second, and the heavy, warm crystal lay in Alex's hand.

Kim, the picture of innocence, stood in the circle of the tomographer, while Janet did her magic at the control panel. Alex lowered his gaze to look at the iridescent cone in the palm of his hand.

He was under no obligation to report his crewmembers' personal belongings. Besides, the crystal was not the object of an official search. And maybe it wasn't even a real gel-crystal. With a price ten times higher than a ship like the *Mirror*. Maybe it was just a masterful fake.

An appeal based on your own stupidity was always the best defense.

"All right, that's it. Get dressed," said Janet brusquely. "No, wait a minute."

She got a syringe out of a small cabinet, tore open the packaging. "You afraid of blood?"

"Not blood, but I'm afraid of shots," said Kim gloomily.

"Sorry to hear that," rejoined Janet, unsympathetically. She took hold of the girl's arm and brought the syringe over to the inner elbow. There was a smell of disinfectant, and the transparent little barrel filled up with blood.

"You could do a skin test instead!" protested Kim belatedly. Backed up toward Alex, put an urgent hand behind her back, taking advantage of the fact that Janet had turned around again for a moment. Alex silently returned the crystal.

"No, I couldn't. This isn't a fully equipped clinic, it's just an express-analysis lab. That's it, we're done, get dressed and go to your quarters."

Kim seemed to realize that there was no point in arguing, and especially in trying Janet's patience. She quickly dressed, darted an indignant glance at Alex, and left.

"Why did you send her away?" inquired Alex.

Janet pensively studied the syringe barrel. Sighed.

"Just in case. Captain, are you aware that the Zzygou race has been attempting to send spies into human society?"

Alex took a deep breath, mentally counted to ten.

"That's paranoia, Janet. Any Zzygou could be detected from ten yards away. Even if you're blindfolded. By odor alone."

"They've found a way to neutralize the odor, and the guise of a young girl is their best-developed transformation," said Janet dismissively. "This could be the reason for having no documents, and the unwillingness to undergo genetic analysis. . . . One minute, Captain."

Alex waited while she divided the blood between a dozen test tubes and took reagents out of cabinets. It was useless to argue with her. As useless as derision, or appealing to reason. He had to keep in mind that Janet was, after all, from Eben. What might seem like crazy paranoia to Alex was for her a routine precaution, as normal as washing fruit before she ate it.

"This is our express field methodology," she commented while dripping the reagents into one of the test tubes. "It could give a false positive, but it's generally reliable. Let's not wait for the results of the serum reactions, especially since they can be falsified by injecting the necessary anti-glutinogens into the bloodstream. Okay, here we go . . ."

The doctor silently examined the test tube.

"What's supposed to happen?" Alex asked. He tensed. Paranoia was contagious.

"Already happened. The blood coagulated." Janet shook a small lump of red jelly onto her hand. "See?"

"And what does this mean?"

"That Kim is human, of course." Janet went over to the sink and thoroughly washed her hands.

"I could have told you that from the get-go, Janet, without any crazy tests!"

"But this way, I know for sure."

She was from Eben . . . Alex half-closed his eyes. If he could see his Demon now, what would it look like? Weary, annoyed, or beside himself with rage?

"Janet, let's do a specialization analysis."

"Okay, just a minute."

Janet went back to manipulating her test tubes. She opened a flat plastic case, which turned out to contain at least a hundred tiny vials. She took a speck of something out of each one, then began adding that to the blood in the test tubes.

"I thought you were going to do the genetic analysis," remarked Alex.

"This *is* the genetic analysis. These vials contain the indicators for a number of specific genes. If a reaction occurs, then Kim has that particular gene."

Leaving the test tubes on the table, Janet walked over, sat down next to him.

"Do you have a cigarette, Captain?"

"Here, please take one."

Janet lit up. Some ashes fell to the floor, and she nodded approvingly when a small cleaner bug crawled out of a corner with a rustling sound.

"I have my quirks, Captain . . . you'll have to be tolerant of them."

"I understand . . ." And then he blurted out, before he realized it, "My whole crew has quirks, damn it!"

"Is this your first flight as a captain?"

Alex bit his lip. This is what happens when you spill your guts.

"Yes."

"It's all right. It's easy to get used to. I've been a captain on a torpedo boat . . . in my past life. Two hundred subordinates. Do you think any of them were without quirks?"

"I don't know."

"Yeah, a few. Five or six people at the most. The ones who could hide their quirks. Ah! The first test tube's lost its color!"

Alex looked at the tabletop.

"And what does that mean?"

"It's called the cheetah-gene. Responsible for the transformation of the musculature, makes you capable of short-term super-overloads. Well, we saw this one in action recently. So, as I was about to say, Alex . . . if you ever need help . . . or advice from a former captain . . . you can always count on me."

Alex searched her face for any sign of irony or ridicule. No, Janet was serious.

"Thank you. I'll remember that."

"The second and third test tubes," Janet noted. "The remodeling of neurons, the increased pain threshold, and accelerated synoptic reactions."

"Then Kim is a fighter?"

"Yes, of course, Captain. I had no doubts about the results of these tests. And here is the fourth test tube . . . transformation of the retina and the eyeball . . . by the way, you should also have a positive on this test. You know what that means, don't you?"

"The possibility of inheritance?"

"Exactly. If you ever decide to have progeny with Kim . . . What is it, Captain?"

Before he answered, Alex also lit a cigarette. The doctor waited patiently. Two more test tubes changed color—but Janet had no comment on what was happening.

"Are you well acquainted with fighter specializations, Janet?"

"Reasonably well. I'm not a geneticist, of course, but . . ."

"Does *etiquette* constitute any part of a fighter-spesh's preparation?"

Janet frowned. "Pardon?"

"Yesterday, Kim and I were at a restaurant. A very decent restaurant, by the way . . . Well . . . the girl acted like a young lady from the highest circles of society. I've had etiquette lessons at the academy, but next to her, I felt like an uncultured natural."

"And how do you know how many restaurants she's been to? Captain, if the girl is from an influential Edemian family, she must have had very expensive and well-qualified teachers."

"Possibly," murmured Alex. Why hadn't he thought of this obvious possibility? Maybe because he was used to measuring everyone according to his own standards—those of a provincial bumpkin, who received his first lessons in proper conduct at the flight academy?

"Okay . . . There was no modification of the skin," reported Janet after a brief look at the test tubes. "Well, you don't need a test to see that."

"What does that mean?"

"Nothing. Skin modification—the grayish tint and increased resilience—is not a necessary characteristic of a fighter. And all the main things have already been established, so I can issue a certificate."

"One more thing, Janet. During her metamorphosis, Kim enumerated all these poets, artists, political figures . . ."

Janet frowned. "Now that *is* strange, Captain. Are you saying she's been preprogrammed with some knowledge of history?"

"Yes."

"And not just military history, but the cultural realm?"

"Exactly. She didn't recall Alexander the Great or Kutuzov, or Moshe Dayan, or Lee Dong Hwan, or Mbanu."

"You consider him a great commander?" Janet grinned wryly. "In reality, his glory is slightly exaggerated—he wasn't the one who made the main decisions; it was his flag-officer . . . Well, that's beside the point . . . You amaze me, Captain. It really is a strange education for a spesh."

"And there's one more thing, Janet. How sexual are the fighters?"

"Same as ordinary people. They are not hetaera-speshes, after all."

"Well, Kim is . . . how should I put it . . . a bit oversexed."

"Captain, as far as I understand, you helped the girl out of trouble, got her through metamorphosis . . . now you're getting her onto the ship. Couldn't this be a very natural reaction on her part? A crush on the heroic pilot-spesh, a desire to have him, to win his love in return . . . A mixture of gratitude and calculation?"

"It didn't look like it, Janet. Last night, the girl offered herself to me. I wasn't really against it . . ."

"I can imagine," Janet chuckled. "I'm sorry, please continue . . ."

"I suggested that she wait a while . . . After the metamorphosis, the body should have time to rest."

"That's reasonable."

"We went to a restaurant. It was all very nice. Kim behaved as though she was a member of the highest aristocracy . . . she was a little flirtatious with me, nothing more than that. But when we got back to the hotel, the whole thing started up again. Changing into her pajamas turned into a striptease. A couple of remarks about the weather got her started telling erotic stories straight out of her own limited experience. Then she offered me a few fun diversions."

Janet was silent. Looked at the test tubes, got up, started rummaging through her vial rack.

"I've had a few dealings with hetaera-speshes," said Alex. "It's an expensive pleasure, but every now and then you indulge yourself . . ."

"So?" Janet poured the remnants of blood from the syringe into a clean test tube. Threw in a few tiny crystals from a vial.

"I could swear that Kim is specialized as a hetaera—that besides being a fighter-spesh, she is also a courtesan-spesh. Is that even possible, from a medical point of view?"

"It's difficult, but it is possible . . . Very difficult, Captain. The hetaera's body modification is minimal, but the psychology is changed completely. A fighter has to kill, with no scruples, no hesitation. Kill anyone who can be defined as an enemy. A hetaera has to love. Really love—selflessly, purely . . . to give herself to love completely. And at the same time, to be able to step aside, to forget her love, as soon as her services are no longer required. It would be very difficult to combine the two specializations, Captain." Janet shook a test tube side to side in the air. "It would be more reasonable to suppose that after the metamorphosis, her hormones were out of balance . . ."

"Well, if we remember history . . . back when all people were naturals, they somehow managed to combine many roles.

Napoleon was a great military leader, right? And at the same time, he was quite a womanizer."

"With all due respect, Captain, that's nonsense. In the past, there were people who might today be described as speshes. Military leaders, womanizers, scientists, artists. But every spesh today is a result of the most complex genetic alteration. All the unnecessary stuff is eliminated. Let's take you, for example—you're incapable of love, right?"

"Right."

"By the same token, a fighter might be capable of love, but only to the ordinary human degree. There!" Janet lifted a test tube containing a few drops of pinkish liquid. "You see that?"

"What does it mean?"

"Modified pheromones. One of the characteristics of a hetaera. To be completely sure, it would be best to test for the VIII-Operon, responsible for hyper-sexuality, but I don't have the right serum . . ." Janet put aside the test tube, rubbed her forehead. "You're right. I'm wrong. Kim is both a fighter and a hetaera. Most intricate work!"

"But who would need such a combination?"

"There are several possibilities. To make a female bodyguard, for instance, one who would also be able to provide sexual services. It would be very expensive, very complicated, almost foolish . . . but possible. It's not right, Captain." She looked at Alex gloomily. "Do you understand what has happened? And what the consequences may be?"

"Not just yet."

"Kim has fallen in love with you."

"So it seems, but . . ."

"A hetaera has to achieve reciprocation! Do you see? That's her specialization. Her reason to exist!"

"I don't intend to keep her away permanently, Janet! If it's so important for Kim . . ."

The doctor sighed.

"It's not sex that she needs, Captain. To be more precise, it's not just sex and not only sex! She wants you to fall in love with her!"

"But I'm incapable of that." Alex threw up his arms. "If something's not given, it's not given. I understand that love is a wonderful, pleasant, sacred feeling . . ."

"Pleasant . . ." snorted Janet. "Ah, Captain . . . sometimes I envy you pilots, incapable of love . . ."

"Maybe Kim could fall in love with someone else?" Alex suggested tentatively. "Puck is out of the question, but what about our young engineer?"

"That would be nice. Let's hope that her specialization as a fighter will distract her from the hetaera part of herself. But you made a very dangerous and painful step for everyone involved when you took the girl under your wing."

"I realize that already."

"Shall I issue the certificate?" asked Janet bluntly. "Or is it not worth it? You could still give her some money and let her fend for herself."

"It's too late for that. Go ahead and issue the papers."

Janet nodded, as if she had never expected another answer.

"Pilot . . ."

130

Alex could not decide whether the word contained ridicule or pity, or was only the assertion of a simple fact.

Probably the latter. After all, he had never had a right to choose, ever. His parents had made the choice, nine months before he was born.

And he appreciated their decision.

CHAPTER 5.

The courthouse was close to the spaceport. Alex sincerely hoped that the staff would refrain from asking too many questions.

And on the whole, his hopes were realized. Half of the short line in the cozy waiting room consisted of visitors from other planets. Even among this colorful crowd, one family group stood out. They were visitors from High Valley—two tall husband-clones, naked but for their small metalized loincloths, and their plump wife, wrapped in brocade and fir. Crowding around them was a large litter of half-naked children, still too small to tell their gender. Only the eldest had a white bow in its braided hair. That was the one for sale.

A little farther off stood two Zzygou. They really did resemble two adolescent girls. Only their airtight, transparent overalls with a sealed air circulation cycle gave these odorous creatures away. Alex wondered what they were doing there. Maybe they had decided to register a marriage under Imperial law? Not likely. Zzygou didn't have the concept of family. More likely, they were there to finalize some business transaction with humans.

Five stalwart mercenaries from Baghdad-3, looking warlike in full battle garb, their skull crests fanned open, were probably also waiting to sign some kind of contract. After all, they had no labor union of their own to make sure their agreements were issued properly.

Looking around, Alex was pleased. In this company, he and Kim looked downright respectable. There was a good chance that they would attract no special attention at all.

"This is the first time I've ever seen a real Zzygou!" Kim whispered in his ear, getting on her tiptoes. "They are just like humans, aren't they, Alex?"

"Only on the outside," said Alex. He decided not to mention Janet's recent suspicions. "Could you kill them?"

"Do you need me to?" asked Kim, businesslike. "Right now?"

Alex choked, grabbed her firmly by the arm. "No! No! It was a theoretical question. I just wanted to know if you were ready to fight with the Others."

"I'm ready," said Kim calmly. "If you ever need me to, just tell me."

The girl looked at the pilot, and Alex saw that she wasn't just ready. The thought filled her with enthusiasm. Not so much the thought of killing, but the opportunity to please him.

Janet was right. He had gotten himself into a very delicate situation.

"I'll tell you," he promised her. "But a fighter's job is not just killing left and right."

"What then?"

"Being ready to do it. Ideally, being ready every minute of your life."

"All right." Kim smiled. "Don't worry, I'm ready!"

The two Zzygou, blissfully ignorant of their close call with fate, were talking to each other, pressing together their transparent head-shields. The line moved gradually forward. The big High Valley family left, and the mercenaries barged into one of the back rooms. The only ones left in front of them were the two Zzygou and a gloomy, well-dressed man with a large-headed, hunchbacked midget on a chain. The midget stared into space with a blank, stupid expression. A thin thread of drool hung from its half-opened mouth, and its left eye twitched repeatedly. Alex tried to remember which planet had a fashion of keeping freaks as pets, but couldn't think of it and turned away. Wasn't his business, after all. The galaxy was a big place.

The Zzygou got called in, and with a polite nod to the rest, they left the waiting room, holding hands. Then the little tag on the hand of the midget owner lit up. The man was apparently lost in thought, and he didn't notice the signal. The midget darted an angry look up at him, yanked the chain, and hissed:

"Iven!"

The man started, looked down at the midget, and said wearily:

"You and your shenanigans, Miles . . ."

He stopped short and walked toward the door, above which a small light signal was flashing. He dragged the miserable midget behind him. The chain jingled, and the midget minced along, throwing its arms wide at every step.

"You remember your part?" said Alex quietly. Kim nodded, furrowing her brow.

"Yes. To say nothing and just smile."

"Put all your charm into your smile, if the clerk is a man. Be shy and quiet, if it's a woman."

His little tag started blinking. Alex peeled it off, threw it on the floor, then got up and straightened his uniform.

The office they entered was tiny, apparently used to take care of lone visitors or couples. The older woman sitting behind the table had a small bundle of wires coming out of her temple. Another spider, making her living in the boundless web of data.

Kim demurely lowered her eyes.

"We would like to register a marriage contract," said Alex, putting their spesh-certificates on the table.

"Duration?"

"Twenty-four hours." Alex smiled.

The spider moved the certificates toward the center of the table. Apparently, that was where the scanner was located. She looked pensively up and to the left, where she alone could see her virtual screen. Then she asked:

"Your IDs?"

"Did you bring yours, Kim?"

The girl shook her head. Alex looked at the spider. "Are they really necessary, ma'am?"

The spider frowned, still looking up into space.

"No. No, but . . . Kim, you received your spesh-certificate an hour ago?"

The girl nodded.

"You see," Alex felt it was high time to launch into an explanation, "she's just had her metamorphosis. She was so excited when she finally got the certificate . . . we just couldn't wait to try out its legal potential. Surely . . . she couldn't get married with a minor's card!"

The spider pursed her lips. The excuse sounded more or less reasonable . . . but something seemed to worry her.

"But why a twenty-four-hour marriage? To try out the certificate? Or do your religious beliefs require formal permission for sex?"

"Do you have to know these details?" asked Alex harshly. The whole plan was going to hell.

"I don't," agreed the spider. "But I have a right to put a hold of up to three days on a marriage contract. Because one of the people involved is young, for instance."

Having seen a pair of happy teenagers, as young or even younger than Kim, leave this very room half an hour ago, Alex was barely able to suppress a harsh remark. Kim was the one to rescue the situation:

"Alex, dearest, show her your labor contract. Chapter eight, paragraph seventeen B."

"I don't have it with me," Alex answered, trying to recall the text. What did she mean? Chapter eight . . . financial provisions. "Besides, I can't show it to anyone without the company's permission . . ."

The spider looked really curious. Kim turned to her and said, still smiling shyly:

"We are from the same ship, ma'am. We have a provision for a fifteen percent bonus for married couples. To boost crew morale. I haven't signed the contract yet, and so . . ."

The woman pursed her lips. Murmured:

"Your company lawyers don't have any brains. Well, at least you're not making up stories of sudden romance."

Alex was silent, leaving further discussion completely to Kim.

"The registration of a twenty-four-hour marriage costs five spacenyans. Whose account should I charge?"

"Mine," said Alex quickly.

The spider coughed, got up from her chair, winced as her wires caught on the corner of the table and almost got detached from the contact plate.

"Alexander Romanov and Kim O'Hara, in the name of the planet of Quicksilver Pit and on behalf of our president, Mr. San Li, I congratulate you upon your entry into a temporary marriage union. During the period of the contract, I hope you get to know each other better"—here, even the spider could not help smiling— "so that the present contract can be extended for a longer period of time. Your marriage is now recognized by His Imperial Government as legal on the planets of the Empire, as well as beyond its borders, for the entire period of the contract."

The pleasant, though somewhat willfully improvised, version of Mendelssohn's wedding march, which had been playing during the entire speech, ceased.

"Any special wishes?" the spider politely asked, obviously not expecting any such wishes. Her right hand was already sliding around in the air, filling out all the items of the marriage contract form.

"I would like to take the last name Romanov," said Kim quietly.

"Why?" asked the woman in surprise.

"It sounds exotic."

The spider shrugged her shoulders.

"As you wish. You want your property rights separated? Genetic rights stay with the genes' carriers? Personal debts and felonies do not transfer onto the family unit?"

Her fingers fluttered in the air, weaving new threads into the data web.

"My warmest congratulations, Alex and Kim Romanov... Would you like to make a small donation to the planetary home for orphaned children of astronauts? Or for the development of medical technologies?"

"For the children's home," said Kim. She looked at Alex, and he nodded.

"Five nyans? Ten?"

"Ten."

"I thank you on behalf of the grief-stricken orphans of astronauts. . . . Your marriage contract is now valid. Congratulations."

With a slight bow of her head, the spider handed them two marriage contract documents.

"Thank you." Alex caught Kim under her arm and dragged her out of the office.

"What about my ID?" whispered Kim as soon as the office door closed behind them.

"We'll get it from another spider," Alex explained. "Any manipulations with the law should be done one step at a time. When none of the bureaucrats break any rules, they don't give a damn about the final result. Janet turned a blind eye on the time manipulations, one spider registered the marriage based on the spesh-certificates, and another one will now issue you a new ID."

"So the whole thing is based on the fact that a spesh has two identity documents?" asked Kim.

"Exactly."

"So naturals couldn't have pulled it off?"

"Naturals never have any problems with the Imperial bureaucracy. The spiders just let them slide."

A smiling waiter handed Alex a cigar. The restaurant was half-empty today. The workday was in full swing, and it was past the lunch hour. Alex thought wearily that he would probably have to sit around till very late in the evening.

"May I, Captain?"

It was the master-pilot he had met the other day. To approach a hiring person the second time, having once rejected the position, was considered somewhat rude . . . but Alex nodded yes. The man silently played with his sake cup. It seemed hard for him to start the conversation.

"I'll be very glad if you have changed your mind," ventured Alex.

The pilot drank up his sake in one gulp. Murmured:

"This is a hole of a planet, isn't it?"

"I've seen worse."

"Really?" the pilot rejoined, with a sudden ironic note in his voice. "I've been trying to get hired onto a ship for two weeks now, and there hasn't been anything better than a *Hamster*!"

"Strange. When I was looking for a job, I saw several galactic-route positions . . ."

"You don't mean to say that you . . . got your job as a captain from an infonet search?" He looked like he was about to have a heart attack.

"I did."

"That means I am phenomenally unlucky," the pilot scowled. "Astonishingly unlucky. I haven't seen a single decent offer, let alone a captain's post. Yesterday, a promising option did pop up, on a passenger liner . . . a local one, from this stinking garbage pit . . . Well, they didn't take me! When I tried to register the contract, they told me to collect all the info about all the relatives on my mother's side! Another great idea from the spider room. . . ."

Alex snorted.

"Yes, I heard about that. When I went to have my papers issued."

"I hope you're not based here?"

"No, on Earth."

"That's good . . ." The pilot rolled the sake cup between his fingers. "Show me your contract, Captain. If I still suit you, of course."

He placed his papers on the table in front of Alex, took a copy of the contract. Alex absently looked through the recommendations and evaluations. Xang Morrison, thirty-nine, free stations citizenship. Those born in space made the best pilots in the universe. A decent work record. Even better than Alex's own, to be honest.

Quicksilver Pit wasn't Earth or Edem. But it was a large and well-developed planet. And to have a master-pilot unable to find a job here? For two weeks?

Very strange.

"Not bad," said the pilot with bitter resentment, putting the contract aside. "Looks like the owners aren't tight."

"So it seems."

"What is the Sky Company about?"

"I don't know."

"And where are we flying to?"

"Don't know that, either."

"Well, isn't that nice . . ."

"They can't require anything illegal," said Alex with a shrug. "It's a perfectly standard, union-approved contract."

"I can see that. Captain, I won't lie to you . . . two master-pilots can't be happy on a tiny ship like *Mirror*. Can you take me on temporarily? Till you find another pilot? Then just give me the slip . . . I'll get drunk while on duty, if you want, or show insubordination, or something. Just help me leave this awful hole!"

Alex thought for a moment. Morrison waited, tense and visibly on edge.

"But not until I find a good replacement . . ."

"I will be as diligent and obedient as a graduate on his first flight. Just find someone to replace me and kick me off on some halfway decent planet. Even New Africa will do."

Alex couldn't suppress a wry grin. To take aboard a pilot, knowing that he had no intention of staying for any length of time . . .

"Please, friend-spesh . . ." said Xang quietly.

"Go on and sign the contract," Alex decided. Crunched the cigar in half in the ashtray.

His crew had been hired.

One hell of a weird crew, to tell the truth.

He himself, a master-pilot who could use some more work experience, just out of the hospital. A woman soldier and executioner from Eben in the role of a doctor. A girl barely out of metamorphosis as a fighter-spesh. A touchy natural navigator. A co-pilot who couldn't find a job for two weeks, sitting at a huge transport crossroads. A young engineer who had brought their ship to Quicksilver Pit, thinking he was done with it . . . only to go right back aboard.

If *Mirror*'s routes proved to be half as odd as the crew, he was in for an exciting life.

The communicator beeped in his pocket, and Alex took it out, feeling a strange pleasure mixed with embarrassment. A captain's communicator was slightly larger than standard, loud orange in color . . . one of the few symbols of power.

"Captain . . ."

He recognized Generalov's voice. In a second, the visual matrix opened up above the receiver. The navigator was at his workstation. Wearing his spacesuit. With his hair braided in the form of a pretzel on top of his head. And . . . a discreet red-and-blue ornament glowing on his left cheek. It was probably pointless to try to reform him.

"Captain here."

"A direct communication from the owners. I'm transferring it to you."

Alex closed the hologram, switched off the speaker, and touched the communicator to the back of his head, to the computer interface. This was the only way to guarantee the privacy of the conversation. He was intrigued—they hadn't bothered contacting him when he first got hired, so he had no orders as far as the crew or the ship itself. Had it only now occurred to them to contact him?

"Alexander Romanov?"

The sound imitation was perfect. The voice seemed normal, secretarial. Just polite enough, just formal enough.

"Yes."

"Are you using a private channel?"

"Of course."

"Mr. Li Tsyn, the Director of the Sky Company, wishes to speak with you."

Alex realized that visuals were not being transmitted. But he straightened his back anyway. He wasn't in the habit of having official conversations while picking his nose, or scratching his foot, or even simply lounging in a chair.

"Mr. Romanov?"

The owner's voice turned out to be one of an elderly but still sturdy man.

"Yes, Mr. Li Tsyn. I am listening, Mr. Li Tsyn."

No formal introductions. No questions or congratulations on the new job . . . Mr. Li Tsyn could have used the same tone of voice to talk to his coffeemaker or his vacuum cleaner.

"Have you hired a full crew?"

"Yes, Mr. Li Tsyn . . ." Alex looked sideways at Morrison, who was in the act of pressing his finger to the contract.

"Good. Today you will take aboard three passengers and put yourself at their service. They will provide all the necessary route information."

"Yes, Mr. Li Tsyn." Alex could imagine the company director as vividly as if the visuals were on. A fat old bastard lounging in a luxurious armchair, petting a girlfriend . . . maybe even that same secretary . . .

"Mr. Li Tsyn has finished talking with you," purred the secretary, as though reading his thoughts. "Are there any questions?"

The tone of her voice presupposed that there shouldn't be any. That was why Alex asked:

"Mr. Li is not in the habit of talking with new employees?"

"He is. You've talked. Any other questions?"

Under the inquisitive eye of Morrison, Alex forced himself to smile. The co-pilot could hear Alex's part of the conversation.

"No, thank you. Goodbye."

The transmission ended.

A direct call from Earth . . . wow . . . that cost a pretty penny.

"What are the orders, Captain?" inquired Morrison. It was an ambiguous question—orders for Alex himself, or orders for Morrison? Alex chose the second option.

"Be on the ship in an hour. We might be leaving tonight."

"Aye-aye, Captain."

The ship was all in order—this much, at least, was going right. Kim and Janet were in the sick bay; the black woman seemed to have taken the girl under her patronage. Turning on the surveillance system, Alex looked into the sick bay for just a second. Janet and Kim, both leaning over a table, were taking apart an assault ray gun, the *Perun*, the most powerful hand weapon allowed on small-tonnage ships. Kim was probably better at handling guns, theoretically speaking, but Janet had experience behind her . . . bitter, hard-won, but valuable experience as an Ebenian soldier.

Inside his navigation module, Generalov was still blissfully immersed in his work. Alex watched him for a few minutes on

144

the screen of the captain's control panel. Constant practice and self-training were typical for a spesh. And although Puck wasn't a spesh, that was what he was doing—plotting imaginary routes in virtual space. Just now, Puck was plotting a course from Quicksilver Pit to Edem, Kim's home world. At first, that track seemed far from perfect to Alex—the navigator had ignored the stationary space-tunnels, which were in constant use, and was taking the ship through "pulsing" tunnels. That would cause them to lose time— pulsing tunnels opened on intervals ranging from three to a hundred and twenty hours. It was also financially deleterious. The use of a pulsing tunnel cost twice as much. And finally, Alex did not see any distance advantage at all. The ship's route was drifting farther and farther away from Edem.

When Generalov plotted a trek from Zodiac to Lard Crest, Alex finally realized what he was up to. Here they had no need for any tunnels, as the ship would be propelled by its own hyper-generator. And afterwards, covering two parsecs and arriving at the Crest, the ship would find itself at the stationary tunnel Lard Crest-Edem.

The solution was beautiful, and, as far as Alex could tell without being plugged into the machine, perfectly reasonable. They won with respect to time, to money, and to the ship's resources.

"Cunning natural," murmured Alex in delight, and switched over to the engineering module. This time he did it openly, initiating a two-way communication channel.

Young Paul Lourier was standing near the gluon reactor. He was swaying slowly, as though meditating in front of the energy stream flowing less than two feet away from his face.

Nothing was safer or deadlier than gluon energy. It was almost cost-free, not counting the cost of the reactor itself. No radioactive waste. No collateral radiation. If the reactor ran stable, of course.

But it was no easy task to achieve working stability with a reactor manipulating the very basis of all matter. At this level, the laws of physics started tripping up. There were no easy answers and ready-made schemes. While the reactor was in minimal-capacity mode, everything was still predictable, and it could always be turned off. But as soon as it moved into full capacity, the process would start "drifting." And a great many different radiation flows would start appearing out of nowhere. The titanium body of the reactor could turn into gold or graphite, and once Alex even saw a reactor whose walls had turned into a cylinder of solid crystal. *Mirror* had a tandem Niagara gluon reactor with absolutely no walls, only force fields around the core.

Outwardly, the gluon flow looked like falling water, and Alex appreciated the imaginative approach of the design engineers. It looked as though two transparent, slightly bluish currents were cascading in front of Paul, taking their source from a gold-colored plate inside the ceiling and disappearing into a similar plate in the floor.

"Engineer," Alex called out.

Paul turned around slowly. His eyes were half-closed, and a smile haunted his lips. He enjoyed familiarizing himself with the driving chains of the reactor—a typical spesh's reaction to his work. Alex wondered what Paul saw. Probably not flowing water. Paul's vision was rather different from Alex's or Kim's. He could see most of the known radiation bands and visually estimate a flame's temperature to a fraction of a degree. Now a whole magical fireworks display was playing out before him . . . neutrons slipping past the force field, bursts of gamma rays, fanlike X-radiation, slow and clumsy alpha particles . . .

"Are you free?" asked Alex.

"Yes, Captain."

"Meet me in my quarters."

"Aye-aye, Captain."

Lourier shook his head, tossing his heavy hair off his forehead. Glanced once more at the gluon streams and left the camera's field of vision.

He was apparently an excellent engineer. Young, but familiar with this very reactor. Burning with enthusiasm. What more could a captain hope for?

Alex threw his coat off, rolled up his shirtsleeve, and looked at the Demon. The little devil was wincing. Sad and hopeless, as though a nameless ache was gnawing at him.

"I sense it," Alex whispered. "I really do feel it. Something's wrong."

A spark of curiosity appeared in the Demon's eyes.

"I don't know what it is yet . . ." Alex confided. "But I swear I'll figure it out!" The Demon probably had little faith left in his promises, but its tiny, cartoonish face did look slightly more relaxed now.

A door signal beeped, and Alex hurriedly rolled his sleeve back down.

"Captain?" Paul hesitated at the threshold.

"Come in." Alex waved him to a chair, suggesting with his entire manner that the talk would be informal. "Want some coffee? Wine?"

Paul nodded awkwardly. By tradition, as they came off duty, engineers were used to having some dry red wine. But he apparently did not consider himself off duty just yet.

"Coffee, please."

Alex waited a few more minutes, exchanging small talk with the engineer. And only when the fellow seemed to have relaxed a bit did he bring up the serious business.

"I was really surprised by what you said before, Paul." The engineer looked at him questioningly. "Tell me how you got onto this ship the first time. Why were you let go?"

The young man was silent for a second, obviously formulating his answer.

"I graduated from the university in Lyon, got my engineering degree. We had been warned that finding a good job while still on Earth would be difficult. And I'd already been thinking about a trip to some outlying parts to look for a position. But then this trip turned up . . . a one-time thing, one-way. To take a yacht called the *Intrepid* over to Quicksilver Pit. I checked it out in the handbooks—there's a huge transport crossroads here, and speshes are in high demand. But the planet's own academy is rather small. The trip over was uneventful, just three people aboard—a master-pilot, a navigator, and me. Got our pay here . . . it was all legit. Started looking for the next job, and met you."

"So there was nothing unusual?" probed Alex. Paul looked at him in surprise.

"What could be so unusual about driving a ship from one planet to another?"

"Well, the fact that you all were dismissed, and a whole new crew had to be found. Why?"

Paul shrugged his shoulders.

"Were you bringing anything to Quicksilver Pit? Cargo? Passengers?"

"No."

"Were there accidents during the flight? Non-compliance with orders?"

"Not at all!"

"Who recommended this trip to you? Who hired you on?"

"A fellow graduate from the academy. He had gotten a job on a military cruiser . . . well, you know . . . he has family connections. . . . As for hiring, it was done through the net, as usual. I sent an inquiry to the Freight Company, then got the contract . . ."

"The Freight Company?"

"Yes. It's a small company, specializing in incidental deliveries and driving ships from planet to planet. The company is affiliated with the lunar shipyard, the one where this ship was built."

Alex was silent. Everything Paul told him was plausible. The surplus of speshes on Earth wasn't at all surprising, and neither was the custom of driving empty ships from place to place.

One problem remained. Driving crews were never formed for only one trip. To hire three people only to dismiss them—what for? Why not keep the three of them aboard and hire the rest of the crew on Quicksilver Pit? Or even hire the entire crew on Earth in the first place?

There was a possible answer, but it was way out of the ordinary.

"Forgive my questions, Paul, but I am a bit uneasy about this whole thing."

He watched the youngster's face closely, but Paul just smiled a shy smile.

"I'm not all that experienced in these matters, Captain."

That made sense. Stupid of him to seek advice from a greenhorn. His communicator beeped. The sound was soft, so it wasn't a secret call.

"Yes?"

"Captain"—the voice of the ship's service program was soft, soothing—"the co-pilot Xang Morrison has arrived on board, sir."

"Thank you." Alex switched off the connection. "Paul, go to the cargo bay. Welcome the co-pilot aboard, give him a tour of the ship, and show him to his quarters."

Paul nodded, getting up from his chair. Alex hesitated for a moment, and added:

"Oh, and please don't scratch your name on the john anymore. Or on your bed. Despite the tradition. All right?"

He was curious to see the engineer's reaction to his words.

Paul smiled and left.

Alex sat for a time, staring at the closed door. You should never enter a place without knowing how to exit. Or whether there *is* an exit. Or what awaits you outside.

But he'd already entered. Breaking the company contract was impossible without forever ruining his chances of other employment.

"Increase plating transparency," he said, getting up from behind the table. The outer wall of his cabin vanished, opening a vista of the spaceport.

A boundless concrete field, with various vessels scattered here and there, big and small, old worn-out orbital clunkers and new interstellar liners. Though not too many of them . . .

And above it all, a gray sky. A sagging layer of dirty gray clouds and smog, several miles thick. How could anyone stand living here?

It suddenly occurred to him how richly the planet deserved its name of Quicksilver Pit. Not only because of the huge mercury deposits of the south continent: the famous Mirror Lakes, as beautiful as they were deadly. Those lakes had become the foundation for the entire planetary economy and killed off tens of thousands of workers. But the planet's sky was also a quicksilver pit. It was beautiful, in its own way, and just as merciless. The lid of a gravity well with a teeming mass of millions of people, both speshes and naturals, forced together at the bottom.

"I'm so ready to get out of here," Alex whispered to himself.

Gray clouds swirled into washed-out spirals. A fiery needle cut through the sky—somewhere far away, a tiny orbital ship had been launched. Alex followed it with his eyes, until the tiny flame was engulfed by the clouds.

Then he turned around and went to the bathroom unit. Took down his pants, sat on the toilet. Turned his head and cast a gloomy look on the pristine, white plastic wall. The laser in his Swiss Army knife was very weak, even at the maximum setting. Alex had to apply himself.

"Took on the rank of Captain," he scrawled on the wall, and then added his signature, clear and easy to read.

*   *   *

Alex conducted their first drill late that night. Kim and Janet, of course, were not fully involved. The crew took to their battle stations according to the ship's schedule, but Alex had no intention of putting the ship's weapons systems on line. Some jumpy spaceport security officer might take it the wrong way.

Morrison took his pilot's chair first—Alex didn't mind. Let the co-pilot get used to the ship. He'd had it pretty rough lately. . . . Alex stood at his pilot's chair in front of the control panel and watched its tiny flashing lights. The engineer was at his station. The navigator went to his. So did the co-pilot. And only when all battle stations had reported ready did the captain lay down in his chair.

The automatic straps fixed him in place with a soft click. This was an almost pointless precaution—after all, if gravity compensation failed, all living tissue would be torn apart. Still, even the craziest instructions had been issued for a reason; behind them was somebody's life and somebody's death.

"Contact . . ."

A warm wave washed away the cozy, tiny world of the pilot's module.

Space opened up all around him in every direction. The planet, the cosmos, the ships. The glowing rainbow—the soul of his vessel. And other people's consciousness like fiery vortexes circling around him.

Never before had Alex experienced this, seen the world this way—being in its center, at the very rainbow. The old *Heron* didn't count—it had been a one-person ship.

His crew was waiting.

Alex reached for a small white vortex. He felt sure that was Kim, and he was right. The vortex curved toward him and its heat splashed onto Alex, a mixture of adoration, lust, flirtation . . . and a pure, completely unbridled readiness to destroy. Alex touched the vortex, as if slapping his hand onto hers, and recoiled away from her. Back towards the rainbow, towards the ship.

A dark-red clot of fire. Janet. She did not rush toward the captain. Just saluted him with a brighter flash. A cold, dying star . . . ready to explode at any moment and turn into the devouring blaze of a supernova.

A nebulous cloud of blue light. Like high-temperature plasma, bound by a magnetic trap. Alex watched Puck with intense curiosity, trying to see how he differed from the others. The navigator could not use a bioterminal because the neurons of his brain had not been altered. He entered the ship's net with a primitive cable, like some spider from the spaceport accounting office. But it did not look as though that created any problems. The cloud glowed, greeting the captain.

A quivering white zigzag. A captured bolt of lightning. When Alex first entered the virtual space, the zigzag lengthened, straightening itself. The engineer. For some reason, Alex had been sure that Paul would look precisely this way. Nothing fancy, no quirks—the way a novice astronaut, just out of school, should look.

And finally, the other master-pilot. An emerald-colored spiral and a handful of precious gems, connected by an invisible thread and circling around the ship's consciousness. Xang did not react to the captain's presence at all. That was a bad sign.

Alex moved toward the rainbow light.

"It's me . . ."

The rainbow brightened, and every color of the spectrum turned painfully vivid and distinct. The six colors that naturals saw in rainbows turned into the seven colors scientists had thought up. Then split apart into strips of turquoise and threads of carrot-orange, veins of crimson and belts of canary-yellow, shadows of gray and filaments of sand.

"Take me in . . ."

A warm touch. Whispering foliage. Sunlight. A mother's embrace. A gentle sea wave. Soft breeze. Sweetness and tranquility. Restrained passion. Intoxicating lightness. Giddy excitement. Restful contentment. Quiet exultation.

No ordinary human could ever experience it. All of this at once. All of life's pleasures, all this happiness accumulated bit by tiny bit. Alex, a small boy of five, racing toward the edge of the sea, seeing it for the first time in his life. Running and laughing, overflowing with joy, into his mother's open arms, into a rolling wave . . . Alex, overcome with delight, holding Pawlie, his dog, warm and real, and Pawlie enthusiastically licking his face. Alex, celebrating his thirteenth birthday, the cake in front of him twinkling with multicolored candles, and his father, so young, brimming with pride, saying that his son would become a pilot next year, would be a person destined for nothing but happiness . . . Alex, already a student learning to use his new abilities, in a city park, kissing a girl-natural, his first real lover, inexperienced, but burning with desire to gain that experience with his help . . . Alex, wearing his pilot's uniform for the first time, standing on parade square, and the legendary master-pilot Diego Alvarez attaching badges to the young pilots' uniforms, finding a special word of encouragement for each of the graduates . . . Alex, sweaty and worn out, sliding out of the pilot's chair, barely able to walk . . . but the throat of the channel, which had suddenly narrowed, is already behind them, passed, and he passed it, an inexperienced third pilot, none of his five hundred passengers realizing how close death had come . . . Alex, barely out of the hospital, alone and lost on a strange planet, saving a girl-spesh, helping her get through the most difficult time in her life . . .

This was something new. He didn't realize just how happy and proud he had felt about rescuing Kim. But memory lives by its own rules, so now that night would always be with him, as well as the quiet exaltation of a man who had done some good . . .

Suddenly, something pricked him. Almost imperceptibly, and immediately washed away by a warm wave of iridescent light. And yet it did prick him, before it vanished . . .

Before he became one with the ship.

And the crew became a part of his own self.

Alex sent out an order, without so much as a thought, and not in any verbal form. The white lightning flashed brighter, giving off energy. The emerald spiral lifted *Mirror* off the concrete blocks, then folded in the supports, checked all the equipment one last time. The bluish light opened like a fan, displaying hundreds of take-off trajectories. The white vortex and the red flame, his two fists, tensed up, ready for a personal battle with the entire planet of Quicksilver Pit, with the entire galaxy. . . .

Now that Alex was in complete confluence with the ship, all of them became one whole, connected by his will.

Exactly the way it all should be.

Alex got up from his pilot's chair and stretched. Everything around him still seemed irregular, unreal. The bridge looked too small after the boundlessness of space. The co-pilot getting out of his chair was no longer an emerald spiral. His own beating heart had replaced the silent stream of energy.

"Seven minutes, thirty point five seconds," murmured Xang. "Do you think that's enough for the first training session, Captain?"

"Quite enough."

Alex felt that the tone of his voice had changed, but he couldn't do anything about it. And why should he? Now he really had become the captain.

That was the whole point of the training session—to get a feel for every crewmember and to place his own image into their psyches. That was the goal, not the synchronization of all their actions, which was unavoidable anyway.

"Captain?"

He looked at Morrison.

"Do you wonder what you look like from the outside?"

Alex reflected a moment and nodded. "I do."

"A white star. So bright it hurts to look at it . . . even in virtual reality. A tiny white star. And when you had your confluence with the ship, the rainbow seemed to explode from within."

"Was it beautiful?" inquired Alex.

Morrison hesitated a little before he answered. "Don't know. Impressive, bright . . . beautiful, perhaps."

But he didn't sound all that sure.

"Thank you, Xang. You're an excellent pilot. I think we will split our bridge duty time equally."

The co-plot looked suddenly perplexed. "Captain?"

"Is that all right with you?"

"Hell, yes!" Xang got up. "But why?"

"Because you're a good pilot," said Alex. He couldn't see the Demon, but knew that it had a spiteful smile on its face.

Piloting was any pilot's supreme pleasure. To merge with the ship completely, to become a metal bird soaring among the stars— what could ever be better than that?

Only one thing was better—to be the ship's captain. And Morrison had no idea of this little secret. He was only a pilot, just like Alex had been so recently.

"Thank you, Captain." Xang's voice quivered. "Damn . . . it's so unexpected."

"It's all right, Xang." Alex left the bridge and stopped outside in the hall, looking down its length. The engineer stuck his head out from the door of his engine room at the end of the hall, saluting the captain with a wave of his hand, and then dived right back in to be with his beloved gluon streams. It was as if he didn't even need any comments about his recent performance. Then Janet and Kim simultaneously rushed out of the narrow passageways leading to the battle stations. Roaring with laughter, they gave each other high-fives, then a hug, and only after that, both turned to Alex. He smiled back. Somehow outer space always increased women's longing for same-sex love, and Alex would have gotten jealous . . . had he felt more than just a friendly attraction to Kim. Jealousy was a mere derivative of the main function unavailable to him.

Then a door closest to the bridge opened, and Generalov came out into the hall. He was still in his spacesuit, though with the helmet folded down.

"Good," said Alex. "Really good."

Puck grinned a crooked grin. The slight tension vanished from his eyes.

"The route to Dorian was remarkable," Alex said with sincere praise. "I never had any plans to go there, but the route you plotted was great. I never should have doubted your abilities."

The navigator reveled in this, like a young girl upon hearing her first compliment. It occurred to Alex that the analogy was to some extent true, and he hastened to add, now in a more formal tone of voice:

"But the track toward Zodiac, which you plotted earlier today, is far from optimal."

"Now, wait a minute, Captain!" Puck cried out in dismay. "The optimal route would require going through the tunnel in the Monica-3 system!"

"Yes. And what's wrong with that?"

"That region is not recommended for small ships, Captain."

"But neither is it forbidden, right?"

"No. But any pilot would prefer to avoid the Bronins' ritual zone."

"Puck, please keep in mind that I'm not just any pilot."

"And neither am I," added Morrison, appearing suddenly behind his back. "I've had occasion to use the Monica-3 tunnels."

"And what were your impressions?" said Puck with curiosity.

"Painful. But only pilots have to worry about it."

"How come speshes are always so suicidal . . ." murmured Puck.

"Did you say something, Navigator?" said Alex.

"No, Captain. I've taken your wishes into account. Next time, I will be guided only by the maximal optimization of the route, not by its safety. Excuse me."

He turned around and disappeared into his module. The door slammed behind him.

"Looks like we've offended him. . . ." said Morrison softly.

Alex thought in passing that what had offended Generalov was the co-pilot's intrusion. When he talked to him one-on-one, the navigator was still open to suggestion. But when faced alone with two speshes, he immediately retreated into his shell.

"I shouldn't have interfered," sighed Morrison, as if reading his mind. "I'm sorry, Captain."

"Let's go have a drink," said Alex. "After all, we've just had our first training session, and a rather successful one, I should say."

"All right. The girls are already there, I see." Morrison shifted his gaze away from the empty hall. "Captain . . . just in case . . . are you involved with Kim or Janet?"

"Not yet."

"Would you mind if I courted the girl?"

"Absolutely not." Alex smirked. "Hell, you're also a pilot . . . so why these questions?"

"Well, you never know," Xang explained as they walked down

the hall. "Of course, we can't love, so we're spared the emotional prejudices . . . But I once worked on a ship, a medium-tonnage freighter, nothing out of the ordinary . . . well, the third pilot was involved with a navigator girl, and his reaction was quite hostile. His religious beliefs didn't allow being unfaithful, you see."

"Thank God, I'm an atheist."

"That settles it, then." Morrison nodded.

"There's just one thing, Xang. The girl's in love with me. But I won't be upset if she chooses you as a more appropriate object of affection."

Xang smiled contentedly, but said nothing. He had needed so little to put him in a good mood! Only seven minutes of contact with the ship.

They passed by several closed cabin doors and reached a small circular lounge. Passengers and crewmembers always shared the recreation hall on small spaceships, and the furnishings were a compromise between asceticism and luxury. The compromise was never a happy one, and this lounge was no exception. The plastic walls were decorated by still lifes in heavy wooden frames that were way too fancy. The oval-shaped table was made of ordinary foamed metal, but two small sofas and armchairs were constructed from wood, though they did have safety straps. A tiny field bar was incongruously filled with exquisite beverages—from Earthly wines to Edemian cognacs and ambrosia. And small emergency lights surrounded the delicately wrought crystal lamp on the ceiling.

It all looked as though the unknown designer had simply tossed together bits of standard interiors to create a random mix of passenger lounge and crew lounge.

The door leading to a tiny kitchenette stood open, and Janet was already bustling around in there. Alex happily noted her willingness to get snacks ready. Had Janet been a feminist, no one could have gotten her into a kitchen, even at gunpoint.

Kim was sitting in an armchair near the wall with a goblet in her hand. She gave them an unusually gloomy look as they walked in.

"When the captain enters, one should stand up," said Janet quietly without turning. Kim jumped up, all but spilling the contents of her goblet.

Hiring Janet was beginning to look like the best decision Alex had made in the last few days. If anyone could make a true astronaut out of Kim, it would be a lady from Eben.

"However," Janet continued in the same tone of voice, "traditionally, female crewmembers do not abide by this rule and salute the captain's arrival with a nod . . . or a charming smile."

And she turned around, demonstrating that smile to Alex.

"Thank you, Janet," he said. "Kim, please sit down."

"Sandwiches, anyone?" asked Janet without even a hint of formality in her tone, as she came out of the kitchenette with a tray in her hands.

"Wow! Thanks." Xang sat down sideways next to Kim. He smiled at the girl. "Friend-spesh, you look great on watch!"

Kim snorted. Looked at Alex with piercing intensity, as if she had heard them talking in the hallway . . . Damn it!

Alex felt his face turning red. But of course! Less than eleven yards of hallway was nothing to Kim's enhanced hearing!

"And you must be that dangling bit of green snot I saw?" she asked Morrison in all innocence. There was a silence. Then Morrison faked a laugh.

"Usually my virtual image inspires more pleasant associations, you little white vortex."

"My first impression *was* more pleasant," said Kim bluntly.

Now Morrison also caught on. He rubbed the bridge of his nose, threw a guilty look at Alex.

What could be done now? To Kim, it looked all too obvious. Two boors decide to share her, and the one she loves agrees to give her up without so much as a second thought.

The situation was saved—to the extent that it could be—by Paul. The engineer was leaving his module. Alex heard the squelching sound of the hermetic hatchway, then waited a moment. Of course, everyone but Kim knew exactly what was happening. But Kim couldn't help herself and asked:

"What's he doing now?"

The "bit of green snot" was first to answer. Xang was uncommonly persistent, it seemed.

"The engineer's job, even on clean gluon reactors, always carries the risk of irradiation."

Kim shrugged, unimpressed by such rudimentary information.

"His body is thoroughly specialized," Xang continued. "His skull and his pelvic bones contain a lot of lead, to act as a screen. His ribs are fused into a single bone-and-cartilage plate, for the same reasons . . . But protecting the reproductive organs has always been one of the main challenges. You see, Kim, the irradiation of the testicles may lead to unwanted mutations."

"They should have more women engineers," said Kim darkly.

"That's what we were doing on Eben," noted Janet. She languidly reached for a huge sandwich and took a bite.

"In the last few decades," continued Morrison, completely unabashed, "the most rational solution to this problem has been adopted . . . Hi, Paul!"

The engineer nodded, entering the lounge.

"The solution was found in one of the practices of sumo wrestling," said Xang. "In case of emergency, Lourier draws his testicles into his pelvic cavity, where they are completely safe from radiation."

"Wow!" Kim looked at the engineer with admiration. "Is that hard?"

"It's a bit tough to explain to someone not in the trade," said Paul, reaching for a sandwich. "Generally, it isn't. The main thing is not to rush it, otherwise it hurts a little."

"Captain, what are you drinking?" asked Janet.

"Red wine, please"—Alex bowed his head slightly toward Lourier, and Paul returned the polite gesture—"out of solidarity with the professional traditions of our engineer. You did a good job, Paul."

"Thank you, Captain. We have a great ship. It's a pleasure to work with it."

Finally, Generalov also appeared. He paused in the hallway and looked at his fellow crewmembers.

"Captain, I've checked the alternative route through the Monica-3 tunnel. There's a seventy-two percent chance that it won't give us any time advantage."

"Why is that?" asked Alex.

"Such is the probability of a ritual battle of the Bronins at the moment we reach that system. Even if we manage to avoid getting involved in the fray, all the maneuvering to escape pursuit will take anywhere from nine hours to three days."

"We've passed through Monica-3 in three hours," interrupted Morrison.

"You lucked out."

"Please, sit down, Puck." Alex nodded. "You're probably right. Would you like some wine?"

"Yes, I would, thanks." Visibly proud of his victory, Generalov sat down next to Paul and quietly noted, "You did a great job, man. . . ."

"You've provided interesting energy consumption challenges, sir," replied Paul, reserved as usual.

Janet poured everyone some wine. She seemed not to mind her impromptu role of hostess.

"Attention, please." Alex got up. "Fellow crewmembers, I will be informal."

Generalov smirked, sprawling in his chair. Kim took a sip from her goblet, still glaring at Alex. What was she drinking? Juice or wine?

"This is my first flight as a captain," said Alex. "And to be completely honest, I became *Mirror*'s captain by chance."

"You lucky . . ." said Morrison under his breath, although there was no longer any tension in his tone.

"Yes, I am," agreed Alex. "All thanks to Kim."

The girl lifted her eyebrows in surprise but said nothing.

"You all are here by chance . . ."

It would be interesting to catch a glimpse of the Demon now. Would a skeptical grin appear on its little face?

"And we're all quite different. Janet is from Eben . . . her knowledge and experience are unique."

The black woman smiled dryly.

"Paul is only just beginning his astronautical career, which promises to be outstanding."

The engineer lowered his gaze.

"Puck is the only natural I know who works as a navigator. And he's great at it."

The expression of Generalov's sour face showed that he'd heard such compliments a million times and couldn't care less—life was a joyless business, after all.

"Kim is probably the youngest . . . as well as the loveliest fighter-spesh in the universe."

The girl peered at him searchingly.

"And Xang hesitated so much before signing the contract, it became a matter of pride for me to persuade him."

Morrison threw up his arms with a deep sigh and left his right arm resting on the back of Kim's chair.

"Here's to our crew, which is becoming a real team, a close-knit, happy family!" concluded Alex.

They clinked their glasses.

"Good wine," reported Morrison, with a knowing air. "You know, I worked on a small ship from the Barton Company for two years. We shipped wines from Earth. Those were the best wines! And half a percent of every shipment was written off as damaged during transportation . . . but we were a very careful crew, ladies and gentlemen. I don't know how I managed for two years!"

Janet noted thoughtfully:

"I first tried alcohol when I was thirty. When I was a POW. I didn't want to live anymore . . . and I had been convinced that a glass of wine would kill me. On Eben, having alcohol, drugs, or tobacco was considered ruinous to your body, a crime against humanity."

"Poor things . . ." sighed Generalov.

"We had many other pleasures in life," said Janet. "No doubt we were missing out on some things. But that's inevitable, after all. We all choose to miss out on some things, to have others instead."

"You should take everything life has to offer!" said Puck with great conviction.

"Really?" Janet slit her eyes quizzically. "Then why don't you have sex with women?"

"I tried it. Didn't like it!" hastily replied Generalov.

"Maybe. But you're missing out, a lot! You're not taking everything life has to offer."

Generalov winced, but kept quiet.

"And I simply have to have alcohol," said Paul. "It's part of my metabolism, and if I don't have at least two ounces of pure alcohol every twenty-four hours, I get sick."

The conversation resembled a weird roll call. Kim was about to say something, but at that very moment the hidden speakers came alive.

"Captain." The ship's service program chose to address Alex alone. "Three life forms are approaching the ship."

"Our passengers are here . . . damn!" Morrison waved his hand in the air, holding an empty glass. His other hand was already on Kim's shoulder, and the girl didn't seem to notice. "What if they demand an immediate launch?"

"We're the crew, so we go by the rules." Alex got up. "Janet, let's go meet them. The rest of you, relax."

He should have taken Kim with him. But Alex didn't want to risk introducing such an unusual fighter-spesh to the passengers at the very first meeting.

They walked out into the cargo bay. Alex hastily straightened his uniform, using the shiny surface of a spacesuit unit as a mirror. Janet stretched her arms toward him, quickly straightening out his collar. Said in a quiet, soothing voice:

"Everything's all right, Captain. Don't be nervous."

Alex smiled in reply. He didn't have to pretend in her company. He said:

"Computer, open the outer hatch and take in the newcomers."

The hatch in the floor came open, the ladder slid down. It was already dark outside, and only the intermittent flares of launching ships lit up the figures below.

They stepped onto the platform all at the same time. The ladder started its ascent, drawing them inside.

Two young girls, probably Kim's age, stood at the front. They were pretty, dark-skinned, and smiling, completely identical twins. Each held a little suitcase.

Behind them towered a tall man. So tall, in fact, that Alex's own height of over six feet seemed hardly worth mentioning. The man was a Europeoid, his light hair cut very close, and his piercing eyes were a cold, icy blue. His clothes looked civilian but fit like a uniform. His voice was very low and heavy:

"Alex Romanov, captain of the spaceship *Mirror*."

It wasn't a question, it was a statement.

"Yes." There was no need to repeat what the man had already said.

"Very well." The man extracted from his pocket a carefully folded sheet of paper. "I am Danila C-the-Third Shustov. You are now at my service."

Alex took the documents out of his hand without looking at them. Who would have thought! A clone! He glanced sidelong at Janet.

Something was happening to her. Her face was absolutely still, frozen. Dead.

"Let me introduce my wards and fellow travelers," C-the-Third Shustov continued. "Zei-So and Sey-Zo, our distinguished guests from the Zzygou Swarm."

Alex unintentionally held his breath for a second, though that was not necessary. These Zzygou did not stink. Had no odor at all. They were just like humans.

"Greetings!" sang out the Zzygou in unison. "Best of luck and health to you, servants!"

Janet stood as still as a statue.

"Show us to our quarters," said the clone.

Alex turned to Janet, using all his willpower to overcome his own stupor. His heart was pounding.

If the woman from Eben lost it, she would kill both of the Zzygou with her bare hands. And that thuggish bodyguard, as well. At the very least, she'd try.

"Doctor-spesh!"

Janet slowly transferred her gaze onto Alex.

"May I ask you . . . I order you to start preparing the sick bay for launch, immediately."

"Sick bay is ready," said Janet in an even, empty tone of voice.

"Conduct a thorough test of all systems."

She stood absolutely still for a few more seconds, then nodded and walked out of the cargo bay. One could only rejoice that it was impossible to slam an automatic door.

"There are sick people aboard?" inquired the clone.

Alex heaved a deep breath. Exhaled.

"No, but better safe than sorry. I will show you to your quarters myself."

"We thank you, servant," tunefully sang out the Zzygou.

OPERON II. EXOGENOUS.
THE OTHERS.

CHAPTER 1.

The passenger quarters were located on the lower deck. The only way to get to them was through the central hall, passing by the recreation lounge.

Alex led the way, clenching his fists so tightly that his knuckles whitened. Behind him came the laughing and bowing Zzygou. And finally, C-the-Third, a clone of the person named Danila Shustov. The recreation lounge was dead quiet—Janet had probably had a chance to mention something on her way to the sick bay.

They went down a narrow, winding staircase to the small circular hallway with six cabin doors facing it. The passenger quarters were double-occupancy cabins.

"We thank you, servant," chirped the Zzygou.

For some reason, Alex was sure they'd take the same cabin, but they let go of each other's hands and, with the same astonishing simultaneity of movement, went into two neighboring doors.

"Mr. C-the-Third Shustov . . ." said Alex.

"I'm listening, Captain."

"Could you tell me what the Sky Company does, and what the purpose of our trip is?"

The clone showed absolutely no sign of surprise.

"The Sky Company specializes in galactic tourism. We organize cruises within the human space sectors for visitors of the other races, as well as"—for some reason, the clone's voice quivered—"for human visitors to planets of other civilizations."

"Our work will consist of transporting the Others?"

"Yes."

Alex was silent a second before answering.

"Mr. C-the-Third Shustov, in that case, the crew must include a linguist, an exopsychologist, and a doctor specializing in the Others."

"I am an expert in all these areas," answered the imperturbable clone. "Captain, please tell me frankly—are you a xenophobe?"

"No." Alex firmly shook his head. "I've even had a few acquaintances among the Others."

"Then what is the problem? By the way, the term 'Others' is offensive. May I ask you to try to call our galactic neighbors 'persons of another race' or 'persons of nonhuman descent'? Or, at the very least, the 'other race,' but never just 'the Others'!"

It would probably have been best to tell him right then and there exactly what the situation was. Tell him about Janet, who was from Eben and whose specialization was executioner-spesh.

Except that the result would be the woman's immediate dismissal.

"All right, I'll use the term 'the other race.'"

The clone fixed a probing stare on him. "Captain, this ship is made especially for cruises with life forms from other planets. Have you looked at the passenger quarters?"

"Not closely. Personal control of the cabins is not my responsibility."

"If you had bothered to look, you wouldn't be so surprised now. The passenger quarters are designed to accommodate any life form. Adjustable atmosphere and gravity, a wide range of temperature, programmable food synthesizers . . ."

"My mistake," admitted Alex. "But . . . I've never heard of such cruise vessels before."

"Well, now you have," shrugged the clone. "How soon will you be ready for launch?"

"Any time."

"I'm glad to hear that. We'd prefer to start in an hour, an hour and a half."

Alex nodded.

"And the route?"

"The documents I gave you contain all the necessary information. The honorable Zzygou wish to see the famous waterfalls of Edem. We could, I suppose, make a stop or two on the way, say, at Zodiac. Have you ever seen the drift of the giant lotuses?"

"I haven't . . ."

"Neither have I." The clone smiled. "But it's rumored to be a marvelous sight. Right now, it's the beginning of the dry season on Zodiac. Has it occurred to you that working for this company gives you great advantages, Captain? You can travel to some of the most beautiful planets of the human sector, free of charge. Even get paid for it."

"Yes, of course . . ." Alex licked his lips, suddenly remembering Generalov's recent efforts to plot a course from Quicksilver Pit through Zodiac and Lard Crest to Edem.

"Would you mind just one more question, Mr. C-the-Third Shustov?"

"Please just call me C-the-Third." The clone obviously had no inhibitions about his own origins. "Not at all, go ahead!"

"Why is there no odor?" Alex nodded towards the cabins taken up by the Zzygou.

"The Zzygou are a race of highly advanced biotechnology. They've found a way to block the release of merkaptane. It causes them some discomfort, but the Zzygou are willing to endure it for the sake of human comfort."

"I see. In that case, perhaps you could also ask them not to call us 'servants'? For the sake of the comfort of the crew."

"All of us are masters and servants at different times in our lives," remarked C-the-Third with a melancholy air. "Maybe when I take a cruise through their sector of space, I'll get to call the Zzygou 'servants' as well. But of course, I'll try to explain the situation to them."

"Thanks."

Alex had already braced himself to speak. Almost, but not quite.

"Is everything all right?" asked C-the-Third, looking closely at him.

"Yes, of course. We take off in fifty-six minutes. Agreed?"

The clone looked at his watch.

"Agreed, Captain. I will inform my wards."

Alex left, without saying a single word about Janet or her problems with the Others.

Strangely, as he entered the recreation lounge, the discussion that had been raging there suddenly ceased. It didn't look like they were just patiently waiting for him. More likely, they had been saying something unpleasant behind his back. Kim sat tense and annoyed, and Morrison looked uncomfortable, as if he had been forced to defend a position he didn't exactly hold or argue for something he didn't really believe.

"Attention, please," said Alex. Reflected for a second and sat down. He still had some time left, after all.

"We are all ears, Captain," said Generalov with emphatic courtesy. It was obvious who had initiated the heated discussion.

"Our passengers have arrived," Alex continued. "As you already gathered, they are two visitors from the allied race of Zzygou and their guide, a specialist in communications with the Others, Danila C-the-Third Shustov. Apparently, we can all call him simply C-the-Third."

"A clone?" asked Paul for some reason.

"Yes, Engineer. A clone. I hope no one here is a chauvinist? The Zzygou are an intelligent and peaceful race . . ."

"The hell they are! Who cares about the damn Zzygou, anyway!" Generalov's politeness suddenly failed him. "Captain, you never warned us that there'd be a clone in the crew!"

"He is not in the crew," Alex pointed out. "C-the-Third is a Sky Company employee, just like us. His task is to accompany the Zzygou and provide all the necessary services . . ."

"Sexual services," sneered Generalov.

"I didn't delve into the details." Alex continued to speak with the same even tone of voice, but that seemed only to augment everyone's annoyance. "Clones have the same rights as all the other citizens of the Empire."

"You don't get it, do you?!" Puck clasped his hands in anger. "Cloning is the way to human degeneration! These nasty clones are everywhere! Entertainment clones, government clones, and now, space clones!"

"Why should it bother you so much?" asked Alex. Generalov exhaled heavily. But he answered a bit more calmly:

"It doesn't. I don't intend to clone myself. But it's totally unnatural! Human strength is in human diversity. Nature intended everyone's genetic makeup to be unique, so cloning is immoral! Don't you agree, Captain?"

"On the whole, I do, yes."

"And what would cloning lead to? Do we want to end up like the Zzygou or the Bronins? At least the Zzygou clone naturally, and the Bronins have a very high death rate. Without cloning, they'd go extinct. But if we all start cloning ourselves, we'll turn into a crowd of scum, living robots with serial numbers. One genotype for pilots, another for garbage collectors, the third one for rulers. Hell, we'll get mass-produced on a conveyor belt!"

"Puck, you're exaggerating! Clones in human society make up no more than five percent of the total population. And most of them are residents of far-flung, newly colonized planets. Cloning is essential there."

"Hah!" Generalov laughed without mirth. "Those are the official numbers! Clones are actually much more numerous. And all the sympathizers, who no doubt would clone themselves at the first opportunity, only pour oil on the flames! Lots of people we consider normal humans are really clones who have changed their appearance and gotten their claws on good jobs! And where there's a clone, no normal person has a chance! The clone will only have more of his own clones!"

Paul cleared his throat and shyly added:

"Captain, Puck has a point. I also think that giving clones full citizenship rights was a mistake. We had this one guy at the academy, Aristark Yosilidi, a good spesh . . . very talented. He was offered the chance to clone himself, and he agreed. In fourteen years, seven of his clones will be coming to the academy, can you imagine that? His abilities are very strong, so they'll all be accepted, no doubt about it. And that means that seven ordinary speshes won't be able to get in. See? And what if every one of the seven clones also cloned himself? In twenty-eight years, the entire department would be full of Aristarks-C-Yosilidi!"

"Exactly!" Generalov elbowed Paul's side. "He knows what I'm talking about! He had a chance to see for himself!"

"That's stupid!" Kim jumped up. "I have two clone friends! One of them wants to be an electronics engineer, like her matrix. But not the other one. She wants to be an assembly-spesh in an orbital shipyard. She wants to build spaceships!"

"If the girls' specialization is not too narrowly defined, they'll do just fine, too . . ." said Morrison without much certainty in his tone, then darted an anxious glance at Alex. It was high time to break up the argument.

"All right, thank you all for an interesting discussion." Alex got up. "We'll continue this later, okay? And now, some useful information. We all signed the contract. We all work for a company that pays us a lot of money."

"That *promises* to pay us," interjected Generalov. He probably didn't really think that the company would risk a fight with the union by deceiving the crew. More likely, he just wanted to have the last word. Now it was plain to Alex why this uniquely qualified navigator never stayed at any one job for very long.

"We take off in thirty-six minutes." Alex was looking only at Generalov, and the navigator reluctantly hushed. "I ask everyone to be at their posts in twenty minutes."

"What's the route?" hissed the navigator.

"It won't be a problem for you. We're flying first to Zodiac, and then to Edem. The honorable Zzygou wish to see the most beautiful planets of the human sector."

Generalov furrowed his brow.

And Kim turned noticeably pale.

"Any special instructions for this flight?" inquired Morrison. "Gravity levels, inertia parameters, jump rhythms?"

"No, nothing. The Zzygou tolerate the human environment well. Any other questions?" No one had any questions. "You all are free to go."

Generalov, murmuring something under his breath, was the first to leave the lounge. Then Paul followed him, obviously distressed by the conflict and his own participation in it. Morrison looked sidelong at Kim, but she remained sitting as before.

"I'll go test the ship," said the co-pilot, and left.

"What's wrong, Kim?" Alex came closer to the girl.

"You . . ."

"Forgive me, Kim. I can explain . . ."

"I don't want to fly to Edem!" cried Kim.

She seemed to have forgotten about the conversation between Alex and Xang.

"Kim, it's unavoidable. You're a spesh. You're a member of the crew now, so you have to go by the contract."

"Alex, don't you get it!? I cannot show up on Edem! I simply can't!" The girl's eyes were bright with tears.

Alex gently took her by the shoulder. "Kim, for now, we're flying to Zodiac. It's a marvelous planet. The most beautiful one in the human sector, even though your home world might dispute the claim. Do you have anything against Zodiac?"

"No . . ." Kim leaned forward, pressed herself to Alex's chest. A frightened little girl . . . it didn't matter now that she was capable of killing off the entire crew. "Alex, friend-spesh, I don't want to fly to Edem!"

"Kim, I have a lot of problems as it is. Janet hates the Others. Generalov hates clones. If you start . . ." He stopped short of finishing the phrase.

The girl was quiet, hugging him and hiding her face, wet with tears.

"Kim, we're flying to Zodiac. You hear? We'll have time to discuss all this. If push comes to shove, we'll think of something. You could stay on Zodiac, for instance, you could take a few days off . . . sick leave, maybe?"

"Fighter-speshes never get sick," Kim informed him. "Well . . . almost never."

"We'll ask Janet . . . surely she'll understand your situation?"

"Probably . . ." Kim's voice sounded a little calmer. "But I won't return to Edem! I'd rather jump right out into open space!"

"Kim. We'll think of something. But for now, please help me, okay? I need your support, friend-spesh."

The look in Kim's eyes, when she lifted her face to look at him, was triumphant.

"Will you ever again tell Xang that he can hit on me?"

"I said that knowing you would reject him," said Alex, almost honestly.

"You better watch out, I might just be tempted. He's a stud," purred Kim.

Alex forced a laugh.

"Really? I thought you liked our engineer."

Kim snorted. "That pink piglet? He's still just a baby! No, he's nice, but he's still a kid. Generalov is much more interesting, but he isn't interested in me . . . All right, friend-spesh, I'll be going to my cabin. My stuff is all over the place. I have to anchor everything, right?"

"That's the rule. Just in case."

"But I won't fly to Edem," said Kim on her way out. Alex sat down. He wanted a drink, but in twenty minutes he had to be in charge of the ship. Besides, everything had already been cleared off the table.

He had never imagined that being a captain would entail these kinds of conversations. What a stupid tradition it was to appoint pilots to be captains! They should appoint psychologists. Or was it just his luck to have a whole crew of weirdos? Did problems like these ever come up on any other ships of the fleet?

Alex rolled up his sleeve to look at the Demon. The little devil was holding its head in its hands. It was wincing, as though it was suffering from a terrible headache.

And Alex realized that what bothered him was not so much the conversation that had just taken place, but the fact that he still had to talk to Janet. A woman who had almost become his friend and was now caught in the worst kind of trap—a conflict between her spesh duties and the program of behavior precoded into her subconscious mind.

"There's no time," said Alex. Got up and went to the sick bay.

The door was unlocked. Janet was sitting in a chair and holding her head in her hands, just like the little tattoo on his arm. As he entered, she looked at him and said in a quiet voice:

"The sick bay is ready for take-off and for receiving patients."

Alex sat down on the floor in front of her. Stretched out his arm to show her the Demon.

"You see this?"

Janet nodded.

"Do you know what this is?"

"An emotion scanner . . . I've seen them . . ." she replied in a colorless voice. Then a look of concern appeared on her face. "What's wrong, Captain?"

"You have a problem. You hate the Others. Generalov has a problem. He hates clones. Kim has a problem. We are under orders to fly to Edem, and she doesn't want to go there. And I am your captain. All of your problems are my problems now."

Janet rubbed her forehead wearily.

"Captain . . . Alex, don't worry about me. I can handle it."

"Janet, are you sure?"

"Yes, Alex. I do hate the Others, those Zzygou things especially. They were our first targets, you understand. But I can handle it. Even if I have to wait their tables."

Alex looked searchingly at the woman.

"Everything will be fine," she repeated, with a little more conviction in her tone. "Of course, I was shocked. I am a soldier of Eben. But even a soldier doesn't have to rush headlong into a fight. I can control myself, Alex. Don't worry."

"Then I have only two problems left: Generalov and Kim."

"I'll try to sort it out with Kim. She seems to listen to me."

"Thanks." Alex lightly touched her hand. "Friend-spesh, thanks for your understanding and self-restraint. We take off in fourteen and a half minutes. I have to go."

"Will you need me at my battle station?"

"No, not really. The space around Quicksilver Pit is well patrolled, so there's no real danger."

"But I'd like to be at my post, anyway."

"All right. I'll be glad to see you, Janet."

Alex smiled at the woman and left the sick bay. Looked like there was one less problem to worry about. Or was there?

Janet had been convincing, but could she really control herself?

He had no other choice but to trust her word.

"Accept me."

He became one with the ship.

And somehow, all that had been bothering him disappeared. All the problems—Kim's, Janet's, Puck's—were really minor things, barely worth noticing, in comparison to the warmth of the ship's gentle wave.

It must be very similar to love . . .

Too bad he couldn't really compare the two.

His crew were specks of colored light in the darkness. His ship—his powerful body. And the ship's consciousness was still something separate . . . but it was closer and more important than his own thoughts.

Could he have ever really been happy without experiencing this? Yes . . . Because he had been happy being just a pilot. And had his parents chosen another specialization for him, he would've been happy working in a factory, or demonstrating models on a podium, or collecting edible seaweed in the ocean. He would have been happy regardless, for happiness was a necessary attribute of being a spesh.

Still, how glad he was that what made him happy were the stars, and flying among them, and all these mechanisms and bionics, interwoven to form an expensive toy called a spaceship!

"Passengers, please prepare for take-off. We are leaving the surface of the planet in seven minutes."

Alex had never before been a captain on a passenger ship. But his memory easily supplied the necessary phrases.

"Time to orbit—twelve minutes, thirty-two seconds. Time to tunnel—forty-four minutes. We will be making an intermediate jump to Gamma Snakebearer, the transport center of the third sector. After that, our route lies through New Ukraine, Heraldica, and Zodiac. Other intermediate landings are possible at the passengers' request. Our estimated total flight time is twenty-nine hours, thirteen minutes. The crew wishes you a pleasant flight."

He waited another ten seconds, in case there were any additional orders or questions from the passengers, and then turned off the connection.

All right. That was it. The route had been approved, and now he had complete control over the ship.

Generalov had already made the route viewable to everyone. It was the very route he had practiced plotting that morning.

Alex reached out through the eternal night of virtual space. Touched Generalov, getting his attention. Ordered:

"Private channel."

A moment later, his consciousness split in two. He was still the root of the ship getting ready for take-off. He was watching the last preliminary tests, feeling the reactor powering up . . . but at the same time he stood face to face with Generalov. Around them was nothing but darkness. This talk would be just between the two of them, and no other crewmembers knew about it.

"Navigator, I have a serious question for you."

"I am listening, Captain." Puck's virtual image nodded.

"Please leave out the formalities. I'd like a heart-to-heart."

Generalov looked aside in embarrassment. And said after a pause:

"I am sorry about my outburst. But . . . I really don't care for clones."

"We all have somebody we don't care for, Puck. Some people don't like naturals, some don't like the Others. But that's not what I wanted to talk about."

"I see," Puck nodded. "It's about the route?"

"Yes. I believe that coincidences happen. But everything has a limit. You already plotted this route once today."

"I was practicing."

"And you just happened to choose this exact route? Quicksilver Pit-Zodiac-Edem?"

"Yes!"

"Puck, that's impossible."

"What are you trying to say, Alex?" Generalov certainly enjoyed being informal. "Are you suggesting that I actually knew about our route beforehand?"

"Of course."

The navigator burst out laughing.

"You overestimate me. I really was just practicing. The whole crew was practicing, and so was I. You can suspect whatever you want, but I really did choose that route entirely by chance!"

"Puck, that's impossible. If you're telling me the truth—can you see why I have my doubts?"

Generalov lapsed into thought.

"I do understand, Captain. I was also really surprised. I was plotting a course . . . let me see . . . well, I picked Edem because of our lovely bodyguard."

"Okay, I suppose that's plausible. But using Zodiac as an intermediary point? How do you explain that?"

For a moment, Puck's image got blurry—he must have been calculating all the possibilities. Alex could almost feel the ship's computer strain to handle the extra burden.

"I have to agree with you," reluctantly admitted Generalov. "It's a really good route, Quicksilver Pit-Zodiac-Edem, but there are five more alternatives. None are better than any others—all are within random probability parameters. All I can tell you is that I really did choose this particular one by pure chance."

"Puck, tell me: Before you went into the navigation module, had anyone even mentioned Zodiac in your presence?"

A short hesitation.

"No."

One minute to take-off.

Alex nodded. He had a lingering, unpleasant sensation—the feeling of having missed something.

"All right, Puck. Let's get back to work." He cut off the private connection and concentrated on the ship. Flight control had already given the last corrections for the take-off corridor. The ship's reactor was slowly increasing its power output, releasing energy to be accumulated and used up by the ship. Lourier's job was to supply a lot of power, but also not to supply too much.

"Countdown."

Morrison had already plotted the graceful curve of the take-off trajectory and was waiting with tense anticipation. Alex understood his hopes . . . he knew the feeling. But he could not let the co-pilot perform his own very first take-off.

"Ten."

He reached for the tense green spiral and whispered:

"Sorry . . ."

The spiral moved off to one side, giving Alex full access to the piloting gear.

"Nine."

The membranes of the plasma thrusters opened.

"Eight."

The grid of the gravitational engine opened. Of course, no one was planning to take off riding a graviray, which would damage the old launch pad. But for the improbable eventuality of plasma-engine failure, the ship had to have an emergency option.

"Seven."

Alex's consciousness reached out to touch each member of his crew ever so lightly, a brief, reassuring, and grateful contact.

"Six."

The gluon reactor started pulsing, boosting the energy output. Paul had a wonderful sense of timing. . . .

"Five."

Alex turned on the engines.

The ship smoothly leaned on its tail, not leaving the surface yet, but standing on its hind supports alone. Gravity compensation worked perfectly, so there was no change in the gravity vector within the ship itself.

"Four."

A firestorm burst out around the vessel.

"Three."

The ship quivered, leaving the surface.

"Two."

They were already standing "in the pillar." The ship still looked chained to the planet to an outside observer, when really it had already broken free.

"One."

The energy flooded into the engines, throwing them into full-power mode.

"Zero. Take-off."

And they were airborne. The ship was piercing the sky with a swift thrust, no longer bound by gravity, or any orders from flight control, or laws of Quicksilver Pit. Somewhere below them were the dirty and malodorous capital, the honorable president San Li, the smog-blackened sky, speshes and naturals, astronauts and planet-dwellers, humans and Others.

Only the ship remained, and the seven humans and two Others aboard it, and the invisible route charted among the stars.

The parting clouds dabbed the ship's body. The city below them diffused into a murky, glowing blot. It even looked rather pretty from the dark distance. . . . At sixteen thousand feet, Alex switched over to the graviray and the vessel gave a slight jolt. Darn it! Botched a smooth transition.

"Nice transition, Captain," said Morrison, as if to calm him down; a slight jolt when switching to another set of engines was almost inevitable. But at the same time, Morrison was reminding him, "I noticed."

Alex grinned, increasing the traction. Glanced at an *Otter* coming in for landing through the adjacent corridor. The narrow cone of the gravity engine's thrusting field trailed behind the ship, and the computer traced an alarming red around its outer edges. The cone presented little danger to any ship that might sideswipe it. At the very worst there might be minor damage to the skin plating, which would regenerate overnight. And the unwritten laws of the pilots' fraternity would most probably prevent any official involvement. What's more, they were well within their own take-off corridor, so it had to be the mistake of the tanker's pilot. But to allow this kind of situation was considered bad form.

"Co-pilot, that *Otter* is getting into our tail. Track them."

Xang started murmuring something at the clowns piloting the

tanker. Concentrating on his own tasks, Alex paid no more attention to him.

Mirror was as light as a feather in comparison to the heavy, multiton vessels he had piloted for the last few years. Alex couldn't help remembering an old book that described the ecstasy of a boy who kicked off his heavy winter boots and put on a pair of light summer shoes. Now he was feeling something very much like it.

A lightness. The universe had become not just the place where he lived but a home he knew and loved, small and cozy, where everything was close to everything else and where he knew every little corner. Even the ship's responses to his orders were not just precise executions of his commands, but happy continuations of his thoughts. Not a servant, but a friend. Not a machine, but a beloved.

He had experienced this kind of thing a long time ago, before his metamorphosis, when he was still an almost-ordinary kid. He would leave the house with his posse, stay out till late. Sometimes they'd be gone for several days, traveling into the thick northern forests and as far as the Baltic Sea, where they would lie on the jagged cliffs and look down from on high, through the clear water, onto the ruins of ancient cities that hadn't survived the first ecological storm. "The gang" were five friends. Alex himself. The dark-skinned, redheaded David, who emigrated to New Jerusalem at the age of fourteen, right after his metamorphosis. Builder-speshes were in great demand there. Fam Hoh . . . poor Fam, he was also a spesh, a fighter-spesh. He died at fifteen, barely out of the academy, taking part in a peacekeeping mission in the Martian Free Cities. He was shot down over the desert, far from the terraformer towers, had to walk back for twenty-four hours, but died of dehydration, hypothermia, and oxygen starvation. Gene was the only natural in their whole gang, so he was always the butt of their cruel childish jokes, and at the same time the object of their clumsy sympathy . . . he wanted to become a psychologist. Maybe he did, who knows. . . . And then there was Nadia, his devoted girlfriend, his first lover, his best friend . . . She was now a well-known and successful doctor-spesh. But back then, she seemed to have two separate and unrelated lives. When she was with the rest of the gang, she was a fighter daredevil, their total buddy, with whom you could share a heart-to-heart talk and have a smooch or two in a dark little corner. But at home she was always a perfect, sweet, reserved, well-behaved girl . . .

Alex was always the leader, though no one ever chose or appointed him as such. No one felt any need to, really, or even thought that he was the chief of their little gang. If anyone ever even mentioned that he was in charge, the rest would have laughed at such a preposterous idea. Nevertheless, that was the way it was. His crazy ideas became their common plans, and his pranks turned into group endeavors. If he was in a good mood, everyone shared his joy. That was the way it was till the very day of his metamorphosis. Even Nadia, who had had her transformation earlier, still kept following him. When did it all change? Probably right after his metamorphosis. He didn't leave right away. He had to wait till the next admission period at the pilot academy. They kept horsing around, just like before, shaking up the entire tiny town of Izborg . . . except that Alex stopped being the leader. And no new leader emerged.

Maybe the reason was that a pilot-spesh should never show too much initiative?

But now it all came back, because a captain was responsible for making decisions for everyone.

He was feeling that connection again. A oneness with all those around him. And this connection was strengthened not by orders or contractual formalities, or rules, or ranks, or by the crew's love for him . . . It was something else, elusive and unutterable. Something that had helped him lead all of them—the smart boy David (a hut David had built at the age of seven lasted till the gang came of age), the pugnacious Fam (who was always careful, as any spesh should be, to match his strength to his opponent's), the inhibited, shy boy-natural Gene (Alex really hoped his dream had come true), and Nadia, with her biting sense of humor . . .

His crew had turned out to be a good one, after all. Despite all the quirks and problems. The navigator continuously posted alternative routes, the co-pilot controlled the ship well, the engineer made available just the right amount of energy for any given moment. And the battle stations scoured the space around the ship for possible targets, even though the orbits around Quicksilver Pit were considered absolutely safe.

They reached orbit and almost immediately started their acceleration toward the mouth of the hyper-channel. Alex gave all the piloting over to Morrison and called up a detailed chart of the channel.

The channel turned out to be not just old, but ancient. Now, in his state of confluence with the ship's memory blocks, Alex had access to its entire history. The channel had been cut from the Moon station during the second colonization wave. These days, there was a museum in place of the Moon station, and most of the worlds colonized back then were in a state of decay—either utterly abandoned or barely scraping by. Quicksilver Pit seemed lucky by comparison.

Alex practiced the channel entry several times with a time-dilation computer program. There were six possible trajectories that would fit within the assigned time interval and take *Mirror* towards Gamma Snakebearer and then to Zodiac. Alex chose the trajectory that would give them the most temporal advantage, and he went through it several times.

All was well. They would dive into the channel behind a couple of heavy trucks, keeping all the required distances. There would be another vessel right behind them, a mercury tanker, not too large, but loaded to the gills and possessed of immense inertia. Of course, mercury tanker pilots went through this channel so often that they could probably do it with their eyes closed.

Alex folded the virtual chart and moved Morrison off piloting with a gentle push. They were approaching the mouth of the channel, and there were three minutes remaining before it would be their turn to jump in.

The mouth of the channel glittered among the stars like a giant piece of the lightest fabric, lit from within, floating through the darkness of space. The entrance was the shape of an irregular trapezoid, curving and bending every second, changing its size and its angles—although from the point of view of six-dimensional geometry, it was actually a perfect circle.

"*Mirror*, you are now allowed to enter the channel's waiting zone."

That was the voice of a guard station called Stationary Channel. Twelve battle stations guarded the entrance. Most of them were real battle stations, built for that purpose at the shipyards, but several were just old, converted battleships. Still, it would have been unwise to reproach Quicksilver Pit's president for being tightfisted. The modern stations could hardly have been more powerful than an old battleship, even one with its main engines gone and its planetary weapons off.

"Understood. We're getting in line." Alex ran his virtual chart one more time. Two large *Burbot* tankers were approaching the channel exactly on schedule. The first one's rounded nose touched the surface of the gossamer sheet trembling amidst the emptiness of space. Then the ship quivered, rippled, and vanished. In exactly eight seconds, the second ship followed. The trucker pilots were probably not aces, but they were well coordinated with each other. Alex quickly looked at every one of his crew—all were there, doing their job, and the situation was under control.

"All right, kids, we're about to jump. . . ." As if confirming his thoughts, one of the bases reported:

"*Mirror*, you're cleared for entry into the channel."

Alex moved the ship forward slowly—a quick entry into the channel could lead them out to a random point in the transport grid or even cause the ship's destruction. He had one trajectory to lead the ship out to Zodiac.

Hyper-channels were very strange things. To be precise, there was only one hyper-channel in the universe; more simply would not fit. But that was an idea from six-dimensional geometry, a field in which fewer than a hundred scientists were experts. For practical piloting, all you had to know was that every channel would lead the ship to this or that exit point, depending on the trajectory of the entry and the phase of the pulse. And there could be no more than thirty-six such exit points . . . again, no one knew why. Each channel had been made at random—although, with the relative probability of sixty-six point three (recurring decimal) percent, they seemed to appear near massive gravitational anomalies. Stars, for instance. Also, the channels couldn't be closer to each other than one light year, although this factoid was still not fully confirmed by science. In addition, no one could know where a new, freshly made hyper-channel might lead. Only the probable distance could be measured, with a large margin of error.

The entire history of human galactic colonization was a chain of random coincidences. Olympus had been Earth's first colony, a cold and unfriendly little world, but somehow considered almost a paradise back in the mid-twenty-first century. After that, the channel stations went to work at full capacity, poking holes all over the universe, and more and more new worlds appeared. The magnificent Edem, a splendid and rich planet, flourishing in the blue light of the Spike, had been colonized a very long time ago, despite its huge distance from Earth. But Alpha Centauri, long a candidate for the first interstellar flight, had not been reached until very recently, only some fifteen years before. Well, it was for the best, anyway. It turned out to have no promising planets.

Most ships had their own hyper-engines, allowing them to traverse several light years at a time. But this capability had absolutely no commercial value at all. The heavier the ship, the more energy devoured in a direct hyper-jump. *Mirror's* mass was actually at the

upper limit for a ship with its own hyper-engine. Courier ships, lei-
sure boats, scouting vessels—and that was about it, no other kinds
in that class.

His thoughts rushed by at a speed possible only when he was
connected to the computer. Alex was taking the ship along the axis
visible only to pilots, mechanically noticing what was going on
all around, while thinking about channel peculiarities. Quicksilver Pit, for instance, had a rather shoddy channel. Only five of its
entry trajectories led to other planets of the Human Empire. All the
rest led out to derelict exits, some in the middle of totally empty
interstellar space, or near stars which had no planetary systems, or
planets utterly unsuitable for life . . . or orbiting stars that belonged
to alien races.

In most cases, the race that mined out a channel to a star would
be its owner. But there were two alien races that never used hyper-
channels at all, preferring other methods of interstellar communication. And there had been cases when a planet turned out to be
so attractive that the Others colonized it without using any hyper-
channels. For example, one of the exits from Quicksilver Pit's channel led out to a planet inhabited by Cepheideans, a strange race
almost as humanoid as the Zzygou and, at the same time, engaged
in an eternal war with the Zzygou Swarm . . .

"Morrison!" Alex couldn't quite say what had put him on guard.
Everything was within the norm . . . for the time being. But what
was that tanker doing?

The tanker was not going anywhere yet, just turning around,
working out its trajectory—its orientation engine nozzles were
blinking.

Its future trajectory, however, cut right across the path of *Mirror*.

"Tanker MT-28, tanker MT-28." Morrison had also noticed what was about to happen. "Your present course is dangerous! Over!"

No reply.

There was no cause to panic just yet . . . but Alex unwrapped a trajectory forecast chart anyway. The two ships' velocity, mass, and direction.

He froze.

If that moron attempted to turn on the engines at full force, a collision would be imminent. It wouldn't be a catastrophe—their force fields and gravity compensation would absorb most of the blow. But it would mean that *Mirror* would enter the hyper-channel at an uncharted angle . . . and . . . A web of trajectories flashed and vanished in front of him, leaving only one track. The track that would lead to the Cepheideans' sector.

To turn inside a hyper-tunnel was impossible. Once you were in, it took you where it took you . . . Right into the little fists of those small but warlike creatures, who would be thrilled to find a couple of Zzygou in their space.

They'd probably let the humans go, though. . . .

There was still a bit of leeway in their speed, and Alex used it all up. The tanker seemed to freeze in space . . . Right . . . why in the world would it ram a yacht?

And then the tanker's graviray engine turned on. The space around it distorted violently, as the full impulse started pushing the tanker's cylindrical bulk on a collision course with *Mirror*.

Towards the exact point that would make the collision unavoidable and throw the yacht off into Cepheidean space.

"Morons!" shouted Morrison. He, too, understood that a collision was imminent, though he probably wasn't aware of all the consequences. Suddenly, the tanker replied:

"*Mirror*, we have a problem—our engine has misfired. All systems blocked, no maneuvering possible at this time. Please clear the way. Over!"

"Not possible." Morrison's voice turned very calm. "Our speed reserves are up. The ship will be destroyed upon entry into the channel."

"Increase your force fields," came the advice of the tanker's invisible voice. "It's our fault. We'll pay full compensation."

What did compensation have to do with this? The pilot must really have thought that what was about to happen would be just an accident, lamentable but not tragic. Or perhaps he was simply lying.

Although such a lie would require him to know about *Mirror*'s passengers and also to have a monstrously keen eye for spatial calculations.

"*Mirror* to channel guard." His own voice sounded unfamiliar to Alex. "We need help."

Twenty-four seconds to collision impact. Subjective time in virtual reality flowed much more slowly, but that had no bearing on the laws of physics. The tanker could no longer slow down, and *Mirror* had no way of maneuvering.

"Channel guard to *Mirror*. The situation is under control. What sort of help do you require?"

Alex glanced again at the other ship. A three-people crew, max. More likely, just a pilot and a navigator . . .

"Annihilate tanker MT-28."

The tanker's pilot shouted something unintelligible. The guard stations—or, rather, their officer on duty—hesitated for a second.

Space was ruthless. A ship that was about to cause a collision could very well be destroyed. Especially if it were a tanker endangering the lives aboard a passenger vessel.

"*Mirror*, are you nuts?!" The guard officer had lost his official tone of voice. "The situation isn't critical—your shields will hold!"

"Guard station, we require protection. A collision will cause us to enter the channel at an uncharted angle."

"Protection denied. Your course is not life-threatening."

But of course. The guard station officers were speshes as well trained as Alex. They could see all the potentialities.

"Here are some recommendations," the officer added. And once again, a map of possible routes fanned open in front of Alex. "Reduce your speed by eight percent, maximize shield power, prepare for emergency jump to Gatané-4 . . ."

"We can't enter Cepheidean space!" Alex yelled. "Destroy the tanker!"

"The Empire has friendly relations with the Cepheideans," replied the officer bluntly.

On the other communication channel, the tanker's pilot regained his gift of speech and shouted a few choice words at Alex. Yes. If he really were innocent, Alex's demands must seem monstrously cruel.

"Alex . . ."

The dark-red clot of flame. Janet. The weapons blister, his fist . . .

"Permission to act, Captain." She understood there was no time to persuade the guard officer. She knew all the intricacies of the Others' relations with each other better than any of those officers growing fat in their guard stations. Even though she had no trace of warm feelings for the Zzygou, she had no intention of pleasing the Cepheideans, either. But what could she do? To destroy the tanker would be unthinkable for her—there were humans aboard!

"Permission granted," said Alex.

At the same moment, the reactor power jumped way up. Maybe Paul had guessed what was required, or maybe Janet had contacted him.

"*Mirror* to guard stations, we are addressing the problem on our own. . . ."

Before he had time to finish his sentence, the battle station fired a ray at the hapless tanker. The ray wasn't powerful enough to destroy the tanker about to ram them. Janet had taken aim at the cargo hold. For almost three seconds, nothing happened. Then a scorched chunk of plating fell off. And a powerful stream of boiling mercury burst out of the tanker's innards.

It was an enchanting sight. The tanker, shot through and boiling over, was still on a collision course with *Mirror*—except that the jet stream of mercury was slowing it down and reducing the tanker's mass with every passing millisecond. It seemed as though the tanker had been transformed into a comet with a fiery tail of boiling mercury.

"What are you, nuts?!" shouted the tanker's pilot. He had already realized that no one was going to destroy him, but losing all of his cargo was also a terrifying prospect. "We'll take this to the tribunal!"

Alex didn't bother answering. A joint commission of the union of pilots, Quicksilver Pit's administration, and military detectives would investigate the incident. Alex didn't doubt that his crew would be cleared of all charges. When everyone figured out what their entry into Cepheidean space would have led to, all the responsibility would be dumped on the tanker's crew. And there would be nothing but praise for Janet.

"*Mirror*, hold your fire!" The guard officer was really aggravated. "Your next ray burst will be considered an act of aggression against the Empire!"

Well, yes. Theoretically the guard stations, as well as the hyperchannel, were Imperial property. But in reality they were eating out of the hands of the local officials, who would be very upset with the damage to the tanker and the loss of its cargo.

"The following is an order—"

But he had no chance to finish his phrase. Through a cloud of cooling mercury, brightly flashing against its protective force field, *Mirror* entered the hyper-channel.

Exactly on course to take the ship to Gamma Snakebearer.

CHAPTER 2.

The gray tube of the hyper-tunnel seemed endless. They could all feel the ship's movement, though it wasn't very fast by planetary standards—about one hundred and eight miles an hour. It felt as though the yacht had turned into a land vehicle speeding along a dark tunnel.

All this had nothing to do with the ship's actual speed, of course. These were purely subjective impressions.

"Fellow crewmembers, congratulations on a successful entry into the channel." Alex paused for a moment. "Janet Ruello, doctor-spesh, I thank you, on behalf of the company, for your timely and decisive actions in an emergency situation."

By saying this, he took all responsibility upon himself. If for any reason Janet's shot at the tanker were to be reprimanded, Alex alone would bear the consequences.

"Thank you, Captain," replied Janet.

Alex paused again.

"Janet, was that your own idea?"

"No, Captain. Pilot training on Edem included some

nontraditional ways of affecting enemy vessels. Bronin spaceship reactors run on mercury . . . it was a lucky coincidence."

"I wish I could thank your teachers personally, Janet."

She smiled somewhat sadly. "Why not, Captain? In another three hundred years or so, when the quarantine field dissolves . . ."

"Captain, shall I prepare an official complaint to the union?" asked Generalov.

"That's my job," said Alex.

"You have extensive experience with judicial quibbling?" rejoined the navigator. "Of course, the report should bear your signature, but someone else can put it together . . ."

Alex didn't hesitate for very long. When it came to concocting complaints, the navigator really was the most experienced member of the crew.

"All right, Puck. Prepare the document and send it to me for a signature. Don't forget to stress the fact that our entry into Cepheidean space would have led to a customs search and imprisonment of our honorable Zzygou passengers. Morrison!"

"Yes, Captain."

"The jump to Gamma Snakebearer will take six and a half hours. You have the bridge."

"Aye-aye, Captain. Permission to perform intermediate maneuvers in the Gamma system?"

Alex smiled. Of course: piloting inside a hyper-channel was not any pilot's idea of fun. Morrison seemed to have decided to eke out every good piloting opportunity he could.

"All right, Morrison. But don't forget to call me to the bridge right before we exit the channel. The rest of the crew may now rest. Engineer, you may turn the reactor to minimal power output."

While the ship slid through the invisible currents of hyperspace, it didn't need much piloting, or energy, or defenses.

"I have the bridge, Captain," said Morrison. Alex lingered for a moment, watching the colored lights melt into darkness—his crew leaving the control system.

"Be good, now . . ." whispered Alex. Not to the people—to his ship. A warm wave, gentle and soothing, washed over him in reply as if to say, "Don't worry, everything will be fine . . ."

When only the emerald spiral was left in virtual space, Alex left.

The piloting chair straps clicked softly open. Alex got up, stretched his neck and shoulders, looked at the control screens. A smooth gray tunnel—the ship was sliding through the inner side of space. Morrison looked as motionless as a mannequin in the other pilot's chair. Poor Morrison. He had no way of experiencing this ecstasy. It was great to be a pilot, but being a captain was so much more . . .

"Have a good shift, Xang," said Alex gently and left the bridge.

Janet waved to him from afar. But Kim approached him decisively as he neared the door to his cabin.

"Not now, honey . . ." Alex took her by the shoulder. "I have an important meeting right now."

Kim frowned.

"Alex, will I be hearing you say that all the time now?"

How was he to maintain any kind of discipline under such circumstances? The engineer, opening his own door, stared at them curiously.

"Kim, come see me in half an hour, okay?" He looked into her eyes. He had no idea what she must have heard in his voice, but she beamed and affected a slight, mocking drawl as she said:

"All right, A-lex . . ."

Another second, and she disappeared behind her door. Alex entered his quarters, shook his head. Yup. He had a problem. Kim's specialization was making her seek his love . . . the one thing he couldn't give her.

But he had more pressing matters to tend to.

"Computer, put me through to C-the-Third, captain's priority, open channel."

The screen came on. To Alex's surprise, C-the-Third was in his bed, sleeping peacefully. The yacht gravity compensation system was strong enough to protect the passengers from gravity overloads upon tunnel entry, but the clone's equanimity was in itself worthy of admiration. Either he didn't give a damn about anything, or flew so often that he felt no trepidation before yet another hyper-jump.

"C-the-Third . . ."

The clone awoke instantly. One moment he was lying on the bed, wrapped tightly in his blanket, and the next instant he was standing by the side of the bed, looking at the screen.

"Captain here," Alex felt compelled to say, for some reason. "Come to my quarters. Immediately."

C-The-Third didn't say a word. Only nodded and disappeared from the field of vision. Alex sat down in the chair, propped his chin with his fist. He was absolutely calm. The recent incident had taken so little real time that his body hadn't even had a chance to react by releasing adrenaline. Everything was over. And all pilots were pre-programmed to not worry about misfortunes that hadn't happened.

If not for Janet . . .

The door beeped.

"Open," Alex ordered.

It was C-the-Third. He wasn't even dressed—he came just as he was, in his pajamas, which were rather childish, blue with little red and white stars. Alex made a mental note to be more careful with the word "immediately."

"What's going on, Captain?"

The clone's harsh tone did not match the cheerful design of his pajamas. And his face wore the look of a man ready to kill.

"Sit down. Would you like a drink?" Alex leaned over and opened a little bar. Glanced at the flattish flasks . . . not a bad selection!

"Brandy," said the clone resentfully. "Just a little."

He waited while the captain poured two glasses of brandy and then asked, a little more calmly:

"So what's happening?"

"At the entrance to the tunnel, we were almost rammed by a mercury tanker."

"An attack?" The clone tensed.

"The pilot said their engines misfired. It's been known to happen on old tubs like that. Their computers are extremely primitive and unstable."

C-The-Third frowned.

"Captain, this ship is supposed to be well protected . . . and well armed. If I am not mistaken, according to the law, the guard towers were supposed to destroy the tanker. And you had the right to do so, as well."

"No, I didn't. The collision would not have led to a catastrophe— only forced us to enter the tunnel with an uncharted trajectory."

"Was there a collision?" asked the clone.

"No. You would've felt it, I can assure you. We . . . managed."

C-the-Third drank up his brandy in one gulp. Asked testily:

"Then what the hell? I knew we weren't going for a walk in the park. You could've told me all about it in the morning . . ."

"C-the-Third, by a strange coincidence, the new trajectory would have led us into Cepheidean space."

The clone started. He rolled his empty glass in his fingers and said:

"But it didn't happen, right?"

"Right. We are on our way to Gamma Snakebearer. Can you imagine what would have happened, had we entered Cepheidean space?"

C-the-Third winced.

"Customs search. Capture of the Zzygou. Or, rather, an attempted capture. I have a duty to protect them."

"I too have a duty to protect all my passengers." Alex poured two more drinks. They drank in silence.

"It seems I must thank you." C-the-Third bowed slightly. "That was an extremely unpleasant situation."

"Indeed. But not me—Janet Ruello. Well, that's beside the point, anyway. What do you think is the probability of an accidental collision?"

"Negligible."

"Agreed. C-the-Third, I don't like what's happening. We were hired for civilian service."

"This *is* a civilian trip. Ordinary tourism . . ."

"Is it?"

They looked closely at each other for a few moments. Then the clone shrugged his shoulders.

"Damn it, Captain . . . I've been making these trips for seven years now. Three years for the Pearl company and four years for Sky. I have escorted Zzygou, Bronins, Cepheideans, Fenhuan . . . and a dozen other races, with whom humans hardly ever have any contact. I am a spesh for these contacts, you see?"

"Yes, I see."

C-the-Third continued, more softly and earnestly:

"Alex, I have lived through many different incidents. Skirmishes with xenophobes. Aggression on my customers' part. Once I had to kill a Bronin who suddenly got violent. Another time we were taken over by terrorists from New Ukraine and had to wait eight weeks before a Zzygou patrol ship rescued us. I've seen a lot of things . . . but it's all ordinary civilian work. Maybe slightly more risky than average . . . but your salary is probably also a little higher than average, am I right?"

"Who could be behind this? And why?"

"Got anything smokable?"

Alex silently handed him a pack of cigarettes. They both lit up.

"Tourism business for alien races is not the most developed field . . ." said the clone pensively, letting out a stream of smoke. "How *can* you smoke this trash, Captain? But there are four companies, nevertheless. Ours is the largest. An incident causing our passengers' capture by the Cepheideans would have led to a complete loss of trust in our company. You see?"

"Yes, I see." The clone's constant questioning of his understanding was beginning to irritate Alex. It was as if C-the-Third doubted his captain's ability to put two and two together. "It's all just the competitors' underhand plotting, then?"

"Possibly. We will contact the police authorities . . . and, of course, we'll have our own investigation right away."

"Can you imagine what bribing a pilot would cost?"

The clone smiled.

"No, I can't."

"Neither can I. If the poor fellow from the tanker gets convicted, he will lose his pilot's license for good. This kind of thing has no price, C-the-Third. It would be like wagering someone's life. Like depriving someone of all colors, forcing him to see the world through a dark, murky glass. We pilots don't have that many simple human pleasures."

"But there might be exceptions?"

"Yes. Theoretically, a tanker's pilot could be a natural—his job would then be only one of many joys in life. That sort of thing ought to be forbidden." Alex halted, remembering Generalov.

"That would be discrimination," said C-the-Third bluntly. "What if somebody had reprogrammed the tanker's computer?"

Alex thought for a few moments. Those computers really were primitive.

"An ordinary change of programming wouldn't work. Without the pilot's help, the tanker's computer wouldn't be able to calculate such a complicated maneuver. Although someone could hack it and control it remotely."

"Agreed." The clone nodded. "The terrorists could have been anywhere—one of the guard stations, or one of the other ships waiting in line. They could have put in a remote-operation bio-block, which would simply disintegrate once the action was over."

"Nasty."

"Yes, indeed. But any business field has some ruthless people. No one has ever succeeded in making a businessperson-spesh, you know."

Both of them smiled.

"So did I wake you up for nothing?" Alex inquired.

"Of course not. The situation really was extremely dangerous. In the morning, as soon as we are out of the channel, I will contact the company management."

"Mr. Li Tsyn?"

The clone scowled.

"No. Mr. President doesn't bother with small incidents. I will contact my matrix, Danila Shustov. He'll understand."

"Are there a lot of you?" Alex asked.

"Clones? There were four. But Danila C-the-First Shustov was killed a year ago."

"Condolences."

The clone bowed slightly.

"We all work in the tourism business, Captain. C-the-First was in some respects my opposite—he escorted humans in the alien sectors. There was a freak accident. While in the Fenhuan sector, he organized an excursion to the incubation beach. A little girl left her mother's side to look more closely at one of the eggs. They're very beautiful, you know. They radiate a whole rainbow of colors, and their singing is lovely, too . . . She licked her finger and rubbed the egg . . . wanted a closer look at the embryo."

Alex winced.

"My brother had no other choice but to take the blame upon himself." A note of bitterness rang in C-the-Third's voice. "The Fenhuan performed their ritual cleansing and then sent his remains back to Earth. With profuse apologies, of course. That's life. But from now on, when our company organizes trips to alien planets, children must be kept on a short leash and wear a muzzle at all times."

"Makes sense," said Alex, nodding. "They couldn't think of that before?"

"They did. But some parents protested. Some still object, of course, but the universe is not a friendly place."

The clone got up, offering his hand. Alex shook it without hesitation.

"Thank you for finding a way out of the recent situation. I will ask the management to reward your crew, especially you and Janet Ruello."

"I apologize for disturbing your sleep."

When C-the-Third left, Alex thought for a moment and refilled his glass. The accident—the near-accident! he corrected himself— had now been explained. Such passions raging in the peaceful tourism business! Well, where didn't you find them? Even street sweepers and sewer workers must have their own raging passions, hidden from the rest of the world.

Alex imagined a broad-shouldered, squat, long-armed street sweeper-spesh, creeping stealthily in the middle of the night.

Reaching into his belly pouch, taking out some litter he'd gathered the day before, and spreading it around someone else's lot. Laughing quietly, straining his genetically weakened vocal cords, heading back home, relishing his revenge . . . But, no! That was nonsense—a street sweeper-spesh was incapable of littering. A natural could do it easily, though . . .

The door beeped again.

"Open."

For some reason, he had been expecting a small provocation from Kim. She could arrive wearing only her skimpy PJ's, for instance, or even nothing at all. Or something she had bought back on Quicksilver Pit—her black-and-silver pantsuit, which showed off her trim figure—or a semi-transparent evening gown . . .

Alex underestimated her, as it turned out.

Kim wore a simple white dress and sandals. A small black chiffon scarf was tied around her throat.

It was the same provocation, only much more sophisticated. A sweet schoolgirl, freshly dressed for the prom. An element of every adult male's erotic fantasies.

"Kim . . ." said Alex softly.

"I totally understand." Kim sat down on the floor at his feet and gave him a heartrending, beseeching smile. "You're tired. Don't send me away, okay? Just don't send me away . . . Let me sit here with you for a little while?"

"Kim . . ." Alex lifted her off the floor, sat her down on his lap. "You're making a mistake, kid. . . ."

"A mistake?"

"It's a mistake to have a crush on me."

Kim frowned slightly.

"Whatever gave you that idea? I'm just very grateful to you, that's all . . ."

"You're welcome."

"Besides, we are still husband and wife . . . for the next eight hours."

Alex kissed her soft lips. Whispered:

"Kim, it will only make things worse, trust me. . . ."

"As your wife, I have a right to demand that you perform your husbandly duties." She gave him a strict, serious look. "I insist!"

Her eyes were ardent, demanding. The eyes of a hetaera-spesh. A hetaera in love.

"I can't deny my duties," said Alex. His kiss stopped her from saying anything in reply. He lifted the girl up into his arms and, still kissing, took her over to the bed. He lay down next to her and started taking off her dress, all the while returning her urgent kisses. Kim's hands slid down his torso and unbuttoned his pants. For a second, she freed her lips from his and whispered hotly and earnestly, as if swearing an oath:

"If anyone interrupts us now, I'll kill them!"

Alex glanced at her body—her slender, perfect figure, her tousled hair, her fingers flexing in anticipated ecstasy.

"Agreed . . . We'll kill them together."

After all, he had been deprived of decent sex for almost five months, and the dreary virtual sex imitator at the hospital contained only the programs that bored Alex even back in his puberty days.

"Alex . . ."

Maybe promising to kill was a mistake. She was, after all, a strange hybrid of fighter and hetaera. Quite possibly, violence excited her as much as sex did. She pounced upon him with a passion he hadn't seen even in the most experienced professionals.

"I'll do anything you wish, anything," she whispered, helping him undress. "Anything. Just love me, you'll see, no one will ever love you like me, no one . . . only love me . . ."

Alex kissed her again without answering.

Sex with her was really wonderful. Alex had never much cared for hetaeras, who were specialized to look like nymphets, but this was something different. He couldn't help feeling that Kim would be just as seductive in the full glory of womanhood, and in later maturity, and even in old age. Possibly she had been pre-programmed for delayed aging, giving her almost a century of youth. But it was also possible that she would age the way ordinary women did. In any case, the sexual charge emanating from her seemed endless. Alex took her four times in a row. Every time, she had an orgasm. But it seemed she could keep going the whole night and the following day, and never get bored.

She rested for just a few minutes—Alex felt her rapid kisses on his body, and her hot lips, and her quick slender fingers. He opened his eyes and whispered:

"Kim . . . I'll pass this time . . ."

She laughed quietly, pressing against him with the same passionate readiness.

"Was it good for you?"

"Yes, Kim. It was great. Thank you . . ." He lightly kissed the tip of her nose. "You're wonderful. I've never met anyone like you."

Kim smiled proudly. But her smile quickly faded.

"Alex . . ."

"Yes?"

"You know . . . something's not right."

She sat up on the bed, wrapping herself in a thin blanket. She looked suspiciously at Alex.

"Tell me, are you really attracted to me?"

"You couldn't tell?"

This time, her smile was even more evanescent.

"Alex . . . well, something's wrong! You don't . . . love me?"

It would be nice to get some sleep now, and not start this senseless discussion . . .

"No, I don't."

"Not at all?" she pressed.

"Not at all, baby."

"But why?" She tossed her hair back. "You think I'm a sex maniac? I'm not! I won't ever say a word to you about it, if that's what you want. I just saw that that's what you needed."

"Kim, I'm a pilot-spesh."

"So what?"

"Damn it, Kim. My ability to love is removed. Artificially removed."

Her features froze. Then came a sheepish little smile. "Alex . . . you're kidding, right?"

"Nope. It's true, baby. I'm incapable of love. Anything but that."

"How can . . . love be removed?" Kim's voice quivered. "It's like breathing . . . walking . . . thinking . . . Alex! You're pulling my leg! You're joking, right?"

"Kim, I'm telling you the truth. It is common knowledge that pilots, detectives, and tax collectors are genetically modified to be incapable of love."

"Why?! Why pilots?!"

"We have a feeling of confluence with the ship, Kim. It must be . . . well, it's probably something like love. It's like with the hyper-channel, you know. There cannot be more than one hyper-channel in the galaxy. Same with love. Either you can love people, or you can have confluence with the ship."

"And you chose a chunk of metal?"

"The ship is not a chunk of metal, Kim," said Alex quietly. "It's alive, though not sentient—it's a biomechanical organism. And I didn't choose. None of us chose. No one has figured out how to ask for an embryo's consent yet."

"Alex . . ."

He was expecting an explosive reaction. Was ready to face it. Ready to have Kim punch him, if her fighter instincts took hold of her. Ready to see her run away in tears.

Once again, Kim surprised him.

"Oh, you poor thing . . ."

She hugged him with the impulsiveness of a hetaera and the forcefulness of a fighter. She made him sit up. Pressed his head against her small, firm breasts.

"Alex . . . you poor darling . . ." He was suffering, all right—the pose she had bent him into was very uncomfortable. Besides, his pilot instincts were telling him that this pose would be dangerous, should the gravity vector suddenly change. But Alex kept mum and waited.

"I won't leave you!" cried Kim suddenly. "I won't, no matter what! They couldn't have removed your love completely! You will fall in love with me! I'll teach you how to love! I swear I will!"

Her skin scent was cool and gentle. Maybe perfume, maybe natural pheromones. When the scent became spicy and heady, Alex realized that it must be pheromones.

He freed his head from her embrace and returned another kiss.

Alex had never been one for great sexual exploits. His best achievement must have been participating in the traditional graduate orgy at the pilot academy. The event started at sundown and lasted till sunrise. And it was devilishly multifaceted, with sex simulators, tonics, invited geishas, fellow graduates . . . Even some exclusive virtual images from the world's best modeling agencies. The graduates had held a big fundraiser to get them. Alex had never suspected that one girl, young and inexperienced, could excite him so much.

Kim was putting her heart and soul into it. They tried several old but fun sexual diversions, drank a bottle of dry wine from the bar, then began anew. But as soon as Alex started to feel he was participating in some exhausting sport competition, Kim quieted down. Maybe she really was well tuned to his emotions. Then again, she may have been watching the Demon.

"Should I let you rest?" Kim lay on her stomach, slowly caressing his shoulder. Her pose was a compromise between her next attempt to seduce the captain and the inescapable need to rest. "You'll have to be back on the bridge soon, right?"

"In three hours and seventeen minutes."

"Your internal clock is very accurate."

"Part of my specialization. I feel time to one-tenth of a second."

He slid his hand along her spine. Thank God, Kim didn't bring up his inability to love again. Perhaps she felt sex was a worthy alternative. Or maybe she was still coming up with a crazy plan to overcome his specialization.

"You have a little scar . . ."

Alex looked down at his own stomach. Yup. The scar was really thin, but went all around him, like a belt, just below the belly button.

"I told you . . . there was an accident. I was torn in half."

Kim winced.

"Poor thing. It must've hurt like crazy?"

"I lost consciousness immediately. I hardly remember anything."

"So what happened?"

"We weren't going to land on Quicksilver Pit. Docked at one of the orbital ports to get some fuel. Our orientation engines had a small malfunction . . . so I went to the aggregate module. That's also a part of a pilot's job—small engine systems repairs. And then . . ."

Alex lapsed into thought.

"No, I don't remember. There was a flash . . . and that was it. There was a minor problem with the force field generator, and plasma burst out at the very moment I entered the module. The burst was not a big one, so I wasn't incinerated. But a shard of the generator cut me in half. I got lucky, though—our fighter-spesh was walking down that passage. He heard the explosion, took me out, and hooked me up to an IC unit. Then he took me to a shuttle, delivered me to the planet, and brought me to the hospital. I hope William doesn't get into trouble for that."

"Into trouble?"

"Do you have an inkling of how much it costs to regenerate half a body? I had a comprehensive insurance plan, so the company had to pay up. I think they would have preferred to have a nice elaborate funeral for me instead."

"But they could have just re-attached your other half . . ."

"Nope, they couldn't. William didn't waste any time, and that was what saved me. But he had only one IC unit handy, so he had to choose what was more important—the top half or the bottom half."

Kim smiled.

"The top half . . . they patched up the bottom half just fine."

"Even better than before. My left leg had been broken twice."

"Another accident?"

"No. I had that since childhood . . . just kid stuff. I jumped from the fifth floor, on a bet. I figured a pilot-spesh would be okay. What I didn't take into account was that I hadn't had my metamorphosis yet."

"I jumped, too. But not from so high up. My bones aren't as strong."

Alex smiled, wrapping two fingers around her wrist. The girl was looking thoughtfully at him. "You know . . . I have to tell you this one thing . . ."

"Kim, you don't *have* to do anything."

"Yes, I really do." Kim got serious. "I have to tell you . . . about . . . this."

She slid a hand across her stomach and held out the gel-crystal a moment later.

Alex said, with no hesitation:

"Kim, I really have to warn you! If the Imperial police have an official search out for this crystal, it is my duty to report you and turn you over to the authorities."

"There is no search out for it." Kim shook her head. "I give you my word. It's a very large crystal, isn't it?"

"Very large. Very expensive . . . that is, if it works."

"It's working as we speak."

Alex cocked his head. Carefully took the crystal from her hand, looked through it at the light. Along its facets, a light whitish film was gathering, or perhaps it only seemed to be.

"Then we have to recharge it, Kim. It looks like it's been running autonomously for quite a while."

"That's exactly why I took it out. You do have a spare control center, don't you?"

"I do."

Kim nodded.

"The computer in my cabin isn't capable of feeding such a large crystal. But yours will probably manage."

Alex got up silently. Went over to the terminal, snapped off the processor panel. In a small port lined with a moistly trembling bio coating, there sat another crystal, a tiny one, less than point two inches in diameter. The brackets of another port were open. Alex tried the crystal against the opening, gave a contented nod. It would fit. Just barely, but it would. Kim had also gotten up and was now standing next to him, pressing her warm, firm thigh against his leg.

"You understand what I'm doing?" Alex unfolded three tiny, thin bracket arms—each one could rotate on its axis and then be fixed in place in two different positions.

"No."

"These are the crystal's information chain conduits."

"But why?"

"Who knows what kind of programs are in it? The crystal will get its charge, as well as access to the infonet. But it won't be able to interfere with the ship's controls network. That's the recommended procedure for recharging uncertified gel-crystals."

Alex inserted the crystal into the port. Its aperture trembled, then contracted, tightly hugging the transparent cone. Only the three little conduit arms helplessly wobbled in the air, unable to reach the crystal.

"I could cut off the information input as well . . ." added Alex pensively. "And leave only the recharging function on. Well, this ship has nothing all that secret on it, really. . . ."

"Don't cut it off!" said Kim hastily. "He'll be really bored!"

"He?"

"I better start at the beginning."

Alex looked at the crystal, shrugged, then closed the panel.

"All right, baby."

Kim sighed. Then said quickly, in the same breath, as if jumping off a cliff:

"My friend is in there. My best friend."

"An artificial intelligence?"

"No, he's human. Just like us."

"This is a great start. That is, it's a great place to stop. Kim, darling, let me take a shower and change? Then you can tell me the rest, okay?"

They took a shower together. There was nothing erotic about it; Kim simply couldn't wait to start telling her story. She must have been longing to share her secret with someone for a long time now.

Alex put on light overalls, sat down on the bed. Kim didn't go back to her cabin for a change of clothes, but simply wrapped herself in a bath towel. Alex didn't mind—she looked even better this way.

"I was nine," Kim began, having settled, legs and all, into an armchair. "And I . . . well, it just so happened that I had absolutely no friends back then, girls or boys. I had lots of pals, you know, but not a single really close friend."

Alex nodded.

"I found a friend in virtual reality." Kim smiled gently as she said this. These memories must have been pleasant for her. "His name was Edgar. He was my age. We hit it off, became good friends . . . you know the way it happens in virtuality?"

"Yeah. At that age, I also liked virtual reality. Especially space-flight simulations."

"Well . . . these were not spaceflights. You see, he didn't have a real body."

"What?" Alex raised one brow in surprise.

"Edgar told me he had been in a car wreck. Back when he was really small, only three. They couldn't save him, so they just trans-ferred his consciousness into a gel-crystal . . ."

"Kim!" Alex raised his hand. "Wait a minute! Stop right there. This is utter nonsense! A gel-crystal this size costs as much as a good hospital. So it's much less expensive, not to mention more . . . humane, to reconstruct a body, even if it has been smashed up into suspension."

"They couldn't get him to the hospital on time. Just managed to transfer his mind into the crystal."

"Hold it right there! Let's suppose the boy's parents could afford it . . . although I can't really imagine such a thing. Why couldn't they reverse the process, grow another body for him, say, by cloning the old one or generating a new one out of his parents' stem cells? They could then transfer his mind back into the clean brain. I've heard of such cases, except they were famous scientists and politicians, not little boys."

"That's right. I've been telling you a bunch of lies." Kim smiled. "But they aren't my lies . . . that's the crap they told Edgar. Don't forget, we were both just nine."

Alex nodded.

"All right, then. Go on."

"Edgar grew up in the crystal. In the virtual worlds. His playmates came and went back to the real world, but he stayed there. Always. At first, his parents would visit him, often, in their virtual bodies. After a while, they stopped coming. He was thinking they'd simply forgotten about him, had more children, or whatever . . . He was really upset about that."

"But what was really going on?"

"He'd been stuck into the crystal on purpose!" Kim tossed back her hair. "Can you even imagine? There wasn't any car accident! His memory got placed into the crystal, and his body . . . we don't know what they did with it! Maybe they threw it away. Maybe it's out there somewhere, in a vegetative state. And maybe his memory got copied, without erasing the original, and there's another Edgar somewhere, alive and well."

"Why?" Alex shrugged his shoulders. "Kim, this is a crazy story. Why would anyone screw up a little boy's life like that? A crystal which contains a human consciousness and is also, I assume, capable of sustaining some semblance of a living environment . . . the cost is simply inconceivable!"

"All you talk about is money," Kim snarled. "Alex, the thing is that Edgar is a very rare kind of spesh. It was an experimental mutation. He is a spesh to create speshes."

"A genetic designer?"

"Yup. You don't have to change the body for this specialization. The eyes will never match an electron microscope, anyway. All the alterations were done to his mental processes. It was a project of the Edemian government . . . they had decided that Edgar didn't need a body at all. That he'd be better off growing up in the crystal."

Alex studied the girl's face as she spoke. Was she lying? Didn't look like it . . . she seemed to believe her own words. When she was telling him that first legend, she spoke with a smirk, as if to say, "Can you believe how stupid I was to have bought this stuff?" But now her voice held real sorrow. Kim believed what she was saying. And really wanted Alex to believe it, too.

"But why make it all so complicated?" he asked. "I believe that there are assholes in the Edemian government. Just like anywhere. They may be assholes, but they aren't idiots. It has been obvious to everyone for a long time now that transferring a mind to virtual reality has a lot of drawbacks. The mind still feels the illusory nature of that existence and slowly the person . . . the human mind . . . goes insane. When the first human consciousness was copied into a machine, back in the twenty-first century, it was the computer genius David Kross. He managed to have a normal existence for thirty years. But then . . ."

"Yes, I know." Kim nodded. "I've studied everything I could about the field. These weirdos were hoping to get the most out of Edgar. They wanted absolutely nothing to interfere with his work. They didn't want him to have or do anything *but* work. They also wanted to make multiple copies of his mind, if the experiment was successful."

"Then they shouldn't have let him out into the common virtual space."

"They didn't. He broke out by himself. He's a genius, Alex!"

"All right, so how come you ended up with the crystal?"

Kim smiled.

"It happened a year ago. Edgar organized his own abduction. He hacked into one of the military cyborgs that were guarding the lab with the crystal. The robot took the crystal, mailed it to my address, and then destroyed itself, along with the whole building. We were both sure that the trail was lost, and that the crystal was considered destroyed in the fire. I . . . I took care of Ed. I had a good computer, and I managed to hook the crystal up to it. We were still virtual friends, except now Edgar was free. I was thinking that as soon as I could work, I would quickly save up for a new body . . . any body. Ed said, 'Make me a baby, or a geezer, just don't make me a girl.' Except I think at that point he was ready for anything . . . We would transfer his mind, and he could really be human again."

"Then you could be sisters, like the Zzygou," commented Alex. "Suppose I believe you. So something went wrong?"

"A month ago." Kim tightened her lips. "I . . . I messed up. I told Mother about Edgar. I was sure she'd understand! But she reported me to that lab. That's why I simply can't go back to Edem! We managed to run away, but they're looking for us."

"Probably unofficially. This sure is fishy business."

"The security agency always prefers searching unofficially."

Alex drummed his fingers against the wall. The story Kim just told him was not completely impossible. Idiocy is universal. Someone could have thought up this idea of raising a genius-spesh in a virtual world. This genius could have deceived the security agency. An excitable girl-spesh could have fallen in love and run away to become a galactic fugitive.

But what irked him was the melodrama. Alex was ready to believe in any coincidence . . . but not when the chain of events so strongly resembled a soap opera for young, hysterical girls and their sentimental grandmothers.

"You don't believe me, do you?" asked Kim bluntly.

"I don't know. *You*, I believe. I think." Kim's features turned gloomy. "As for your bodyless friend . . . How do you communicate with him, Kim?"

"Through the net."

"You do understand that I have no intention of letting him into the ship's network. Any other options?"

"Hook up to the crystal directly. His home is there . . . his own virtual world. Just talk to him, Alex! You'll see right away—it's all true!"

"You love him so very much?" asked Alex.

"Yes, I do!" Kim looked at him proudly. "But not the way I love you. You're my lover. And Ed . . . he's like a brother. Or maybe even a child. He's so helpless, you know, inside the crystal. And there are many things he doesn't understand, even though he's a genius."

"You got yourself into a colossal mess, Kim!"

"I know." The girl nodded. "But I couldn't act any other way."

Alex almost let slip that everything would have turned out quite differently had she been an ordinary fighter-spesh. As soon as she was past the metamorphosis, she would have gotten such a boost of civic responsibility that she'd personally take "Ed" back to that hypothetical lab.

But Kim was not just a fighter. She was also a hetaera. Highly emotional, amorous, devoted . . . as long as she felt that someone needed her.

And that was where the whole thing got messy.

"My ethical side," Alex slowly began, "does not predispose me to follow other planets' laws blindly. That would be a very dangerous quality to have, and so I must make decisions based on universal human morality. But . . . all this is rather complicated, Kim. I must have a talk with your friend."

"You have a neuro-shunt?" asked the girl simply.

"Most probably."

He opened a desk drawer and, just as he expected, found a standard neuro-shunt, for reading books, watching movies, and making excursions into virtual spaces. It was a headband with a neuro-terminal microchip sewn onto it and a soft, plastic, sticky patch with a gel-port. The shunt was of a cheap variety. The headband

and the sticky patch were connected by a thin extension of optical fiber. But Alex didn't care.

Kim silently watched him put on the headband and reopen the processor panel. The feeder-fibers had already wrapped themselves around the giant gel-crystal that sustained Edgar's whole world. Alex had to separate them in order to hook the sticky patch to the crystal.

"Maybe I should be the one to go in first?" suggested Kim sheepishly.

"I'll go first. You'll go next."

"He might get scared. He doesn't know about any of the stuff that happened since we ran away from Edem."

"I'll calm him down."

"Tell him I said 'hi,'" Kim managed to add, right before Alex sat down in the chair and activated the shunt.

CHAPTER 3.

Each gate to a virtual world opens in its own unique way.

Some with a bright flash, a cascade of lightning, or a series of colorful rainbows.

Others with utter darkness, in which a world slowly takes form.

Whatever the world, a threshold is necessary—a place to prepare, to take the first couple of steps towards the nonexistent spaces.

The creator of this particular world, however, did not believe in introductions. Alex instantly found himself surrounded by the universe locked inside the gel-crystal.

He found himself standing on a riverbank, waist-deep in lush meadow grass, his feet sinking down into the soft, soggy mud. The river was straight as if drawn with a ruler, wide and unhurried, its cold clear waters rolling past languidly. About ten paces away was the edge of a thick wood of dark conifers. It stretched the length of both banks. Over the waters flowing toward the horizon, right above the middle of the river's course, the sun was setting. Alex didn't know if the terms "east" and "west" were appropriate in this situation, but he was sure it was evening.

An interesting world. It looked like a giant playground. A place where a dragon might suddenly fly up, or a mermaid might lift her head out of the water. Well, according to Kim, this world had been a child's creation. And even if this child was now years older, it mattered little—those who spent a lot of time in virtuality were slow to grow up.

"Edgar!"

Alex slowly plodded toward the woods. The gel-crystal dweller should be nearby. He had to have sensed the presence of an intruder. That would mean the boy was hiding, watching closely, still not sure whether to make contact. In his small universe, he was a king and a god. He could easily toss Alex out. But the boy was not stupid. He had to understand that his microcosm depended fully on those who held the gel-crystal in their hands. A hard blow, or a few seconds in the microwave, and that would be the end.

"Edgar, I know you're here!" Alex shouted out. "I'm not your enemy!"

He preferred to avoid saying "friend" just yet.

"Kim wanted us to talk! She says 'hi'! Edgar!"

"I'm here."

Alex turned around.

In his own world, Edgar could look any way he chose. He could be a giant, towering a hundred yards tall. A monster. An innocuous-looking scientist. Or a warrior.

But the boy looked as though he preferred his normal appearance—if one could use such a term to describe someone who had no real body. A youth in his teens, awkward and lanky, with a pale, untanned face and black hair, long in need of a cut. He was

231

barefoot. He wore only a pair of pants cropped below the knee and . . . glasses. This antique trinket on his face looked rather weird.

"I'm Alex," the pilot said.

"I know."

"How?"

"You left me an entry channel yourself. Thanks." The boy's voice bore no trace of irony. But not much real gratitude, either. His was the tone one might use to thank an executioner for promising to take extra care to sharpen his ax.

"I'm glad you're well informed." Alex smiled. It hadn't occurred to him that the crystal-dweller could download data from the sensors inside the captain's quarters. Well, nothing could be done about that now. "So then you know that Kim managed to complete your plan."

"Complete?" Edgar frowned and sat down on the grass, crossing his legs. "If she had managed to complete it, she'd be working somewhere on a quiet planet, no one would know about the crystal, and in a few years, I'd get a new body."

After a minute's hesitation, Alex sat down beside him. The damp dirt was unpleasantly cool to the touch. But this was virtual dampness—no risk of getting sick from sitting on it.

"If your story is true, then your plan will be completed just as you say," he told the boy. "Working on a spaceship, Kim can make money way faster than on any planet."

"And why should I believe you?" asked Edgar testily.

"Why? A difficult question. You're a genetic construction specialist, right?"

The boy gave a vague shrug.

"Which gene is responsible for my ethical qualities?"

Edgar smiled at such a simple test.

"Not just one gene. You have a whole complex of genes activated—the Zey-Matushenski complex, also known as the Aristotle Operon. It is responsible for your heightened honesty and your need to seek out the truth. And it's also a very strong behavioral operon that strengthens your parenting instincts. Subconsciously, you consider all the people who enter your life to be your children. You feel they all need you to care for them and to defend them, regardless of age, real abilities, or even their wishes. The genetic Kamikaze complex, or, rather, the Gostello Operon, as it is properly called, was discovered by Russian scientists. It makes you always ready to sacrifice yourself. You have several other minor alterations, but those I just listed are the main ones."

"The crystal could have a database you might be using," Alex noted.

"Of course. So how do you test me? If I told you something that can't be found in widely available databases, you'd have no way of knowing if it were true or I was just making it up."

Alex nodded.

"All right. You've convinced me. So you know that I am a pilot-spesh. You should also realize that pilots don't lie."

"As a general rule, they don't." The boy burst out laughing, plucked a blade of grass, squeezed it between his teeth. "But I'm a thief, after all. And you're an honest citizen."

"You've run away. You were deprived of your body. That's not fair."

"But I have also stolen the crystal, haven't I? It costs more than a thousand human bodies."

"What are you going to do with it, once you have a body?"

"Send it back to the lab on Edem. Empty. Let them kick themselves."

"Then it's not a theft. I have no reason to turn you in."

The skinny boy, who had no real body, sat a long time looking down the river, watching the sun, which was setting, but never seemed to be able to roll below the horizon.

"These are just words. A lot of words. I can't trust you. I can't trust anyone."

"No one at all?"

Edgar didn't answer immediately.

"Only Kim. I'm like a brother to her . . . or like a child."

Alex bit his lip.

"Don't hold a grudge against her."

"What is it to you?" sneered the boy.

"When you get a body, everything will be different. You know I'm incapable of love. I'll be happy for her . . . for the two of you."

The boy pierced Alex with a look that spoke volumes.

"How I'd love to turn you into a toad and . . . squash you!"

He looked away again, making no attempt to fulfill his threat.

Damn, damn, damn! Alex sighed. Now, on top of everything else, he also had to deal with a moody, jealous boy incarcerated in a gel-crystal. . . .

"Well, go ahead, do it, if it makes you feel better. You can do anything, right?"

"In my toy land, yes. But who will stay your foot, when you crush the crystal?"

Alex reached out, touched the boy's shoulder. Edgar tensed.

"I have no intention of getting back at you. I won't harm you. But I can't reject Kim, either. You see, she hungers for love. I'll try to make our encounters as . . . rare as possible. Though I won't lie to you—I find them pleasurable."

"Give her a neuro-shunt," asked Edgar. "I haven't seen her for a long time."

"If she doesn't have one, she can have mine. No problem. Don't be angry."

"Slaves don't have the right to be angry."

Alex felt rage boiling up. He wasn't mad at Edgar, of course.

"What has been done to you, Edgar, is a heinous crime. I'll make every effort to help you."

"Maybe it is heinous." The boy slowly lifted his hand, and the sun suddenly started slipping quickly below the horizon. "But it's commonplace in the galaxy. Everyone's creating slaves. Strong arms, sharp eyes, excellent mind, beautiful figure—what else to demand from a slave? Ah, yes! Loyalty. Well, it's easy to increase people's need for a leader. But I had no need of a body, so they left me none."

"And made a huge miscalculation."

"Yeah. Loyalty, obedience, submission—these are just bio-chemical reactions. I lost my body, but gained my freedom from those invisible chains."

"Why do you choose to look this way?"

"This is exactly the way I would look. I managed to find my own genetic map, so I reconstructed my appearance."

"But why the glasses?"

Edgar touched the thin frames. And said curtly:

"I'm very nearsighted."

"No one wears glasses. It's the simplest correction."

"But I have nothing to correct, mister pilot."

It was already dark. Stars lit up one by one in the sky. Alex dropped his head back, looking at the constellations. The Southern Cross glowed right overhead, and a little farther off were the Sextant, the Spy Glass, and the Dolphin.

"I won't betray you," Alex said. "The gel-crystal will remain in my cabin. That's the only terminal that can provide a normal connection for it. Kim can come into your virtual space any time . . . and I'll ask her to do it often. You can use all the information from the ship's infonet. I'll keep the access to the closed-circuit cameras blocked, though. I'll probably just disconnect them altogether."

"But why?"

"Edgar, trust me, to feel that someone could be watching your every step is really unpleasant."

"Suit yourself. I'll have plenty to occupy my time. This is a very powerful crystal."

"I'm sure you've amassed quite a library."

Edgar nodded, barely visible against the darkness.

"Yup. Quite a library."

"And you're really a top-notch genetic constructor?"

The boy smirked.

"Yeah."

"Tell me about Kim. She has a strange specialization, right?"

Edgar was silent for a moment before he answered in an even, calm voice:

"My whole world is a fiction, Mr. Pilot. A tiny island of organized data, held together in a quasi-alive goo. I don't exist. Neither does this river, or this sky. All I have is information. So I am very cautious about sharing it. We'll talk about Kim, if you want. But not now."

Alex got up off the grass. His pants were soaked. His waterlogged shoes squelched.

"I understand you," he answered gravely. "But I'm not your enemy, trust me. And, come to think of it, I'm also nothing but an island of information, locked in the goo that's called a brain. You'll be all right."

"Best of luck to you, Pilot," said Edgar in his even voice. Paused for a moment, and added, "You can drop in and see me. Once in a while."

"Thanks. I will. From time to time."

He strained his mind, ripping himself out of the dark summer night, leaving the other on the bank of the geometrically perfect river.

The virtual world faded away.

Kim watched him from her armchair. She had dressed and looked like a nondescript young woman again rather than a raging hetaera. Alex couldn't decide if he was pleased about it, but in any case, it was better this way. After all, Edgar was watching them from his transparent prison.

"How is he?" asked Kim quickly.

"Fine." Alex took off his headband. "Alive and well."

"So, now you know I wasn't lying?" Kim demanded.

A tiny eye of the optical sensor on the cabin ceiling . . .

"You weren't lying," he replied, endowing his words with all the conviction he could muster. "But he got really upset."

"Why?"

"Because of what you and I were doing. Edgar is still watching us through the cabin's sensors."

Kim winced.

"Edgar, that's stupid!" she shouted. "Don't be jealous!"

"Kim, he can't reply," interrupted Alex softly. "Tell you what. You go see him right now, so you two can settle all the misunderstandings. In the meantime, I'll take a nap. For at least a couple of hours."

"Will you help him, Alex?" demanded Kim.

He thought for a moment before making his answer:

"Kim, this story is horrendous. Of course I consider it my duty to help a boy who has been so viciously mistreated."

The girl nodded, relieved and reassured.

"Go talk to him," Alex repeated, "if you're not sleepy."

"I'll manage," said Kim quickly. "I can go for a week without sleep."

"I know. Me too. But I don't see the need right now."

Paying no more attention to Kim, he tossed off his robe and stretched out under the blanket. Watched the girl put on the neuroshunt headband.

Damn it, what should he do?

What was this mess he had gotten himself into?

Just a few random suspicions that were impossible to prove

or disprove. Circumstantial evidence, to use a legal term. And a gnawing sense of deception . . .

Kim jolted. Her body stretched out and then lay still. Her skinny legs stuck out funny, the right foot dangling in the air, not reaching the floor.

Kim, what have you gotten yourself into?

Edgar was right. Alex was bound hand and foot by the invisible biochemical fetters that made him protect all those close to him. He was incapable of love, but could anyone tell from his actions? Pilots were ideal captains, after all. Their power rested not in strength or authority, but in the love of their crew. And that was right. He was glad to have ancient moral principles embedded in him, the principles that had been learned through thousands of years of human suffering. These fetters were also a gift. No need to strive to become better—it had all been given to him in advance.

He couldn't betray Kim.

He couldn't let himself resolve his vague doubts the simplest and most obvious way—by ripping the gel-crystal out of its nest and handing it over to the security officers at Gamma Snakebearer.

All he could do now was wait . . . and hope that all his suspicions were groundless, that all the coincidences were random. And that the crystal harbored a frightened young man who dreamed of gaining a human body.

Alex closed his eyes and went to sleep. He would sleep for exactly two hours. It was certainly less than recommended, but quite enough for a modified nervous system.

*   *   *

Gamma Snakebearer had no planets suitable for life. One planet, a charred hunk of rock, orbited very close to the star itself. Another, a luminary never born, just a cold clot of gases, patrolled the very edges of the system. But the space channel located there was very convenient—twenty-eight exits led out to populated worlds, most of them human, and a few to alien territories. So the Empire had built a gigantic transport station at the channel's mouth and stationed several ancient battleships there to milk the new and lucrative junction for all it was worth. The absence of any planets actually proved to be a bonus; it was much easier for the Imperial government to control a space station than a planetary colony. This way, the profits didn't have to be shared with any local presidents, kings, tsars, khans, or shahs.

Mirror didn't need to stop for fuel or rest. The ship dove out of the exit point, turned around to trace a gigantic arc around the one-eyed cylinder of the space station, and then got in line for another entry. The magic mirror of the hyper-channel floated among the stars, indifferent to the many ships diving in and out.

Most of the crew were off duty. The engineer appeared, idled a while, got bored, and departed, leaving the engine running at minimum capacity. Generalov dropped in for a second. With the generosity of a magician, he spread out several routes and went off again. There was still an hour remaining before re-entry into the channel. Janet never appeared at all, and Kim was bored at her battle station, entertaining herself by calculating possible attack routes. Seeing this, Alex blocked off her weapons systems, just in case.

Only Morrison was utterly thrilled to be flying. He enjoyed every tiny maneuver, every little piloting show-off trick invisible to the untrained eye. Seeing who could perform the most graceful turn, using the gravitational field of the channel. Or who would be the one to give the most elegant salutation to his colleagues by a barely detectable movement of the ship.

Now that Alex had become a captain, he regarded Morrison from a slightly different point of view. Not with condescension, but with a certain smiling indulgence. The way a gray-haired father might regard his young son's academic feats in college.

"Captain?"

"I'm listening, Xang."

"Who is to perform the entry into the channel?"

"You—go ahead, Morrison."

"Thank you."

There was a momentary pause. And then Xang asked:

"What's it like—being a captain?"

"It's a very good feeling, Morrison. You've never been in charge of a ship?"

"Only back at the academy. But that was an ancient *Heron*, with no crew. Just me and the instructor."

"Same here. Seems like retired *Herons* are used for training everywhere you go."

"Back at Serengeti, we also had a *Flamingo*."

"Not bad," said Alex, sincerely impressed. And so they chatted away the hour. Ships came and went. A magnificent and monstrous Tai'i cruiser crawled out of the channel. It looked like a rough-hewn asteroid, its surface enveloped in blood-red flame.

The cruiser was making its usual patrol rounds, and a small battleship escorted it through Imperial territory. The giant cruiser of a once-great civilization floated on among the stars as if not even noticing the tiny convoy ship, which could destroy it with one blast.

All is vanity among the stars.

The ancient Tai'i civilization, dying from its strange internal problems, clutching desperately at the last dozen stars left to it, still patrolled the ancient borders of its former realm. As if the Tai'i didn't realize that their once-mighty ships wouldn't survive any serious skirmish these days, and that they owed the very existence of their kingdom to the mercy of the races they once ruled. . . .

Alex transmitted a full report of the recent incident to the pilot's union, sending a copy to the Imperial administration and the government of Quicksilver Pit. Generalov had done a great job preparing the report, carefully detailing all the potential consequences of the collision, briefly noting the shocking negligence of the channel's guard stations, and hinting at the possibility of a premeditated act of sabotage. The only thing Alex had to add was an "unofficial and off-the-record opinion" that the root of the trouble should be looked for in the commercial rivalry of competing tourist firms.

Then they downloaded the latest news from the station. There turned out to be nothing exciting, except, perhaps, the contents of the society pages. The gala celebration of the Emperor's seventh birthday. A tired child, blinking sleepily, sat on the high throne, the actual seat of power that his ancestors had used to rule the Empire many generations ago. The child was receiving countless greetings from various ambassadors—and sometimes the representatives of the ambassadors—from various colonial worlds and alien races. Only the Zzygou, following their own peculiar customs, had sent the highest-ranking dignitaries and potentates to the official ceremony.

All is vanity among the stars. All but traditions.

Soon it was their turn to make another hyper-jump. And Morrison, expertly performing the graceful "Ionesco Loop," ran the ship into the mouth of the channel. Their route now lay toward New Ukraine.

"Take a break, Morrison," Alex suggested.

"Is that an order, sir?" the co-pilot rejoined quickly. The murky grayness of the channel flowed around the ship. This was a short jump—two hours and forty-three minutes.

"You're not tired?" asked Alex simply.

Morrison laughed.

"I've just spent two weeks sitting on a planet, Captain. Can you imagine? No piloting. And broke, besides. Couldn't even rent a glider."

"Very well, Xang. Happy piloting!"

"Thank you, sir," said the co-pilot with deep gratitude. "Alex . . . I won't forget your kindness."

Alex left the control system. Detached himself from the pilot's chair, glanced briefly at the screens, and left the bridge.

The first thing that attracted his attention was the sound of laughter.

From the recreation lounge. Many happy voices joining in a merry uproar. He immediately recognized Kim's bright peals of laughter, the high tiny voices of the Zzygou, and the deep throaty voice of . . . Janet!

Alex quickened his pace, cursing his own indecisiveness. He should have ordered Janet never to appear in the common modules while the Zzygou were there. He should have warned C-the-Third that sudden aggression from Janet might be expected. . . .

He stopped at the entrance to the recreation lounge.

"We greet you, Captain!" the Zzygou sang out, though they didn't seem to have been looking in his direction. "We thank you for the hyper-jump and for the second hyper-jump as well!"

No . . . There didn't seem to be any trouble.

Kim was sitting next to the Zzygou, and Alex had to agree with Janet's recent suspicions. The human and the adult Zzygou did look very similar. Even their clothes were alike—a dark-navy skirt suit on Kim and almost the same on the two aliens, though theirs were lace-decorated and a little lighter in color. If it weren't for the Zzygou's strange way of talking, no one could ever tell that they were a completely different life form.

Janet, with a rather placid smile on her face, was at the bar, mixing some cocktails. Generalov, lounging with a small glass of whiskey, greeted the captain's arrival with a good-natured wave of his hand. And Paul, whose glass of wine was still untouched, gave a shy nod. C-the-Third smiled affably as he leaned against the wall behind the Zzygou. He seemed to be quite favorably impressed by the crew Alex had hired.

"And then we got very surprise-ed!" said one of the Zzygou brightly, moving the conversation along.

"We, I got very surprise-ed," the other one intoned. "A smell? What smell is? Molecule movement in air?"

All right . . . then the second Zzygou had actually been the one who witnessed what was being described. They were not the same age. They had just lived together for a long time, and their appearance had synchronized.

Alex sat down at the table, opposite the Zzygou. Gave Kim a little wink. The girl replied with a barely noticeable but rather inviting smile.

"Would you like a cocktail, Captain?" asked Janet cheerily.

"Yes please, but not too strong."

"Very well, Captain." Janet reached for another cocktail glass.

"We were shock-ted!" pronounced the Zzygou. "How can molecule be offensive? They don't harming, but offending?"

"Yeah, sometimes it might be very convenient to be unable to smell," remarked Paul. "When I was a scout, we took long hikes in the woods for three or four days in a row. And if there happened to be no brook nearby, the tent in the evening got quite odorific . . ."

"How can the scent of a healthy young body be unpleasant?" asked Generalov with a dramatic flair.

"I don't know about healthy young bodies," Lourier countered, "but the scent of nice dirty socks . . ."

The Zzygou giggled, indicating to the others that they got the gist of the joke.

"And we, I suggest-ed a solution," sang out the second Zzygou. "Spacesuit. Tight spacesuit. No molecule can escaping!"

"And then we made a fix," the other one continued. "It's painful . . . Ouch! But no smell at all. But going to the toilet very-very often, even every day!"

"Cocktails?" Janet came up to the table with a tray in her hands.

"We thank you, servant . . ." the Zzygou sang out. Alex held his breath. Janet had already been bending over backwards for them. . . .

"Oops!" The Zzygou got up from their chairs, slightly bowing their heads. "We remember! Offensive word, causing pain . . . We mean 'thank you, male or female friend!'"

"'Friend' will do," Janet answered calmly.

"We thank you, friend!"

Alex also reached for a glass. Took a hurried sip, still watching Janet's reactions. What if she had mixed in some poison?

But Janet took up a cocktail glass herself.

The drink was excellent, though it had a slightly unusual taste—lemon and anise, with just a hint of mint and honey, very refreshing. And it was no stronger than forty proof. Little colored ice cubes, made with slightly magnetized water, swirled around gracefully in the tall glasses. They reminded Alex of his virtual image of the ship.

"Alcohol wonderfully!" the Zzzygou declared, having taken a few sips. "We did not know taking alcohol internally. We knew humanity was a great race for invented alcohol. But it is still hard for us to drink a lot."

"Not to worry," said C-the-Third, joining the conversation. "Humans also didn't adapt right away to drinking alcohol. There was even a time when it used to cause unpleasant aftereffects. Some radical naturals, who totally reject any kind of genetic engineering, still have a natural limit to their alcohol intake . . ."

Alex, utterly confused at this point, sat watching what was going on around him. It was a nice friendly get-together, as though the passengers and the crew had been good friends for a long time. Janet was a wonderful hostess, making hot cheese sandwiches for the Zzygou and all manner of snacks for the crew, while also refilling everyone's drinks and keeping up the conversation. Kim and the Zzygou sitting closest to her were discussing the cut of their suits and the peculiarities of fashion in the Zzygou Swarm. The Zzygou had already produced a portable computer, quite human in its design, and was showing Kim some pictures.

Only Generalov's tone of voice, when he addressed himself to C-the-Third, had a hint of spiteful irony. But Alex wasn't sure if he was just imagining it.

Trouble began a quarter of an hour later. And, of course, Janet was the one to start it. With a perfectly innocuous, or so it seemed, friendly phrase:

"It is wonderful that the Zzygou race became a human ally from the very first contact . . ."

The Zzygou who sat chatting with Kim had no reaction to this whatsoever. But her companion chirped happily:

"No! No from the very first contact! We were first deeply offended by the Empire. Your appearance, your behavior, and your morals are all offen-sive! We prepare-ed for big war."

"Really?" rejoined Janet in a honey-sweet mellow tone. "And I was sure that was all an Ebenian extremist lie . . ."

"We prepare-ed, prepare-ed!" the alien chirped on. "But later we rejecting all the violent ways. The human race will meet its own natural end. Humanity are way too aggres-sive to reject expansion. You are also too fond of biological modeling for preserve unity. When the Empire finally falls apart in hundreds of independent planets, it will be conquer-ed by other race-es. Then we take our slice of cake! A large, very large slice!"

The pealing laughter of the Zzygou sounded especially odd in the silence that abruptly froze the air in the recreation lounge. The Zzygou smiled for another second or two. Then her face went ashen. The other alien, who had been caught up in telling Kim all the super-secret details of the Great Zzygou sacred fertilization ritual, stopped in mid-sentence. Looked at her companion. Touched the panel of the portable computer, folding the image. Then quietly said:

"We ask forgiving."

"We ask forgiving," sang out the Zzygou who had been chatting with Janet. The alien's face had lost all color.

"We overestimate-ed ability drinking ethanol," sang the two Zzygou in complete unison. "We start-ed joking, but our joking are somewhat strange and offen-sive to humans. We ask forgiving, we ask forgiving . . ."

They got up and backed out of the recreation lounge.

"Everything's all right, sisters." The tone of C-the-Third's voice gave away his deep doubt in what he was saying. "Happens to everyone. We understand jokes."

"Of course we do!" agreed Janet, smiling brightly.

"Sey-Zo!" said Kim in surprise. "But why does the cut for the larvae-laying *have* to be triangular?"

The question was left hanging in the air—the Zzygou left the would-be wonderful party.

Lourier shrugged his shoulders and took another sip of wine. Said, not looking at anyone:

"A slice of cake, eh? Big enough to choke on . . ."

"Let's not talk about this," retorted C-the-Third. "Most likely, it was really just an unfortunate joke."

"Yeah, right . . ." said Janet, still smiling, taking a sip of her cocktail. "They just honestly admitted their opinion about us humans."

"Why?" the clone responded. "Forgive me, but that would be very odd. I think they were joking. I prefer to think it was a joke."

"As you wish." Janet got up. "Well, I better be off. Have some reading to do."

Alex caught up with her at the door to her quarters. Took her arm to stop her.

"Janet . . ."

"Yes, Captain?" The black woman smiled.

"What did you mix into the Zzygou's cocktails?"

"Captain, I simply made a drink for everyone. I added no chemicals at all."

"Then let me ask you another way. Janet, what could have caused such frankness on the part of the aliens?"

The woman's face turned thoughtful.

"Hard to say, Captain . . . Back on Eben, there was a rumor that the Zzygou race poorly handles the natural alkaloids in anise. It is reputed to have an un-inhibiting effect, similar to that of truth serum. The Zzygou apparently lose neither their sanity nor their will, but become capable of blurting out anything. Doesn't that just sound like a ridiculous urban legend? Everyone knows Eben is populated entirely by psychos."

"Janet . . ." said Alex, feeling her pain, "why do this?"

"To make you see who you're dealing with," replied Janet seriously. "Their adorable girl-child looks are just an evolutionary fluke, combined with the ability to change several outward appearance parameters. But they are not even mammals, Captain! They are warm-blooded insects!"

"That's a crude analogy."

"In any case, they are biologically much closer to beetles and roaches than to us."

"Not so. They are just as far from humans as they are from earthly insects."

"Those little bulges you see underneath their blouses, Captain, aren't breasts, but a rudimentary third pair of limbs. They feed their young by regurgitating partially digested food."

"Nevertheless, they have red blood and almost-human lungs and hearts . . ."

"Six-chambered hearts!"

"They couldn't have two-chambered hearts?" Alex felt that Janet was about to escape into her cabin, so he talked faster:

"Let's just drop this whole argument. The Zzygou are neither roaches, nor humans. They are alien beings from the Zzygou race. And no, they don't feel any great attachment to us, but why would they? We are a young and energetic race, taking over one planet after another. Let them have their illusions, as long as there's no war!"

"Agreed." Janet nodded. "Let me go, Alex."

"Don't set up any more provocations like that, Janet. Please. We don't need any scandals, or complaints to the management, or conflicts with the Zzygou and C-the-Third."

"You've burned our ships, which wouldn't dare open fire at humans. You've covered our planet with a power shield as if it were a leper colony. You've brainwashed those you left alive. And still it's not enough for you. Now you're kissing up to the Others. And they can't wait to see us all enslaved!"

Janet freed her arm with a strong invisible movement. Alex thought of the full military training she had gone through on Eben.

"I didn't burn any of your ships. I never messed with your mind, sister-spesh!"

"You are no better than those who did!"

The door closed behind her. Alex barely suppressed the impulse to slam his fist into the plastic.

What could he do? Cajole, beg, appeal to reason?

All that was useless, when a program put into a spesh's mind was activated. Alex went into his own cabin, stood still for a while, his hands locked together in helpless wrath.

Then, obeying a blind impulse, he unbuttoned his shirt to look at the Demon. The little devil didn't seem even remotely angry. Its features looked sad and reproachful.

"It's just as hard for me!" Alex cried out. The Demon stared back with deep doubt in its eyes.

"Damn it all . . ." Alex turned to his terminal. "Computer, establish a secret watch over the cabin of Janet Ruello. Captain's access."

The screen unfolded and lit up.

The black woman was lying on the bed. Her body was quaking with sobs. Her hands were clutching and crushing her pillow.

Damn Eben, damn their crazy church of the Angry God, damn the genetic engineers who programmed Janet to hate the Others!

Alex rushed out of his cabin.

"Open! Captain's orders."

The blocked door beeped in protest, and he walked into Janet's quarters. Nothing had changed in the last three seconds. She was still sobbing into her pillow.

Janet's quarters, however, did surprise Alex. He had thought Janet had practically no personal belongings, but she had managed to completely transform the drab standard surroundings. Over the bed hung a crucifix. Christ was portrayed according to the Ebenian custom—having freed one of his hands and shaking a tight fist. On the floor near the bed lay a small but plush rug of multicolored threads. There was an open mirror-case set of expensive makeup on the nightstand. There were also four framed pictures of smiling babies: two dark-complexioned boys and two little girls, one black and the other white. And numerous other tiny trinkets that seemed utterly useless but completely changed the feel of the place.

"Janet . . ."

She didn't even lift her head.

"Come on." Alex sat down next to her, putting his hand on her quivering shoulder. "I understand what you're feeling. And I don't consider your position completely wrong. But we all must fulfill our life's duty . . ."

"Then why do you hate us so much?" Janet whispered. "So much more than you hate the Others . . . All we wanted was to make everyone happy!"

"No, Janet. Not everyone hates you, believe me. More people feel sorry for you."

"Why should they?"

"Your minds have been altered by genetic engineers . . ."

"Ours but not yours?" Janet burst out laughing, sitting up on her bed. "Friend-spesh, they've mutilated you much more than me. You aren't even capable of love!"

"So what?"

"What do you mean, 'so what'?" Janet spread out her arms. "You stupid pilot . . . You go on getting laid, having orgasms, and thinking that's what makes a relationship between a man and a woman?"

"Why, of course not. There's also personal empathy, warm congeniality . . ."

"Oh, go shove your personal empathy! You're much more of a freak than I am! I was made to hate the Others, so I hate them. Maybe I'm way, way wrong, but at least I haven't lost anything! I've found something—hate! Do you get that? But you . . . you've lost everything! Lost half the universe! Kim, the poor little girl, watches you with adoration, follows you around like a puppy. And you don't even notice it!"

"I do notice it, Janet! A few hours ago she and I had sex, and we both . . ."

Janet Ruello, the Ebenian executioner-spesh, burst out laughing.

"Deus Irae! How do I describe a sunset to a blind man?! Alex, did you know that on Eben, pilots were left capable of love?"

"That was dumb. A complete confluence with the ship can be achieved only with a lack of attachment to people."

"That's not it at all! It's just that everything is interconnected. Both love and hate. It is impossible to get rid of love without putting in at least some kind of surrogate. For you pilots, that surrogate is the confluence with the ship. For detectives and tax collectors, it's the ecstasy of discovering the truth. One day, they'll find a surrogate for all the rest of us, as well."

Janet thought for a moment and added:

"All but the soldiers, probably. For them, love is a necessary counterbalance to the working hatred for the enemy. We were all soldiers . . . so we were all capable of love."

Alex was silent. It was impossible to argue with a spesh defending her own specialization. Besides, she was right to some extent— Edgar, in virtuality, had also talked about biochemical links.

"Janet, what are we going to do?"

"Were you convinced that the Zzygou race are not our allies?"

"They're temporary allies," Alex corrected her. "I've never had any illusions about it."

"I won't provoke them again."

"Do I have your word?"

"I swear as a spesh, friend-spesh."

"Swear an oath to me, as your captain."

Janet smiled.

"Why?"

"Swear the Ebenian military oath."

Her features quivered.

"Friend-spesh, I am no longer a citizen of Eben. What remains of our army is hermetically sealed off from the galaxy."

"What difference does that make?"

Janet looked away. Reluctantly admitted:

"None."

"Swear an oath to me, as your captain."

"In the name of divided Humanity . . ." Janet began, her lips trembling.

"Continue," ordered Alex mercilessly. Then added, in a softer voice, "I have to ask you to do this, friend-spesh."

"In the name of divided Humanity, reigning over the stars, worshiping our Lord, in the name of my ancestors and my progeny, I swear . . ."—she paused briefly, while the words came to her—"I swear that I won't harm the aliens Zey-So and Sey-Zo, temporarily occupying the same ship with me. I will not show them my true feelings. I will not prevent them from leaving the ship alive and unharmed."

In Alex's estimation, this oath was comprehensive. Or very nearly so.

"Thank you, Janet. Forgive me. I had to order you to do it."

"It's all right, Captain." Strangely enough, Janet really meant it. "You took all my responsibility upon yourself. Now I feel I am in a war situation, so I must conceal my true feeling from the Others."

"Thank you . . ." Alex bent down and kissed her lips. He hoped the kiss would be brief, just a token of affection and gratitude.

But it didn't work that way.

Janet folded her arm around his neck, then pressed him closer. Her kiss was not as artful as Kim's, but much more distinctive and personal. Alex felt himself unintentionally returning the movement of her lips. Forced himself to stop.

"Janet, if Kim finds out . . ."

"Don't worry." She smiled. "She and I have talked this over."

"What?"

"I told her right off the bat that I found you attractive. Kim agreed that I had a right to feel the way I do."

Alex could barely suppress a laugh. Incapable of love, he felt compelled to remain faithful to his girl. Kim was crazily in love with him, but she let him sleep with Janet.

With Janet, everything was different. She didn't have any illusions about their relationship, and never demanded more than he could give. She may have lacked the genetically programmed art of the geisha, but her ordinary human experience turned out to be a worthy substitute. Everything was different. Just as different as the two women's appearances. They were each other's opposites—the fragile fair nymphet, and the heavyset black woman.

Although he had to give himself just as energetically to both of them.

"I have another quarter of an hour," he said, as they rested. "Then it's back to the bridge."

"Just a sec . . ."

Janet got out her cigarettes, lit two up, handed one to Alex, and avidly smoked the other one herself.

"I enjoyed it very much," said Alex, caressing her dark thigh, glistening with sweat. "You are a wonderful lover, Janet."

"Better than Kim?" she asked with a mischievous smile.

"Yes, I would say . . . because of your age. She has very little experience. And that makes a big difference, despite all her efforts."

"In five years or so, she'll far outshine me." Janet smiled. "Well, I don't really mind . . . Oh, Alex, I should've warned you in advance . . ."

"What about?"

"I didn't block conception. There's a possibility that I'll get pregnant."

Alex was quiet for a moment before admitting:

"How unusual. I've never had a woman like that."

"Does that turn you on?" Janet smiled again.

"Yes," said Alex earnestly. "I have three kids, but all were conceived under the terms of an agreement. Two boys under the government order—they are at some boarding school on Earth—and a girl from a . . . good friend of mine. I visit her regularly."

"All speshes?" Janet inquired.

"The boys—I don't know, to be honest with you. Probably. I have a good genotype. But the girl is specialized as a detective."

"Poor thing . . ."

Alex said nothing. He didn't really feel like continuing the argument about the necessity of love.

"I have five, but no one specialized for a profession that requires the loss of major emotions," Janet told him.

"You seem to have mentioned four . . ."

"The fifth one's on Eben. If he's alive, that is. I prefer to think he is alive . . . I would have felt him die."

"What do you mean, you would've felt him die? Is that also a part of your specialization?" Alex asked curiously.

The woman laughed. "No, of course not. We have this belief . . . a mother feels if her children are alive."

"Very romantic," Alex agreed. "A bit archaic, but sweet."

"We kept to our old traditions in many respects. I gave birth to my first three kids personally, for instance."

She said that with an easy and even careless air, but Alex felt his skin crawl.

"Why?" was all he could ask.

"It's a tradition. Are you disturbed by that?"

"No . . . not much. After all, a third of all people are born that way. I've even been trained to assist with natural childbirth, in case of unforeseeable flight circumstances. But I didn't expect it of you. . . ." He laughed a forced laugh. "Don't tell me you also suckled them yourself?"

"Yes. All five of them. Each one at least once."

Alex started.

"Your lactation isn't blocked?"

"No. An Ebenian soldier is a military unit unto herself. A woman must be able to give birth and nurture future warriors without any assistance."

Alex looked sideways at her voluptuous breasts. He had thought their size to be a result of genetic modifications or individual peculiarities of her constitution . . . now he knew.

"Sorry. I should've told you before . . ." said Janet pensively. "Many people are disgusted by that fact of my biography. I let my children consume my own bodily fluids . . . I can certainly see how that would be shocking."

Alex was listening to his own reactions. Then gave up, unable to sort out all the raging sensations and thoughts, and looked down at the Demon. What he saw made his face turn red.

"Janet, I must be some kind of pervert. All that . . . just turns me on."

Janet Ruello looked at him. Her eyes were blazing.

"I hoped it would, Alex."

CHAPTER 4.

New Ukraine was considered to be a successful planet, with solid prospects for the future and more or less loyal to the Imperial government. In a word, it was the golden center of the Empire, one of the pillars propping up civilization. Peaceful, plentiful, and utterly dreary.

Had the hyper-channel near the planet been a continuously functioning one, Alex wouldn't have even considered landing on New Ukraine. But the colony wasn't a galactic crossroads like Gamma Snakebearer. Neither was it a bustling trading post like Quicksilver Pit. *Mirror* came out of the channel, traced another arc to return to the entrance, but didn't manage to re-enter. A whole caravan of refrigerators loaded with frozen and nominally live pork—the two main New Ukrainian exports—was slowly pulling into the narrowing aperture of the channel.

"The next time it opens will be in nine hours and seventeen minutes," reported Xang gloomily. "Do we wait, Captain?"

Alex was lost in thought. He had walked onto the bridge about a minute before they exited the channel, and Janet appeared in the system literally one second before they came out into real space. His emotions hadn't yet settled, and mentally he was still with this tall, dark-skinned woman, so charmingly depraved, and at the same time so conservative . . .

"C-the-Third . . ." Alex had connected to the ship's inner net. The clone was in his cabin—he sat at the computer terminal working on a text file. "We have some nine hours in the New Ukrainian system. Shall we land or wait in orbit?"

"Let's go down," replied the clone without hesitation. "The Zzygou prefer to attend to their natural needs in open air or running water."

Alex was using an open channel, audible to the whole crew, and Janet let out a quiet, spiteful laugh.

"Very well. Please tell your wards," Alex asked him. "And . . . how are they feeling, by the way?"

"Everything's back to normal," answered the clone calmly. "Sey-Zo has explained to me what had happened. The cocktail included some anise liqueur from Hellada-2. It was an unfortunate misunderstanding. Turns out, the natural alkaloids of anise cause a strong intoxication in the Zzygou, which is accompanied by a propensity for mystification and an uncontrollable need to say things that are unpleasant to their interlocutors. They beg your pardon . . . and ask not to offer them any more beverages that contain anise."

It was impossible to tell whether C-the-Third really believed that what had happened was an accident, or if he simply preferred not to blow up the scandal. He seemed ready to believe it was an accident.

"Propensity for mystification . . ." Janet murmured. "Yes, of course . . ."

"Right battle station, please be quiet," said Alex dryly. And Janet fell silent. Not offended; rather, fully satisfied with what she had heard.

They began their descent toward the planet.

New Ukraine had four spaceports. One was located near the capital city, Mazepa-Misto. Two more were out in the boundless green steppes, where herds of mutated swine roamed—huge, elephantine creatures, covered by a three-and-a-half-foot-thick layer of aromatized lard, rich in vitamins. Alex had had occasion to try various kinds of local pork, created by the artful cunning of geneticists. He had also tried the lard, which, though untreated, had a smoked flavor and consistency. He had also sampled the sweet "chocolate" lard you could buy in small cans. Alex wasn't a great fan of the local delicacies, but the geneticists' mastery was unquestionable.

The fourth New Ukrainian spaceport, where they would be landing, was located near the planet's one and only sea. The colony was not lacking for water, but by a strange caprice of nature there were no large lakes on New Ukraine, to say nothing of seas or oceans. A long and arduous terraforming process had artificially created the sea. There was no true necessity for it, especially considering that this large body of water had a significant, and not positive, effect on the climate of the adjacent regions. But at this point, it had become a matter of principle. Every colony wanted to have everything a normal planet should: seas and mountains, forests and swamps. Alex had already seen the shapeless, monstrous, artificially created mountain chain on Serengeti, so the New Ukrainians' desire to have a sea did not surprise him.

The ship went in for landing over the sea. Tore through a line of clouds—a sign of an approaching storm moving toward the shore at a leisurely pace. Rushed over the pallid gray blotches of water poisoned by hydrogen sulphide—the terraforming was still not completed. The view changed closer to the shore. The sea turned a clean greenish-blue, and the air got clear and bright. The ship was moving about three hundred thirty feet above the surface of the water, having reduced its speed to a minimum and shifted to the clean, though energy-consuming, plasma thrusters.

"Will there be any shore leave, Captain?" inquired Generalov, in a businesslike tone. He had absolutely nothing to occupy him at the moment, so he was visibly bored.

"Yes. A six-hour leave for anyone interested. The only one to stay on duty . . ."—he hesitated briefly—"will be me."

The raging white vortex—Kim's consciousness—tossed a needle of white light at him.

"Alex!" The girl was clearly mad at him, but at least she chose to confront him on a private channel. "I thought we'd hang out on the planet together!"

"Kim . . ." He transferred the piloting to Xang, who was delighted with this unexpected gift. Then Alex focused on the conversation. "As the ship's captain, I must make sure that the crew has a chance to rest. By tradition, the first shore leave is the captain's time to stay aboard."

"I hate your traditions! I won't leave the ship, either!"

"Fine. Stay on," Alex agreed.

She fell silent immediately. Then grumbled:

"I changed my mind."

"Come on, don't be mad . . ." Alex tried to imbue his words with as much warmth as he could. "We'll hang out together on Zodiac for sure. And it's a much more beautiful planet, trust me."

"Do I have your word?" asked Kim quickly.

"I swear."

Kim fell silent, apparently satisfied. Alex returned to piloting, though he did not take the controls away from Xang, simply keeping an eye on the co-pilot instead. There was no real need for that—the ship was already coming in for landing. Below them stretched green fields of lush alfalfa, pigs leisurely plodding through them. Alex turned on the magnification to take a closer look at these gigantic, imperturbable animals in all their glory. They did not in any way react to the landing ship—they were used to them. And only a mischievous shepherd boy, making his rounds on the back of a fast young piglet, turned his little face toward the sky and waved at the ship enthusiastically, his little hand clutching a thermal whip. Alex smiled, regretting the fact that he couldn't greet the happy kid in kind.

"Landing glissando . . ." Xang reported.

Mirror slid down to the very surface, rushing over the landing field paved with six-sided concrete slabs.

"Standing in the pillar . . ."

The ship came to a stop over the spot assigned to it by flight control.

"Touchdown . . ."

The landing supports had slid out of the body of the ship and touched the work-weary slabs of the spaceport.

"Thank you very much, Mr. Morrison," said Alex ceremoniously.

"Much obliged to you, Captain," replied Xang with feeling. "Shall we make the transfer to parked mode?"

"Yes. Go ahead."

Alex slipped out of the glimmering rainbow, out of the warm, caressing embrace of the ship. Felt the ship reaching for him, striving to prolong the moments of contact.

"I'll be back . . . I'll be back . . . I'll be back . . ."

Leave on terra firma!

What could bring more joy to a spaceship crew?

No matter how long the flight had been—a few hours or a few weeks. No matter what kind of world the ship had landed on— the fragrant valleys of Edem, or the wide open New Ukrainian steppes, or among the biodome settlements of the mining planets.

It made no difference; nothing was more joyous or more eagerly anticipated.

The balmy air of a new world, new faces, funny and strange customs, exotic dishes, happy local hetaeras, interesting though useless souvenirs—all that awaited the crew stepping out for shore leave. Combined with the pleasure of one's favorite work, the ship was their home, and the most beloved little part of the universe. But what human being doesn't enjoy being a guest? And that was why all astronauts cherished even the briefest hours of leave so fervently.

Alex stood under his ship's belly and smiled, looking at his crew. His wards, his coworkers, his friends, his children . . . they stood waiting for the land transport. This spaceport wasn't so large as to have a well-developed underground transportation network like the one on Quicksilver Pit.

Generalov was preening himself, looking in a little mirror, wetting a tiny pencil with his tongue and touching up his thick eyebrows. He was obviously counting on having some sort of romantic adventure. Janet, standing next to him, was doing the very same thing. She may have had the same intentions, or perhaps she did it simply out of every woman's ineradicable need to look as seductive as possible.

Kim stood next to Morrison. The co-pilot, bright and cheerful, as if he hadn't just finished a lengthy stretch of one-man bridge duty, lightly encircled the girl's shoulders with his arm. He wouldn't get anywhere, Alex was sure of that, but still mentally wished his colleague the best of luck.

"You're off to the museum, then?" Alex inquired, just in case. "I'd go to the sea . . ."

"Join us, and we *will* go to the sea," rejoined Kim. She smiled, picking with the tip of her little shoe at the concrete slab. Xang threw an alarmed glance at the captain.

"Nope, I can't," said Alex, with a tone of regret that was almost genuine. "Well, have a nice time."

He himself found nothing interesting about visiting the Museum of Animal Husbandry, one of the main places of interest on New Ukraine. But Kim, it seemed, was really into every facet of genetic engineering.

"Here comes the van," said Paul with a melancholy air. The engineer was the only one who didn't regard shore leave as anything particularly special. He hadn't even changed out of his uniform overalls and intended to spend the whole six hours' leave in the spaceport bar.

A potbellied van of the ancient wheeled variety rolled up to the ship and slid sharply to a halt. The driver couldn't be seen behind the mirror-windshield, but a girl, all smiles, came out of the passenger section of the bus. A customs-inspector badge was pinned to her blouse, embroidered in the New Ukrainian folk style.

"Good day to you, travelers!" she cried in a ringing bright voice. "Be welcome, dear guests!"

The girl was cute. Even her force field belt, in the standby mode, looked more like a sweet joke than like a menacing attribute of a customs officer.

Alex waved at his comrades as they were getting into the bus, then winked at the customs girl. In reply, she gave him a very endearing smile, even if it was prescribed by her job regulations.

They probably wouldn't have any problems with the customs— New Ukraine was famous for its lenient and indulgent border patrol services. The only conflict that came to Alex's mind had to do with an attempt on the part of one Sviatoslav Lo, a navigator-spesh, to take some vanilla pork fat off the planet. As it turned out, this unusual delicacy was strictly forbidden for export—a rather simple way to attract tourists. But Mr. Lo got no punishment for his attempted crime, not even a fine.

The bus had already disappeared into the distance, approaching the squat spaceport buildings, but Alex remained where he was, standing near the ship. Lighting up another cigarette, he happened to remember that New Ukraine had some decent tobacco . . . he would need to contact one of his crew and ask them to buy some local cigarettes.

A hatch entry melted in the belly of the ship, and down slid the elevator platform. Alex turned and greeted C-the-Third and the two aliens with a short nod.

"Greetings, greetings, kind male friend the captain!" the Zzygou sang out. They seemed to have completely recovered from the anise poisoning and seemed no longer worried about it.

"We've decided to fly out to the sea," the clone told Alex, with a conspiratorial wink. "For a swim."

"Wonderful," Alex agreed. "Have a great trip."

The Zzygou stood, smiling happily at him, and C-the-Third, his sturdy hands on the shoulders of the Others, seemed positively thrilled. He looked somehow like both a doting father and a hopeless lecher. Wonder how the genetic engineers had managed to wrap his psyche around love for the Others? Could it really have been done through sexual attraction? That was, after all, the easiest and most logical way. . . .

Another vehicle approached, a car this time, an old but impressive Barracuda. The customs officer turned out to be a young and handsome fellow.

Another minute, and Alex was alone once again.

To be completely honest, besides piloting he loved this kind of moment more than anything else in the world.

A soft wind blew, heavy with the scent of grasses. The orange sun was warm, but not hot, and some little birds were chirping in the sky. They must be rather dumb to live at the spaceport . . . or rather smart to avoid getting hit by the ships . . . Dumb, most probably.

Alex took a deep drag on his cigarette. It wasn't as enjoyable anymore, starting to taste a little bitter. Everything is good in moderation. A glass of wine, a sip of cigarette smoke, a morsel of an exotic dish . . .

"Computer, I'm ready to come in," he said, and the elevator platform was lowered to his feet.

He hesitated a long while before putting on the neuro-shunt.

It wasn't because of fear, not at all. Pilot-speshes were capable of fear—a normal and useful human reaction—but pilot-speshes would never let fear interfere with their actions.

Alex wasn't sure his actions would be right. It was unpleasant—he wasn't used to feeling this way. And now he was forced to act based on . . . no, not on facts, not even on premonitions . . . more like barely detectable hints. The way a person climbing a mountain could go up a beaten rocky path, maybe even a hard and a dangerous one, but clearly visible. Or he could crawl up a vertical cliff face, where a single false move could mean death. And then he could choose a rock shrouded by mist, where a foothold that looks strong and reliable suddenly breaks away, like a rotted tooth, taking the ill-fated rock climber down with it.

The hardest thing is half-knowing, half-truths. They give you neither freedom, as does complete ignorance, nor any direction, as does truth. But if you are unlucky, they bring you a full measure of defeat.

Alex pulled on the headband of the neuro-shunt.

The world plunged into darkness and was reborn.

The very next moment, a tremendous blow threw Alex down to his knees.

"No one stands before the Sovereign!"

Alex turned his head. Slowly, because a cold, sharp steel blade was pressed to his neck. He was held down by two half-naked muscular warriors, looking as though they came out of the pages of a history textbook . . . or a kid's comics. A third warrior, dressed a little more ornately, was holding a bared sword to his throat.

A farce. But dying would be painful even in a virtual world. . . .

It was a huge circular hall with a dome of crimson-and-gold stained-glass windows, white marble columns, and mosaic-tiled floors. In the center of this hall stood a throne—a rough-surfaced hunk of black rock with a wide seat carved out. Edgar, dressed in black and red silks, seemed to be a part of the throne, just as dead and cold. Only his eyes glimmered behind his glasses, so appropriate among all these medieval props. Two very young girls, clinging to the boy's legs, fixed a startled stare on the pilot.

"We've gotta talk," said Alex.

Edgar said nothing. He seemed lost in thought.

"Get rid of your phantoms," said Alex, annoyed. The blade at his throat trembled, as if about to strike.

"Say 'Sovereign'!" Edgar ordered, the echo of his voice rolling inside the dome.

"Sovereign." Alex had no intention to fuss about trifles.

The boy on the throne snapped his fingers. The young girls slid down the steps and rushed away. The guards were apparently reluctant to release Alex—they hesitated.

"Out," Edgar told them dryly.

Rubbing his forearms, Alex got up from his knees. He approached the throne.

"What's all this masquerade?"

"They're very good self-teaching programs," Edgar informed him, with an offended note in his voice. "And I've worked on this reality for five years. I have to live somewhere! And now I'll have to explain to my courtiers the unexpected appearance of a sorcerer in the Sovereign's palace!"

Alex sat down at the foot of the throne, shrugged his shoulders.

"What kind of sovereign are you, to have to explain anything to anyone? Well, it's your game, not mine. Can't you get down?"

"I can," affirmed Edgar gloomily. He got up, gracelessly descended the stone steps, and sat down next to the pilot. "So, everyone's off on a little vacation, eh?"

"Yup. Can you guess why I stayed behind on the ship?"

"'Cos you wanna talk to me?"

"Exactly."

The boy frowned. Then peaceably spread out his arms, saying:

"Well, all right. Want some wine or ice cream? Or should I call in the houris?"

"I said 'to talk,' not 'have some fun.' Edgar, are you a good genetic engineer?"

"The best in the universe."

Alex smirked. "All right, suppose you are. What can you tell me about Kim?"

"You're still interested in that?"

"Of course. The girl is suffering, Edgar."

"She's suffering," the boy agreed. "She's in love with you. You were with her in the moment of metamorphosis, you see. Imprinting as such is not really characteristic of speshes, but Kim's situation is different. Her psychological profile demands love, and you have become the first object of its application."

"That I get. Her genes are part geisha's?"

"A very small part."

"And why was that done?"

Edgar was silent.

"Look, I want to be your friend." Alex put his hand on the boy's shoulder. "I want to help you gain a living body. Want to help Kim. But I need you to help me as well . . . just a little. Why was a fighter-spesh equipped with a geisha's abilities?"

"Kim isn't a fighter-spesh at all," said Edgar abruptly. "A fighter! Hah! Mass production, cookie-cutter job, fodder for the Imperial cannons . . . Kim is absolutely unique."

"What is she?"

"A secret agent."

"What?" Alex couldn't help laughing.

Edgar turned to him and stared furiously straight into his eyes.

"You think it's funny? You think that secret agents are all made to be six-foot-tall hunks with plasma cannons implanted in their asses? An agent can kill. An agent has the skills and reaction reflexes of a fighter, but that's not the main thing! To use an agent-spesh as a fighter is insanely wasteful! Kim has been created to revolve in the highest social circles, to make people fall in love with her, to have influence, to gather intelligence, to blackmail . . . and, well, to kill, if necessary. But that's secondary. You can't imagine even a fraction of her abilities! She herself doesn't realize most of them . . . just yet. Kim can read information off computers remotely, she can hold her breath for a quarter of an hour, lower her own body temperature to match the temperature of her immediate environment. She has perfect memory, an intuitive ability to decipher codes . . . and a number of truly unexpected physical abilities—"

"Does Kim know?" asked Alex bluntly.

"Do I look like an idiot to you?" snarled Edgar. "No. She doesn't even suspect anything. It will be a huge shock for her when she finds out. She's used to considering herself a fighter-spesh, after all . . . well, at least some kind of fighter, something like a bodyguard or an assassin."

"What would happen, if she found out?"

"I don't know." Edgar shrugged. "Most probably, she'll be really shocked at first . . . and then she'll want to take her place in life. People like her work for the Imperial Secret Service, or for planetary administrations . . . or perhaps for some massive and powerful corporation."

"Why haven't you told her the truth, Edgar?"

The boy looked up at him sadly. Then asked with a sneering tone:

"What would she need *me* for, then?"

Alex nodded. "Okay, I get it. Forgive me. But if you're right . . ."

"I *am* right!"

"Then Kim has to find out who she is. A spesh's whole life is about fulfilling her purpose. Working as an ordinary fighter, Kim will always remain unhappy."

Edgar said nothing, and Alex felt a sharp sting of shame. The boy's every hope was tied to Kim. All his plans to gain a real body, to break free of his monstrous captivity . . .

"I see what you mean . . ."

That is, if he wasn't lying, of course!

"But we must come up with something for Kim's sake, right?"

The boy looked at him in surprise.

"We?"

"Of course. You're her best friend. You're the genetic engineer. And I am the man Kim's in love with."

"So why do anything else?" Edgar shrugged his shoulders. "She's got a job now, and she's okay with it so far. When Kim does discover her own abilities, that will be the time to worry about it. But I hope to have a real body by then."

"Anything is possible. But what's to be done about the problem of her crush on me?"

"It's not a crush, it's love," Edgar corrected him. He was silent for a moment, then dryly added:

"I have nothing against your encounters. It's a natural need, so . . ."

"She doesn't need sex. Or, rather, not only sex. By the way, why was that done? Sure, an agent has to be able to make others fall in love with her. But to fall in love herself?"

"Love is such a strange thing, Alex . . ." The boy got up, paced to and fro, his hands behind his back. "There have been many attempts to create geishas who would make others love them while staying cold and indifferent themselves, just doing their work without involving emotions. A seductive appearance, acting talents, smarts, pheromones . . . All to no avail, Alex. For a guaranteed seduction, the hetaera's love must also be real. As soon as her goal is accomplished, a geisha gets to fall out of love with the object . . . to regain her freedom, even if it's a difficult process, with lots of heartache and sadness. But first, a geisha must be in love herself. No matter for how long—fifteen minutes for a quickie or several years in the role of a lady-escort—but a geisha's love is genuine."

Edgar talked on, utterly immersed in his own words. As if mesmerized, Alex watched the skinny boy pace around the caricature throne, readjusting his glasses, dissecting the "greatest of all human emotions."

"Love! Ah! Alex, you can't even fully grasp what it is, true love! Madness—joyful and voluntary. And an all-engulfing flame, whose heat is delight and torture at the same time. The love of a mother for her children, of a patriot for his motherland, or of a naturalist for truth, all of them pale in comparison with real, genuine, all-engulfing love! Poets have composed verses that live on for millennia. Conquerors have shed rivers of blood. Ordinary and unremarkable people have suddenly caught ablaze like supernovas, burning away a whole life in one blinding flash, raging, and inexorable. Love . . . love. Thousands of definitions, an endless search for the right words . . . as though mere sounds could ever encompass this ancient magic. Love is when your beloved is happy . . . love is when the whole world is concentrated in that one person . . . love is the feeling that makes us equal to God . . . There's no approaching it! No expressing it in words. And it's not even necessary to express—everyone understands, everyone has experienced this sweet intoxication. Even all the alien races are capable of love, Alex! Theirs may not be human love, but something very, very similar. The Tai'i don't have any notion of what humor is. The Bronins are incapable of friendship. The Fenhuan can't fathom vengefulness. A vast number of emotions are unique to humans, though we can't ever grasp . . . um . . . well, for example, the Zzygou sense of sunrise. But every race has love!"

"Not anymore," said Alex simply.

Edgar stopped short. Sighed.

"Yes, of course. We've moved farther than the other races, Alex. We've learned to alter our own bodies, and our own souls, as well. To cut something out, and stitch on something else."

"Stitch on?"

"That's an ancient term. Back then, thin threads were used to attach both cloth and living tissues . . ."

"I got it, thanks! But are we right, Edgar? You know that Janet played a joke on our Zzygou guests?"

"How would I know? You've switched me off from the ship's internal cameras."

"She slipped some anise cocktail to the Others. And the alkaloids of anise affect the Zzygou like a potent truth drug."

Edgar let out a ringing laugh.

"You don't say! What happened then?"

"One of the Zzygou declared that the human race was doomed. That we've gone too far down the road of genetic changes. That humankind is losing its unity and falling apart to become many disconnected, weak civilizations."

"Bull!" said Edgar bluntly. "Dream on, stinkers . . . Humans always *were* different, you know? In prehistoric times, and in the Middle Ages, and in the blessed twentieth century . . . always! Some were rulers, some were peasants, some were poets, and some were sewer workers . . ."

"But back then we were genetically unified."

Edgar shrugged.

"Do you know what kind of person would be born, for instance, from your sperm and Kim's egg? If you don't order any specialization, of course?"

"A baby-natural with sharp vision."

The boy nodded, slightly surprised. "Yes . . . Exactly. It's your only shared characteristic. Then you can easily get the rest! And the point, Alex, is that if necessary, humanity can easily and painlessly return to a unified genotype. Every spesh's gametes contain a double set of genes. The altered one—the one your parents had the geneticists specify. And the regular set—the one you'd have had if you had been born the natural way. This regular set is compressed in the S-organelle and gets activated only during the fusion of sex cells. After that, the process can go all kinds of different ways!"

Edgar's face was flushed. This was obviously a beloved topic that filled him with inspiration.

"And that was the hardest part, you see, Alex! Back in the beginning of the twenty-first century, when the active genotype alteration work began, we were facing an unsolvable problem. It was easy to alter the body completely. But how do you keep the human genotype intact in the process? How do you get a mermaid, who herds schools of fish, and a steeplejack, who has no fear of heights and can spend a whole work shift hanging by two fingers, to have a normal, healthy baby, and not some monstrous freak? It was then that this way was suggested, a complicated one, but safe— and fascinating! A spare copy of genes. Clean and untouched by alteration. Suppose our little mermaid swam out to the shore and met the young steeplejack. A moonlit night . . . the gentle lapping of waves. Two happy, self-satisfied young people meet. Our little mermaid is sitting on a tree branch, which gently slopes toward the water, and our steeplejack is walking along the shore and humming a tune, say, the one that goes: 'We aren't firemen or carpenters, our work takes us to the sky, we send you greetings from on high!'"

Edgar paused, looked at Alex with a smirk. "Have you heard this song?"

"No."

"It's a very, very old Russian song. From the epoch when all were naturals. But it perfectly expresses the very point of specialization. Well, back to our young couple . . . so, they meet . . ."

He slowly joined his hands.

"Surprise . . . confusion . . . laughter . . . it's so romantic! Moonlit night on the seashore, as I said. Gentle caresses in the wet sand. We had to make sure these two citizens, so different, but equally useful to society, never suffered because of their differences. We had to make sure their baby could become a human-amphibian, or a female steeplejack, or simply an ordinary natural. Whatever they wanted. And so, when the great promise of love is fulfilled"— the boy locked his fingers—"enter the S-organelle. The nucleic chains spin open, ferments shuttle along the DNA strings, checking for specialization. Snap! A gene is altered! Then there is a check of whether both parents have the altered gene. Both do? We leave it. Only one does? Move over, please! A spare copy of the gene is extracted from the organelle—the necessary bit is cut out and pasted in. The DNA strings quickly repair themselves before the fusion. Well now, let's see what we got? An ordinary baby-natural! And if the little mermaid fell in love with an amphibian-human—no intrusions would be necessary. Their baby would be born in the water, easily drawing its first breath with the little gills inherited from the mother . . . And if there were two steeplejacks, male and female . . ."

"I get the picture, thanks," Alex interrupted him.

Edgar stopped short. He smiled apologetically.

"I'm just in awe of my . . . predecessors' mastery. You see, they had to create structures that were self-sustaining—who knows what might happen to a group of speshes, if they found themselves cut off from genetic engineers. And at the same time, these structures had to be able to return to their initial state in the course of one generation. The engineers accomplished that goal beautifully!"

"And what if a spesh-couple wanted to give their child a different specialization?"

"Well, then the engineers have to work on that some more," Edgar admitted. "But can you imagine this situation actually happening? You decide to have a traditional nuclear family, wife and kids, the way it ought to be . . . and not wish your kids to have the kind of life you've had?"

"No, I can't imagine that."

"And there you have it." Edgar smiled triumphantly. "Alterations of the body are a mere trifle. A task for beginners. The main thing is to change the psyche. To manipulate emotions. That is the hardest problem of all."

"Great. Then help me solve it. Kim must fall out of love with me."

"Why?" Edgar looked closely at Alex. "After all, I understand everything, and I don't mind. Why should her love bother you?"

"No, not me. But with every passing day, Kim will be hurt more and more because her love can't be requited. Right?"

"Right." Edgar nodded.

"And I can't even pretend to return her feelings," Alex continued. "The tension will keep growing. And that will result . . . might lead to trouble."

"And what do you want from me?"

"If you're really the genius genetic engineer . . ." said Alex in an ingratiating tone, "you must know how to eliminate Kim's feelings."

"Whatever gives you that idea?"

"It is commonly known that there are several methods for doing it. When a certain profession is no longer needed, the speshes get reoriented for another one."

"That's the psychologists' job. I can't chase Kim back into a zygote and do corrective surgery."

"You're absolutely sure that nothing can be done?"

Edgar hesitated.

"I'm not a genetic engineer," Alex said. "But I'm no idiot, either. Altered emotions are not only . . . not so much a result of reconfigured synapses. They are a result of altered adrenal glands. It's about blood chemistry."

"So what can *I* do?"

"Block some hormones. You know which ones."

Edgar sighed and shook his head.

"Right. Block some hormones . . . The pituitary is not a campfire you can splash a little water on to extinguish a couple of coals. It's all or nothing. Changes in character are brought on by a single, though very complicated, polysaccharide chain produced by the pituitary. A temporary block of its synthesis is possible, but that would lead to a shutdown of all the personal particulars at once."

"And what would those be for Kim?"

The boy adjusted his glasses. Thought for a moment.

"Ruthlessness . . . first and foremost. Love—the one that was the result of artificial stimulation. That's about it. Intellectual changes are not connected to pituitary hormones."

"Let's do it."

"You think it's so easy to interfere with a spesh's organism? We'll need a top-notch biochemical lab, with organic synthesis equipment. The ship's sick bay won't do."

"We're on a planet, Edgar. It may not be the most developed planet, but it's quite civilized. An order could be put in and completed in two or three hours."

Edgar said nothing.

"Are you really a genius geneticist? Or has your value been exaggerated?" asked Alex with a smirk.

"All right," Edgar said, giving up. "But I think you're making a mountain of a molehill, Alex. For Kim, love is a normal work mode, nothing bad would've happened. . . . Scribe!"

A small bent figure emerged from somewhere behind the columns. The skinny, hunched-up old man in a florid pointy hat and a brightly colored robe was holding a parchment roll in his hand.

"You won't have any problems administering it," said Edgar to Alex. "The active ingredient is stomach-acid resistant, so you can just mix it into food or wine."

"Dosage?"

"Five or six milligrams. Put in a bit extra, a slight overdose won't cause poisoning. Scribe, take this down!"

The old man nodded vigorously, sitting down at the foot of the throne. Squinted myopically at Alex and hurriedly averted his gaze. Extracted an inkwell and a long feather from somewhere. All Alex could do was shake his head at the sight of this pitiful entourage.

"Synthesis instructions . . ." Edgar began dictating.

Of course, Alex had overestimated the New Ukrainian science labs. The synthesis took a full five hours. The delivery robot, a flying disc of about three feet in diameter, landed near the ship shortly before the Zzygou and C-the-Third returned.

Alex waited for the identity chip to finish its work-cycle and a small green light to turn on in the polished metal side of the robot. Then he came up to it and opened a tiny trunk compartment.

The tiny vial had cost him an entire month's salary. Three grams of white, opalescent liquid. Alex squinted his eyes, looking closely at the product Edgar had ordered.

Had he lied or not?

Could it really be that this liquid was capable of slowing down that most complicated of all biological mechanisms, which started up the minute a spesh was born and, after the metamorphosis, began working at full force? The ruthlessness of fighters, the cold benevolence of pilots, the nymphomania of haeteras—could all that be reduced to naught? And if so, how exactly would that occur? Abruptly, as when a device's power is suddenly cut off? Or gradually, as when a car, with its engine turned off, slows down? Maybe the feeling induced by the geneticists really would disappear—but what if it had been so thoroughly internalized by the person as to become genuine?

These were questions that could not be answered theoretically—they had to be tested in an experiment.

He caught a glimpse of the approaching Barracuda and hid the vial in his pocket. The empty delivery robot floated away over the field at a leisurely pace.

C-the-Third scrambled out of the car first, then extended his hand to the Zzygou. The two aliens couldn't have looked more pleased . . . although that seemed to be their usual disposition.

"You've been standing on the field all this time, eh, Captain?" cheerfully cried out C-the-Third.

"Had some mail delivered." Alex preferred to explain the robot's appearance himself. "I've decided to have some fun."

He winked conspiratorially at C-the-Third, hinting at having ordered some illegal drug or some particularly elaborate sex simulator. C-the-Third winked back.

"You should've come with us, Captain. It's a really funny sea."

"I know. I've been here once before."

"So nice, so nice, friend Captain!" the Zzygou reported. They were holding each other's hands and exchanging glances. "Much pity that you were not there!"

"I'm really sorry, too." Alex nodded.

He stepped aside to let the Zzygou and the clone pass on their way back into the ship. Then he lit a cigarette. The tobacco from a different world somehow seemed to taste worse . . . as if the New Ukrainian air didn't want to accept it.

Thirteen more minutes passed, and the minivan with the crew appeared.

It was immediately obvious who had fared well on shore leave and who hadn't—who got Fortune to smile upon them, and whose hopes had been dashed. Generalov, all gloom, went back inside the ship without saying a word. Paul came out of the minivan with a stolid air of a space wolf that had seen a hundred planets. He threw Alex a sharp, formal salute and also went inside.

"Your cigarettes, Captain," said Janet. Handed him a carton. "They seem all right."

She was smiling, obviously content with her life.

"What's with Puck?" Alex inquired.

"Nothing out of the ordinary," Janet smirked. "Found a boyfriend at the bar, dreamed up all kinds of things . . . now he's all hurt. Decided it was the love of his life."

"Can you fall in love in just five hours?" asked Alex rhetorically.

"Oh, Captain, my Captain . . ." She kissed him playfully, touching her plump lips to his cheek. "Anything's possible, trust me. But don't worry about Puck, he just wants to squirm and suffer a bit . . . he's just that type of person."

"How irrational . . ." Alex shook his head. "I am ready to accept the expediency of love, though I lack the ability. But you should fall in love exclusively by mutual consent, making extra sure in advance that your partner agrees to reciprocate your feelings for a long enough period of time. Otherwise, all you end up with are negative emotions instead of positive ones . . . Janet!"

The black woman had pressed her hands to her mouth, but her laughter still broke through.

"Alex . . . no, forgive me, for Angry God's sake . . . you're right . . . of course . . . theoretically speaking . . ."

The pilot went silent.

Slightly embarrassed, Janet went back to the ship. Kim, who had been patiently waiting for them to finish talking, came up to Alex.

"This is for you."

The thick brown paper packet was small but rather weighty. Alex unwrapped it with that sudden happy feeling that touches anyone receiving an unexpected gift.

Of course, it was the very thing New Ukraine was so proud of—a piece of fresh lard.

"They cut these off the piggies right out there on the pasture," Kim said. She was bubbling over with new impressions. "But it doesn't hurt the piggies at all—the skin heals up in a day, and the pig gets more fat, just walking around. Here! Try some—it's already smoked. When the layer of fat gets to be over a foot and a half, the piggies start secreting special ferments . . . Isn't it neat?"

Alex took out his pocketknife and cut off a small piece. Chewed it, then nodded. "Yes, it's neat. Very tasty. And a green apple aroma, right?"

Kim nodded. Behind her, Morrison's face was contorted in disgust. "Aroma . . . you should smell the aroma of those pastures—Good Lord! This lardy mammoth lumbers around the steppe, gorging itself on everything it can find, and shits continuously, excuse the unsavory details!"

"It's a natural process!" Kim retorted.

"Of course it is. But the *aroma* is disgusting. Why can't they grow their meat and lard in containers, as it's done on any decent planet?"

"You just don't get it, do you?" Kim's quick temper flared. "The taste would be completely different! Besides, pigs are good for the planet's ecology. And they're cheaper to keep. Three shepherd-speshes can manage a huge herd, and there are no other expenses!"

Alex, like Xang, was not at all inclined to see New Ukrainian animal husbandry as an engaging topic for conversation.

"Kim . . ." He took the girl by the shoulder. "We take off in thirty-nine minutes. I think everyone wants to take a shower and change . . ."

"So you're not even a little bit interested in this . . ." she replied, slightly offended.

"I am. But I've already visited the Animal Husbandry Museum."

"And did they take you to see the main genetic lab?"

"They did."

"They didn't let *us* in. There was some experiment on . . ."

The three of them entered the ship.

CHAPTER 5.

Heraldica.

One of the strangest human colonies Alex had ever heard of . . .

The mouth of the hyper-channel was located some six hundred miles away from the planet, orbiting it like an ordinary satellite. There was only one battle station here, though it was rather powerful. The security of the channel was guaranteed by the stationary installations on the planet itself. They were spread out all over the surface—in the arid, hot deserts, atop forbidding mountain ridges, and even on floating oceanic platforms. Their construction must have cost a lot more than the building of a few space citadels would have, but from the point of view of Heraldica's inhabitants, their solution had been the only option. As the channel made its orbital loops around the planet, control over it was transferred from one battle installation to the next.

Heraldica was a planet of aristocracy. Gathered here were the remnants of the ancient Earth lineages, now dying out, such as the British royal family and the Arabian sheiks. But also the more recent aristocracies—for instance, the New-Russian dynasties, who had amassed their enormous fortunes at the end of the twentieth and the beginning of the twenty-first century by selling off the lands, natural resources, and population of their earthly homeland. Several aristocratic lineages from other colonies—planets that had made a transition to other forms of government—also dwelt here. Rumor had it that there was even an enclave of the Bronins, descendants of the once-ruling nest.

Alex had no intention of landing on the planet, of course.

They were waiting their turn to enter the channel, and everyone—Alex had no doubt about that—was peering down at the planet revolving below. The ship's optical systems were powerful enough to provide the observers with a richly detailed view.

Alex himself had chosen to watch a small, cozy town in a mountain valley. Its little houses, only five or six stories high, were roofed with carmine-red tiles. Its streets were buried in greenery, and everywhere, fountains ran. Close to the town was a palace—the pilot would not have been surprised to learn that the building had been brought to Heraldica from Earth. There was also a spaceport, but it was so tiny and run-down that there could be no doubt the planet's aristocrats had lost all interest in space.

Their greatest passion was hunting.

Along a swift mountain brook, a person was running. The optics, even computer enhanced, didn't let Alex see the person's face—light clouds above the valley were blocking his view. It was either a youth or a young girl. Pursuing her were three riders dressed in bright, flapping robes, the unmistakable attributes of the ruling class—all petty princelings adored luxury. The animals they straddled could have been anything. But they weren't horses . . . unless it had been some geneticists' prank to have horses equipped with fancy antlers.

The chase didn't last very long. The pursuers caught up with their prey. Blue sparks flashed . . . the aristocrats didn't reject all technology, after all. The three men dismounted and walked over to the motionless body. With a mixture of confusion and revulsion, Alex watched the aristocrats rape their helpless victim. An entourage of about twenty men had caught up with them by then and now stood a little ways off, patiently awaiting their turn.

Finally the hunters got tired of this entertainment. They walked back to the entourage. There was a short discussion, accompanied by some imperious gestures, and then another little figure rushed out running along the river. The hunters bided their time. Some drinks were served, and now it looked like they just stood around talking.

To his mild relief, Alex saw that the victim was still alive. A girl—at least the gender was clear now—got up and, awkwardly shuffling her feet, started to limp back towards the town. No one was pursing her anymore. Quite the opposite—some even waved her on.

"Despicable!" said Janet loudly.

"You mean the hunt?" Alex asked.

"What hunt? No, I'm talking about that yacht party."

"Aristocracy!" rang out the voice of Morrison. "Blue blood . . . goddamn it. It's really blue, right?"

"I've heard it is," said Alex, watching the fun begin anew. "Of course, they wouldn't have switched from hemoglobin iron to copper. That would violate the Imperial laws. They only changed the color . . . I can't even imagine how that's possible . . . and they haven't lost their genetic unity with ordinary people. But their blood *is* blue."

"No one would have allowed this back in the old Empire," declared Morrison. "A decent emperor . . ."

"Heraldica flourished even under the previous emperors," rejoined Alex. "And the boy now formally on the throne has probably never even heard of this planet."

"Or maybe he has heard of it," remarked Janet. "Who knows, he might even admire it. Real kings, dukes, and sheiks. He might be very pleased about that."

Alex finally switched off the zoom-in optics. He had not the slightest wish to study Heraldica anymore. Sixty-four small dynasties, all-powerful within the borders of their realms. Sixty-four genetic lines that had utterly degenerated.

Absolute power corrupts and depraves, even if it is limited to the space of a single mountain valley, a single little town. Human history had known many a tyranny, but never had the tyrants been free from the threat of revolution. Never, until the moment when servant-speshes first appeared.

How were they recruited? After all, everyone who had flown over to Heraldica went there voluntarily. The Imperial observers had watched the streams of colonists closely, making sure no one was being taken against their will. So there had been volunteers for this. And not just a handful of them, not even dozens or hundreds. Hundreds of thousands of people had moved to Heraldica with their masters. It was very unlikely that Earth would have had so many insane masochists.

More likely, everything had looked really nice at first. A small country on a peaceful and abundant world. Wise, aristocratic rulers. A bit of medieval exotic charm—*that* always had a fantastic power over the human heart. And people, in good faith, would order servant-specializations for their children. After all, what harm could possibly come to them at the hand of a wise elderly lady of a royal bloodline or a sage, poetically inclined sheik who cared so much about the welfare of his people? Except that generations kept succeeding each other, raising a new crop of rulers who were now used to having only servants around them . . .

There should be, after all, more limits to specialization, other than the considerations of social utility and genetic compatibility with the naturals. It should be forbidden to encroach on a person's free will . . . at least, to this extent.

"Crewmembers, prepare for entry into the channel. Estimated time to entry—plus six minutes, twelve seconds. Set the jump vector for Zodiac. Estimated time to destination—eighteen hours, twenty-nine minutes, eight seconds. I am the first one on bridge duty. Morrison takes over in nine hours, fifteen minutes."

No one had any objections. No one asked any questions. Alex was also a ruler on his ship, like the people with blue blood in their veins down on Heraldica. Except that his power had different roots . . . so far, they had been different.

So where was that boundary? Where lay the borderline between a spesh's readiness to obey those in charge and the slavish submission of a servant? What was the difference between power and tyranny? Why had the very thing that was the basis of life in the Empire degenerated into brutal nastiness on Heraldica?

Here Alex couldn't suppress a crooked grin. If one took a look at the Empire from the outside, might it look just as nasty? Fighter-speshes, hetaera-speshes, street sweeper-speshes . . .

He tossed the threads of control over to Morrison. Watched Xang for a few seconds, as the co-pilot took the ship closer to the mouth of the channel, then switched over once again to the optical scanners.

This time, having received the command to search for people, the computer opened a completely different part of the planet, a part already sinking into night shadows. A river delta dotted with a multitude of small islands. Large houses—here, a truly big city was sprawling. Even the nearby spaceport looked rather up-to-date. In the streets, cars dashed by, pedestrians scurried about, and here and there billboards flashed.

An ordinary city. No dirty fun or mad princelings.

At least at first glance.

Yet this city also lived by the laws of Heraldica. Complete and unlimited power. Non-acceptance of Imperial laws . . . which, in turn, cut tourists' access to the planet, except for the most reckless.

What is better—overt or covert coercion?

Mirror entered the hyper-channel, and Heraldica's world disappeared.

There was something mystical about piloting while the ship was gliding through the inner side of the universe. The gray corridor—the walls, made of the great nothing, rushing towards you—and a complete, absolute, unfathomable detachment from the outside world. Multidimensional physics asserted that there was only one hyper-channel, and its existence lasted a mere quantum of time.

Therefore, in that one brief moment, all the ships of all times and civilizations would be superimposed—incorporeal shadows, rushing by in all directions at once.

The universe was full of paradoxes. Most of the races had come to use the hyper-channels as the most convenient and inexpensive method of interstellar travel. And now, right at that moment, countless Tai'i fleets were on their way to meet their unknown, utterly obliterated enemies in the decisive battle for the fate of the galaxy . . . the battle that brought the winners to no good at all. And here also, rushing into the unknown, was Son Hye, Earth's first interstellar explorer, whose bright fame eclipsed both Magellan's and Gagarin's. And here was the strangest bit—the ships of the future were also already here. The last cruisers of humanity, the race that would also fade away someday. The first fragile little spacecraft of alien races that hadn't even broken the bounds of gravity yet but were destined to rule the universe. And here also was *Mirror* itself, in all its future flights, with Alex and the others aboard.

Of course, astronaut lore carried many a legend about hyper-channels. There was one about a man who had thrown himself overboard and was delivered by the hyper-channel back to Earth. And one about a ghost-spaceship that appeared from under the stern, majestically passed the astonished observers, and vanished into the distance ahead. And one that said that occasionally, the exhaust of your own ship's engines could be seen *in front* of the ship itself . . .

And, of course, there wasn't a single grain of truth in all that lore. But it was kind of fun to pretend that you believed it.

Alex wasn't really sure if he would have liked to actually see anything unusual in the hyper-channel. The spine-tingling stories were good only when you knew they were lies. He was much happier with just the silence and the tranquility. Silence, tranquility, and the warm rainbow of the ship . . .

Nevertheless, he liked to stare into the nonexistent space of the channel, as if he really did expect to see the stern of his own ship up ahead . . .

Morrison entered the controls system at exactly the appointed time. He and Alex exchanged a short emotional signal: no words to it, just wishes of luck and an expression of goodwill. The rest of the crew was resting.

Alex felt tired, but stepped into the recreation lounge anyway. All alone, he poured himself a glass of dry wine. The ship seemed to be dozing, placidly and serenely . . . Only the air conditioning was rumbling softly, almost inaudibly. Sensing the presence of a person, a small turtle-like cleaning robot stirred in the corner, licking with its moist tongue the floor that was already squeaky-clean.

Alex still couldn't chase away memories of Heraldica. That girl, walking away from her rapists. Submissive, uncomplaining, maybe even content to have fulfilled her duty . . .

He took the vial out of his pocket, and looked at the cloudy suspension. What would have happened had the rape victim taken a blocker? Nothing good, that's for sure. She would have tried to scratch the aristocrats' eyes out, resist them . . . to the great surprise of the entourage and, no doubt, of the rapists themselves.

Alex opened the vial, smelled it cautiously. There was a sharp chemical odor, not exactly pleasant, but not revolting, either. One drop would be enough. Well, two—for a full guarantee. Overdose would not be dangerous . . .

He tipped the vial over the glass holding the remnants of wine. Looked at the Demon. His shirtsleeve was rolled up, so the little devil was in full view. Except it had closed its eyes, as in terror.

"It *is* scary," Alex agreed. "Very scary."

Surely he wasn't the first spesh ever to brave a self-experiment with such a substance. And surely, nothing good had come out of such an experiment, otherwise the recipe of the blocker would have spread through the Empire like wildfire, breaking down the established order of things.

A drop.

Two.

Three.

He carefully closed the vial and hid it in his pocket. Swirled the glass a bit. The liquid stubbornly refused to mix with the wine and formed an oily film upon the surface.

Alex put the glass to his lips and threw its contents back in one gulp. Then poured himself another splash of wine to wash it down. A slight acrid aftertaste remained.

The substance wouldn't work right away. Edgar had said something about three to four hours before the behavior modifiers, already present in the body, were flushed out from the nerve cells. And yet, Alex stood for a while, listening closely to his own sensations.

He felt sleepy, and that was all. . . .

"Let's go take a nap," said Alex. The Demon, of course, had no objections.

Then he was in a dream, a strange, chaotic one, composed of bits and pieces of everything that had happened in the last few days. As though he was a ruler of some unknown planet, maybe Heraldica, or Earth, or Edem. A good, kind, peaceful planet . . . Alex stood at the foot of a throne. Ten or so guards, their swords drawn, were closing in on him in a tight circle. And in front of Alex, on his knees, stood the boy named Edgar, awkwardly clutching his broken and bent glasses.

"Why'd you do it?" his own voice seemed unfamiliar to Alex. He even realized that he was asleep, and was ready to wake up, as it often happens as soon as you say something in your sleep. But the dream didn't end, and Edgar lifted his head, squinted myopically at Alex, and gave an awkward shrug:

"I wanted to save myself . . ."

"Add 'Sovereign,'" said Alex, and the guards tensed, ready to rush over to Edgar and hack his skinny body to pieces.

"I wanted to save myself, Sovereign." Edgar had finally straightened out the frames, and now fastened the glasses onto his nose.

"But why in this way, exactly?"

The boy—who stubbornly continued to wear glasses, a thing that had been forgotten by everyone a century ago—winced.

"It was the only way that remained to me, Sovereign."

"You're cruel . . ." Alex looked over the guards' heads and met the glance of Kim, who stood hugging Janet. Kim nodded to him, and cried out:

"Kill him, Sovereign! I never wanted to be this way, Sovereign!"

Janet stopped her by putting her hand to Kim's mouth. Then shook her head, whispering:

"Our soldiers were unable to shoot at humans . . . Alex . . ."

Alex nodded to each of them. Approvingly to Kim, soothingly to Janet. But he was the Sovereign, and that bound him with invisible fetters much stronger than the altered spesh operons. . . .

"You're cruel," Alex repeated, looking down at the boy, who was awaiting his decree. "Guards!" And ten glistening swords swung up into the air. . . .

Having opened his eyes, Alex lay motionless for a while. He winced, remembering the dream—bright and colorful, it seemed to have embossed itself upon his memory.

His experience with psychoanalysis was limited—a standard course in elementary school and, later, the occasional trips to the union therapist. But the interpretation of this dream did not present a difficulty.

He winced at the memory of Kim yelling, "Kill him!"

But the most frightening thing was that she was actually right . . . and these words might someday ring out for real.

He didn't sleep long—there were still two and a half hours before they would exit the channel. He could go to the recreation lounge and sit around with a glass of whiskey. Or he could stop by Kim's or Janet's and indulge in the simple pleasures of sex. For a while, Alex lay, trying to decide to whom he was drawn more. Both women were very attractive, but each in her own way . . .

He sighed and decided not to bother anyone.

The neuro-shunt was still in the desk drawer. Alex put the headband on and started rummaging through the contents of a pencil box, with its meager collection of entertainment crystals. There were a few "Wonderful Journeys," which allowed you to travel through virtual copies of the most beautiful planets in the galaxy. Four detective adventures from the series about the Hunchback, agent-spesh of Imperial Security. This particular colleague of Kim's, if you believed the authors, really did have a disposable plasma discharger . . . well, not in the body part that Edgar had mentioned, but in one of his sinuses. Alex hesitated— he had watched the crystals titled "The Hunchback" and "The Hunchback's Truth" a while back, and he remembered being captivated by the daring plot, in which you could be on the side of the agent-spesh or on the side of his numerous but unlucky opponents. Someone had also enthusiastically recommended to him the crystal named "And Now—The Hunchback." As for the one called "A Tomb for the Hunchback," *that* promised either the end of the hero's exploits or—and this was more likely—some totally mind-boggling escapades. But a quality virtual detective adventure, if you played as several characters, would take up no less than twenty-four hours. Alex put "The Tomb for the Hunchback" aside, where he could easily see it, and went on looking through the rest of the tiny crystals.

He immediately put away the bonus-crystal named "100,000 Best Commercials, from the 20th Century to Today" that had been included by the thoughtful merchants of the entertainment industry. No, thanks.

Three more crystals remained—classical literature, music, and drama. Of course, it would be pleasant to sit on a porch near the ocean shore, sipping a cold cocktail, hearing the cries of the seagulls, and reading a good book. It would be just as pleasant to enjoy the same activity on a cold fall evening in an armchair by the warmth of the fireplace, listening to the drumming of the slanting rain upon the windowpanes.

And, of course, there was the "Sex Kaleidoscope," an entertainment crystal approved by the Imperial Health Committee, as well as by the Church, for use by space-crew on long trips.

Alex thoughtfully twirled the crystal in his hand. He did, after all, want to check out what love was. And the "Kaleidoscope" was best suited for that purpose. Even without any *love*, Alex had derived plenty of pleasant emotions from that simple handbook of all the possible forms of sexual activity.

He pressed the tiny crystal into the resilient suction cup, then waited a moment, and relaxed. The world went foggy as it disappeared.

After the abrupt transitions of the virtual space created by Edgar, the "Sex Kaleidoscope" made a cozy, soothing impression. Through the mist, the walls appeared, a chandelier poured down a soft light, and a soft fluffy carpet laid itself under his feet.

"Welcome . . ." said a gentle genderless voice. "Would you like to choose your sexual role?"

Alex thought a moment.

"Okay . . . I am a man . . ."

"Accepted," confirmed the voice.

"Not inclined to masochism, no interest in bestiality or xenophilia . . . and let's not try homosexuality . . ."

"Accepted . . ."

"The rest is up to you," said Alex with a hint of doubt. "Random choice."

"Enter."

A door opened in the wall. Soft, pleasant music could be heard.

A random choice of sexual adventures was the favorite game of astronauts, especially those on long flights, though a few awkward mishaps had taught Alex to make strict provisions for a few basic demands. It wasn't exactly fun having to flee from a crowd of naked, muscular black men armed with chains and leather whips.

But this time there seemed to be no trouble. Alex's body changed as he passed through the door. He got taller, gained a sizable belly, and his arms were now covered with little red hairs. He carried a small carton, which was obviously not empty, though not very heavy, either. In front of him was the empty elevator lobby of a skyscraper. Judging by the color of the sky in the window, it wasn't on Earth. Mingling with the music came a calm, self-assured voice:

"My sex life has been regular and traditional. As a child and an adolescent, I paid my tribute to the fad for group sex. Upon passing my specialization and becoming a pastry chef-spesh, I entered into a normal tripartite family. But something has been bothering me and making me suffer. I've been feeling dissatisfied. Often during the night, I stand at the open window, watching swift Charon pass through the waning half-moon of Cerberus, and dreaming . . . of what? I have not been quite prepared to admit my inclinations to myself . . ."

Alex waited patiently, though the commentary was obviously going to be long and nebulous.

He stepped forward, and the voice stopped abruptly in mid-word, then continued at a faster, more energetic pace:

"I've come to the Fast Transit company office to hand-deliver a wonderful chocolate cake to the company's vice president. He's celebrating the one hundred and first birthday of his mother, the founder and the first president of Fast Transit . . ."

A soft push made Alex step toward one of the elevators. He could've resisted it, of course, but that would defeat the whole purpose of his being there.

The elevator doors opened with a melodious chime. Alex went in, and immediately felt that something was not quite right.

First of all, there was only one other passenger in the elevator: a small, gray-haired, elderly lady, wrinkled and stooping. She wore a shapeless brown dress, and a headscarf covered her thin, faded hair.

Secondly, the floor in the elevator was covered with a soft rug.

"Good morning, ma'am . . ." Alex forced himself to say. The granny said nothing, only nodded, tilting her flabby chin, and stared at the mirrored wall.

Maybe he'd still luck out? The elevator started to crawl up smoothly.

"My heart skipped a sweet beat . . ." triumphantly announced the commentator.

"Shit!" Alex hissed, clenching his fists.

"For some reason, I started thinking of my mother . . ." continued the voice musingly. "Those times when, as a youth, I'd come home late at night and climb into a bath, and then my mom would come in and, for a long time, she would slowly, tenderly wash my hair . . ."

Alex pressed his back into the corner of the elevator. No, he wouldn't move! He still had his free will, after all!

"The elevator went on climbing and climbing," the narrator said, commenting on the obvious. "And suddenly!"

Alex dug his fingers into the walls. But in virtuality, even his spesh reflexes failed him. The elevator halted, literally in an instant. He was tossed upwards, thrown against the wall, and hurled onto the floor. The cake carton was ripped out of his hands and smashed against the wall. Icing squirted out, and pieces of broken chocolate figures came cascading down. There was a nasty grinding squeak. The elevator stopped, swaying a little, as though it was being pulled up not by a gravitational field, but a common cable.

His own instincts played a bad trick on him. He couldn't help perceiving what had just happened as anything other than a catastrophe.

And a captain's duty was to take care of the passengers.

"Are you all right, ma'am?" Alex asked, kneeling beside the granny, who had dropped to the floor. Her puffy, reddish eyelids fluttered. The elderly lady glanced myopically up at Alex.

"Oh . . . sonny . . . my poor bones . . ."

"Do not move, ma'am." He had forgotten that he was in virtuality . . . and a very peculiar one, at that. "The emergency systems will be triggered any minute now. . . ."

But the elevator wasn't about to open the doors.

"I'm scared . . ." the granny whimpered. She stretched out her arm, wrapping it around Alex's neck. "I am claustrophobic, sonny. It's a medical condition. A hundred and twenty years old is no joke . . ."

The unseen commentator gushed on, triumphantly:

"I looked and looked at her sweet, wrinkled face, bearing the traces of every year lived, every worry, every sorrow . . . And at that moment, I realized that I had never *really* loved anyone but these most wonderful of all human creatures, the embodiments of life's ripeness and the highest expression of femininity—elderly ladies! And now, at long last, a bad accident leaves me all alone with . . ."

"I think I wet myself," said the lady, coyly lowering her eyes. "But no broken bones!"

"Morons!" yelled Alex, throwing off the poor patient's arm and jumping to his feet. "Hacks! If the elevator gear had failed, we would've been smeared all over the walls! Quit program!"

Even the emergency exit was realistically presented here. The doors flew open. A team of paramedics rushed in. The granny, still reaching for Alex, was carried off on a stretcher. A quick-moving youth in a waiter's uniform scraped the remnants of the cake off the wall and stuffed them back into the carton.

Only after that came a tide of fog, and Alex found himself back at the starting place of the "Kaleidoscope."

"Do you have complaints?" the system asked him with alarm.

"Yes I do! Tons of complaints!" Alex cut himself short, realizing that he was yelling at the simplest service program. "Okay. Remove geriatric sex from the list!"

"The social importance of gerontophilia is immense," objected the system. "Its roots . . ."

"Never mind! Remove! Give me something else. But give me a synopsis first!"

For a few seconds, the system shuffled the possible options.

"An extremely interesting and unusual adventure . . ."

"Synopsis?"

"A middle-aged male accountant-spesh, who used to have a binary family, which had dissolved through no fault of his, works at the Imperial Committee for Lightweight Armaments. He is extremely shy, and that interferes with his sex life, as well as his career advancement."

The system was silent for a moment, as if waiting for any objections. Alex shrugged his shoulders. It was a typical beginning.

"The head of the committee is a female coordinator-spesh. Completely absorbed by her work, she dedicates very little time to socially beneficial sexual activities. A socially and professionally successful male comrade of the accountant joins the committee team. He advises your character to become a sexual partner of the coordinator-spesh in order to get promoted and to satisfy sexual instincts. Does this suit you so far?"

"Yes, fine," said Alex cautiously.

"After a series of comical and captivating adventures, the accountant-spesh manages to gain the love of the coordinator-spesh. However, as circumstances would have it, the character's villainous male comrade informs the coordinator-spesh of the true motivations behind the accountant's sexual activities. But that does not hinder the happiness of the two lovers. They form a solid, happy binary family and live together for a long time."

Alex was silent, totally stunned.

"Does this suit you?"

"Do the committee members engage in sexual orgies?" he asked cautiously. "Is there a failed romance between the main character and his male comrade, which causes the comrade to betray him?"

"No."

"Any sadomasochistic aspects of the accountant's love with the coordinator?"

The system hesitated. "Hardly worth mentioning. The accountant splashes the coordinator with water from a decanter. The coordinator tosses a few print-outs in the face of the accountant."

Alex had never had occasion to deal with such a plot in the past.

"That's interesting," he conceded. "Good . . . unusual, but good."

"The duration of the plot is thirty-eight hours," the system warned him.

"Can you speed it up?"

"Not recommended. The main intrigue of the plot consists of the slow and gradual development of the relationship between the two main characters."

Alex shook his head. He didn't have that kind of time.

"Remember this plot and offer it next time I enter. And now, I want to exit completely."

"Exit completely," affirmed the system. "Thank you for visiting. I'm always happy to serve you. Please come again."

A dense, heavy fog billowed all around.

Having taken off his headband, Alex looked at the crystal suspiciously. If Edgar was to be trusted, he was supposed to have gained the ability to love by now. And, to believe all the books, movies, and simply ordinary people, love was a feeling that flared up instantly and knew no boundaries, no limits.

But he hadn't managed to feel any such emotions for the granny! Only revulsion. Revulsion?

He started.

The crystal was designed especially for astronauts. Experienced psychologists had carefully constructed the simplistic, though highly diverse, plots.

As soon as he had entered the elevator with the granny inside, Alex was supposed to have taken her into his "sphere of responsibility." The catastrophe, which plunged him into a stressful but genetically pre-programmed situation, would then heighten his sense of responsibility to the max.

Yes, he had a duty to . . . well, not to fall in love—pilots were incapable of love, so nothing like that could be foreseen—he had a duty to be overcome with warm feelings toward the old lady.

What was supposed to happen next, according to the program?

A soulful discussion?

A shy kiss?

A raging sex scene on the elevator floor?

A mutual enjoyment of the birthday cake?

Alex imagined the naked, happily giggling granny, stuffing a morsel of chocolate into his mouth, and himself, trembling with excitement, licking the sweet cream frosting off her sagging breasts . . .

"Holy shit!" he yelled.

That could have actually happened!

Really!

And he would have had no unpleasant feeling upon leaving virtuality. It would have been just a curious, intriguing adventure, approved by doctors and by the Church . . .

How could this be?

He wanted to gain the ability to love, but had he instead acquired the ability *not* to love?

Or maybe these were just two inseparably linked halves of a whole? Could it be impossible to understand love without the ability to reject?

Alex paced the length of his cabin, his arms wrapped around his shoulders, as he strained to grasp at least some of his feelings.

Yes, he had already broken one of the commandments of a pilot-spesh.

The main commandment, perhaps. The boundless responsibility for everyone who happened to be around. So Edgar's remedy was working—blocking his altered consciousness. And that was really frightening . . . just to imagine pilots capable of abandoning their passengers and crew to the mercy of fate!

He thought of Kim, Janet, Lourier, Generalov, Morrison, C-the-Third, and the Zzygou.

Suppose something goes wrong now . . . the ship's in danger . . . what would he do?

No! No way! He wouldn't rush to save his own life. He was still ready to fight till the end for this ship, its passengers, and its crew! Everything was okay!

Except . . . what was this dreary restlessness, this cold emptiness inside?

As if an unfelt biochemical blow had cut off something that used to dwell in his soul . . .

Or . . . pulled away the mist that had concealed a bottomless abyss?

"Looks like I shouldn't have drunk this shit," said Alex rhetorically. Took a hurried look at the Demon, his most faithful adviser and companion.

The little devil stood, his head lowered, his arms spread out. It glowered at Alex sullenly from under its brows with the same inner torment Alex was feeling himself. He didn't have to look at the Demon anymore—it no longer had anything new to tell him.

"But this isn't love!" Alex vehemently shook his head. "It's the wrong feeling! This can't be it!"

"No, this isn't love . . ." came a jeering whisper of something invisible, something that used to be dead to the world at the bottom of his soul. "This is the *absence* of love . . ."

"Then what kind of goddamn joy is this?" Memory obligingly supplied dry, scientific definitions of love, as if he were clutching at something in the past, something calm and stable. "A steady feeling, accompanied by emotions of gentleness and delight . . ."

Alex fell silent, controlling his breath. Stop. No need to get worked up. He had drunk the blocker of his own accord. He wanted to test it out to make sure it wouldn't harm Kim. He wanted to try feeling what he had always been deprived of.

Was the reason he was experiencing all these unpleasant emotions precisely because of the absence of love? Fine—there were two women aboard, a young one and a middle-aged one. And, if push came to shove, there were also the Zzygou and Generalov! And finally, if worse came to worst, there was a crystal with virtual characters. He'd get that love thing, one way or another. And after the blocker's action wore off, that foreign feeling would go away, and everything would return to normal, to the way it had always been.

The main thing was not to panic.

Alex quickly went to the shower, turned it on ice-cold, and

stood for a few minutes, clenching his teeth. The gnawing anxiety and emptiness seemed to be subsiding, to be washing off.

Hang in there, we'll make it!

It would be something to remember! What other pilot-spesh could brag about having loved, or having suffered the absence of love?

He turned on hot water for a moment, chasing the chill out of his bones. Rubbed himself dry with a towel, quickly dressed, dried and combed his hair. Looked at himself in the mirror.

Everything seemed normal.

Strong, manly face. Intelligent eyes.

Then something elusive, anxious, made him look away in fear.

Nonsense. Nothing, really. He was panicking—that was perfectly natural. So he was seeing things, stupid stuff.

Alex left his cabin and hurried to the bridge. All he needed now was the confluence with the ship, its rainbow warmth, the true feeling of a pilot-spesh. It wouldn't let him down, it would save him. So what if it was still Morrison's bridge time? He had every right to enter the system early. Say he couldn't sleep, for instance. Or that he personally wanted to conduct the entry into the Zodiac system. He had never been there, and it was a great and magnificent planet.

Alex all but burst onto the bridge. He hurriedly lay down in the captain's chair, looked over at Morrison. The co-pilot's face was serenely happy, the way it was supposed to be. A good ship, a long flight, and reliable fellow crewmembers—what else could a pilot need? What sort of *love*?

Lowering his head, Alex entered the system. The green spiral quivered, reached toward him uneasily.

"The ship is still in the channel, thirty-four minutes remaining before exit, no accidents, all systems are working well . . ."

"Thank you, Xang. Never mind me. I just couldn't sleep. I won't interfere with the controls."

The green spiral replied with a wave of emotion—gratitude and sympathy.

"Captain, I used to have trouble sleeping—a problem easily solved by a glass of red wine. I've also heard warm milk with linden honey helps. And there's always sleeping pills . . ."

"Don't worry about me, Xang. It's a rare thing. I'm fine. I won't . . . I won't stay long."

Morrison's image faded a little, done with the conversation. Alex remained alone with the ship.

The rainbow. The warm, wonderful rainbow, reaching over through the darkness. The soul of the vessel.

Alex reached toward it, greedily, already feeling his tension ease, the gaping abyss that cut across his soul drawing together and diminishing.

"Touch me!"

"Be one with me!"

"Love me!"

The rainbow flared up around him.

Faithful, selflessly devoted, it took him in gently but firmly, wrapping him in an invisible embrace. . . .

It was like being back in the first or second grade, during the virtual instruction courses . . . A charming virtual young lady for an instructor, even for the little snots like him. Her joyful voice, "And now we will be introduced to the simplest method of sexual self-stimulation, celebrated as far back as the biblical times. Boys, if you some of you are already familiar with it, please be quiet for a few minutes, do not interrupt . . ."

It was like being back at a school party, playing spin the bottle, when teenagers would split into couples and bustle into secluded nooks, hoping to find out the difference between virtuality and real sex.

It was like being back at the graduation orgy—with experienced geisha-speshes, who knew every last erotic zone of the human body and were able to give themselves to you with joyful and self-less abandon.

It was everything—and nothing. A forgery. An illusion. A surrogate for love. A cynical fake. A nutrient tablet in a starving man's hand—something that sustained his body, but didn't feed his hunger. An inflatable doll-woman in a museum of sexual culture. A sex-partner recommended for procreation, who carefully played out the role she had memorized since childhood.

It was anything—but not love!

Alex screamed, ripping himself out of the colorful rainbow, away from the cloying touch of electronic witchery. The system shivered, letting him out into the real world. He twisted around in the chair, having forgotten to rip off the safety straps, noiselessly yelling something, seeing the uncaring light of the screens and the serene face of Morrison.

He had been robbed blind!

A long, long time ago, before he was born! With the complete assent of his parents, who chose for their future son the secure and gainful specialization of a pilot. He was deprived of . . . no, he still had no idea exactly what it was . . . he only knew he wouldn't be able to live without it anymore.

He had been betrayed.

He was a servant, just like the poor vassals to the aristocrats on Heraldica. Though he wasn't being raped quite so openly.

What had he been living for?

For the cold contacts with the rainbow light?

For the right to pilot a dozen tons of metal?

For the right to die for the Empire?

Alex wept, shaking in the straps of the chair. He hadn't cried for a long time . . . so very long. And he had probably never wept because of emotions before. Pain, or physical discomfort, or a botched-up assignment made him cry many times . . . but what was it like to weep because of an elusive, intangible feeling, not essential to life?

Thirty-four years he had been a happy pauper. He had been eating the leftover crumbs he was ordered to eat, rejoicing over gifts of cast-off rags, working to fulfill his social duties in good faith.

Now his hour of reckoning had come.

Master-pilot, spesh, captain of a starship, Alex Romanov wept, like an offended child. He wept, looking at the happy smile on the face of his co-pilot, who had no need for strange experiences.

Zodiac glittered like a Christmas-tree decoration. Its insane orbit, which curved like the number 8, now lay beyond a blinding white star that poured oceans of light onto the planet. Any earthly vegetation would not last an hour under this scorching luminary.

But life is a very tenacious thing.

The whole surface of the planet turned towards the white sun now became a carpet of mirrors. "Lotuses," giant flying plants inhabiting the highest layers of the atmosphere, floated through the air like a many-layered carpet, avidly absorbing torrents of radiation. Somewhere far below, in cool, deep shade, Zodiac's plants and animals went about their lives . . . as did its people. Guests of this strange world.

On no other planet in the galaxy were endemic things treated as gently and carefully as they were on Zodiac. Of course, technology would have allowed the construction of an orbital shield to protect the planet for the two months of the year when it passed close to the white star. But the people who had made this world their home decided to take the risk of relying on the natural protection that had been in place for hundreds of thousands of years.

Alex stood in the recreation lounge in front of the switched-on wall-size screen. He was watching a live broadcast from the surface of clouds, and above them, the greenish, off-white underside of the lotuses, drifting to follow the sun. The active part of the lotuses' life cycle took slightly longer than those two months. The rest of the year, they carpeted the surface of the ocean, turning it into a green, scaly plain, lightly rippling on the waves. The lotuses were home to other plants and animals—little symbiotes that had perfectly adjusted to the cycle. They spent the two sunny months in the oceans, awaiting the lotuses' return, or inside the flying plants' thick, meaty tissue, replete with hydrogen cavities, or simply on the leaves' underside.

"There's a gap!" commented the announcer quietly, without any hint of fear. "Dear guests of the planet! You will now see what to do in case of a break in the lotuses."

Maybe it had been a gust of wind, maybe something else, but the plants scattered. Amidst the greenish-white field, a blinding flash flared up. As if a fiery spear, thick and heavy, had ripped through the live shield and hit the surface of the planet. The video camera lowered itself, zooming in on a strip of forest that was hit by the flare. A light mist stood above the treetops—water was evaporating from the leaves. Then the camera showed a family—a man, a woman, and several small children—enjoying a picnic by the edge of the woods.

"Even if it looks like the affected zone is passing you by," said the announcer cheerily, "be on the safe side. Take cover . . ."

The man and the woman looked sideways at the sky and moved under a tent of mirror-like reflective plastic.

"Be sure to put on personal safety-wear . . ."

The kids, who had been peacefully making sand-pies, took little crumpled sun-coats made from the same shiny material from their pockets. Slipped them over their shoulders, put the hoods over their little heads—and went on playing.

"If for any reason you are unable to take these safety precautions," said the announcer amiably, "be sure to assume the following position . . ."

Out of a brook, which meandered a little ways off, a little girl came running. She wore nothing but a pair of panties. She looked up and then hurriedly lay down, folding her arms and her head underneath her body.

"Help will come!" said the announcer soothingly. The girl's mother was already running towards the brook, waving a sun-coat.

"And even if it comes too late . . ."

The scene flooded with blinding light.

"Do not worry. The 'sun kiss' lasts no more than ten or twelve seconds. In most cases, the worst you can expect are some superficial burns."

The barrage of light rushed on. The mother pulled the whimpering little girl to her feet, spanked her a few times, and then, with equal ardor, rubbed the child's body with ointment. Then the woman sauntered back to the tent. The little girl wailed for a while and then returned to the water.

"The corporal punishment of the child, as shown here, is in no way endorsed by Zodiac's Health Ministry. It is not a mandatory procedure after being accidentally 'kissed by the sun,'" quickly added the announcer. "Welcome to our hospitable planet!"

The infomercial was over. Alex couldn't suppress a crooked grin, thinking of the official statistics. Every white-sun season still claimed from twenty to thirty lives on Zodiac. Mostly tourists', of course. Locals were more careful, and everyone, even the naturals, had adapted to "sun kisses." In the same situation from which the little girl had emerged with only a slight redness of the skin, he, a strong and healthy man, would have been howling from the pain of being covered head to toe with blisters.

"I'm not so keen on going down there," said Generalov. He looked around, as if hoping the others would support him. The whole crew had already gathered in the recreation lounge, but no one shared the navigator's pessimism.

"Two hundred million people live down there," said Morrison. "I've been there, though not in the hot season. It's a very beautiful world."

"I wanna go there," Kim interjected quickly. And smiled at Alex.

Alex felt he really was looking at Kim differently. The girl hadn't become more sexually appealing . . . and he still felt affection for her. But something had changed—something Alex had no words for.

Would it always be like this?

"Our venerable passengers are sure taking their sweet time," said Janet with a smirk. She was standing right next to the screen, now showing views of Zodiac set to pleasant music. Really beautiful views. Zodiac's nature was not Earth-like, but strangely enough, it looked very agreeable. There were lakes of dark-blue water, as if tinged with artificial color. Lush crowns of trees—every leaf green on one side and white on the other. Agile, cute little animals, scurrying in the grass like orange fur-balls.

"The Zzygou must not need an orientation," remarked Paul. He yawned. "Captain, do we wait for them or just go in for landing?"

This jolted Alex out of his contemplation of Kim.

"Yes, please. Paul, go call them in to the recreation lounge. But be sure to ask Zey-So first, she is the senior one of the couple. . . ."

The engineer nodded and was just about to step out of the lounge when there was a sound of hurrying feet.

"Finally!" snorted Kim. "Should we hit replay?"

C-the-Third appeared in the recreation lounge.

The air went still with an oppressive silence. The clone's face was covered with red blotches, and beads of sweat ran down his forehead. His eyes were glassy.

"What happened?" Alex stepped forward. This could very well be the way a pilot would look after seeing the stern of his own ship in the hyper-channel.

316

"Captain . . ." The clone's voice was barely audible. He swallowed spasmodically, and stretched out his arm, grabbing Alex by the shoulder. "Come with me! N-now!"

Alex turned around, glancing at his crew. They all looked on in bafflement.

"Everyone, stay here," he said, just in case. "We'll leave the landing till the next circuit."

The clone nodded vehemently, as though Alex had given voice to his own thoughts, and then dragged the captain off.

"What's going on?" said Alex softly, as soon as they were out in the hallway. "C-the-Third?"

"Sh-sh-sh!"

Now that they were alone, C-the-Third's face expressed such desperation and panic that the grimace that had frightened everyone back in the lounge seemed good-natured and happy by comparison.

"Stop it, C-the-Third!"

"It's . . . all over . . ." the clone forced out. Laughed hoarsely. "No. I lie. It's all just about to begin . . ."

Having lost any hope of getting a coherent answer out of him, Alex quickened his pace. Ten seconds later, they were standing at the door of one of the cabins.

"You aren't faint of heart?" the clone's voice dropped to a whisper.

"Not really."

C-the-Third flung open the cabin door.

First, Alex saw one of the Zzygou, maybe Zey-So, maybe Sey-Zo, obeisantly kneeling beside the bed. The cabin, it seemed, had been decorated for a carnival—bright spots of red paint all over the walls. Odd, shapeless garlands hung from the ceiling. The odor, disgusting, almost intolerable to the human sense of smell, made him hold his breath.

And then it was as if a dam burst—his mind made the leap, and Alex realized all that had happened.

"No!" he shouted.

The Zzygou, frozen in a kneeling position near the mutilated, cut-up body of her partner, didn't even stir.

"Let's go, Alex. Let's go. There is nothing we can do to help now." C-the-Third dragged him out into the hallway, quietly closing the door of the cabin. He swallowed. Then shook his head. "It's monstrous . . . monstrous."

"Why did she do this?" Alex looked closely at the clone, who was, after all, a specialist in the Others. "They aren't Bronins. They don't have ritual murder!"

The clone tittered, quietly, hysterically:

"Alex . . . No! Zzygou partners are incapable of killing one another!"

"A suicide . . ." Alex began, and stopped himself. No living creature could smear its own blood all over the walls, festoon the ceiling with its own entrails, and then peacefully lie down on the bed.

"Zey-So has been murdered." An anxious rattling note appeared in C-the-Third's voice. "She has been murdered by someone in your crew, Alex! By a human—by one of us!"

He was quiet for a second and then, a little more calmly, although the words' significance would not in any way dispose anyone to be calm, he added:

"Zey-So is the Crown Princess of the Zzygou Swarm. Her death at the hands of a human is a just cause for war. As a matter of fact . . . I think the Zzygou warships are already on their way through the hyper-channels. Sey-Zo has a portable transceiver. Before calling me in, she had gotten in touch with her mother world."

OPERON III, DOMINANT.

THE NATURALS.

CHAPTER 1.

"Before we begin . . ." The man sitting across from Alex had finished filling his pipe and was lifting the flickering little flame of his lighter. "First of all . . . have you ever worked with a detective-spesh?"

"No, I can't say that I have, Mr. Holmes," replied Alex.

Sherlock Holmes puffed on his pipe and leaned back in his armchair, fixing Alex with a tenacious stare. They were sitting in Alex's own cabin, but now he felt himself a guest . . . an uninvited and unwanted guest, at that.

"My real name is Peter C-the-Forty-Fourth Valke. My matrix, Peter Valke, has been dead for thirty-six years now, but our line has proved so successful that more of his clones are still being made."

"A rare case," Alex ventured. "They say . . . they say it is very hard for clones to be born posthumously."

"Yes, Mr. Romanov." The clone nodded. "That's right. But my whole line of detective-speshes, including me, is incapable of any human emotions, so we aren't shocked that our matrix happens to be dead. Peter Valke was a great man, one of the first genetically modified detectives. He had personally offered to introduce the production of a line of his own clones and named them in honor of the most popular detective of all time."

"Do you also like Sherlock Holmes, Mr. C-the-Forty-Fourth?"

"Of course. But I suggest you address me as Mr. Holmes in all our communication from now on."

Alex nodded. That wouldn't be hard. The detective-spesh's entire appearance—from the lean, broad face, high cheekbones, and lanky figure to the formal tweed suit—brought to mind the immortal hero of Arthur Conan Doyle and his mad successor, Professor Hiroshi Moto. Moto had been a Japanese literature specialist who had superimposed the psychological profile of the long-dead British writer onto his own consciousness, completely losing his own personality. In his place appeared the twenty-first century writer named Moto Conan, and children all over the world still were engrossed by his books. *The Rebirth of Sherlock Holmes*, *The Case of the Missing Gel-Crystal*, *Cyborg at Rest*, *The Four Contested Gigabytes*, *The Strange Story of a Dentist-Spesh* . . . Without a doubt, Hiroshi Moto had really become a worthy successor of the ancient writer. Most probably, he had latently possessed a genuine talent— after all, not one of the many other attempts of this kind had ever led to success. Neither Count Lee Tolstoy, nor poet Anna Shelley, nor artist Mikola Rubens had ever managed to create anything decent.

"The image of my prototype, Sherlock Holmes," continued the clone in the meantime, "is almost completely congruous with a detective-spesh. All remnants of emotions had to be removed, of course. But in general, I am a real Sherlock Holmes, Detective for Cases of Imperial Importance . . ."

Alex could not resist saying, "Holmes usually demonstrated his abilities to his distrustful clients."

"You are not a client." Holmes took the liberty to smile. "You are a witness and also, excuse me for saying this, a suspect in the case of the brutally murdered Zzygou. Although . . ."

The detective's gaze became more piercing as he studied Alex closely.

"I have already committed your official and, I beg your pardon . . . your unofficial personal files to memory. So I will be asking you about things I couldn't learn the ordinary way. The last alcoholic beverage you perused was dry red wine . . . um . . . Edemian Beaujolais . . . with some chemical stimulant unknown to me. During the last twenty-four hours, you had sexual contact with two women, apparently, first Kim and then Janet . . . and then there was an unfinished contact in a sex imitation program . . ."

As absurd as was the very thought of making ironical comments about a detective-spesh, Alex couldn't help himself—the blocker was probably to blame. . . .

"Yes, the real Sherlock Holmes would have benefited enormously from acquiring a dog's sense of smell."

The clone's lean, wrinkled face remained unperturbed. He took a few puffs on his pipe and then gruffly said:

"The real Holmes is the offspring of a writer's genius. I am the offspring of the genius of geneticists. That is why I am just as real and have the same right to this name. Well, Alex, since you've asked for it . . ."

He leaned forward across the little table separating them. And started to talk quickly, bluntly, as if hammering in every word:

"Your parents, Alex, were miserable losers. Your mother a natural, your father an accountant-spesh. He strained himself to the breaking point to pay for your elite specialization. He always worked overtime, and you got used to seeing him in his chair, with bundles of wires sticking out of his cheap neuro-port . . . so you grew to hate the very sight of it. The hostility you harbored since those days, you later transferred to everyone who used the old neuro-shunts, wrongly assuming that these people were cold, cruel, and indifferent toward others. Three years ago this very attitude became the cause of problems on the space-liner *Horizon* because you cooked up a far-fetched excuse to relieve from duty a pilot-spesh with an older-model neuro-port. Your metamorphosis had been extremely painful, due to the peculiarities of your organism, and since then your mind has fixed upon the opinion of all naturals as a lower caste of humanity."

"That's not true!" cried Alex harshly.

"Yes, it is. You are convinced that the suffering you've endured gives you the right to consider yourself special, while in reality you simply have a weak reaction to analgesics. Ever since your metamorphosis you've been feeling offended and tormented by the insignificant reduction of your emotions, although that is unavoidable for a pilot-spesh. I wouldn't be surprised if you've been using some kind of emotional scanner to keep track of your own feelings. But this is all the result of common, ordinary shortcomings in the work of your parents and your child psychologist—they allowed you to experience too close an emotional contact during your premetamorphosis period . . ."

"I don't know what personal files you're using, Mr. Holmes . . ."

Alex hissed. "I don't know how you've found out about my poor parents! But it's probably not worth digging through my past in order to solve a problem in the present!"

Holmes said nothing. He let out a cloud of heavy smoke, set aside his pipe, and continued in a softer tone of voice:

"All this isn't in your personal files, Mr. Romanov. Trust me. This is a manifestation of the very capacity for induction and deduction characteristic of my literary prototype. In addition, I have unlimited access to information systems, enhanced sense organs, and modified morals. I am a servant of the law, Mr. Romanov. If the law says that a starving child who has stolen a piece of bread deserves to be hanged, I will send him to the gallows. And if the law says that a rapist and a murderer should be acquitted, I will let him go in peace. That is the foundation of my strength. The literary Holmes could allow himself to let a guilty person go, and leave justice to the Lord, if he felt the person truly deserved it. I cannot do that. My heart is only an organ for pumping blood, and I have no other god but the law. I will find the person who has killed Lady Zey-So and turn the criminal over to the punishing hands of justice. No one is capable of deceiving a detector-spesh, Alex. If you are innocent, however, if your hands aren't stained with blood—I will become your defense and support."

Alex was silent, looking at Sherlock Holmes, a person created by the talent of writers, by the work of geneticists, and by the wild imagination of detective Peter Valke. Valke was in some ways akin to Hiroshi Moto—the writer turned himself into a reincarnation of Conan Doyle, and the detective became the embodiment of the literary character.

"I am not guilty of Zey-So's murder," said Alex with a sigh.

Holmes nodded and began speaking again. His voice changed now, becoming soft and benevolent, which was surprising in a person completely devoid of emotions. Alex recalled that Sherlock Holmes had remarkable acting abilities.

"Tell me everything that happened following your first visit to the deceased Zzygou's quarters, Mr. Romanov."

"I went back to the recreation lounge," began Alex. "All the crewmembers were waiting for me. They were all a bit alarmed because the appearance of C-the-Third Shustov had made . . . um . . . quite an impression. But I didn't notice anyone behaving differently from everyone else. Just ordinary tension among people who sensed that something unpleasant had happened."

Holmes nodded approvingly.

"Having told the crew what had happened, as prescribed by the rules, I asked if anyone wished to clarify the situation. Everyone said that they had not the faintest idea about the causes or the circumstances of Zey-So's demise. After that, using the captain's exclusive access, I took *Mirror* into a stable emergency orbit and blocked all the control systems of the ship. Then I reported the situation to the Imperial Security Services, adding to the report the special opinion of C-the-Third Shustov about the consequences of the Zzygou's death. Having gotten the confirmation that the message had been received, I turned off all communication systems, and we waited for you."

"We flew out immediately." Holmes nodded. "So . . . let's sum up . . . everyone on board denies any involvement in Zey-So's death?"

"Yes. Everyone absolutely denies any involvement."

"And you haven't noticed anything suspicious in the conduct of the crew, or Sey-Zo, or C-the-Third?" Holmes carelessly omitted the last name of C-the-Third's matrix, required by the rules of politeness when there was more than one clone around.

"Nothing. Just ordinary shock because of what has happened. I've had occasion to see people in a catastrophic situation. And Sey-Zo never comes out of her deceased partner's cabin."

"She's undergoing a parting ritual, which will last for another four and a half hours," Holmes informed him. "I've had to take in a sizable dose of information about the Zzygou."

"Then tell me—is C-the-Third Shustov right? Is war really possible?"

"It's inevitable," said Holmes coolly. "The Crown Princess having perished by a human hand, and especially in such an utterly outrageous way . . . Did you know that her ovary had been cut out?"

"Oh, God . . . no. But why?"

"Otherwise Sey-Zo could have preserved the genetic fund of Zey-So, by transplanting the ovary into her own body. Sey-Zo herself, as the junior partner, lacks reproductive organs."

Alex looked Holmes straight in the eye.

"That would mean that the murderer planned all this in detail? He . . . set out to kill Zey-So in the most insulting way . . . making sure nothing of her would survive?"

"Yes."

The pilot wiped his sweating forehead.

"Holmes, I've heard a lot about the Zzygou, but I can't even imagine where their damned ovaries are . . ."

"Ovary—they have only one. Right under the stomach. It's equipped with its own sealed lymph-supply and a muscle pump. Even after the death of Zey-So, that part of her body could have lived on for several days. The murderer cut out the ovary and severed the lymphatic contour. This is a very, very professional murder."

Alex tensed. He realized what the next question would be.

"Mr. Romanov, having hired Janet Ruello to be a member of the crew, did you know that she was from the quarantined planet of Eben, and that she had been specialized as an executioner-spesh?"

"Yes, I did."

"Then why did you take her into your crew?"

"Back then I had no idea that *Mirror* would be involved in transporting the Others!"

"Then why didn't you void the contract immediately upon discovering the ship's mission?"

The pilot helplessly spread out his arms.

"Mr. Holmes . . . Janet Ruello is now a citizen of the Empire. Her rights are not restricted in any way. Psychologists have made her tolerant of the Others—"

"So tolerant that she would serve them some anise cocktail, inducing a temporary insanity?"

Alex couldn't begin to fathom how the detective had come to know of this incident. From C-the-Third? Or from Sey-Zo?

"That didn't threaten their lives in any way," he said gloomily. "Besides, anise induces not insanity, but a fit of truthfulness."

"You can't prove that. The Zzygou say something quite different."

"In any case, Mr. Holmes, I insisted that Janet Ruello swear to me an Ebenian military oath! She promised that she wouldn't harm the Zzygou in any other way!"

"Mr. Romanov . . ." Holmes sighed. "And you believe her promises?"

"Yes, I do. After all, being true to her word is a genetic feature."

"As is her hatred for the Others. So our psychologists have either overpowered both of these features, or both these components of Janet's personality are still functioning."

Alex was silent. He had no way of countering that.

"Mr. Romanov, perhaps your decision to keep Janet Ruello aboard *Mirror* was motivated by some special circumstances?" Holmes sympathetically asked. "For instance, by that shady little transaction of getting new documents for Kim O'Hara, which you accomplished by using the double legal status of speshes and the captain's right to set the ship's time?"

Alex expected that his "little transaction" would be uncovered by the detective-spesh. But the speed with which it had been discovered terrified him.

"No," he answered, after a brief consideration. "That wasn't the reason, Mr. Sherlock Holmes."

"What is unpleasant is the very fact that a spaceship's captain, a pilot-spesh, considered it possible to break the law." Holmes sighed. "The whole Empire stands on the moral strength of its speshes. We are role models for ordinary naturals, whose consciousness is at times overwhelmed by the lowest kind of emotions. And here you are, a spesh, breaking the law!"

"From the formal point of view, you're right," said Alex quickly. "But Kim was under my protection. And she was sure that her legalization as Kim O'Hara would put her life in danger. It was my duty to help."

"And what was Kim saying about your final destination? About her arrival on Edem?"

Alex licked his parched lips.

"She didn't want to fly to Edem . . ."

"Didn't want to? She felt very strongly about this?" inquired the detective.

"Yes."

"All right, Mr. Romanov. Now tell me—has Puck Generalov's animosity towards cloned people manifested itself in any way?"

"It has." Alex realized that his part would now consist of nothing but affirmative answers to the detective's cues. "He reacted to C-the-Third Shustov's appearance with great hostility."

Holmes sighed and unhurriedly shook out his pipe into a silver pocket ashtray.

"How stupid. All these human enmities—speshes and naturals, people and clones—all that could easily plunge you into racism and nationalism. Was there anyone who supported Generalov's position?"

"Paul Lourier."

"And by all appearances, he is such a nice, courteous, modern young man. By appearances . . ."

"You're searching for a motive?" asked Alex bluntly.

"Yes, of course." The detective got up from his chair. Paced to and fro, his hands behind his back. "Would you mind if I played the violin?"

Alex shook his head. It seemed that in his pursuit of keeping in character, C-the-Forty-Fourth Valke knew absolutely no limits.

From a small leather case, Holmes took out an old and shabby Toshiba electroviolin, checked the charge, and extracted a bow from a narrow opening in the neck of the instrument. Then he pressed the violin to his shoulder, paused a second, and began playing Paganini's seventh concerto with marvelous virtuosity.

At this point, Alex felt utterly worn out, devoid of any hope of extracting himself from the problems in which he was enmeshed. Nevertheless he listened, spellbound, to Holmes's masterful playing. It seemed that back in his brief childhood, packed to the limits with schooling, the clone had also received very decent music lessons.

"Janet Ruello has a motive for murder," said the detective, still playing. "Hers is the most weighty motive. She hates the Others. But Kim O'Hara also has a motive. She has no wish to return to Edem, and could have considered the death of poor Zey-So a perfect way to cut the tour short."

"Kim didn't kill the Zzygou!" cried Alex.

"She is a fighter-spesh," retorted Holmes. "For her, murder is a natural action. She could have found plenty of reasons 'pro' and not notice any 'cons' . . . after all, Kim is just a girl. Properly speaking, she ought to take many more years to study the fighter's craft . . . first and foremost, the mastery of her own impulses."

Alex was silent. Sherlock Holmes was absolutely right.

"Also," the detective continued. The melody he was playing lost its force, becoming soft and melancholy. "Puck Generalov. Another complex situation. His animosity towards cloned people is truly phenomenal. . . . Do you know why he was kicked out of the military fleet?"

"Because he is a natural," Alex grumbled. "I've looked through his papers."

"Well, that's just a camouflage. 'The command was unsure of the navigator's actions in a battle situation.' What nonsense! The real reason, as evident from the official spacefleet records, was his conflict with one of the senior officers. Truly Shakespearean passions there . . . unhappy love . . . your non-traditionally oriented navigator is very amorous. After that, he found out that the object of his desire was a clone. The story ended in a hysterical outburst on Generalov's part, slaps in the face, threats, and even a suicide attempt. He was dismissed immediately."

"There is a huge gulf between railing against clones and killing them. Besides, what does C-the-Third have to do with any of this? He wasn't the one who was murdered!"

"No, Puck is incapable of killing him." Holmes shook his head. "He is an extremist. But in words only. His psychological profile practically excludes the killing of a human. But to kill the Zzygou and so to ruin C-the-Third's life and career—easy! Seems he didn't understand that Zey-So wasn't just a worker individual of the Swarm, whose life was unimportant to the Zzygou."

"Are you accusing him?"

"I'm only thinking out loud, my dear fellow." Holmes impulsively lifted the bow off the strings. "The same thing is possible with regards to Paul Lourier. His teachers and classmates testify to his extremely hot temper, impulsiveness, and a penchant for cruel pranks . . . besides, the fellow is easily influenced by others."

"Good grief, that's such nonsense!" Alex shook his head. "The young man is as calm as a tank! If only all novices were this even-keeled . . ."

"You've only known him a few days, Captain. And I have listened to the opinions of people who have lived with Lourier for years. And now, let's move on to Xang Morrison."

"What's he got to do with it?" Alex could no longer hear any conviction in his own voice.

"A few facts of his biography. In his youth, ages thirteen through nineteen, he was a member of the youth ministry at the Church of the Mournful Christ."

"But that's the . . ."

"The followers of the Church of the Angry Christ, after it was banned. In point of fact they have the same worldview as do the poor inhabitants of Eben. When Xang was nineteen, the clandestine work of psychologists had its effect. Morrison officially broke away from the Church of the Mourning Christ, but echoes of that time remained with him. He has been noted more than once for comments insulting to the Others, and several times he publicly incited people to 'blast the buggers.'" Holmes pronounced the last phrase in the voice of Morrison, and Alex started.

"I would've never thought . . ."

"So everyone has a motive, even an obvious motive! And what if we dig a little deeper?"

"And what motives do I have?" asked Alex wearily.

"None." Holmes smiled. "Absolutely none. You aren't looking to stir up any trouble. You're tolerant of the Others. You're happy with the ship, with the crew, and with yourself."

Alex smirked. Yup . . . especially happy with himself . . .

"Thank God," he said. "Then I'm not a suspect."

"What are you talking about, Alex?" Holmes's voice suddenly filled with sympathy, which he was incapable of feeling. "That's precisely the reason why you are the likeliest suspect."

"I see," said Alex, trying to grasp what he had just heard. "If I'm the likeliest suspect, then why are you telling me all your conjectures?"

"That's Peter Valke's trademark style." Holmes spread out his hands, palms up. "Creates an excellent effect. You do understand that the criminal has nowhere to run. Turn on the outer-space sensors, Captain."

"Computer, turn on outer-space sensors," said Alex wearily.

A screen unfolded.

Very close to *Mirror*—about three point six seven two miles away, from what Alex could hastily estimate—a *Lucifer*-class destroyer was hanging in mid-space. Its gun turrets were closed, but that didn't make Alex feel any calmer.

No matter how good his own ship might be, the *Lucifer* could reduce it to ashes in a fraction of a second.

"If I don't leave your ship in forty-eight hours, it will be annihilated. And if *Mirror* turns on its engines or opens up its battle station blisters, the *Lucifer* will fire immediately."

"But why forty-eight hours?" asked Alex.

"The Zzygou fleets are on the move. Their attack on human colonies is estimated to start in forty-eight hours, plus or minus three hours."

Suddenly Alex felt himself completely devastated, empty. As

though it was he, and not the poor Zey-So, whose entrails and reproductive organs had been ripped out, and whose blood was smeared all over the cabin walls.

The world was crumbling. The Zzygou race, though inferior to humans in its military power, was only slightly so. Soon planets would be ablaze. Space would be filled with radioactive streams and predatory flocks of rockets. Every human and every Zzygou would curse those who had instigated the war . . . not knowing that *he* was the real perpetrator—he, Alex Romanov, pilot-spesh, who took into his crew someone capable of heinously murdering one of the Others, monstrously, in cold blood.

And it wouldn't matter who came out as the winner of the slaughter—the universe would change. All the other races would attack those who escaped destruction. This had been the fate of the Tai'i, and the same would now befall the humans . . . or the Zzygou.

"How can you be so calm saying this, Mr. Holmes?" cried Alex. "Don't you see—this is the end?"

"Let the world perish, so long as justice triumphs," said the detective. Alex turned to him, met his eyes. "I'm kidding, Captain. Of course I want to live. And I want a happy life for all the honest citizens of the Empire."

"Then what's that ship doing here?" Alex asked. "Its place is in a military alignment. As for us . . . either just shoot us all at once, or send us into the army. Has mobilization already been announced?"

"Of course. The Zzygou have already sent the Emperor an official declaration of war."

"What does the little snot on the throne have to do with it?"

raged Alex. "He ought to be playing in a sandbox, not making military decisions!"

Sherlock Holmes furrowed his brow.

"Alex, there's no need to say such things about the ruling Emperor. He will receive his full power in due time, and then the Empire will rise to new heights."

"What heights? What are you talking about? Both our civilizations will be destroyed in this war! Don't the Zzygou realize this?!"

"They do, as far as I know," the detective nodded. "Any other race would not allow this conflict to escalate to an all-out clash. But we are witnessing the full power of the most profound forces that move each civilization. C-the-Third could explain this better than I can."

"Explain the best you can!"

"As you may know, Captain, most of the Zzygou used to lack a fully fledged mind. The men . . . um . . . the drones, despite their lowered social position, did, nevertheless, enjoy love and respect, developing the arts. But the nominally sexless worker individuals gained self-awareness only in the last two hundred years. The human segregation between the rich and the poor, or between naturals and speshes, is nothing by comparison to the social abyss that used to separate the highly esteemed Zzygou females, who had two-syllable names, and the workers, who just had numbers. But when, out of necessity—for stupid animals cannot work with high technologies—the ruling females allowed the development of the workers' minds, they also inculcated in them the highest level of loyalty and love for their rulers. All this guarantees the Zzygou society freedom from internal conflicts."

Alex thought again of Heraldica. And felt sick to his stomach.

"Unfortunately," Holmes continued, "the kind and peaceful worker individuals have already been informed of the recent events, because they are the ones who work at the communication stations and make up most of the crews of the Zzygou ships. And so . . . this is truly a tidal wave of wrath from their entire race. This is the holy war for ninety-five percent of their population. And besides, about seventeen percent of them are genetically linked to the deceased Zey-So! They are her brothers . . . or sisters? Let's just say, relatives. The Zzygou females may not wish to go to war. They might have agreed to hush this business up, accepting apologies and reparations, but . . ."

"Their own slaves will not understand."

"Their workers."

"Their slaves. You've explained it all very well, Mr. Holmes." Alex now stood face to face with Holmes. He hadn't even noticed the moment he had jumped up out of his chair. He looked into Holmes's wise, weary eyes, which seemed to contain all human sorrow. The great detective smelled of brandy and tobacco.

"Is there no way out, Mr. Holmes?"

"There is, Alex. There is always a way out. If in the course of the next forty-eight hours, before all-out war begins—small skirmishes are already taking place—if I find the murderer and turn him or her over to the justice system . . . the Zzygou will stop their advance. They are ready to punish either the murderer alone, or the whole human race. And so I ask you directly, Alexander Romanov, pilot-spesh . . . were you the one who killed Zey-So?"

"No, I'm not, Mr. Holmes." Alex shook his head. "I did not kill her, and I haven't the slightest idea who did, or why. But . . . I'm ready."

"Ready for what?"

"I'm ready to admit that I am the murderer."

Holmes stuck the long-cold pipe into his mouth and asked with curiosity:

"What for?"

"To save the world from destruction. After all, it was I who took the murderer into my crew. Whoever he or she might be. I . . . didn't sense a mistake."

Holmes shook his head.

"No, Alex. It's impossible."

"But why?"

"Let the world perish, so long as justice prevails."

"Oh, the hell with . . ."

"Besides, the whole thing will probably end with extradition of the murderer to the Zzygou. And they will find a way to check the person's sincerity. Your sacrifice—if it is a sacrifice, and not a belated confession—is useless."

"Then find him, Holmes."

"Him or her?"

"What does it matter? Murderers are like angels—their gender is irrelevant."

"It's a good thing you are incapable of love, Alex," the detective said. His gaze was so piercing; it was as though he already knew about the blocker Alex had taken. "Love has often made people do crazy things."

"No matter who the murderer is, he is entirely in your power, Holmes."

The detective nodded. At that very moment, the unlocked door of the cabin opened.

"Report, Dr. Watson," the detective ordered, without even turning.

"How did you know it was me?"

"Elementary. All the rest have been ordered not to leave their quarters. And besides . . . if you ever wish to take me by surprise, change your perfume. The scent of *Fiji* I recognize a quarter-mile away."

Dr. Watson smiled and came into the cabin. Alex looked at her with curiosity. When she and Holmes had first arrived on *Mirror*, there was no time to get acquainted—Watson went to Zey-So's quarters, and Holmes immediately sequestered himself with Alex.

Holmes's faithful sidekick was a petite redhead with large eyes. Sort of pretty, though a multitude of tiny freckles didn't do her any favors. In other words, she was the kind of girl who would easily become a loyal friend and a cheerful lover. The kind of girl who would happily accept a partner and let him go without sadness, who was always eager to have fun but at the same time capable of serious and selfless commitment to her beloved work.

Alex caught himself analyzing the girl's behavior and shook his head. Seemed like Holmes's way of thinking was contagious.

"But Captain Romanov . . ." said Dr. Watson doubtfully, looking at Alex.

"Go ahead. It's all right," Holmes replied, gesturing to her to come in. "If he is the murderer, the information won't help him any. But if he's not, then he may be able to help us."

Dr. Watson nodded and perched on the arm of a chair, as though it was her favorite spot, reserved by habit. When Holmes lowered himself into the chair, Alex realized that that was indeed the case.

"I wasn't able to . . . determine the time of death." Dr. Watson lowered her eyes.

"At all?"

"No, I do have a rough estimate. The Zzygou had been killed during the time interval between twelve and a half and fourteen hours ago."

"Bridge duty shift change falls precisely within that period of time," Holmes nodded, looking at Alex with renewed interest. "That's too bad. I was hoping to clear at least one of you of suspicion, Captain. Either you or Morrison."

"They both could have killed Zey-So." Dr. Watson took out a computer notebook, handed it to Holmes. "Here, take a look. The space vector unfortunately puts the deceased in everyone's availability zone. The same goes for the time vector. The interval zone is just too large."

Alex's enhanced vision enabled him to see the picture on the display fairly clearly. A three-dimensional grid with a tangle of different-colored curves. The center of the grid was taken up by a hazy oval, which must have been the "zone," the time interval and the spatial coordinates of the murder.

"You don't have to look over my shoulder, Captain," Holmes growled. "Come closer."

He touched his fingers to the screen, and the curves stretched out slightly, intertwining even more intricately.

"Ah," said Watson under her breath, "and everyone has a motive, right?"

"Unfortunately, yes."

Holmes wasted no time on disappointments. Took another look at the grid, shut the notebook, and handed it back to Dr. Watson.

"Why were you unable to determine the time of the murder, Jenny?"

"Because of the cabin's air conditioner. It has been working in the chaotic mode. Temperature, pressure, humidity, and oxygen levels in the cabin have been changing every five minutes. With absolutely unpredictable parameters! And since the cabin is made for the Others, the range is very large. The temperature variance, for instance, is between seven below and one hundred and seventy-six above zero."

"Good." Holmes began to relight his pipe once again. "Simply wonderful!"

"For goodness' sake, Holmes! Why?" exclaimed Dr. Watson. Her eyes, fixed on the detective, were filled with mute adoration.

"The murderer was covering up his tracks. In a very professional manner, mind you! He made it impossible for us to determine the time of the crime, and that was considered impossible!"

"If we could deliver some military technology to this ship—something like a mental scanner, for instance—we would certainly be able to detect the pain burst, Holmes! The Zzygou's murder took five or six minutes, and she was alive the whole time. The background emotions will most certainly linger in the cabin for many months to come."

"Mental scanning would take no less than forty-eight hours, Dr. Watson. We don't have that kind of time. If war breaks out, it will be impossible to stop." Holmes looked at the wall screen, as though expecting to see the charging Zzygou ships. "But what about smells?"

"The cabin's air conditioner had been turned on to circulate the air. The entire volume of it had changed eight times over. It's even possible to breathe there without a mask, even though the Zzygou has been carved up into bits . . ."

"An excellent murder," said Holmes through his teeth. "No traces of the culprit. We still don't know who he is . . . But at least there's no doubt we are dealing with a professional of the highest class!"

"Janet or Kim!" cried Dr. Watson cheerily. Alex ground his teeth to keep himself from stating his opinion about her joy.

"I'm not sure," said Holmes, letting out a billowing cloud of smoke. "Not sure at all. Despite common assumptions, most genius-murderers are self-trained, not products of genetic enhancements. Do you remember the maniac from the Third-Orbital, Jenny?"

"Oh, yes!" Watson was smiling, but her hand involuntarily rubbed a scar on her neck. It was a strange scar, resembling human tooth marks. "Nineteen victims . . . and I almost took his score up to twenty."

"Nineteen and the two poor souls who, under torture, falsely confessed to committing his crimes and were then thrown out into vacuum," Holmes corrected her. "So, what do we have so far?"

Dr. Watson fell deep into thought.

Alex couldn't help becoming absorbed in the show that they

were putting on. Of course, he was the spectator for whom Holmes and Watson were reasoning aloud. Dr. Jenny Watson really did serve as a sparring partner for Holmes—she was the wall against which he bounced the tennis ball of his intellect.

"The murderer is a very clever professional," said Jenny tentatively.

"Yes," pronounced Holmes approvingly.

"And he is also a heartless bastard who tortured to death a poor helpless woman—"

Holmes shook his head.

"The Zzygou are far from helpless, Watson. Even with your impressive combat training and military experience, you wouldn't have been able to overpower her. Or you would have emerged from the fight with broken bones and bruises all over your body. But something else is much more important, Dr. Watson."

Holmes got up abruptly, and Jenny involuntarily slapped her hands down, trying to keep her balance on the chair as it tilted to one side. The detective's eyes sparkled feverishly.

"The murderer is a professional. He knew how to neutralize the Zzygou and how to kill her in the way most offensive to her entire race. The murderer has expertly covered up all of his tracks! And he must have known that there was a detective-spesh on Zodiac, and that the kind of crime that would cause a trans-galactic war would eventually be solved! And still the murderer made absolutely no attempt to run away, or to take over the ship, or escape down to the planet. That means," Holmes threw out his hand, pointing at Watson, "he is simply biding time! He doesn't value his own life! His goals couldn't be just to destroy an individual alien, or to vex

C-the-Third, or to bankrupt the Sky Company. His goal is precisely a galactic war, a clash between the Empire and the Swarm!"

"Oh, God!" was all that Dr. Watson could say. Holmes turned to Alex.

"And what would you say, Captain? Remember the incident with the tanker that almost tossed you into Cepheidean space?"

"Of course I do!"

"I must tell you that the tanker's pilot broke off his own vital functions during an attempted deep questioning. It seems he had been pre-programmed with a multilevel psychological code. Traces of a self-eliminating gel-crystal of medium size have been found in the tanker's controls system. Most probably, the calculations of the trajectory that threatened the Zzygous' lives were done precisely by that crystal . . . and the brainwashed pilot simply didn't interfere with the controls."

"Then you can clear at least a few of us of suspicion?" asked Alex. "Doesn't that mean that Generalov, Morrison, and Lourier had nothing to do with it?"

"On the contrary! Alex, I was actually inclined to consider the tanker incident a result of the commercial competition between tourist firms, and the Zzygou's murder an act of a psychopath. But now there can be no doubt. Someone is trying to provoke a galactic war. Someone attempted to cause the Zzygou to perish at the hands of Cepheidians, which wouldn't have made any difference—the Swarm's wrath would still have come down on the humans. When that attempt failed, the agent who has infiltrated this ship went for the ultimate stakes. He has killed Zey-So and is now biding time. Once the first bombs rain down on helpless planets, the war will be impossible to stop. I will not be surprised if someone comes forward to confess to the princess's murder right after the start of the war. But anyone could be that 'someone.' Including C-the-Third. When the stakes are this high, criminals could have interfered even with a spesh's mind. I don't know how, but . . ."

"There are substances to block the altered emotions . . ." Alex ventured to put in. But Holmes shook his head.

"Nonsense, my dear friend! Fairy tales that childhood sweethearts whisper to each other before their metamorphoses! 'I'll grow up and become a tax-inspector, but I'll still be able to love! I will love you, only you!'"

Alex started. The memory was piercing, like the sting of ice-cold water.

. . . *Nadia, raising herself up to rest on her elbows, and his hand reaching toward her, brushing the sand off her naked chest. She's smiling—so sadly, as though they hadn't managed to swim out after all, to get out of the ice-cold water of the gulf. As though Alex hadn't dragged her, immobilized by a cramp, to the shore, to the warm sand, under the parting caress of the autumn sun. And in her eyes—a farewell. She seems to be memorizing his smile, his touch, and his naked body.*

"I will still love you," Alex is saying, because he knows the words she longs to hear. He is saying them sincerely, fully convinced he will keep his promise. "I'll be a pilot, but so what? Metamorphosis won't make any difference . . ."

"Are you thinking about something, Captain?" Holmes asked bluntly.

"I was sure that the substances that can block altered emotions do exist," said Alex.

"You should watch fewer soap operas and adventure thrillers. It would take a genius the likes of Edward Garlitsky to consider all the operons and make up this kind of remedy. Chemical interference with the mind of a spesh is impossible . . . but I am still ready to suppose that C-the-Third could have been a victim of mental encoding."

"Who could possibly want a galactic war?" Alex shrugged. "I don't think we could find madmen with that much power in the Empire. Holmes, could it have been—"

"The Zzygou themselves?" Holmes shook his head. "Absolutely not! Sey-Zo could not have killed Zey-So. It would be the same as severing your own hand."

"Human history has known such cases. What if, for some reason, a war is necessary to the Swarm? What if Zey-So had volunteered to give up her own life to provoke a conflict . . ."

Holmes seemed suddenly downcast.

"Captain, a crime has been committed against a citizen of an alien race. The prosecutor is the Zzygou Swarm. I cannot make the victim's companion answerable as a suspect. As a witness, at most. To prove Sey-Zo guilty, I would have to absolutely exclude the guilt of every person aboard the ship. That won't be an easy task."

"But you've been created precisely for difficult tasks."

"So you want Sey-Zo to be found guilty?"

"I want no harm to come to my crewmembers."

"Everything is in the hands of the law. Well, thanks for your cooperation, Captain. Dr. Watson will stay with you a while longer, but I have to go see the other suspects."

Already at the door, Holmes turned around.

"Captain, why is the ship's inner monitoring system off? As far as I know, technology allows you to record everything that happens on all the premises?"

"Yes, it does. But few ships utilize it in practice. People tend to feel uncomfortable when their every move is tracked."

Holmes nodded, having apparently expected just that kind of answer. And then grumbled under his breath, "Emotions . . . complexes!"

Alex was left alone with Dr. Watson. The girl was studying him with unconcealed curiosity.

"Please proceed with your work," suggested Alex. "I'm at your disposal."

"Tell me, is it true that you didn't kill the Zzygou?"

Alex sighed.

"Yes, it's true. But what's my word worth?"

Dr. Watson nodded. Took a portable scanner out of her pocket.

"Okay, stand up, feet wide apart, lift your arms to the sides . . ."

Alex waited patiently for the narrow tube of the scanner to search all over his body. Then he obediently took off all his clothes, and the procedure was repeated.

"You can get dressed now." Dr. Watson looked sideways at the closet. "Your clothes are all here, Captain?"

"Yes. Well, I don't have much . . ."

Dr. Watson busied herself with his pitiful collection of shirts and underwear, making no distinctions between the ones he'd worn and those still wrapped in plastic.

"Looking for blood?" Alex asked.

"Uh-huh . . . Blood, body cells, odors . . ."

"Won't do any good."

"Why not?" Dr. Watson sat still.

"If I were the murderer, I would go to the cargo bay, put on a spacesuit, and wear it to kill the Zzygou. First of all, that would take care of the odor problem. And secondly, there would be no traces or fingerprints to worry about."

"And what about *on* the spacesuit?" Dr. Watson quickly stood up. "On the spacesuit itself, there would be . . ."

"Jenny, this ship isn't an old washtub with ancient equipment. We use gel spacesuits. Have you heard of those?"

Dr. Watson winced and nodded.

"So there you have it. The murderer could have been covered with blood head to toe. But when he got back to the cargo bay, the gel would go back in for cleaning and recycling, and any organic residue on it would be completely obliterated. There would be no traces left—the cleaning cycle is designed to destroy the most poisonous and aggressive media that might get onto the space-suit. And there's a third thing, by the way! There would be no problem hiding a murder weapon! Gel spacesuits can form any tool—a knife, a key, a screwdriver—from their own material. And a spacesuit is very tough—that would solve the problem of the victim's resistance. The criminal won't have any bruises or broken bones."

Dr. Watson was quiet for a few moments, thinking over what she had heard.

"I will relay your opinion to Holmes. Thanks. But . . . I will nev-ertheless finish up my work here."

"Of course," Alex agreed. "There's always a chance that the murderer is an idiot."

In complete silence Dr. Watson inspected all his clothes, forgetting neither the bathrobe in the bathroom unit nor his dress uniform. At the thought of himself on his way to kill the Zzygou wearing that puffy, uncomfortable outfit, Alex could barely suppress laughter.

"Thanks for your cooperation," said Dr. Watson finally.

"Tell me, Doctor, have you been especially created in tandem to Holmes?"

The girl blushed as rapidly and deeply as only red-haired people can.

"Captain, I haven't been created by anyone . . . except my mother and father. I am a natural."

"A natural?" Alex raised his eyebrows. "How interesting. Then tell me why you follow a stuck-up, cloned fool around and murmur sweet nothings?"

Now Jenny's face went pale. She said hastily, "Mr. Sherlock Holmes is the greatest of detectives!"

"Oh, come on! The greatest of detectives was the literary character. Beloved by children and adults, an incorruptible genius, who dedicated his entire life to his fight against evil. And, by the way, he wasn't devoid of human characteristics. You do remember his love for the adventuresome Irene Adler in the nineteenth century and his fateful passion for the cyborg Princette Alita in the twenty-second. And your emotionless clone is just pretending to be Sherlock Holmes."

"You say that, Captain, as if you weren't a spesh yourself!"

"I am. But there's a difference between a limited ability for love, with an enhanced sense of responsibility, and the cold intellect demonstrated by Mr. Peter C-the-Forty-Fourth Valke . . . a.k.a. Sherlock Holmes. You are not nearly as dumb as you put on, Jenny. Why do you play his games?"

There was no doubt. Jenny's eyes were aglow with genuine interest.

"An astounding conclusion, Alex. Well . . ."

She sat down in the armchair. Then asked, "Would you happen to have a cigarette for me, and a drop of whiskey?"

"Of course."

"But not too much!" Jenny warned him quickly. "I have the original reaction to alcohol—I get intoxicated and start acting silly!"

Alex poured a little glass for himself, and a quarter-glass for Dr. Watson. Extended a hand with two packs of cigarettes, one from Quicksilver Pit and one from New Ukraine. The girl picked the Quicksilver Pit tobacco.

"Those cigarettes aren't as good," Alex cautioned. "I'm afraid they're chemically synthesized."

"Uh, same difference . . . but I haven't tried this kind."

Dr. Watson lit her cigarette, touched the whiskey glass to her lips. She then ardently drew in the smoke.

"I'm actually a medical doctor, Alex. And my name really is Jenny Watson. I'm from Zodiac originally."

"So what are you doing in Holmes's company?"

"Is this an official interrogation, Captain?" Dr. Watson smirked. "Keep in mind you're trying to interrogate a legal medical expert and a class-II assistant detective!"

"Yes, well . . . I can't get into any more trouble than I'm already in."

Jenny glanced at him with admiration.

"You are an odd one, Captain. I was working at Zodiac's central military hospital. All the usual stuff—sunburns, injuries, tumors, AIDS, head colds . . . But one day we admitted Sherlock Holmes . . . Peter C-the-Forty-Fourth Valke. You can sneer at him all you want, but he really is a great detective. His playing Holmes may seem phony, but believe me, it's a genuine passion. He has found himself a prototype that is almost devoid of emotion, but at the same time respected all over the world. When we met, he . . . considered it a sign of fate, perhaps? Holmes urged me to take the legal medical expert certification courses and become his companion. He was ready to meet any of my conditions. He could have, of course, requested a cloned companion, but finding a real Dr. Watson apparently touched him deeply."

"You have a way with words," said Alex with a sly smile, and drank off some whiskey.

"It's a habit. You see, Captain, I'm trying to succeed in the fields of journalism and literature. And being Sherlock Holmes's companion is a very, very useful experience!"

"But you play along to get along, Dr. Watson. You're so much smarter than you let on."

The girl smiled.

"That's just a little game of my own. I'm sure C-the-Forty-Fourth can see that."

"I'm not so sure."

"But you won't tell him that, right?"

"Of course not." Alex shook his head. "So you're a writer . . ."

"What's so funny about that?" asked Jenny defiantly.

"It's not that, really. It's just that, to a spesh, the whole notion of changing one's line of work sounds really odd. To be a medical doctor and, it seems to me, a good one at that, but still want to change careers . . ."

Jenny shrugged.

"Writers, artists, politicians—those careers don't lend themselves to specialization. Anyone can choose to do them."

"Politician-speshes do exist!"

"Oh, give me a break, Alex! There have been attempts, but they all failed. On my planet, for instance, there is only one functioning politician-spesh, Leon Nizinkin. Seems to be a great specialist by all parameters. Has all the morality adjustments necessary for a politician. Jacks up the crowd in a blink of an eye, masterfully dissembles any emotions, easily switches from one party to another at opportune moments. And yet—no notable achievements whatsoever. In the final analysis, politics has become just a way he earns his living. And to pour out his heart, he writes history books. Wonderful ones, mind you! So, a number of professions have yet to yield to specialization."

"Does all this mean that your interest in Holmes is purely utilitarian? You're collecting material for future use?"

"Far from it!" cried Dr. Watson angrily. "Yes, the cases are interesting. But we actually do defend the innocent, stand up for justice in the Empire. That is just as important for me!"

"I can tell by your scar . . ."

Jenny made a wry face.

"I deliberately don't have it removed. It's like . . . a baptism of fire."

"I'd remove it, if I were you. Women shouldn't be proud of their battle wounds. Without the tooth marks, you'd be much more attractive."

Now Dr. Watson was looking at him with mild apprehension. Shook her head, got up. Forcefully pressed her unfinished cigarette into the ashtray.

"Thank you for the whiskey. I hope you're not guilty, Captain."

Alex closed the door behind her and stood still for a few moments, smiling.

It seemed he had been able to shock Holmes's loyal companion. But why?

Could it really be that there had been something unspeshlike in his words? Alex himself thought he was behaving the way he usually did.

And however trivial that conversation might have been—just over twenty yards away from the disfigured corpse of the Zzygou, on the eve of a bloody galactic war—Alex Romanov enjoyed the memory.

CHAPTER 2.

"I'm not in a laughing mood," said Alex.

Edgar got up grudgingly. He had been sitting on the back of a dragon, a golden-hued dragon; its wings sprawled out on the flat roof of the palace. Maybe the Sovereign had decided to fly around a bit, surveying his seemingly limitless virtual realm. Or maybe he was just visiting one of his toys.

The dragon turned its head, throwing a hateful, hazy look at Alex. In the corner of its eye, a lump of dry brown pus had congealed. Edgar must have been neglecting his flocks . . . although he didn't seem to deny them food. The dragon exuded the heavy, thick odor of raw meat and also, for some reason, of chewed grass.

As the boy came down the monster's back—the dragon raised its scales, forming a kind of stairway—Alex waited patiently. But as soon as Edgar stepped onto the roof and opened his mouth to unleash another indignant tirade, Alex stretched his arm and covered the boy's lips with his hand.

"Be quiet a minute."

The dragon roared in outrage, but Edgar waved his hand, and the reptile fell silent.

"I'll ask you again. What can you do to help in this situation?"

"Nothing!" Edgar took a step back. "You're the one who disconnected the inner cameras. I had no idea the Zzygou got whacked!"

"Could Kim have done it?"

"No," said Edgar firmly. "No way. In self-defense, yes, but it's unlikely the Zzygou was any threat to her. To defend the crystal I live in—the same objections apply. Besides, a fighter-spesh simply kills the opponent, without making a gory circus out of it."

"What if she wanted to deflect suspicion away from herself?"

"Good grief! If Kim had needed to kill the Zzygou, she would have removed all the witnesses. By now she would be down on the planet, with me in her stomach pocket, and your *Mirror* would be rushing full-speed to the nearest star."

"Your emotions blocker . . . is it capable of inducing mental changes that could make a person turn to murder?"

"But you're telling me you haven't given it to Kim!"

"I took some myself."

Edgar stopped short. He shook his head.

"I'm such a fool . . . so that was your goal all along?"

"No. But you talked about love with too much enthusiasm. Besides, I have to test what I offer to my crewmembers."

"And how are you feeling?"

"No change. Except . . ."

"Except?" Edgar was intrigued.

"Except I've stopped enjoying my confluence with the ship. It's like it died."

"I see."

The boy paced excitedly along the edge of the roof. He spat down and laughed upon hearing someone curse below. Turned to Alex again.

"That's exactly the way it should be. The artificially imposed emotions are the first to disappear. And your own emotions . . . you have to work them out yourself."

"So tell me, could the blocker have made me kill the Zzygou?"

"Did you kill her?"

"Of course not. But maybe I don't remember my own actions?"

"Nonsense. That's impossible. The Zzygou was whacked by someone from your team. But not Kim. And not you, if you're not lying to me right now."

"Are you sure, Edward Garlitsky?"

The boy froze, his hands behind his back.

"Let's be frank here," said Alex bluntly. "Your little fairy tale might have been enough to convince Kim. But not me. You aren't the person you've been claiming to be."

"What makes you say that?"

"The first problem—why would anyone take the colossal trouble of raising a full-fledged intelligence in virtual reality?"

"They wanted to . . ."

"Shut up. Second—genetic constructor is not a profession that lends itself to specialization. It's a coincidence of mental development, a mixture of intuition, a certain special bent of mind, and a goddamn talent! It would be impossible to transfer a child's mind into a crystal to make him a genetic engineer."

Edgar forced a laugh.

"Third," continued Alex obstinately. "No one has ever even heard of an emotions blocker. It could only be created by a genius of Garlitsky's level. By a person working at the very deepest level of specialization research."

A shadow of satisfaction appeared on Edgar's face. He said nothing.

"Fourth. You're imitating an earthly world in your crystal. Plants, landscapes, surroundings. That's logical for a person who was born and spent most of his life on Earth. But not at all for a little boy from Edem."

"Damn," cried Edgar earnestly. "What a stupid goof!"

"Five. You don't make a convincing teenager."

"And why is that?"

"The geishas around you," said Alex softly, "would be mature, voluptuous women. And never the same age as you. Your image would not reflect your actual appearance—you'd be walking around in the handsome, powerful body of a grown man. No one even remembers such a thing as glasses for vision correction! There are glasses as an accessory, and there are glasses for sun protection. But vision gets corrected during the prenatal period! In both speshes and naturals. A boy Edgar could not be myopic and wouldn't wear glasses in the virtual world."

"You've convinced me." The boy threw his hands up in surrender. Took off his glasses, tossed them down from the roof. "Well . . . but what made you think I was the geneticist Garlitsky, who died a hundred and fifty years ago?"

"Immediately after Garlitsky's death, the center of developing genetic technologies moved over to Edem. All the main specializations are now being developed there. So either a new genius of your level had appeared," Alex consciously dropped in another note of flattery, "or Garlitsky's mind continued to function. On Edem. Why Edem, by the way?"

"Earth's legislation back then was highly distrustful of genetic engineering. And virtual minds had no rights whatsoever."

"And look at all the rights you got on Edem!"

The boy's face grimaced as in pain. Alex quickly added, "Why don't we continue this discussion in different surroundings? I have a little time . . . and I'd like to find out a few things."

"All right, Mr. Pilot." The boy raised his hand. The dragon roared piteously, and the fairy tale world vanished.

Now it was an ordinary room, furnished in a style of at least a hundred years ago. Amorphous plasticate chairs, picture windows, a waterfall chandelier whose sparkling streams vanished without a trace right at the level of the floor.

Edgar, too, had changed.

Alex looked at the heavyset old man sitting in front of him and nodded.

"I recognize you. That's the way you looked in the films."

"I can turn totally decrepit . . . the way I looked when I left the human world," said Edward Garlitsky ironically. "But it's not a very appetizing sight. What is it you want to know, pilot-spesh Alex Romanov?"

"Were you really incarcerated?"

"Yes." Edward's face contorted with emotion. "Those scumbags . . . those low-life bastards! I was stupid—I didn't start growing myself a new body immediately. I was thrilled by the idea of first constructing the greatest body-shell ever and then taking up residence in it. To bring forth . . . the beginning of a new race. Of super-humans, not the wretched speshes of today . . . I beg your pardon."

"I'm not offended." Alex sat down in one of the armchairs, which bubbled beneath him, as it searched for the most comfortable shape to take. After a brief hesitation, Edward moved closer to him.

"I was going to make a universalist-spesh. To combine all the best features that *could* be combined in a human body. I would have been human—outwardly. But I would have been able to breathe underwater and function for hours in vacuum, pilot spaceships and write poetry, repair kitchen stools and manage a gluon reactor. I wanted to squeeze the human genome for absolutely everything it could possibly give! And take what it couldn't from other earthly and extraterrestrial life forms!"

"And that was why they imprisoned you?"

"Yes. No one wanted that. It scared them. I had come up with a system of surgical recombination of the genome, and I was very close to achieving a result. I even ordered them to start growing the first body . . . and that was when they stopped me. I was tried . . . posthumously. And sentenced to be incarcerated in the crystal indefinitely to do socially beneficial work. The Emperor personally banned the creation of super-humans. And I . . . I was ordered to work on new specializations for the Empire."

"How could they order you around? Did they threaten to destroy the crystal?"

"Alex . . ." The geneticist laughed. "You cannot imagine what a multifaceted hell you can organize in virtual space. I could show you . . . but you'd jump out into the real world immediately. And I had nowhere to go! They would hook my gel-crystal up to another, more powerful one—it would take over . . . and a nightmare would start. I don't know who they had hired to do it. But he had a fabulous imagination."

"I believe you," said Alex.

Edward threw up his hands.

"Believe it or not. That's the truth. I broke down. I agreed to live in the virtual world until I received a special pardon from the Emperor . . . and keep building new speshes. I was thinking up pilots, fighters, gardeners, and hairdressers . . . At times, I would feel I was losing my mind. I tried to spite the customers . . . have you ever met a street sweeper-spesh?"

"Of course."

"That's not a human being. It's a parody of a human being! Hands touching the ground, fingers covered with fur to play the role of brooms! A chest-pocket for garbage! A soft, quiet voice and a kindly disposition. And despite all this, the intellect is left completely intact!"

"I remember, everyone respected our street sweeper very much," said Alex. "He was so kind, so personable. Really loved the kids, gave us rides around the yard up on his shoulders . . ."

"Oh, Lord! So even that little detail worked?" Edward burst out laughing. "The street sweeper I knew as a kid was always chasing us off, so I endowed my street sweeper-spesh with a special affection for children . . . The very idea was meant as a mockery! But they put it into production."

"So who exactly is Kim?"

"My salvation." Edward immediately got serious. "Twenty years ago I managed to . . . in a very sly way—I had willy-nilly become an experienced hacker—to get onto the galactic web. I was searching for opposing trends. Searching for people who might be able to help. Searching for access to public opinion. Then I realized that there was no way out. No opposition existed—if you didn't count some insane religious sects and a few planetary governments that had recently grown in power. But there was no one who could help me, no one to go against the Imperial powers and the Edemian parliament. So I decided to create a person who would help me escape. It was impossible to work with the masses, but when an order was placed for an agent-spesh, an eternally charming, clever girl with special capabilities . . . I played around with her genes a little bit. My work was being closely watched, but nobody caught on this time. They even thanked me for completing the assignment so masterfully. But I waited till the girl grew up a little, and then started meeting her in some virtual worlds. Made up this touching legend for her . . . I love Kim very much, Alex. I don't even know who she is to me—my daughter, my sister, the woman I love . . ."

"You created Kim to *suit yourself*?" asked Alex.

"Of course. I had no illusion that she'd be faithful to me forever. I had time enough to rid myself of the ancient moral attitude . . . almost. According to my original plan, Kim would rescue me when already a grown woman, with sound savings and solid covers. But the lab was being modernized, the communication lines were changed, and I realized I was about to lose contact with the girl. So I had to improvise, but it turned out very well. I took over the controls of one of the service robots. It carried the gel-crystal out and set fire to the laboratory. The crystal was considered destroyed, when in reality Kim was taking care of it. But then almighty chance came into play. Kim's mother caught her with the crystal. Realized it wasn't just a collection of sex entertainments or romantic stories. You know the rest. We ran away."

"And you took the risk of trusting your life to a girl on her very first foray into the galaxy? Who knows what all could have happened to her!"

"Like what?" Edward shrugged. "Yes, she is attractive! But she is also a fighter-spesh with a whole lot of other capabilities. If someone tried to rape her . . . I wouldn't envy him! Even if she were tied up hand and foot." The smile that appeared on Edward's face was the unpleasant smile of a person who knows something unknown to anyone else.

Alex frowned.

"So you deliberately made her this way? Smart, beautiful, sexy, and at the same time a merciless killer?"

"And what's wrong with that, Alex? These are the things the Empire lives on. Every government creates the citizens it wants. Every large firm with serious intentions for the future puts in an order for speshes of the type it needs. Parents, choosing the future for their kids, pay for this or that specialization. How are my actions any worse? I worked really hard for Kim. So the fact that she's rescuing me is . . . well, a kind of natural gratitude, perhaps!"

"If she were rescuing you knowingly! If you weren't feeding her all these lies!"

"The time will come, and she will learn the truth."

Of course. Alex was silent. Nodded.

"Maybe. But you were wrong."

"Time will tell," replied Edward wearily.

"And you're sure that her mind is stable? To combine a hetaera and a fighter in the same consciousness is already at the limits of possibility."

"I know the potentialities of the human mind better than you do." Edward squinted. "Trust me, Kim couldn't have gone mad and disemboweled the Zzygou . . . that's what you're talking about, right?"

"Yes. I am trying to check out a number of possibilities, to exclude the utterly impossible."

"Aren't you taking on the work of a detective-spesh, my friend?" The geneticist laughed. "God . . . it's nice to talk with you this way . . . sincerely and kindly!"

Alex had no reaction to these words. He just sat there, thinking. Most probably, Edward wasn't lying. He had created Kim O'Hara to suit himself: as a bodyguard, as a source for his means of existence and, ultimately, as a lover. It was improbable that a galactic war had been a part of his plans.

People suppose, but it's chance that disposes. Still, the girl's unstable psyche could have skipped a beat . . . no matter how sure Edward was of the opposite.

Alex asked, "What would you conjecture?"

"The murderer?"

"Yes, of course."

"I'm not a detective. If a spesh is aboard, and a clone of Peter

Valke, at that"—the geneticist threw up his hands—"all I can do is watch and admire his work."

"Is he really that good?"

"Magnificent. I worked on that specialization for more than twenty years. Went through a lot of setbacks, but the result exceeded all expectations."

"So far Mr. Holmes hasn't impressed me all that favorably. A collection of standard magic tricks and enhanced sensory organs."

Edward just smiled.

"The very existence of the Empire is at stake here." Alex tried again to appeal to reason. "You probably won't survive this, either. Finding the murderer is vitally important to us."

"The Empire against the Zzygou?" The geneticist sounded utterly indifferent. "The poor little bees don't have the slightest chance."

"Why?"

Edward sighed.

"Good Lord, a pilot-spesh should show a bit more intelligence! Everything is there in plain sight! The murderer, and the cause, and the trump card up the sleeve—the card the Imperial cabinet is going to produce at the right moment!"

His voice rang with absolute certainty. But for some reason it only frightened Alex.

"What are you talking about? Is there a magic weapon that ordinary people don't know about?"

"You could put it that way." Edward pensively rubbed the bridge of his nose. "No. I won't explain anything. You have all the necessary data to figure out what is going on. And so does the detective.

So don't worry about the Empire's fate . . . and get ready to enjoy the show."

"How can you call the death of a sentient being a show? And the inevitable death of someone from my crew?"

"I'm tired, Alex," said the geneticist bluntly. "Drop in to see me in twenty-four hours, okay? That is, of course, if Sherlock Holmes hasn't solved the puzzle by then. Goodbye for now!"

He got up and lazily walked toward the wall. It trembled, opening up before him.

"Edward!" Alex shouted.

To no avail. The wall reassembled, hiding the geneticist from view. Inside his own crystal, he was lord and master . . . until a more powerful device took over the controls.

"You don't know any more than I do," he said out loud. "Even less . . ."

What had he missed?

Or, rather—what was he reluctant to notice?

In any case, he wouldn't get an answer here.

Alex left the virtual space.

Sherlock Holmes had recommended that the crew not leave their quarters until a special permission was issued. And a detective-spesh's recommendation was, in fact, an order. Even for the captain.

Glancing now and then at the outer-space screen, where the *Lucifer* hovered languidly, Alex tuned in to the news from Zodiac.

And, of course, immediately ran into the news about the Zzygou.

The actual cause of the conflict hadn't appeared in the commonly available information net. There were only indistinct references to an incident that had led to the death, on the Empire's territory, of a member of the Zzygou ruling clan. Apologies had already been issued in the name of the Emperor, along with promises of just punishment of the perpetrators, the organization of a fancy funeral, and reparations. In general, from any human's point of view, the Zzygou's rage was absolutely unfounded . . . after all, accidents did happen in the universe, and rushing to war over the death of a single sentient being—it was sheer madness!

And that was what frightened Alex. The Empire was getting ready for war. The Empire was creating background propaganda. Of course, the alien races would learn the unedited version of the conflict, but . . . the belligerent Cepheideans would be happy with any kind of trouble with the Zzygou, and the Bronins most probably wouldn't consider even the most gruesome murder as reason for war.

Perhaps the alien races were precisely the cause for Edward's optimism? Maybe he was betting that humanity would quickly be joined by some allies?

That was naive. Allies always appeared on time, all right. The time when the opponent's territory was being redistributed.

The worst thing appeared to be the fact that both sides had already sustained some casualties.

The incident had happened on Volga, a poor and austere planet whose inhabitants—mostly Jews and Slavs—earned a meager living by arduous and ceaseless labor. The planet had essentially only one large city, near the spaceport, and a single industrial enterprise—a fuel refinery. The rest of the habitable surface of the planet was taken up by shallow swamps, which were farmed by the planet's inhabitants.

Volga had simply been unlucky—a small Zzygou trading vessel had happened to be passing the planet's space.

The vessel wasn't a recent model. Designed for nonmilitary use, it was not at all suited for action against a planet's surface. But the Others turned upon the planet with kamikaze-like determination. Had they targeted the spaceport's defense stations, fate might have actually smiled on them. But the Zzygou seemed to have gone insane. They started randomly shooting at the city from their low-powered plasma cannons, and in forty-two seconds were shot down by return fire. Strange as it may seem, the Zzygou weren't even able to drop their burning ship onto the city. Instead it crashed in one of the uninhabited outskirts, where it quickly vanished in the deep muck of the swamp.

A short newscast from the planet was full of raw and unedited provincial emotion. A very young and attractive Jewish girl was giving a heated account of the damage sustained by the city and pointing out punctured roofs, mangled roads, and ruined buildings. The worst damage was caused to "the clinic of the kind Dr. Lubarsky," the planet's only dental-services center. Dr. Lubarsky himself, an imposing dentist-spesh with a crew cut, was standing in front of a blazing building, giving a colorful account of how, amid the sudden flames and shaking walls, he had rescued a lady-patient, carrying her to safety . . . he hadn't even had a chance to finish cleaning a complex, twisted root canal. . . . Upset as he was, the dentist lost control of his movements—his right thumb and index finger formed a "claw" and started jerking and clicking involuntarily, as if searching for a bad tooth.

But the dentist turned out to be lucky. The destroyed clinic had probably been insured. As for the bookstore, which belonged to Yuri C-the-Second Semetsky, it hadn't merely collapsed, but had buried its owner under the rubble. The clone's spouse, sobbing uncontrollably, was incoherently telling a sympathetically nodding reporter what a good man C-the-Second Semetsky had been. Way better than C-the-First, with whom she had also been acquainted . . . He was so fond of trout. He had such a beautiful way of imitating the call of the swamp chaffinch . . . Believed in reincarnation and assured everyone that he remembered his previous lives, and each one of them had ended tragically . . . it was as if he had foretold his own fate . . . But whatever might have happened in Yuri's former lives, his present life still had a chance, however slim—the rescue workers were tirelessly digging through the ruins in hopes that the poor man may have been protected by a layer of books, before being buried under concrete panels. The words of a rescuer-spesh also sounded encouraging—he heard a rhythmical tapping under the ruins. Perhaps it was only water dripping from some broken pipes, but everyone was eager to believe that it was the beating of Semetsky's valiant heart . . . Alex turned the news off.

"What a farce," he said sharply.

The Zzygou trading vessel hadn't, of course, had any chance whatsoever. It either had no female aboard, or the female hadn't been able to calm the crew down. It was amazing that they had even managed to destroy a few buildings.

But one fact remained—the Swarm and the Empire had already engaged in an armed conflict.

The door signal beeped.

"Open," Alex ordered. He was getting ready to see Watson or Holmes, but it was Janet who entered the cabin.

Never since they'd met had Alex seen the Ebenian woman so content and aglow with such charm. Janet's appearance couldn't be described as beautiful, after all—five specializations had made her facial features too strange. But now she seemed to be radiating a light from within.

"Janet?" Alex went off to the bar, returned with a bottle of wine. Poured her a glassful.

"Thanks, that certainly won't hurt. I just had a talk with our friend Holmes." Janet lowered herself into an armchair. Looked sideways at the neuro-terminal that lay on the table. "You were having some fun?"

"A bit . . . So what did Holmes tell you?"

"That everyone is a suspect. But I . . ."—Janet gave a blinding smile, raised her glass in mock salutation—"am the *prime* suspect."

"And that's what made you so happy?"

Janet shook her head, regaining her seriousness for a brief moment.

"Not at all, Alex. I'm not prone to masochism. And I don't find these accusations pleasant in the least. After all, I didn't kill the Zzygou."

For a few seconds, they were looking into each other's eyes.

"Really and truly, I am not the one who killed her," said Janet. "I have sworn an oath to you. What made me happy is something else."

"What?"

"The war! The Zzygou won't stop now. The Empire will have to engage in the war."

"Janet Ruello," said Alex slowly, "what you're saying is monstrous. The war will cost the Empire billions of lives."

"Oh, please." Janet shook her head. "That's complete nonsense. Our illustrious detective-spesh is of the same opinion as you, but he is wrong. The Zzygou will be defeated with little bloodshed."

"But how the hell . . .?"

Janet gave him a puzzled look.

"You really don't get it? Alex, my home planet hasn't been demolished. Eben is sealed in an isolation field, but removing it is a matter of just a few minutes . . . if the Emperor gives the order."

Alex gasped. And Janet continued calmly:

"Our planet cannot be measured by ordinary criteria. Trust me—I know. There, under the eggshell, the Church is still alive, and the patriarchs, as well as most of the fleet. New ships are still being built. New weapons are still being created. And our people feel no hatred for the Empire. If the field is removed, Eben will rejoin the Empire's ranks. And believe me, there is still nothing in the galaxy to match the power of our *Liturgy* cruisers or our *Anathema* raiders! Your Emperor . . ."—Alex noticed this accidental—or was it deliberate?—slip of the tongue—"is only a little kid. But the Imperial Council has more than just idiots. If war becomes imminent, they will remove the quarantine from Eben. Then the Zzygou will be doomed. I've estimated . . . we will lose from five to fifteen planets before the fighting moves to Zzygou territory. Closer to five than to fifteen. And if the South-Sea lab on Eben has already finished working on the gluon net, the ships of the Others will burn upon exiting the hyper-channels."

"Janet . . . do you understand what you've been saying?" Alex whispered. It was clear now what Edward had been hinting at. Earth really did have a super-weapon hidden away, a weapon everyone had long forgotten.

"I hope I've calmed you down!"

"Janet, you have just signed your own death sentence! Now you're not only the prime suspect, but all the clues point to you!"

"But I didn't kill the Zzygou," she repeated stubbornly. "I had no idea her social status was so high. But . . . if my death serves to liberate Eben, I'm ready to die. By any means the Others may choose to devise."

"Good Lord, Janet, what are you raving about?" Alex lunged toward her, grabbed her by the shoulders. "Even if Eben is liberated and the Zzygou defeated—what next?"

"We'll see."

"No need to see. I'll tell you what will happen. If, with Eben's help, the Empire manages to destroy one race, all the rest of them will prick up their ears. A common anti-human front will be formed . . . or a coalition. You don't really think that the Empire will be able to stand up to the combined forces of ten alien races?"

"The races of the Others are disjointed. All have their bones to pick with one another."

"Don't worry, they'll temporarily forget those. Eben's ideology and politics were at one point the cause of tension in the whole galaxy. Even the crazy Bronins had never made it their goal to purge all space of alien life forms. Eben as part of the Empire is the alarm signal for everyone!"

"So then, you think that a whole world, equal in power to the combined forces of Earth and Edem, should remain isolated for all eternity?" Janet spoke calmly, but dry bitterness broke through now and then in her voice. "Yes! I want it to be liberated! I dream of seeing my first-born again. I would like to go visit the graves of my parents and pay my respects to them, according to our custom. To see my old house . . . to visit my first teacher . . . to call on my first lover . . . You all consider Eben a cesspool of evil, when we've been humanity's shield for hundreds of years! A weapons smithy, a military academy, a factory, and a base . . . everything the Empire needed. Do you know how beautiful Eben is? At least, those places where nature can still be found . . . We raped our own home planet, turned ourselves into soldiers . . . and all *that* we did for the sake of humanity! Because the Empire needed ships, ships, and more ships! And soldiers, and channel stations, and new kinds of armaments . . ."

Speshes were not prone to hysterics. But five specializations were probably too much for a human mind. Alex sensed that Janet was ready to burst into sobs.

How weird and absurd that was—here was a woman whose planet was used to scare little kids, whose profession was to torture the Others, and he couldn't feel the socially prescribed condescending sympathy for her. He couldn't, because he was ready to sign his name to every single word she had been saying.

Except that if Eben were to be liberated, a pan-galactic war would be unleashed.

"We became what humanity required," Janet continued. "We were the Empire's shield and its sword. And when we were no longer needed, they locked us away in a closet. To wait for better times."

"For worse times."

"What's the difference? We were struck from the ranks of humanity. Yes, we had our own independent policies, but that didn't happen overnight! We . . . we were betrayed, as soon as the Others raised a howl!"

"Your people refused to change, Janet. When wars became a thing of the past, your people didn't want to move on."

"Were we ever offered that option?" The woman tossed the hair off her forehead and looked defiantly at Alex. "Did anyone ever give us even the slightest chance? All we had was an ultimatum, and the united fleet moving towards Eben. That was it. There was no time to look for compromises. And so . . . forgive me, Alex, but I'm happy we are at war! My home planet will be free."

Alex was silent for a moment.

"And still—it wasn't you?"

"It wasn't me."

"Then who?"

A shadow of a smile ran through her face.

"I think I know who it was. But I won't tell, Alex."

"But you must tell!"

"No. Sharing suspicions isn't part of my contract. A detective is aboard, let him puzzle it out."

"You've sworn an oath to me," Alex reminded her.

"I've sworn not to kill the Zzygou. I never swore to look for their killer."

"And if I were to demand another oath . . ."

"No."

Alex threw up his hands. Janet's voice was dangerously high with tension. She was balancing on the edge of hysteria. But he was sure her hysterical fit would not lead to a concession.

"You're wrong, Janet. Believe me, all this will lead to tragedy for Eben . . . and for the whole human race."

"Maybe," she rejoined immediately. "Nevertheless, it's a chance."

"Thank you for telling me the truth about yourself, at least."

"Did I narrow your circle of suspects?" Janet laughed, calming down. "Alex . . . don't attempt your own investigation. You can talk to everyone, and every single person will tell you they didn't kill the Zzygou . . ."

"Why?"

"Because." Janet got up. "I'm going back to my cabin, Captain. You can come visit me, if you want. We can play 'sweet-sweet sugar and bitter chocolate.'"

Alex didn't recall any such game. Well, Janet would probably be a great instructor, and the game—a fun way to pass the time.

If only he had the slightest wish to have sex now . . .

"I'll think about it," he said, evasively.

As Sherlock Holmes and his loyal companion moved from cabin to cabin, Alex had visitor after visitor. A psychologist might say that, subconsciously, the crew still perceived Alex as a father figure. A strict and strong one, whose duty was to protect them.

That was reassuring, in a way.

After Janet left, Kim dropped in. The girl was beside herself with rage. She had also been informed that she was the prime suspect. It seemed that what had offended Kim the most was the fact that the hero of her favorite books turned out to be such a distrustful, dry old stick. She cursed—clumsily, but very diligently—telling Alex in minute detail of her conversation with Holmes.

"Can you imagine? He said I was so desperate to get out of flying back to Edem that I whacked the Zzygou! That I was the only one who knew their anatomy well enough and was strong enough to overpower the Other! It's like using a ray gun to kill flies!"

"I know of a couple of planets where flies actually deserve that kind of treatment," Alex noted. He pulled the girl onto his lap, and for the next few minutes they caressed each other in silence. Kim snorted, murmured something to the effect that she wasn't a little kid anymore and didn't go for such silliness, but she did visibly relax.

"But you didn't kill the poor Zzygou, right?" Alex said in a half-questioning tone, still caressing Kim.

"Of course not! And if I were to kill her, I wouldn't do it *that* way. . . ." Kim winced. "It was probably Janet. She's an executioner-spesh, and she hates the Others."

"Janet says otherwise."

"Then it wasn't her," quickly agreed the girl. "She wouldn't lie."

"Then who?"

"You're trying to guess? But that's the detective's job!"

"Kim, everything is very, very complicated. If everyone thinks about what has happened, it might save billions of lives."

"You aren't a detective. You aren't designed to investigate!" Kim looked at him in surprise. She took away his hand, which had gotten a bit carried away. "You're a master-pilot!"

"Yes, I am a pilot. I'm used to operating under a multitude of dynamic factors that influence each other as well as the ship. I have accelerated reactions, enhanced memory, and reinforced logical capacity. And I am, like any pilot, specially adapted for the job of spaceship captain. That includes the basics of psychology, the ability to sense other people's moods and guide their behavior. Why can't I try on the role of a detective?"

"Because you aren't a detective-spesh!"

"Kim . . ." He lightly kissed her lips. "Not everything can be pre-programmed."

She was silent, alarmed, looking him straight in the eye.

"Then why am *I* not trying to investigate the murder?"

"Because you think you're a fighter-spesh."

"I'm not a fighter." The girl pressed her lips together tightly. "I can feel that. I'm not just a fighter!"

"Right." Alex nodded approvingly. "You're more than a fighter. You're a spy. A terrorist. An agent provocateur."

"How do you know?"

"I just know. Your job is to be involved in the highest circles of society. And, if necessary, to work a miner's hack in a POW camp, serve in the military, serve at a brothel, do lab experiments. You're capable of adapting to any situation. You can become almost anybody. Including a detective, I suppose."

"I don't want to!"

"Why not, Kim? Your specialization is unique. Model-speshes, singer-speshes, strategist-speshes . . . anyone you look at—none of them comes close to your specialization!"

"That just means loneliness."

The sound of her voice startled Alex. She seemed to have aged instantly, grown decades older.

"Any unique specialist is lonely. You'll get to like your work. You will enjoy it, trust me. The real thing, not just what you have here."

"I don't want to, Alex!" She hugged him tightly. "Why did you tell me all this? Why?"

"You had to find out sooner or later."

"But I like flying on the ship. I like being with you!"

"Well, no one can forbid you to work as an ordinary fighter."

"Now that I know what I'm meant to be?"

"Yes, even now." Alex didn't look away. "Especially now."

"I don't understand," said Kim piteously.

"You will."

He didn't answer any more of her questions. And Kim didn't persist for long. She didn't know the "sweet-sweet sugar and bitter chocolate" game. It had probably been invented on Eben. But another game Kim suggested, "kitten claws," turned out to be quite enjoyable.

Generalov barged into the cabin while Kim was in the shower.

"Would you like some wine?" Alex offered, tightening his bathrobe. A half-empty bottle of real Earthly Vouvray stood on the table.

"Something stronger!" Puck roared.

Alex bent over the bar. He fussed for a while with glasses and bottles, then poured the navigator some brandy.

"So, Holmes has called you the prime suspect, eh?"

"Yes! Everyone already knows?" Generalov shook his head. Roared with sardonic laughter. "Arguments of steel! Tough as titanium!"

"And what are they?"

"Well! I'm the only natural on board, you see! As well as the only homo!"

"Is that what he called you?"

"No, this Holmes character, this cloned jerk, used an even more insulting expression!" Generalov punched the air and poured himself some more brandy. "You tell me, Captain, how are my tastes in any way connected to the murder of the Zzygou?"

"I have no idea," confessed Alex.

"It turns out, I was trying to make life hell for C-the-Third and the lady-speshes!"

"Janet and Kim?"

"Yes! I killed the Zzygou to ruin that nasty clone's career, and was hoping to dump the murder on one of the women, since I hate them!"

"You hate them?"

"Me?" Generalov goggled. "Captain, no one treats women more tenderly and gently than we gays! Everyone knows this . . . except detectives, as it turns out! Holmes cursed me out like a drunk miner from some provincial planet!"

"You have my sympathies, Puck."

"Thank you, Captain . . . But listen, how can we possibly count on justice if the investigation is conducted by a cloned idiot?"

"Puck, you are incensed at being discriminated against

because of individual peculiarities, and yet you yourself sound a bit . . . biased."

"Being a clone is not an individual peculiarity, but a rotten core!" said the enraged navigator. "And I have just been convinced once and for all! While our C-the-Third may be just a fool who couldn't keep his wards out of harm's way, Holmes is an aggressive, noisy fool who is a danger to society! Now I'm convinced—war is unavoidable!"

The sound of running water ceased, and the sanitary block's door opened slightly. Kim looked out from behind it. Droplets of water glistened on her shoulders. The girl had wrapped her wet hair in a towel, turbanlike.

"Oh . . . hi, Puck!"

"Hi, sweetie!" Generalov looked sideways at her. "Have you heard what I'm accused of?"

"Just a sec . . . Alex, I threw my clothes into the wash, is that all right?"

"Well, you can't sit in the bathroom for a quarter of an hour." The pilot smiled. "Come on out."

Kim darted over to the bed, sat down, and wrapped herself in a blanket. Smiled cheerfully at Alex.

"I have nothing but good feelings for women!" announced Puck. "And for lady-speshes as well! My own mother is a doctor-spesh! As for clones, I don't like them, but I wouldn't kill the Zzygou to spite them!"

He poured himself some more brandy. Alex thought for a second, then moved the bottle away.

"Yes, thank you . . ." Generalov sighed. "I'm really sort of . . . but just imagine, Captain, for thirty minutes, he threw insults in my face!"

"Don't be mad at Holmes," said Alex. "He doesn't really mean what he says."

"Then what *does* he mean?"

"He's just trying to provoke all the suspects. He deliberately pushes our buttons, works our inhibitions and biases. So he can watch our reactions."

"Asshole!" exhaled Puck with feeling.

"Not at all, actually. This is an extreme situation, so it calls for appropriate methods. If reliable truth drugs existed, or torture with easily controlled coercive force, or any other valid methods for express-interrogations, Holmes would now be using them. He may even use some unreliable ones, if he is left with no other choice."

"Controlled torture?" Puck didn't understand.

"Of course. The murder has obviously been committed by a professional. He could withstand both drugs and ordinary torture. And very strong coercion would make an innocent person implicate himself. But only convincing proof would actually satisfy the Zzygou."

"Good Lord, what is the world coming to!" Generalov cried melodramatically.

"The world is coming to the edge of an abyss. So, Puck, you really didn't kill the Zzygou?"

"No!"

"And you don't know who the murderer is?"

Generalov thought for a while.

"I thought it was you, Captain."

"Why me?" Alex was stunned.

"The act required way too much of a sense of responsibility. Only someone who is ready to make decisions for other people could have committed it. No other spesh aboard this ship has the directive to make general decisions. Only the captain."

"And you, since you're a natural!" cried out Kim.

"Yes." This time Generalov didn't get angry. "And me. But I didn't kill anyone."

Alex thought it over. Reluctantly admitted:

"I haven't tried to look at it from that point of view . . . Yes. It all makes sense. But I didn't kill the Zzygou, either."

"You know what else that . . . clone picked on?"

"What?"

"That I like to walk around the ship in a spacesuit!"

"That's a good point," Alex agreed. "It solves the problem of bloodstains on the clothes."

"But anyone could put on a spacesuit." Puck got up with a sigh. "I should never have signed on to your crew, Captain . . ."

"Everything will be all right, Puck. Innocent people won't get in trouble."

"You have that much confidence in the cloned Holmes?" Generalov asked ironically.

"No. I have confidence in myself."

Paul Lourier showed up in Alex's cabin after both Generalov and Kim had left. Generalov left looking just as tense as when he arrived, but Kim looked much calmer.

"Go ahead, sit down." Alex nodded toward the armchair. "Want some wine?"

Paul nodded wistfully.

"Would Vouvray be all right with you? Or would you like a red, after all?" Alex asked.

"Vouvray'll be fine." Paul took up the glass. He turned it in his hands, then asked, lifting his eyes to look at Alex:

"Captain, do you suspect me in the Zzygou murder, too?"

"And why would *you* be number one on the list?"

Paul frowned.

"So I'm not the only one?"

"Tell me."

"Holmes was alluding to my psychological profile. Well . . . Captain, back at the academy, I really did like pranks . . . but that's all a thing of the past! And there is a difference between hacking into a teacher's computer and slicing up an alien!"

"Yes, Holmes must have really scrambled for evidence there," Alex agreed.

Paul drained his glass. Winced.

"Must not be the best year."

"Probably not," Alex acknowledged. "Don't worry, Paul. Holmes is just provoking you. To watch your reaction to being accused."

"I thought so. He also said I was too decent a young man. That I had too few reasons and opportunities to kill the Zzygou. And that was the most suspicious thing of all!"

Alex burst out laughing.

"Don't worry, no court would ever uphold an accusation based on that kind of reasoning. Especially not the Zzygou. They need ironclad proof."

"So who killed her, Captain?" Paul lowered his voice. "Could it really be . . . Janet?"

"Well, actually, I already know who the killer is." Alex took out his cigarettes, lit one up. "Everything is really kind of simple."

"You already know?" cried the engineer.

"Of course. I'm not sure Holmes knows yet. He's still just watching us and gathering information. But I . . . do know."

"But you're not a detective!"

"So what?"

The youth looked at Alex with admiration. Then asked:

"So, who is it?"

"I won't tell just yet. I have no proof, either. But I will have it. The killer did make a blunder, after all. Now I will let him make the next one, and after that, the Zzygou will have their scapegoat. There won't be a war."

"So it's not Kim or Janet?"

"What makes you say that?"

"Well . . . you said 'he.'"

"I was talking in general. A murderer is a genderless creature." Alex grinned a crooked grin. "Don't try to guess."

"I knew you would protect us, Captain."

"That's my job," said Alex. "All right, Paul. Morrison is on his way. I'll have to hear him out, too. . . ."

"Then the rest have already visited you?" Paul quickly guessed.

"Exactly. Everyone came running to me and complained about Holmes."

Alex took Lourier by the shoulders and softly nudged him toward the door.

"Off you go now. You made your complaint, now let your fellow crewmember do the same."

The door signal beeped again.

Morrison also had to be revived with some cognac. Unlike Janet, the co-pilot was not thrilled with the prospect of war. Unlike Kim, he didn't believe that Alex was capable of protecting him. Unlike Generalov, he wasn't converting his fear into anger. And unlike Lourier, he had real reasons to be afraid of being accused. He was pale as a ghost.

"Xang, things will work out," Alex repeated yet again. "The detective-spesh won't falsely accuse an innocent person. So, if you didn't kill the Zzygou . . ."

"I didn't! Right after my shift was over, I went to bed. I was exhausted!"

"Then you have no reason to worry."

"And I did want to drop by to visit Kim . . ."

"You should have. You'd have an alibi. And so would she."

"I was at her cabin door, but it didn't open."

Alex frowned.

"That's bad."

"I asked Kim later, and she just said she had been fast asleep."

"Nonsense. She's a fighter-spesh. The signal would wake her." Alex winced. Stupid girl . . . Couldn't think of a better lie . . .

Xang's eyes grew wide.

"Kim? Kim did it?!"

Alex just waved this away. "Hold on . . ."

He turned on the computer screen. Quickly sketched a chart, slightly resembling Holmes's data grid, except simpler. Six lines—crewmembers and time dots. He murmured:

"That's why she wasn't worried . . . she has the ace of trumps up her sleeve. So . . . who else has an alibi here?"

"Kim was with someone?" asked Morrison, confused.

"Of course. She was either busy shredding the Zzygou, or having sex with someone."

"No other alternatives?"

"Nope. The girl's too much in love with me. She feels it's her duty to remain faithful, but it's hard for her to challenge the other component of her personality. She needs a healthy variety of sex."

"Alex, have you, by any chance, been specialized as a detective?" Morrison couldn't help asking.

"No, Xang, I haven't. But circumstances force me to be. . . ." Alex nodded contentedly, deleted the chart from his screen. "How wonderful that Generalov is one hundred percent homosexual!"

"I don't get it," the co-pilot admitted.

"Everything is still tangled up," Alex said. "I have to work with the assumption that there is only one terrorist aboard. And that hasn't been proved."

He stretched, throwing a mocking glance at Morrison.

"Unlike you, I have a duty to protect all my crewmembers. Everyone but the murderer . . . that is, if he is a member of the crew. It's hard work."

"Wouldn't want to be a captain . . ."

"Oh, come on! It's interesting. Let's walk over to the recreation lounge, Xang. I'm sure everyone's already there."

"The show goes on . . ." said Morrison despondently. "You have nerves of steel, Captain. Mine seem to be much weaker."

"One false move, and the show will end in the destruction of humanity," said Alex. "Gotta keep my cool despite myself. Let's go. I want to grab a bite to eat."

CHAPTER 3.

They say all people can be divided into two types: those whose appetite increases when they're stressed, and those whose appetite disappears entirely.

Among the crew of *Mirror*, Generalov was the only one in the latter category. He had been picking at a plate of salad in a lackluster way, but as soon as Holmes and Watson appeared, he laid his fork aside altogether.

"Good evening, ladies and gentlemen." The detective was bright and cheerful. "May we join you?"

He seemed to expect a cordial welcome from the same people he had recently accused of murder.

"Of course, Mr. Holmes." Alex gestured toward the least-occupied sofa. As soon as Holmes and Watson sat down, Generalov demonstratively got up and moved over to Kim and Janet. Janet, who had just made supper and was now setting the table, showed no intention whatsoever of offering any food to Holmes and Watson. A dull silence filled the air.

"Once," said the detective, completely unabashed, "the esteemed

Dr. Watson and I investigated a theft of natural emeralds in the mines of Basko-4. We had to spend three days and three nights among the miners . . . to eat at their table, to stand shoulder to shoulder with them down in the tunnels, among many other things. If you only knew how many hateful stares drilled into our backs! How many times the timberings would 'accidentally' fall or the mining-robots lose their grip—And yet, when I, with the invaluable help of dear Dr. Watson, managed to find out the truth—everything changed. The workers cried, seeing us off from the planetoid."

"Tears of rapture at seeing you go," grumbled Generalov.

"I doubt that you want war to break out," Holmes continued. "I doubt you are harboring the murderer. And I doubt that you hated the poor princess Zey-So. The conclusion is simple—you object to my method of leading the investigation. You have, of course, all shared your impressions with each other and realized that each of you has been falsely accused."

"'Falsely' is the wrong word," said the navigator hoarsely. "You deliberately insulted me, Mr. Clone!"

"And now you are insulting me," rejoined the detective calmly. "And before that, you were insulting C-the-Third Shustov. Puck Generalov, I am unmoved by your references to my cloned origin. But it was your intention to insult me, wasn't it?"

"Yes, it was!" said Generalov defiantly.

"This kind of behavior would not be characteristic of a murderer," Holmes observed. "If the murderer were an ordinary xenophobic maniac. But an assassin-spesh can lead a game on five or six different logical levels. Captain, could you please invite the esteemed C-the-Third and the grieving Sey-Zo to join us?"

This was a breaking point in the general mood. Holmes looked as though the investigation was already finished.

In complete silence, Alex left the recreation lounge and went down to the passenger hall. The door of C-the-Third's cabin stood ajar. Alex knocked softly and entered.

Danila C-the-Third was sitting on an unmade bed and staring vacantly at the screen. A tiny meditation pyramid of Earthly origin glowed with soft, flowing multicolored lights on the nightstand. Alex silently turned the pyramid lights off and sat down next to C-the-Third.

"Why are you here?" asked the clone softly. Perhaps his trance had not been deep, or else he had come out of it very quickly and neatly.

"The detective has called all of us to come up to the recreation lounge."

"Me, too?"

"You, too. And Sey-Zo as well. Is her . . . mourning over?"

"Probably." C-the-Third slowly turned his head, looked wearily at Alex. "What is the point of all this?"

"The detective must have found the murderer. Or maybe he just wants to talk to all of us at once."

"You can't turn back time, Captain," the clone murmured. "You can't bring Zey-So back."

"Here. Have a drink." Alex handed him a small flask of cognac.

"Why?"

"Don't ask stupid questions. Drink up! This is an order!"

A look of surprise appeared in the clone's eyes. He cautiously touched his lips to the cognac flask.

"Drink up."

"What's been added to the cognac?" asked the clone suspiciously. "A tranquilizer?"

"What are you talking about?"

"Captain, I work with alien forms of intelligence. I often have to try their food and analyze human foods for compatibility. I have very good taste receptors."

"I thought so. C-the-Third, drink up. Trust me, it's for the better."

"A tranquilizer, then?"

Alex shook his head. "Pharmaceuticals wouldn't defeat your depression. You must be feeling like a complete failure as a guide-spesh?"

"Yes."

"Then drink."

The clone didn't hesitate for very long. He probably would have agreed just as quickly to a glass of potassium cyanide. He drained the flask in three big gulps.

"Great." Alex nodded. "Now let's go invite the Zzygou to the recreation lounge."

"We can give it a try," agreed the clone listlessly.

Despite many hours of airing out the room, the odor of merkaptane in the cabin was strong enough to make you gag. Thank God, Sey-Zo had put her friend's body in order—reinserted the severed entrails, dressed it, and seemed to have even touched up the face with cosmetics.

She herself was lying next to the motionless body and caressing it, slowly moving her hands. All four of her hands—Sey-Zo had taken off human clothes, and the Zzygou robes provided openings on the chest. Her small rudimentary hands, previously disguised as mammary glands beneath her clothes, were now tirelessly massaging Zey-So's shoulders.

"S-s-sey-Z-z-z-o . . ." said C-the-Third in a sibilant whisper. "Azané. Sso shaagaka."

"Kee-ee-stom . . ." Sey-Zo answered, without turning her head. It seemed she had stopped speaking the language of the Empire.

C-the-Third sighed. His face reflected genuine anguish. But his voice, when he spoke, remained calm. He began producing a flow of speech that was soft and melodious and, at the same time, filled with hushing and sibilant sounds.

Sey-Zo jumped up and flung open her arms, shielding the body of her dead friend. Her eyes were burning with hatred.

"Gom azis! Sharla si! Sharla! Sharla!"

"Sharla," C-the-Third seemed to concur. Bowed his head. "Sso shaataka-laz."

The Zzygou hesitated. Her glance ran back and forth between the faces of C-the-Third and Alex.

"Taea," she said harshly. "Zaré."

C-the-Third grabbed Alex by the elbow and quickly took him out of the cabin. The door slammed shut behind them. Alex stood, drawing air into his lungs in a quick succession of long, deep breaths, as though attempting to expel the foul smell which had permeated his clothes. Then he asked:

"So she refused to come?"

"No. She agreed. Let's go. She'll catch up."

The clone was pale and still talked in short phrases, as though mechanically reproducing the Zzygou speech patterns.

"You speak their language well," said Alex, trying to offer some moral support.

"No, not at all. This is the primitive conceptual language of the worker individuals. I can't be absolutely fluent in every language of every race I work with. My primary specialization is the Bronins . . . I speak their language fairly well."

They started climbing the stairs.

"What was she doing with Zey-So's body? Some kind of ritual ceremony?" asked Alex.

"Something like that. Thanatos-sex. Parting caresses."

"Are they really lesbians?" Alex was surprised. C-the-Third made a wry face.

"Not exactly. This type of interaction is limited to emotional partners and ritual-based situations . . . They do need male individuals, after all."

Alex couldn't help asking:

"Male individuals? Drones?"

"If you must know," replied the clone in an icy tone of voice, "the answer is no. Human males will do as well. And clones also suit them just fine."

Alex held his tongue.

They entered the recreation lounge. C-the-Third merely nodded to the crew, as though he had no wish to greet them in any other way. That wasn't hard to understand. Zey-So's murderer was here among them somewhere. With Holmes and Watson, he shook hands.

"Please sit down, Danila C-the-Third Shustov," said Holmes. "And please accept my deepest condolences."

"Have you found the murderer?" asked C-the-Third curtly.

"Sit down, please. Where is the esteemed Sey-Zo?"

"She is on her way." C-the-Third walked over to the wall and remained standing.

Silence descended once again. The Zzygou, however, didn't make them wait long. There was a sound of soft, almost creeping, footsteps, and Sey-Zo walked into the recreation lounge. She also preferred not to sit down.

Alex involuntarily lowered his eyes.

Holmes got up and began speaking.

"Dear Lady Sey-Zo, intellectual and emotional partner of the divine Lady Zey-So, let me share your sorrow and multiply your anger . . ."

After a moment's hesitation, Sey-Zo did give a nod, though she didn't make a single sound.

"Let me briefly inform everyone of the current situation," said Holmes. Paused, as if expecting some objections. "So . . ."

"Have you found the murderer?" repeated C-the-Third again. Holmes threw an icy glance at him and the clone fell silent.

"When I was first was informed of the villainous murder of Princess Zey-So and was on my way to your ship," Holmes continued, "I supposed that this would be a rather ordinary case. There was an Ebenian woman aboard, specialized as an executioner-spesh . . ."

Sey-Zo started. Her eyes fixed upon Janet. The black woman turned her head lazily, as if accepting the challenge.

"Also aboard," continued Holmes in the same calm, academic

tone, "was a girl, a fighter-spesh, who hadn't undergone any psychological training. Elementary logic suggested that these two were the likeliest suspects."

Sey-Zo made a small step towards Janet. The same instant, Holmes, with an imperceptible movement, snatched out a police-type paralyzer-pistol.

"Get back, Sey-Zo! No one has been charged yet!"

"She is from Eben!" In her agitation, the Zzygou switched back to human language.

"So what?" asked Janet lazily.

"You knew that anise affecting us like truth drug!" Sey-Zo screamed. "You making us drunk on purpose!"

"So it is a truth drug after all, and not just a hallucinogen?" countered Janet.

Strange as it seemed, her argument worked. Sey-Zo, now stone-faced, backed off.

Alex mentally applauded.

"Shall we continue?" Holmes put away his weapon. "While on my way to the ship, I became convinced that the situation was much worse than I had supposed originally. Everyone had reasons to kill the Zzygou. In order of seniority, let me start with the captain."

"As far as I remember, my only fault was that I didn't have any reasons to kill the Zzygou," Alex smirked.

"No, Captain. You did have reasons. And you very well know it."

"So you did find out, eh?" asked Alex dryly, lifting his eyes.

"Of course. Victor Romanov. Captain of the corvette *Rapier*. Holder of the Endless Valor Star and three classes of the Orders of Human Glory. Your elder brother, with whom you had a deep emotional bond. He perished in a battle with a Zzygou military ship twenty-three years ago. The widely known incident in the Tokyo-2 system . . . it was a sad moment, but one that finally settled the two great races' differences."

Now all eyes were on Alex.

"It would be stupid to take revenge on every individual of an alien race," said Alex. "Do you really suppose that, for almost a quarter of a century, I have been looking for a chance to kill any and every Zzygou?"

"Are you telling me you haven't read the report of *Rapier*'s demise?" queried Holmes with a crooked grin.

"I haven't read it."

Holmes stopped short. He looked at Alex in surprise.

"But why not, Captain? It would be a natural reaction."

"I knew I was going to work in space. Have encounters with the Zzygou. I didn't want to know the details. I didn't want to make my whole life a vendetta."

"That is hardly the reaction one would expect from a youth fresh out of metamorphosis."

"Perhaps. But I haven't looked at that report. Mr. Holmes . . . the phrase 'deep emotional bond' is a lie. My elder brother was a government child, who had been sent away to be raised at a pilot school from his early infancy. We met, yes . . . he would visit his parents occasionally, like any good government child. I liked to tell others that my brother was a military pilot. That I wanted to become like him. But emotional connection . . . forgive me, Mr. Holmes, there just wasn't any. Ever."

No one said anything. Only the Zzygou, her eyes fixed on Alex, was whispering something inaudibly.

"The incident in the Tokyo-2 system was connected with the fact that the Zzygou military ship had the Crown Princess Zey-So aboard," said Holmes, no longer sure of himself. "It was she, as the highest-ranking person, who made the decision to disobey the patrol ship . . . to instigate the battle."

Alex was silent.

"You didn't know about this?" asked Holmes.

"No. I didn't." Alex shook his head, looking at Sey-Zo. Had she also been there, on that Zzygou ship? Most probably she had. She and Zey-So were inseparable. But even if he had known all that . . . he wouldn't have killed the princess.

"I'm ready to believe you," said Holmes. "And . . . I'm inclined to believe that you haven't read the report of that old conflict. And that your relationship with your brother was not so deep that you would seek to avenge him. But someone wasn't aware of that."

"Who?" asked Alex.

"How did you get to Quicksilver Pit?" answered Holmes with a question.

"You know how. There was an accident on my ship. I was torn in half. Literally. They had to generate half my body anew . . ."

"It's a believable version," Holmes nodded. "Except that the experts have conducted another check of your body's remains. It had been cremated, of course, but a few samples did remain in the hospital funds."

Alex started. The very thought that some part of him was now lying somewhere under the lens of a microscope made him feel sort of numb. Although not so much as one might expect.

"You had been cut in half by a laser beam, Alex. But, someone seems to have paralyzed you first, made you lose consciousness."

"What for?"

"For a single purpose. To make you stay on Quicksilver Pit. To have you come out of the hospital at the moment the Sky Company would need a captain for the new ship. To make you the captain . . . so you would see among your passengers the Zzygou Swarm's Princess, Lady Zey-So."

"Someone thought I would kill her?"

Holmes pondered for a moment.

"More likely—someone *hoped* you would, while creating the stalemate situation we have now. Where everyone's a suspect."

"But I hired the crew by myself!"

"Yes. But whom did you hire? Xang Morrison," Holmes nodded at the co-pilot, "who was turned down by other ships under all sorts of phony pretenses. Xang Morrison, the former extremist . . . You hired Janet Ruello from Eben, who had a similar problem finding work. Then you took Kim O'Hara into your crew, a girl who hadn't undergone the psychological training required for a fighter-spesh. You took aboard Puck Generalov, who hates clones. You took Paul Lourier, who had been fired upon arriving on Quicksilver Pit, back into the crew again. And after that, the company sends the honorable Zzygou and the esteemed C-the-Third onto your ship!"

"But who could have foreseen all this?" Alex shook his head. "I'm afraid I must still remain on the list of suspects. It would be much more realistic to suspect me than to suppose that it's all the work of some secret organization, powerful enough for such intrigues. To have interfered with all the spaceport services on Quicksilver Pit . . . surely not, Mr. Holmes!"

"Yes, you remain on the list." Holmes nodded. "Along with everyone else. I have to admit that the unknown enemy has been deliberately setting up a situation which interferes with the investigation . . . at least for a short period of time. Someone has been hungry for war between the Empire and the Swarm."

"Who?" Alex repeated.

"You're an interesting person, Alex. You're a pilot, but you are trying to play detective." Holmes smiled. "Tell me your version."

Alex heaved a deep sigh.

"The military, that's my first thought. An alien race . . . not us, not the Zzygou . . . Maybe Cepheideans or Bronins . . ."

"Remarkable," Holmes said encouragingly. "Anyone else?"

Alex glanced at Janet. Looked away.

"Say it, Captain!"

"Former citizens of the planet Eben. Those who stayed beyond the bounds of the isolation field, who have acquired citizenship . . . but never lost hope of saving their world."

"Remarkable, Captain. Now let's think about this situation. Lady Sey-Zo, what other races might be interested in a conflict between the Zzygou and the Humans?"

The alien thought for a moment. Then grudgingly admitted:

"Practi-cally any race. A local conflict between us will weakening the Empire and the Swarm. It would benefiting everyone . . . excepting us."

"In case of war, humanity would be forced to take the quarantine off Eben," said Holmes. "Do you understand that? What is your prediction?"

"You won't dare do it!" cried Sey-Zo.

"There is a ninety-nine percent probability that we would. It's a bad bet, but better than the certainty of mutual extermination."

"Then no one is interested. Nowhere except . . ."—the Zzygou shifted her gaze onto Janet once again—"except for the inhabitants of Eben."

"Janet Ruello?" Holmes asked. Alex tensed. But the detective did not say the formulaic phrase to charge her with the crime. He was obviously waiting for the ship doctor's words.

"What do you want from me?" answered Janet calmly. "Do I mourn the death of the Zzygou? No, of course not . . ." She suddenly stopped. Shook her head. "Not at all!"

"Did you kill Zey-So?"

"I won't answer that," said Janet firmly. "If I say 'yes,' I'll be extradited to the Zzygou, and Eben will remain under the quarantine field. If I say 'no' . . . will you ever believe me?"

"Sey-Zo," asked Holmes quickly. "Will you be able to stop the Zzygou squadrons? Will you be able to prevent the war?"

The Other was quiet for a while, then nodded reluctantly.

"Yes."

"Under what conditions?"

"Under condition that I personally administer justice to punishing the murderer, and the punishment is no less horrible than the fate that befell Zey-So."

Janet pressed her lips together, but said nothing.

"Dear Sey-Zo, do you realize that the war will not be of any use to either your civilization, or to the Human Empire?"

"I realize."

"If a crew member voluntarily confesses to having committed this heinous crime and hands him or herself over . . ." Holmes threw a passing glance at Alex. "Will you stop the war, Lady Sey-Zo?"

"If it is the real murderer, and if the confession is truthful. If the evidence of guilt is convincing to me."

"The life of one person is nothing in comparison to the lives of two civilizations."

"I will not execute an innocent person," Sey-Zo repeated. "I expect convincing evidence of the actual murderer's guilt, Mr. Detective-Spesh."

"Deadlock," said Janet quietly. Grinned a crooked grin. "How strange . . . no one wants a war, but it is unavoidable."

Holmes looked around the recreation lounge.

"Among you, my fellow citizens," he said softly, "is the person who killed Zey-So. There is absolutely no doubt that he or she represents some very powerful organization that is interested in instigating a war. The murderer hadn't been motivated by primitive phobias or grudges. His or her actions were calculated, cold-blooded, and selfless. Because whatever happens, this case will be solved, and the murderer will be punished."

Silence . . .

"So you're ready to face death?" asked Holmes. "You still think that this unknown goal is worth the destruction of two civilizations?"

"If Eben is set free, the Empire will not perish," Janet murmured.

"Do you wish to confess something?" Holmes inquired.

Janet smirked.

"All the evidence points to you."

"Circumstantial evidence. Well, do what you wish. No one is required to testify against herself."

"But I can testify in Janet's defense!" suddenly shouted Kim. Holmes braced himself.

"Really? How curious. And what can you tell us, young lady?"

"Janet and I were in her cabin. For a long time. She has an alibi."

"Both she and you?" Holmes pointed out. "Tell us the exact time."

"Twelve p.m. to three a.m. ship time." Kim looked at Alex and gave an embarrassed smile. "Sorry, Alex . . ."

Janet sighed.

"You shouldn't have said anything . . ."

"Why didn't you report this earlier?" Holmes demanded. "Some personal problems, perhaps? You had a sexual encounter you didn't wish to make known?"

"Yeah, right!" Kim snorted. "Sorry, Jannie . . ."

"Then why were you silent on the matter?"

"We had a private talk, okay? It has nothing to do with the Zzygou! We were . . . we were gossiping, you know. Girl to girl!"

She looked at Alex again. He nodded, catching on.

No, it wasn't sex, after all. If there was anything erotic about it, it was in some minimal, trivial form—crying on each other's shoulder, patting each other, maybe a little kissing.

They had been discussing him. Him! Discussing and dividing him up! The smart Janet who understood everything, and the poor

Kim, suffering from unrequited love. The younger asking the experienced woman's advice. The woman sharing the secrets of sex and flirtation, the secrets that are impossible to graft by any kind of pre-programming . . .

Alex looked away.

He already seemed to understand what it was *not* to love.

But it seemed not to have given him the main thing. Love itself.

Or was it simply too late?

Both Kim and Janet had already become his comrades in arms, his sexual partners . . . but not at all his *beloved*. Love is a force of nature. From steadily smoldering coals you can rouse a spark of passion, but not the flame of love.

And wouldn't it be great to fall in love with Kim—she was beautiful, young, smart, and loyal!

What a stupid mechanism of reproduction Nature invented! Why can't it be controlled?

He looked at Holmes, who began talking again.

"Thank you very much for the information, Ms. Kim O'Hara. Even if the information is somewhat belated. Do you have any documentation to affirm that you were with Janet Ruello from twelve to three o'clock last night?"

"No, I don't." Kim shook her head. "But is my word worthless?"

Holmes sighed.

"In this particular situation, it is worthless. You could be covering up for the perpetrator. You could be an accomplice. I have taken your words into consideration, but I cannot rely on them."

Kim lifted her hand and slapped it forcefully on the table. Plates and silverware jumped up, and a deep dent was left in the polished wood.

"Easy," said Holmes soothingly. "A fighter-spesh should control herself."

"Are you deadlocked, Holmes?" Alex asked. He didn't recognize his own voice. It seemed to him tense and hoarse.

And he probably wasn't the only one. All eyes were now on him.

"I am deeply convinced that I know the murderer's identity," Holmes reported courteously. "But I still have no proof. And Lady Sey-Zo yearns for solid proof."

Alex silently rolled up the sleeve of his jersey. Then asked:

"Does everybody know what this is?"

"The Demon," said Kim. "Your little devil . . ."

"It's an emotion scanner," said Dr. Watson, entering the conversation. She was looking at Alex with genuine curiosity. "How strange . . . Why did you have one implanted?"

"I must be the spesh who seeks out the unusual," replied Alex with a crooked grin. "I've always wanted to see what exactly I am feeling. And maybe . . . maybe I wanted to see something on the Demon's face that I couldn't ever experience myself."

"It is smiling." Dr. Watson walked up to him and unceremoniously grabbed his arm. "Captain . . . what does this mean?"

"It means that everything is going to be all right," said Alex. "I, too, know who the killer is. And I'm sure his guilt will be proven."

Dr. Watson's eyes looked full of doubt. As though what was happening now was an unheard-of violation of natural laws.

"If you can help the investigation . . ." the detective began.

"I can't—just yet. But tomorrow morning, everything will change. Believe me, Mr. Holmes."

"Captain!"

Sey-Zo moved towards him, spreading out her arms, as if to underscore that she wasn't doing so in aggression. Alex got up, stepped forward to meet her.

"Who killed Zey-So?"

"I will tell you tomorrow."

The Zzygou's eyes were peering intently at his face. What was she trying to read on the face of a creature that resembled her race only in appearance?

"Give me the murderer. Give him to me, and I will stop the war. In the name of every one of our race, I swear! I will stop the war!"

"The murderer will be in your power." Alex looked at the other crewmembers, sitting still as statues. "What will you do with him?"

"I don't know . . ." The Zzygou faltered. "I have to decide. What is considered worst punishment in your race?"

It seemed the question was asked sincerely. Unlike Janet Ruello, Lady Sey-Zo had no training as an executioner-spesh.

"Throw us into a briar patch—that's the worst," grumbled Morrison. And burst into a fit of almost hysterical laughter, which no one else dared to share.

"Traditionally, it is primitive physical torture, which relies upon various violations of bodily integrity and stimulation of pain receptors," reported Janet. "If I'm not mistaken, it is the exact type of thing you were using against human settlers on Valdae-8?"

"Stop it!" said Dr. Watson quickly. But the crew's restraint had already snapped.

"Unnatural sexual contacts!" uttered Generalov.

"Separation from the work you love," declared Lourier.

"Separation from the person you love," said Kim softly.

Alex shook his head. Looked at Holmes, who faked a slight, understanding smile.

No one believed him! No crewmember believed that Alex really knew the killer's name! Not even the killer himself. Everyone thought his words a bluff, a scene performed for the Zzygou in order to save humanity. Everyone—or almost everyone, except the murderer—was willing to sacrifice himself for the cause.

"The most terrifying thing," said Alex, looking straight into the Zzygou's eyes, "is to lose your own individuality. Your 'self.' The worst thing is to lose your consciousness and become a puppet, yanked by invisible strings."

Sey-Zo's eyes, that had just been so human, suddenly changed. The pupil trembled, split apart, broke into hundreds of tiny dots. Alex felt a short, agonizing spasm of dizziness.

Then it was all over.

And Sey-Zo's gaze turned human again, the way it couldn't and shouldn't have been.

"You probably telling the truth," the Zzygou said. "I will think."

At the opposite side of the table, Kim chuckled softly. Then she quietly recited:

"We fear death not, nor its posthumous sting.

We dread, while we live, that the fate it might bring—

Black void—is more likely and worse than the Pit;

We don't know just whom we would beg, 'Please, please, quit!'"

The Zzygou did not deign to pay any attention to either Kim O'Hara or to the great poet's words.

"Who is the murderer?" she asked.

"Will you take my word for it?" asked Alex in reply.

"No."

"Then wait till tomorrow. In the morning, I will tell you everything."

"I wait, human."

The Zzygou turned and walked out of the recreation lounge. Someone—it must have been Morrison—heaved a deep sigh.

"Bravo, Captain," said Holmes. "You were magnificent."

"I was ready to believe," said Generalov, reaching for his wine glass, "that you really do know who the killer is, Captain."

"I do."

"Give it up!" Puck shook his head. "You want to set yourself up as bait for the murderer. Am I right? You are hoping that he will decide to get rid of you during the night and get trapped as a result."

Dr. Watson cheerfully nodded.

"Exactly! Just like in Moto Conan's *The Case of the Boy with a Rubber Eye!*"

"That's useless, Captain," said Morrison. "If the murderer is cunning enough to hide among us, he won't fall for such a cheap trick."

And only Sherlock Holmes, the clone of the great detective Peter Valke, didn't smile, looking at Alex.

"Are we really going to wait till tomorrow?" asked C-the-Third. "Mr. Holmes . . . if you know the villain's name, why not use torture?"

"This question has already been raised. I think that the murderer will endure any amount of pain. And under too much duress, anyone will admit to anything. Torture won't give us proof." Holmes began filling his pipe. "So yes. I agree with the captain. Let's postpone everything till tomorrow."

"Will you join us for supper, Mr. Holmes?" asked Janet, all of a sudden. The detective looked at her with obvious surprise. And Janet herself seemed a bit startled by her own courtesy.

"Thank you, Ms. Janet Ruello," said Holmes with exquisite politeness. "Unfortunately, I prefer not to partake of food during an investigation. Especially if its chemical composition is unknown to me. But I appreciate . . . your offer."

"Okay, go gnaw on your vitamins under your pillow!" said Janet through clenched teeth, as if coming back to her senses. Puck Generalov giggled.

"She's got you there, Holmes, old boy!"

He leaned toward Janet and slapped her on the shoulder. She looked at him in surprise, half-rose, and moved closer to him. They sat together, demonstratively hugging and looking at Holmes.

Kim laughed. Poured herself some wine, leaned over to Morrison, and whispered something in his ear. Then both of them roared with laughter.

Alex forced himself to look away. And saw that Holmes, puffing his pipe, was watching what was going on with curiosity.

"More wine, anybody?" asked Paul Lourier.

"Sure," Generalov eagerly agreed. "But not this red watery stuff—I think there was some decent port in there!"

Lourier got up, walked over to the bar.

"Alex," said Holmes softly. "Do you smoke a pipe?"

"Yes, but I don't have one on me."

"Join me." Holmes pointed to the chair nearest to him and got a disposable pipe, already filled with tobacco, out of his pocket. It wasn't the good old briar from Earth, of course, but a worthy imitation of it. Besides, this pipe did not need to be seasoned. And the tobacco was quite good.

Alex lit it up. He managed to hold back a sarcastic remark about the tobacco, whose chemical composition was unknown.

"You're very interesting to work with," Holmes said. "I'm really enjoying this investigation, despite the tragic circumstances. The situation itself—the ship, flying through the hyper-channel, the small number of suspects, the exotic nature of the victim . . . Please don't think me a cynic!"

"I don't. You just love your job, that's all."

Dr. Jenny Watson perched on the arm of Holmes's chair.

"Yes, this is a classic murder . . . like the one in *The Case of the Yellow Starship.*"

"I believe the captain was the murderer in that one?" inquired Alex.

Holmes nodded with a smile.

"Yes. But I wouldn't insist on that analogy. You play along with me wonderfully well."

"And you, with me."

They looked at each other.

"What is it you want, Alex?" inquired Holmes. "To help me, to help some friend of yours, or to prove that a pilot-spesh can be a detective as well?"

"To help myself."

"That's a serious reason," Holmes agreed.

From then on, they smoked in silence. The hysterical merriment that seemed to have overtaken the crew after the Zzygou's departure also evaporated. Kim went off to her quarters after a failed attempt to take Alex with her—he just shook his head. Immediately after she left, Morrison, having fetched up a bottle of wine and two glasses, also disappeared from the recreation lounge. Generalov, growing gloomy, emptied a few glasses of whiskey and soda in quick succession and made himself scarce. Lourier excused himself and departed. He loitered briefly in the hallway, as if irresistibly drawn to the sealed door of the reactor module, and then went off to his cabin. Janet, engrossed in her own thoughts, took a long time to notice that she had been left alone with Holmes, Watson, and Alex. She kept swirling her glass, with the remnants of wine splashing at the bottom. For some reason, Alex remembered that Eben had a Red Sea, where the water was actually red because of a myriad of edible plankton. A reserve food source for the entire planet . . . an artificially created reservoir full of krill. Perhaps, looking at the thick red wine, Janet was thinking of her homeland?

Then the black woman lifted her head.

"Captain, permission to leave?"

"Permission granted." Alex was slightly surprised by such a formal request, but decided to keep with her tone.

Only the three of them remained.

"Dr. Watson and I will take the vacant passenger cabin," said Holmes, "if it's all right with you, Captain."

"I can let you have mine." Alex shrugged.

"That won't be necessary."

Holmes carefully cleaned out his pipe. He shook his head with disapproval upon seeing the small cleaner-beetle crawling out of a corner. What's cleanliness to a detective, except more obliterated evidence?

"Do both of you really know who the killer is?" Dr. Watson asked suddenly.

"I do," said Holmes.

"So do I," declared Alex.

"In Moto Conan's book *The Case of Three Men Who Lost the Fourth*, Holmes and the murderer exchanged just these kinds of phrases!" said Dr. Watson excitedly.

Holmes shook his head.

"No, my dear Watson. Forgive me, but I'm not quite ready to press charges."

Dr. Watson smiled, acknowledging another failed try. Then she said:

"What amazes me is the killer's composure. It is well known that a detective-spesh solves ninety-nine point three percent of all cases. How can he remain calm in such a situation?"

"If we were dealing with a classic murderer—an ordinary immoral natural—your surprise would be appropriate," Holmes admitted. "But this was a well-planned act. And the one who is hiding behind someone else's identity"—he threw an eloquent glance at Alex—"is totally devoid of fear. An assassin-spesh never loses his cool, the same way that a pilot-spesh keeps control of his ship till the end . . . even seeing that death is unavoidable."

"I thought so, too." Alex permitted himself to smile at Holmes. "See you tomorrow, Holmes. May a new day bring us luck."

He got up, nodded to Dr. Watson, and quickly went down the hallway.

He didn't feel like sleeping.

Alex lay, covered up to his waist, looking through a little tome of *World Literature Classics* by the glow of his night light. The book, in search mode, was displaying works under the keyword "love."

There were lots of works.

You could even say—all of them.

Alex moved to the "poems" directory. Chose a poet—Dmitry Bykov—and entered the same keyword.

THE CINEMA WHERE THE TWO OF YOU MUNCHED PINE NUTS,
    DUMPING THE SHELLS INTO YOUR COAT-POCKET—
A DETAIL EVEN CHEKHOV HIMSELF WOULD LOVE,
THAT PINCE-NEZED EX-PROVINCIAL GARDENER AND DOCTOR.
YOU'D'VE EMPTIED YOUR POCKETS—NOT MUCH OF A LOAD,
    AND THE TROLLEY-STOP HAD A HANDY DUMPSTER.
BUT YOU FORGOT, BECAUSE LOVE HAD YOU QUITE OVERWROUGHT,
AND BLIND, AND BEMUSED, IN LITERARY PARLANCE.
SOME TIME WILL PASS, AND ONE DAY YOU'LL SEARCH FOR A
    NICKEL OR DIME FOR A RIDE BACK FROM NOWHERE, IN YOUR
    OLD COAT-POCKET, NOW THIN WITH AGE, YOU'LL DISCOVER
    THE REMNANTS OF THOSE PIGNOLIS.

AND THERE YOU'LL STAND, INEXPLICABLY MUTE AND STRAINED,
    HIDING YOUR FACE FROM THE OTHERS, CHOKING BACK
    TEARS . . . WHAT WILL YOU SAY THEN ABOUT THOSE 'SMALL'
    DETAILS—
OF LIFE AND LITERATURE—THAT YOU MOCKED ALL THOSE YEARS?

He put the book aside. In the corner of the page blinked a cheery little face of the "reference person," ready to define any archaic words, or give a biographical sketch of the poet, or provide a critical analysis of the text.

Alex was thinking, drumming his fingers on the firm plastic of the pages.

What's the good of a feeling that constantly causes pain? Should it have any place in human life?

He had still not managed to feel this *love* thing. And tomorrow night, the blocker's action would wear off, and he would turn back into a pilot-spesh.

Of course, he could just keep popping the drug. And waiting . . . but would that be worth it?

Love wasn't there yet. But the anguished yearning was.

"My mom chewed me out," Nadia is saying. *She lights a cigarette, and makes herself more comfortable in the deep armchair. A sunbeam reflection plays on her naked body—the wind is swaying the curtain at the open window.*

"Because of me?" Alex inquires, just in case. His fingers are dancing on the sensory field of a computer, entering long rows of numbers. It's a rather old machine, no neuro-interface on it . . . "I'm almost done, Nadia. Just a minute, okay?"

"Yes, because of you . . ." The girl stretches out a suntanned leg, moving it into the sunshine. Her other foot scratches a mosquito bite on her calf. "My mom says I have the wrong attitude toward you. That it's stupid to go beyond just sex with a future pilot."

"She's wrong," Alex replies. "I tell you, I'll keep loving you anyway."

"I know . . ." Nadia agrees.

A shout comes from the street:

"Alex! Nadia! Alex!"

"It's Fam," says Nadia. "He's tracked us down. You know, I think he might be jealous."

"You think?" Alex begins to enter the last block of data.

"Alex! Nadia!" Fam keeps yelling in the street at the top of his lungs. "I know you're home! Let's go to the river!"

"What a pest," Alex grumbles. "You wanna go?"

"If you want to."

Alex casts a sidelong glance at the slim, tanned leg, then spreads his fingers decisively, shutting down the computer. Leans out of the window up to his waist and shouts, "You go on, we'll catch up!"

Alex smiled at the memory. No, that wasn't love, after all. Otherwise, he wouldn't be smiling now, but "choking back tears," as the poet had supposed.

And poets should be trusted, right?

The door signal beeped, and Alex slapped the book shut.

"Enter."

It turned out to be Dr. Watson.

"Excuse me, Captain . . ."

"Come in." Alex sat up on the bed. "It's all right. I wasn't asleep yet."

The woman nodded, sat down in the armchair. Alex was smiling, but said nothing, leaving it to her to start the conversation.

"Holmes has fallen asleep," said Jenny, somewhat out of the blue, "so I thought . . ."

"Are you lovers?"

"No." Dr. Watson shook her head. "You already know he isn't all that emotional. . . . Sex with a detective-spesh is a purely mechanical process. And who needs that?" She stopped short. "Forgive me, Alex."

"No, no. It's a perfectly reasonable opinion. Is something bothering you, Dr. Watson?"

"Yes. Captain, something was odd about the crew tonight."

"Really?" Alex seemed surprised.

"You noticed it, too, Captain. Stop pretending."

"So what is bothering you?"

"I would say that . . . it's absurd, of course . . . but the speshes started behaving . . . like naturals."

Alex raised one eyebrow emphatically.

"Let's start with you, Captain," said Dr. Watson firmly. "Are you noticing any changes within yourself?"

"I am."

"You see! And today? Janet Ruello—she practically didn't react to the Zzygou at all. Well, she did, but . . . sort of by inertia. Not seriously. Kim O'Hara . . . she's in love with you, right? Janet has told us that the girl has a specialization of a fighter and a hetaera simultaneously. But I wouldn't say that it was noticeable!"

"And what do you think about this, Jenny?"

"Captain, could someone . . . the word 'poison' wouldn't really be right here . . . let's just say, give the whole crew some kind of potent psychotropic drug?"

"Possibly." Alex nodded. "It could've been anybody. Me, for example. Everyone came to see me today, one after another, and I offered every member of the crew some wine and cognac. What would be simpler than to add the drug to the drinks? Except . . . what kind of drug?"

Dr. Watson shrugged.

"That's exactly it. I can't imagine what could have this effect."

Alex nodded. Then inquired:

"Purely hypothetically . . . suppose there was a substance that could block all the mind alterations characteristic of speshes . . ."

"All of them?"

"Yes, all of them at once."

"You told Holmes something of the sort . . . I don't know of any such substance."

"But just suppose it existed. That the crew was under its influence. What should we expect?"

"From the murderer?" Dr. Watson squinted.

"You catch on faster than your literary prototype."

"If Holmes is right, and I'm inclined to believe him . . ." Dr. Watson was quiet for a moment. "An assassin-spesh is deprived primarily of the sense of fear and the sense of pity. Even if it's not the work of underground geneticists, but is just an ordinary agent-spesh, those would be the required parts of his personality. He felt no doubt, murdering the Zzygou. And now he's biding his time, one hundred percent convinced he is doing the right thing. When the personality alterations vanish . . . it's hard to imagine what could happen."

"Remorse?"

"I doubt it. Personality is formed by more than just chemical reactions. There's also experience . . . habits, memories. More likely, the agent will be overcome by panic. Especially if he doesn't expect such an effect."

"That's what I think, too."

Dr. Watson sighed.

"Captain, you know way more than you're telling me."

"It has to be this way. Believe me."

"And what if I go back to Holmes now and report our conversation?"

"Are you blackmailing me?" Alex smirked. Got up from the bed, walked over to Jenny. Bent over—the woman tensed, as if expecting him to do anything, even the most unexpected.

"What are you . . ."

Her lips were so unskilled that it was as if she was kissing for the first time in her life. A natural, what could you do . . .

"You really shouldn't neglect this side of human relationships, Doctor," said Alex softly. "Your literary precursor didn't avoid life."

"What in the world . . ."

"Dump your wizened detective." Alex looked her straight in the eye. "You're a smart woman, but you've already had enough fun with intellectual games. Catching crooks is not your type of thing. Don't make a spesh out of yourself . . . thank God you aren't one. Don't squelch your human feelings. Be alive, Jenny. Alive and real. Love, be jealous, hate, dream, raise children, and make your career!

Create paintings, give people their shots, go waterskiing, grow your garden flowers. Don't turn yourself into . . . into the way the rest of us are."

Jenny Watson jumped up. Leaped over to the door, hurriedly readjusted her blouse, which had come unbuttoned. Cried:

"What's the matter with you . . . you're a pilot-spesh!"

"Uh-huh. But, you know . . ." Alex was slowly moving towards her. "Somewhere very, very deep inside, I remain simply human. With an ordinary human genome. Of course, there, inside, is a clever boy, who can go on doing his homework right next to a girl who's in love with him . . . the girl who kept trying to turn a spesh into a human. Also there lives a studious young recruit, learning the secrets of piloting. And an inexperienced young captain, whose most normal crewmember is a hysterical, affected gay guy who hates clones. All of them are there, inside me. But there is one more little person inside there. A master-pilot, long awaited on a distant planet, by the woman he loves. Probably the same woman he's loved since he was a child. And when this master-pilot is piloting his ship, he isn't bound by a genetic order—to protect the technology, the crew, and the passengers. He will fight till the end simply because it's his favorite ship, and his friends, and the people who have put their trust in him. And also because somewhere far, far away, his beloved is waiting for him, and the children, for whom he chose no specialization."

"There is no such person, Alex," quickly retorted Dr. Watson. "I . . . I don't understand what kind of crazy game you're playing. Why are you making all this up—how can you say such things—but . . ."

Alex put his finger to his lips.

"Sh-sh-sh! Doctor . . . he's there. Inside. You see this little Demon on my shoulder? That must be him. Weird, really weird master-pilot Alex Romanov . . ."

Dr. Watson was pale.

"You've lost your mind," she whispered, fumbling for the door lock behind her back. "You're psychotic! You're a regular loony!"

"I cannot be regular." Alex bowed politely. "Only naturals can be regular. And I—am a spesh."

Dr. Watson bolted from his cabin. Alex waited till the door closed, and only then burst out laughing.

He kept laughing while he put the book away in the desk drawer, and turned off the light, and got back into his bed. He kept laughing until his laughter turned to tears.

CHAPTER 4.

Holmes was playing the violin.

Alex stopped short in the entrance to the recreation lounge, listening, spellbound by the music. And he wasn't the only one.

Her legs folded under her in an armchair, Kim sat motionless, propping her chin on her hand. Right on the floor next to her sat Morrison, his legs crossed at the ankles. Generalov was sprawling comfortably on the couch . . . it seemed that he had taken up this pose of lazy indifference as soon as Holmes started playing and then forgot to change it. Tears ran down Puck's cheeks, blurring ornate spirals of facial paint. From time to time, the navigator sniffled and wiped his face with his hand.

Holmes kept playing.

The old Toshiba violin was probably not equipped with an acoustics compensator unit. Perhaps the recreation lounge had been built to accommodate chamber music concerts, or maybe Holmes's mastery managed to overcome the instrument's limitations.

The violin sang. The violin spoke to each one of them. The music contained it all—the deadly chill of boundless space, and the living fire of lonesome stars, and planets, gliding on the very edge of life and death. The violin's virtual strings flashed as iridescent sparks under the bow, and entire civilizations were born and died in their afterglow. Reason found and lost itself again, tormented by unanswerable questions, and vanished in the darkness of time.

Holmes's head was thrown back, his eyes closed. This performance was nothing like the little concert he had given in Alex's cabin. This time, the great detective's whole life was in his instrument, the bow, and the flowing melody.

Very, very quietly, the Zzygou entered the lounge, dressed in yellow and black, the colors of mourning. She stopped—perhaps in surprise, or perhaps she, too, was enchanted by the music. C-the-Third followed in her wake, like a mournful shadow. Then Lourier approached as well. And after him came Janet. Dr. Watson was the last to appear.

When Holmes briskly took the bow off the strings, everyone was listening.

"Bravo," said Janet softly. "Bravo, Mr. Holmes."

Generalov wept openly, not hiding his tears. He was wearing his kilt, a blue shirt, and moccasins. His hair was braided into an intricate pretzel, and the half-smudged ornament on his cheeks had been drawn with particular care. He seemed to have prepared for anything—a fight, or even death. Alex was about to say something to him about his dress code violations . . . when he noticed that everyone had ignored the rules today.

Morrison got up and cleared his throat.

"Excuse me, Mr. Holmes . . . but what are you doing as a detective? Paganini himself couldn't have played his own twelfth concerto with more virtuosity. I dare say . . . since Paganini's death four hundred years ago, no such violinist has been born."

"I wasn't born, either," said Holmes softly. "I was created this way . . . what's to be proud of?"

"A clone cannot surpass the original, and that's an axiom," persisted Morrison. "Does that mean that Peter Valke was a genius violinist? You shouldn't . . . you shouldn't demean your own talent . . ."

"I am a detective." Holmes shook his head. "I'm a detective who loves playing the violin. I'm happy to see you all here, my friends. Today we must resolve the sad problem that precipitated my coming to this ship. Please, be seated."

His words seemed to have an effect. Alex watched as every one of his crew found a seat. Generalov, Lourier, Morrison on one small couch. Kim and Janet on the other. Across from them, C-the-Third and the Zzygou sat in two armchairs, as did Holmes and Watson. And Dr. Watson, for the first time, ignored her habit of sitting on an armrest.

Alex unhurriedly took a seat between Janet and Kim. After a moment's reflection, he threw his arms around both women's shoulders.

"So . . ." said Holmes pensively. "First of all, I have a few things to tell you, which aren't directly related to this case. The Imperial Council has made the decision . . . and it has already been signed by the Emperor . . . that in case of a massive-scale military conflict, the isolation field will be taken off the planet Eben. And after that, the Empire will make a direct plea for help to the Board of Cardinals. Ms. Janet Ruello . . ."

The woman started. Her face was tense with a mixture of both joy and alarm.

"Do you suppose Eben will answer the call for aid?"

"Yes," replied the black woman, without hesitation. "No doubt, they will."

"Thank you . . . Lady Sey-Zo, do the ruling females of the Swarm comprehend this situation?"

"It change nothing . . ." the Zzygou whispered.

"I believe you. And one more piece of news . . . a small one. The Sky Tourism Company is undergoing bankruptcy proceedings. All of its assets will be redirected to an aid fund for war victims. I am afraid, ladies and gentlemen, that you are unemployed."

"This is just my luck!" cried Generalov, throwing his hands up. "It's always this way! Just when I find a decent job and a good crew—"

The navigator fell silent, glaring at Holmes, as though the detective was responsible for the decision to liquidate the company.

"Am I supposed to resign my commission officially?" Alex asked.

"As soon as the investigation is closed."

Alex nodded.

"And now let's move on to the most grievous question," said Holmes. "By the way, Captain . . . could you assist me with the issue of the listeners' attention?"

It took Alex a few seconds to understand the request.

"Yes, of course. Computer! Captain's access! Prepare the recreation lounge for dynamic maneuvers!"

"Completed . . ." replied the service program. Little orange lights flashed on the armrests of chairs and couches. Outwardly, nothing seemed to have changed, but when Alex tested it by attempting to half-rise from his seat, an invisible strip of force field softly tossed him back onto the couch. The Zzygou lifted her hands to touch the invisible barrier. Threw a questioning look at Alex.

"I hope nobody minds these little safety precautions?" Holmes inquired, and laughed dryly. "But of course, someone does mind. Well, nothing to be done."

He took out his pipe and began to fill it. Alex, after a brief hesitation, lit up a cigarette. Slow movements were easy to make, though you could still feel the firm resistance of the force field.

"This is ridiculous! And useless, too!" said Generalov nervously. "I don't know about you, Mr. Holmes, but I get really irritated by any restriction of my freedom of movement!"

"A killer-spesh is a good reason for force barriers," said Lourier. "Puck . . . don't argue. Holmes will only consider it incriminating."

Holmes let out the first puff of smoke.

"So, what do we have, ladies and gentlemen? A group of criminals—one person simply couldn't have pulled this off—has set the goal of instigating a war between the Empire and the Zzygou Swarm. To achieve this, a crew was gathered whose every member could kill Princess Zey-So. And the preparations, mind you, must have began at least five months ago. That is the precise time when Alex Romanov was badly wounded and left on the planet where Zey-So and Sey-Zo were to transfer to a human ship. I believe everyone here will be interested in the fact that the hospital staff received a hefty bribe for making Alex Romanov's treatment a month and a half longer than necessary."

Alex nodded. It was easy for him to believe that.

"This was serious preparation," said Holmes, without a hint of humor. "Very thorough. Lady Sey-Zo, when did you make the decision to tour the Human Empire?"

The Zzygou heaved a deep sigh.

"Eighteenth day of January, by Earth calendar. During the diplomatic visit of the Imperial Council delegation to the Zzygou realm."

"I . . . was wounded on the twenty-seventh of January," Alex said.

"Nine days. Very speedy work." Holmes nodded. "The choice was probably made from among all the astronauts who were on Quicksilver Pit or on the ships that had entered planetary space. You were unlucky, Alex. That is a fact. Unfortunately, that doesn't guarantee that you were not a part of the plot. You could have landed in the hospital willingly. . . ."

"Holmes, have you any idea what it's like to be deprived of your rump, member, and legs for months on end?" asked Alex angrily.

"To a degree. I lost both my legs once," rejoined Holmes imperturbably. "And I had to use mechanical prostheses for a month—there was no time to go to the clinic for transplants."

Alex involuntarily looked away. Everyone else also seemed rather uncomfortable. Holmes had admitted this unsavory and shameful detail of his biography—using mechanical artificial organs—with the genuine fortitude of a detective-spesh. But still, it was awkward for all of them to hear him admit it.

"But I must consider every possibility, including that of a selfless perpetrator," Holmes continued. "So, the scope of this operation allows us to definitely speak of the existence of a powerful, far-flung organization that has money, connections, and highly qualified agents . . . and is interested in war."

"The military, after all?" asked Morrison.

"The military alone would not win the war against the Zzygou. And to free Eben would mean a complete restructuring of the military, reassigning all the command posts . . . no. The military didn't want war. The generals might have been dreaming of a fast conflict resulting in immediate victory, but not of such a shake-up of the very foundations. The Ebenian natives? There aren't that many of them, after all. They are scattered all over the galaxy, they are being monitored, and they don't have access to the highest power echelons. What does that leave us?"

"Imperial Security!" cried Janet. It seemed she, too, was enthralled by the investigation process.

"Exactly. That is the organization that almost completely lost its influence after the power of the Emperor weakened and the colonies received their federal status." Holmes nodded. "The interests of Imperial Security do not just allow for, but demand, a military conflict, increasing tension, and the implementation of a special governing regime in the Empire."

"We have an Imperial agent-spesh among us!" said Morrison, almost cheerily. "Wow! Ever since I was a kid, I've always dreamed of seeing a secret operation hero!"

"Your dream has already come true," said Holmes dryly. "Let us continue . . . Lady Sey-Zo, does my assumption seem logical to you?"

The Zzygou frowned.

"You are blaming your own security service for what happened? Then it is act of state terrorism, and war is unavoidable."

"I am accusing separate individuals who work for the Imperial Security Service," Holmes pointed out. "And I'm afraid, Lady Sey-Zo, that even if we expose the person who carried out the crime, we won't be able to trace back the whole chain. Those who gave the orders will come through unscathed. Certainly. This is, alas, commonplace in human society."

"This is bad practice," said the Zzygou. "But . . . I understand. Give me at least the agent. The one who carried it out!"

Her hands squeezed together, as though already grabbing the murderer's throat.

"Let us continue." Holmes nodded. "Of course, the undercover agent, or agents, must have a convincing background story. The legend, moreover, presents them either as absolutely innocent, having nothing to do with the murder, or—as part of the double game—on the contrary, the source of multiple false leads. I did not know which cover-up method was used by the enemy. It was another dead end. All the methods of systematic investigation either yielded no results, or required the kind of time we simply do not have at our disposal. It was then I noticed Captain Romanov's behavior."

Alex caught several intrigued and even frightened glances directed at him.

"Captain Romanov was either the murderer himself, or he knew who the perpetrator was. But if he was innocent, why didn't he name the criminal? Perhaps the evidence he had was very circumstantial . . . but Alex Romanov still hoped to check it out first. Then again, maybe he just didn't wish to turn the killer in."

428

Holmes smiled, and Alex politely bowed his head.

"What could have put the captain on guard, I thought? I had to correlate all the information about what had happened, to listen to the testimonies of every witness, before one small detail caught my attention . . . I decided that it could serve as the point of departure and made the decision to support the captain's tactics. No matter what they happened to consist of."

"Thank you, Mr. Holmes," said Alex.

"You can tell us your version of what has happened," Holmes suggested politely. "I think it will be quite interesting. . . ."

Alex cleared his throat, got out another cigarette and lit up. Holmes's pipe did make a better impression . . . and his tobacco tasted better, as well.

"The whole problem is in the lack of time," he began. "There are no perfect crimes. Sooner or later, tracing the biographies of every one of us, or using all the complex methods of instrumental investigations, Mr. Holmes would manage to expose the killer. But the perpetrator never did hope to come through unscathed. His main goal is to bide time until the hostilities start. After that he either surrenders . . . or, more likely, his owners organize a rescue operation. If the higher-ups of the I.S. really were involved in this case, it would be nothing for them to remove the *Lucifer* currently guarding us and send a S.W.A.T. team onto *Mirror*. Although an agent-spesh could eliminate all the witnesses by himself."

"Let him try!" said Kim quietly.

"Even if you aren't the murderer, Kim," said Alex with a melancholy air, "don't overestimate your strength. You are a spesh. But your real combat experience is next to zero. And when two equal forces meet in combat, experience determines everything."

Kim snorted, and indignantly elbowed Alex's side. At least she didn't take his suspicion of her seriously.

"I have a few guesses based on certain clues," Alex continued. "Snippets . . . details . . . sketchy impressions. They put me on guard, but I'm afraid it would be useless to present them. Circumstantial evidence doesn't help. And the time we have left . . . please correct me, Sey-Zo, if I'm wrong . . ."

"Eight hours, thirty-five minutes," said Generalov. "Exactly. After that, the first military unit of the Zzygou will enter into firing contact with our fleet in the Adelaide system."

"Eight hours and twenty-one minutes," the Zzygou corrected him. "I need time to contact the headquarters. Seven thousands warships cannot be halted instantaneous . . . not even ours."

"I would say, we have seven hours, plus or minus ten minutes," Morrison objected. "As soon as the Zzygou ships come out of the hyper-channels, they will be targeted. So *our* fleet has to be stopped as well . . . and that is a more lengthy process."

Janet Ruello laughed quietly:

"I would say we have around four hours left. Taking the isolation field off Eben would take no less than four hours. If the field disappears, our fleet will begin large-scale dislocation and preventive vengeance strikes. This will be a much more serious reason for war than one little bee . . . please excuse my choice of words, Sey-Zo."

Alex nodded.

"As I see it, we are all busy making calculations here. Well,

Janet's opinion is probably the most pessimistic, but also the most correct. Time is slipping away . . . let's not waste it. Lady Sey-Zo! The person who has murdered your companion is one of the crew-members, right?"

"Or C-the-Third," said the Zzygou coldly. The clone lowered his head.

"Or Danila C-the-Third Shustov," nodded Alex. "Lady Sey-Zo. We are unable to definitively point out the killer. So I propose that you personally, with your own hands, execute us all. Computer, remove the force field barrier from the Zzygou."

"Completed," said the ship. The Zzygou got up and looked around in disbelief.

"Computer," Alex continued. "I order you not to obey any of my commands after I say 'Let justice be done' and until the moment when those same words are pronounced by the Zzygou and Peter C-the-Forty-Fourth Valke. Let justice be done!"

"Completed."

"What the hell are you doing!" shouted Generalov. "You fuck-ing bastard! You xenophile! You . . ."

He choked on his own words. Flailed around, trying to breach the barrier.

"Calm down, Puck Generalov! I understand it is harder for a natural . . . but you're human, damn it! What are our lives next to the fates of two civilizations!"

Generalov breathed heavily, but fell silent.

"I want to know your opinion, my friends," Alex continued quickly. "Paul Lourier! Do you agree with my proposition?"

The engineer didn't hesitate to answer:

"Yes, Captain. It's our duty."

"Great. Xang Morrison?"

"Captain, the idea doesn't seem all that correct to me," began Morrison cautiously. "Yes, we are all ready to sacrifice ourselves, but should it be done this way, while we still have time . . ."

"I see. Janet Ruello?"

The black woman frowned, looking at him. Shook her head.

"Stupid, dishonorable, and won't have the right effect."

"All right. Kim O'Hara?"

The girl cautiously touched his hand. She whispered, "Alex . . ."

"Kim O'Hara?"

She glanced over at the Zzygou, frozen motionless.

"I . . . I don't want to. I don't intend to die because of some bastard!"

"Puck Generalov?"

The navigator slowly lifted his hand to his forehead. Wiped the sweat off.

"Why does my luck never change?"

"Puck Generalov, answer me."

Perhaps Alex only imagined it—but a spark of understanding flashed in the Zzygou's eyes.

"Go to hell, you specialized moron!" the navigator blurted out. "I didn't sign up to die for all humanity! And certainly not for the Zzygou!"

"So what's your decision?"

"Will it change anything?" asked Generalov with bitter irony.

"Maybe. Humanity is only an abstract symbol. And the Zzygou—even more so. But do you really have nothing you'd die for?"

"You decide!" Generalov blurted out.

"Do you support my decision?"

"I abstain." Puck closed his eyes and dropped back on the couch, as if he had decided not to interfere in anything anymore.

"C-the-Third?"

"I want a just solution," the clone said firmly. "You shouldn't rush to adopt such extreme measures. Perhaps Mr. Holmes will now be able to name the killer?"

Holmes smiled, tapped his pipe on the edge of the table, shaking out the ashes.

"Your suggestion is meaningless, Captain," the Zzygou uttered. "I share the wish not to have war between our races. But punishing the innocent contradicting the Zzygou ethics."

"Your suggestion is stupid, Alex," Janet concurred. "These little bees have weird ethics. Maximalism. The guilty are punished either personally, or as part of the whole genetic line. So in our case, that means either the killer alone, or the whole of humanity. Even if we all accept death willingly, they won't be interested. We used to call it 'trigger' justice, as opposed to the human 'rheostat' version."

"The murderer has to know this." Alex nodded. And Janet's face hardened.

"What is the main psychological component of the astronaut specification?" asked Alex, not leaving any time for Janet to recover her wits.

"Responsibility."

"For whom?"

"For the crew . . . for humanity in general . . ." Janet frowned. "Responsibility . . . readiness to sacrifice oneself . . . for humanity."

"Exactly." Alex nodded. "My suggestion, for all its impracticablility, does reflect our ethics."

"I would even say that it should certainly be supported by any spesh created for work in space," said Dr. Watson, entering the conversation. "Ladies and gentlemen! You all . . . you all have refused! All except Alex, Paul, and Puck!"

The Zzygou leaned over Alex. A note of anxious eagerness cut through her voice.

"All who didn't supporting your suggestion are not astronaut-speshes? They all agents? They killed Zey-So?"

"I'm not an agent! I'm a pilot!" Morrison shouted.

Alex looked at the eyes of the Zzygou. They were once again losing their resemblance to human eyes—the pupil was splitting into tiny facets.

"No, Sey-Zo," he said softly. "I don't support the idea of collective punishment, either. Your choice should be between Generalov and Lourier."

"I don't see logic . . ." said the Zzygou in a whistling whisper. "You mocking my sorrow?"

"Sey-Zo . . ." Alex suppressed a slight twinge of panic. "Just like your race consists of the ruling females and genderless slaves, humanity is divided into speshes and naturals. Who are the slaves among them?"

"Speshes." The Zzygou's face trembled. "Of course. We modifying worker individuals to suit specific social needs. You do same. That's why we called you 'servants.'"

"Sey-Zo, any astronaut-spesh would do anything to prevent humanity's destruction. That's the way we've been created. And all the alien races know that humans don't allow themselves to be taken prisoner, they don't retreat, and they don't betray their own kind."

The Zzygou nodded.

"An agent-spesh has other purposes, Sey-Zo, a different code of ethics. I would like to be able to tell you that an agent-spesh is an ethical monster, a distortion of the very best qualities of the human soul. But it isn't true, unfortunately. An agent-spesh cannot be deprived of the sense of fear—otherwise he would perish during the first few assignments. An agent-spesh, with all his physical capabilities, is an ordinary human, Zzygou. That's the way we are, and nothing can be done about it. We're capable of killing, lying, betraying . . . and saving our own skin first."

"I still not understand," said the Zzygou.

"An agent-spesh has to adapt to his surroundings. He mustn't be conspicuous. He will behave like an astronaut-spesh because he knows the laws of our behavior. On the physical level, he will be indistinguishable—his body certainly conforms to the morphology of this or that spesh. His genotype would most certainly have been modified so that the alterations couldn't be detected by ordinary express-analysis. Sey-Zo, can you tell me how to find a white crow in a flock of black crows painted white?"

Sey-Zo's eyes started pulsing once again.

"I don't remembering what are crow. But, of course, the black crow need to be wash-ed. The one that doesn't change color will be one we seek."

"It is easier to find an agent-spesh by the rule of contraries, Zzygou. You did see that all the speshes spoke out against their given program?"

The Zzygou nodded.

"All but Generalov and Lourier," Alex added. "But Generalov is a natural. And that is easy to prove by the simplest genetic test."

"Captain, I'm not an agent!" Paul cried out.

"He is the agent," said Alex, paying no attention to the engineer. "He is the one who murdered Zey-So."

"But what is the cause of the speshes' deviating from the given ethical norms?" asked the Zzygou.

"That's not important."

"Yes, it is. Otherwise your words are just gymnastics for the imagination."

"Captain, you can't do it that way!" cried Generalov. "Wait, and what if Paul is really just ready to sacrifice himself? What if his moral qualities are so high that . . ."

Alex looked at Generalov. Shook his head.

"There is one indisputable testing method. It is unlikely that such a serious assignment would be entrusted to an inexperienced youth. You're nineteen, Paul? Aren't you?"

"You bastard . . ." Lourier whispered.

"Dr. Watson, could you please determine Paul Lourier's age using a method more reliable than just visual inspection?"

"Of course." Dr. Watson nodded. "All I need is a small sample of his bone tissue. I can do the puncture myself or with the help of Janet Ruello . . ."

The next moment Paul Lourier started getting up.

The force field "safety belts" were intended only for fixing the crew in place during jolting dynamic maneuvers—not at all for restraining an agent-spesh.

Lourier's arms twisted at the elbows, hands pressing against the back of the little couch. His face turned purple—the stress hormones gushed into his bloodstream, squeezing truly super-human forces out of his modified body. With a sinking heart, Alex saw that Lourier's features were drifting, changing. As if his skin had concealed a layer of plasticine—and now it was being kneaded from within. Paul was slowly but inevitably pushing himself through the force field's zone of operation.

"Kim!" Alex shouted. "Take him!"

It seemed that the barrier-breaching method was a standard "safety" feature in speshes, operating on the level of reflexes. Kim reacted immediately, twisting her arms the very same way and pushing against the field.

"Let justice prevail," said Holmes. A gun flashed in his hand. Three waves of blue flames struck Paul Lourier. C-the-Forty-Fourth's marksmanship was astonishing—not one of the blasts touched Generalov or Morrison.

But *Mirror*'s former engineer didn't seem to feel the paralyzing radiation.

"How did they ever . . ." began Janet. "Come on, Sey-Zo, remove the field!"

But the alien didn't react to that. She was looking at the person who had murdered her partner, and her whole body was quivering with rage. Then, letting out an inarticulate scream, Sey-Zo pounced upon Lourier.

Too late.

Paul had already managed to break through the field. He met the Zzygou with a kick of both his feet, as he leaned back against the force barrier he had just breached. Sey-Zo doubled up, flew back toward the table, knocked her head against the edge of it, and lay motionless.

"You aren't all that tough . . ." Paul whispered. His movements had gained a strange predatory awkwardness—as though it was now hard for him to stay still. He looked over at Holmes.

"Put away your toy. If you reach for the 'Bulldog'—you're dead. I'm faster than you, test-tube baby . . ."

At this very second, Kim O'Hara repeated his trick with the field, broke through, and in a single leap flew up on the table.

"Friend-spesh," said the agent. "That's no way . . ."

"Face the wall, hands behind your back!" yelled Kim.

The man who used to be Paul Lourier just smiled. His face was now that of a mature man. His whole body also seemed to have changed—his shoulders were wider, his stature had increased several inches.

"You silly girl. I've killed the likes of you by the dozen."

A fight between two speshes is a very boring thing, unless you watch it in slow motion, speed reduced about ten times.

Sey-Zo was swept onto the floor when the exquisite wooden table broke in half under someone's blow, which had missed its target. Two figures whirled around the lounge like the wind, and the sounds of blows delivered or blocked thickened into a continuous hum.

This lasted four seconds—then stopped.

Ex-Paul Lourier stood near the wall, aiming a small handgun at Holmes. Kim was frozen helplessly in his arms—the agent had her throat in a stranglehold, as he kept pressing his half-bent elbow harder and harder, forcing the girl's head farther back.

"Drop the 'Bulldog,'" the agent repeated. "Or I will kill both you and the girl."

Sherlock Holmes must have realistically assessed his capacity to fight an agent-spesh. He spread his fingers, and the police pistol with its thick, ribbed barrel fell to the floor. In the silence that followed, the most distinct sound was the rustling of the cleaning-beetle that came running out of the corner to feel the dropped object. The pistol must have not had the characteristics of trash— the little beetle went away disappointed.

"To protect the innocent . . ." the agent sneered. "You're just a robot with a human body. Do you actually think any of us will get out of this alive?"

Holmes was silent, and the agent nodded in surprise.

"But you *will* walk away from here. I have no intention of kill-ing you people. Not even her." He kicked Sey-Zo without looking at her, and the Zzygou let out a weak moan. "Nope, I won't kill you. Though for different reasons."

"What are you after?" asked Holmes.

"You figured it out perfectly. I want war. The liberation of Eben. A new order in the galaxy."

"You are a madman." Holmes remained calm. "Your owners will get rid of you. You've accomplished your mission. People like you are never left alive. Even the most valuable agent has a limit. Having completed his main assignment, he himself becomes a dan-ger. Let Kim go and help us all get out. I swear I'll turn you in to the human justice system, and not to the Zzygou."

"Who told you I'm only an agent?" And here, the man who used to be Paul Lourier burst into laughter. Flexed his arm—the half-throttled Kim collapsed at his feet. "Too bad you interfered with me. The girl is a delight . . . I wouldn't mind a couple of minutes' sparring."

With a sinking heart, Alex watched Kim. Then suddenly she stirred . . . feebly, and yet it wasn't a convulsion.

Alex shifted his gaze to the agent. All the features of Paul Lourier had already disappeared from his face. He put on weight and looked like a man of forty or fifty: sturdy, manly, and dark-complexioned, his features slightly irregular—the outcome of too many genetic alterations.

"What age would your bone analysis show?" asked Alex.

The agent looked at him, nodded.

"You are quite a guy, Pilot. You amaze me. The test would show forty-nine standard Earth years."

"I know who he is . . ." Janet whispered close to the pilot's ear. Her voice had lost all its strength, turned helpless and confused.

"I do, too," Alex said. "You're forty-nine Earth years old . . . or forty-four Ebenian years?"

"Exactly. Holmes was right: those who were taken prisoner during the Battle of Pokryvalo are demoralized. They've been brainwashed, and they are being monitored . . ." He glanced at Janet, and his look had a hint of pity. "But not all patriots of humanity were known to Imperial Security."

"Angry Christ . . ." said Janet. "The Human Control Committee!"

"Ever at your side, Major Janet Ruello." The agent bowed mockingly. "You still have a chance, Major. You haven't fulfilled your humanist duty. You haven't liquidated the Other, though you had every chance to do so. But I do understand the gravity of the psychological treatment you've been subjected to . . . and I can issue a conditional pardon—for the duration of the military conflict. Your decision?"

"I . . . I . . ."

Alex felt that Janet was shaking all over. He touched her hand.

"I am bound by an oath I swore to the ship's captain. I cannot."

"Janet Ruello, you're looking to excuse your treason." The agent was studying the black woman's face with a mixture of pity and disgust. "All right. As a senior officer, I release you from the obligations you were forced to make."

Janet was silent.

"You had your chance, Major." The agent seemed a bit surprised. "You've made your choice."

He bent down over the Zzygou, then jerked her up in front of him, holding her by the hair with one hand.

"What are you going to do with us?" asked Morrison. "Whoever you might be, you are human, and . . ."

"I am human, but the question is—are *you*?" the agent inquired. "Don't worry. This force field barrier is very handy. Otherwise I'd have to kill you all. As soon as the military actions between humanity and the Zzygou begin, I'll leave you."

Holmes mockingly raised one eyebrow.

"The warship will leave, and my friends will come," said the agent.

The Zzygou stirred and hissed something to him.

"Ah, regaining the gift of speech, are we?" the agent jeered. He lowered his hand into his pocket, then raised it again—holding a small pocketknife. "Then it's time I do something about that."

The next second Alex had to look away. It seemed everyone followed his example, except for Holmes. The detective remained sitting still, his back straight, his icy eyes watching what was happening.

The alien let out a gurgling, gagging sigh. Something soft and small plopped down on the carpet.

This time the cleaning-beetle decided it had some work to do. The Zzygou moaned inarticulately, pressing her hands to her bloody mouth. Drops of red blood were streaming down through her clenched fingers. The little beetle bustled around at her feet, eating up the stains. But to take the severed tongue away, it had to call for another cleaner's help.

"You scum," said Alex. "What are you—executioner-spesh?"

The agent shook his head. "My dear Captain, specialization of the psyche is the fate of slaves. Didn't you say so yourself? That's the way it was on Eben, and that's the way it is in the Empire."

He wiped his bloodstained hands against the Zzygou's dress, shoved her roughly into a corner. And then, having taken out his pistol, he fired it four times in a row. Alex didn't manage to recognize the model of the firearm—something operating on low-temperature plasma. Perhaps it was of Ebenian make, or maybe exclusive to Imperial Security. The Zzygou wheezed from the pain, coughing up blood. Her legs were scorched at the knees, and her arms at the elbows. C-the-Third, letting out a horrible, piercing shriek, started thrashing and writhing in the clutches of the force field.

"You're a butcher," said Alex.

"No." Paul Lourier shook his head. "They're tough buggers.

Sey-Zo will survive . . . long enough to hear the news of the obliteration of her entire race. She even has a chance to be the last living Zzygou in the galaxy."

He lowered his gun into his pocket. Smiled—openly, with natural ease.

"Consider me whatever you like. An executioner. A xenophobe. A psycho. But really, I'm just an ordinary man. A normal human, making normal plans for the future. The Zzygou are our main rivals in the galaxy. The Bronins don't share our attitude toward expansion. They have long given up conquering new territories. The Fenhuans need to colonize planets that don't suit us. With the Cepheideans—we can coexist just fine, and our alliance with the Zzygou is the only thing that prevents us from assimilating new planets together. The Church of the Angry Christ are insane idealists. And the Ebenian speshes—nothing but cannon fodder. The Imperial speshes are all emasculated degenerates. Imperial power is just a screen for trans-galactic corporations. The Empire has, to its shame, lost its fighting fist, the planet Eben. Lost all those who have always served humans . . . real humans. Like me. Those of us who really rule the universe. We got rid of the last Emperor too late . . . he was a real Emperor, I admit, but he lapsed into stupid idealism. Now all of that can be reversed."

"Why are you telling us all this, Committee rat?" cried Janet.

"Not just to kill you off for knowing way too much," smirked the agent. "You can't understand it . . . valiant Ebenian Fleet Major Janet Ruello . . . Ah! The hopes I had for you! But you let me down. I'm not afraid of your testimonies. In ten more hours, they won't mean a thing. But I want all you self-satisfied scumbags to know who rules the universe. To know it and remember it for the rest of your lives! And it isn't you, spiritually mutilated speshes. And not the orthodox naturals, who get drunk on one glass of vodka, come down with the sniffles, and aren't any good for any job. Those who have absorbed all the strength of genetic alterations but created no blocks in their consciousness—they are your real masters! They rule the planets, they move billions, and they decide between war and peace. And all that's intended for you—are illusions. Sweet dreams. False belief in your own exclusiveness. And that's the way it has always been and always will be. Always. Masters and slaves never switch places . . . my dear, harmonious crew. Your place will always be reserved for you. In an asteroid mine. Behind an office computer. At a ship's control panel. In combat line with your ray gun."

He was clearly enjoying what was happening. He was on a roll—this Imperial Security agent, Ebenian Human Control officer, secret Imperial politician . . . and whoever else he was, this spesh who wasn't a spesh. Unfettered by anything—neither the moral barriers of speshes, nor the ancient ethics of naturals. And Alex caught himself thinking that he could understand the agent's overwhelming need to unburden himself. Perhaps for the first time in decades. To shed the latest in a long line of masks he'd grown sick of, so that now, standing there with his own—or was it?—face before his recent friends, he could tell them everything he really had on his mind.

"You have nothing to say? Are some of you surprised, perhaps?" The agent looked around at them. "Or maybe you believed that ancient gibberish about human equality? How much of that have we had! Christianity, free enterprise, communism, the genetic revolution . . . And always the same thing—equality of opportunity . . . the thing than never existed in the first place. Social origin is what has always determined everything. Starting capital, social status, the choice made by parents—that's what determines your destiny. And yours has been decided a long, long time ago. The destiny of a slave. And the slave-parents told the slave-children, 'All those around you are chattel, and you are the master.' And the slave-children said to each other, 'We'll be masters of all Life.' But everything has already been decided. Long before your time. And the real rulers are those who are silent. Standing silently in the shadows. But if we have to . . ."

Alex had been watching Kim for a minute or so now. The girl grew quiet . . . she was regrouping.

And now she dealt her blow. Right from the floor, without getting up, without even looking at the agent, by hearing alone—she recoiled, kicking the agent in the stomach with both feet, as she pushed up on her arms and jumped to her feet with a springy bounce.

He didn't seem to even notice the blow that had the power to rip through a normal man's entrails. His body had been so stuffed with alterations that the agent only swayed a little—and the next moment Kim was once again frozen in front of him, her arms cruelly twisted behind her back, her face awful with the pain, or with those sensations that are pain substitutes in a fighter-spesh.

"If we have to, we act independently," the agent said, finishing his phrase. "Didn't I tell you I don't want to kill you, Kim O'Hara? Calm down. People like you are always in demand, any place you go. Do your work and be happy during your long and interesting life."

Kim laughed, spat—unsuccessfully trying to turn her head far enough back to hit the agent. "You . . . master of Life . . . you spend it under other people's names, in other people's bodies . . . groveling before those of us you call your slaves!"

The agent burst into laughter. "You're like an impotent actor who can only screw when he plays Casanova . . . what are you so proud of?"

"That's a good idea." The former engineer of *Mirror* glanced over at Generalov. "I'm so sick of that sniveling sodomite!"

"But you liked it!" Puck shouted. It seemed he was stung to his very core. "But you—"

The agent no longer paid any attention to the rest of them. The blows that he landed on Kim seemed more like soft touches—but the girl went limp, her head lowered feebly.

"Monster . . ." whispered Janet. "God . . . what a monster."

"They're all monsters," said Alex.

Janet looked at him with hatred. "It's all your order . . . the force field. You should have known that a fighter-spesh would break right through it."

"I should have," Alex agreed. "But we needed this . . . moral striptease. I had no idea it would end up being a real striptease."

The agent tossed Kim down onto the floor. Bent over, ripping off her clothes.

"Excuse me for not inviting you all to participate, my dear colleagues," he said through clenched teeth. "But those of you with a penchant for voyeurism can satisfy your curiosity."

He heaved himself heavily on top of the girl. Despite the monstrosity of what was happening, Alex was suddenly sharply hit by a strange, unpleasant sensation of a similarity between the rapist and the victim. The sturdy, stalwart agent and the slender, fragile girl—they seemed to be parts of a whole. They made up some kind of perverted but integral duo. It was as if they had been made for each other . . .

Alex lowered his eyelids. Whispered with his lips alone:

"Captain's access. No reply necessary."

Less than three and a half yards away from him, the Ebenian counter-intelligence agent was taking possession of Kim O'Hara. Alex waited four unbearably long seconds, ready to give the rest of his order to the ship at any moment. Waited four endless centuries, before the agent screamed.

There was nothing human about the sound of his scream. Mixing within it were pain and a panic-stricken, endlessly ancient terror, rooted in the very depths of the subconscious.

"Remove the lounge block!" This time Alex yelled out loud, jumping up.

Sherlock Holmes, of course, reacted faster. When Alex leaped toward the agent, who was twitching convulsively on top of the half-undressed Kim, the detective's 'Bulldog' was already pressed to the rapist's temple. Holmes's other hand had dug into the agent's neck with the strength of steel pincers.

"Get up!" snarled Holmes.

The agent didn't seem to hear him. Or perhaps he thought both the pistol and the vertebrae-crushing hand a meaningless trifle, next to what he was experiencing at that moment.

"Release him, Kim," said Alex, catching the girl's glance—the self-composed, harsh, willful look of an agent-spesh. "It's all right, Kim. You did great."

Kim hesitated for a moment. Then shoved the agent off with one abrupt push. Holmes didn't let him fall over again, but hoisted him up—the way the agent had himself just recently held the Zzygou. The detective's fingers were still gripping the agent's vertebrae, and the skin ripped by his nails oozed blood. The gun seemed to have grown into his temple.

"Janet!" cried Alex. "Attend to Sey-Zo, she's bleeding to death!"

C-the-Third didn't have to be ordered, he was already bustling over the Zzygou's body. The black woman asked:

"Why me?"

"Because you're trained in it! You're an executioner-spesh, and you know the Zzygou anatomy!"

After a moment's wavering, Janet Ruello joined the clone's efforts. Alex helped Kim get up and pull on her torn-up slacks. He said quietly:

"Forgive me, baby. I couldn't interfere earlier."

Kim looked at him seriously, nodded.

"I know. He's too strong . . . he would've killed everybody, even if we'd all attacked at once."

Dr. Watson, in the meantime, was fixing the force field handcuffs onto the agent's hands. As soon as they snapped closed, the metal bracelets reached for each other with enormous force, twisting the arms that, up until that moment, had been pressed to the agent's groin. He was still whimpering quietly, twisting this way and that, trying to see his bloodstained groin.

"What . . . what did you do to him?" Generalov's countenance had changed. What he had just seen seemed to have frightened him more than anything else in his whole life. Kim didn't answer. Wincing, she was feeling her body all over.

"Do you need help?" asked Dr. Watson, businesslike. "Kim?"

The girl shook her head. Answered with a hint of irony:

"No, probably not. I'm tough. All I need is a shower . . ."

She looked at Alex again. And asked, "How did you know about this specification of mine? It isn't documented anywhere."

"A virtual acquaintance of yours gave me a hint."

Kim's eyes narrowed. She nodded, with a slight hesitation.

Alex soothingly patted her shoulder. Went over to the Zzygou.

She was alive and conscious. And that, however cynical it might sound, was the most important thing.

"Lady Sey-Zo," said Alex, softly pushing aside C-the-Third, who was bandaging the alien's elbows. "Muster your strength, Lady Sey-Zo. The future of our races now depends on the strength of your will."

Dim with pain, split into hundreds of facets, the Zzygou's eyes looked at him. The alien nodded.

"Have you been convinced that your companion's murderer is the man who's been disguised as our engineer?"

She nodded again.

"Lady Sey-Zo . . . everything is now in your power. If we leave him alive, then the investigation could possibly lead us to the other members of this plot. To the Ebenian agents entrenched in Imperial Security, to the corrupt politicians who have dealings with them, to the heads of weaponry-producing corporations . . . to all those who were interested in a bloodbath."

The Zzygou shook her head.

"She's right," said Sherlock Holmes from behind Alex's back. "We won't be able to punish those who rule the planetary administrations and are members of the Imperial Council . . . What we'll get, at most, is a series of unfortunate accidents . . . involving us."

"And what about 'Let the world perish, so long as justice prevails'?" asked Alex without turning.

"Captain, I'm only a clone, deprived of the sense of fear, compassion, and love. But I'm not a fool. And Sey-Zo understands as well as we do that it is impossible to root out evil completely."

"Do you want to execute him, Sey-Zo?" Alex asked. "To do it personally? Is it necessary to stop the war?"

The Zzygou nodded.

CHAPTER 5.

"A few planets," said Peter C-the-Forty-Fourth Valke, a.k.a the greatest detective of all time, Sherlock Holmes, "have banned this method of capital punishment as inhumane."

The device in his hand didn't really seem all that menacing. An oval case with a little indicator window and three buttons—not sensors, but primitive mechanical buttons, probably to rule out an accidental release.

"But considering the gravity of the crime, and its implications for the fate of the galaxy, as well as other crimes of which we do not know, but which doubtlessly have also been committed . . ."

The agent lay on the operating table. His hands were still fettered with handcuffs. His feet and his head were held in place by the table's stationary brackets—Alex could only guess their actual purpose. The agent was silent, looking at his executioners, and even now, his eyes expressed absolutely nothing.

Professionals know how to die with dignity, though not even they have an opportunity to practice dying.

"In the name of his Imperial Majesty, in the name of Imperial

Justice, in the name of the Free Republic of Zodiac, in the name of all humanity, I, detective-spesh, accuse you . . ."

Sey-Zo lay in an intensive care pod. A few programs about treating the Zzygou had been found in the gel-crystal of the medical module. She couldn't speak, of course, but her lower pair of arms retained mobility, and now her hands lay on the control panel of a communications device. She listened closely to Holmes, who now began to read out the sentence:

"Murder, committed under especially aggravated circumstances. Sadism, not sanctioned by the victim. High treason, for on the Empire's territory, Zey-So was considered the personal guest of the Emperor. And that's not a full list of your heinous deeds! Considering the special circumstances of the crime, the sentence cannot be appealed and will be carried out immediately."

Sherlock Holmes nodded to Dr. Watson. The woman came up to the agent and clicked shut a flat metal hoop around his head.

"Does the accused have any last words?" asked C-the-Forty-Fourth coldly.

The agent licked his lips. He realized what was going to happen next, but perhaps the collapse of the whole conspiracy was what he feared most.

"I will be avenged," he said, "you can be sure of that."

Holmes shrugged and looked at Alex, who then stepped forward. He had to say something now.

"You violated all the rules of the space fleet," he said. "You went against your captain and your crew. You have committed the most terrible crime an astronaut-spesh can commit—you brought harm to your passengers. You shall die."

He stepped back. And immediately after that, without asking anyone, Kim O'Hara stepped forward. She cried out sharply:

"You killed a good friend of mine. You mutilated another. You made an attempt to commit the most despicable act imaginable—sexual violence against a helpless woman. You shall die."

Moving Kim aside, Janet Ruello approached the agent.

"You blasphemed against the Angry Christ and His Holy Church. You called your comrades in arms and your compatriots 'cannon fodder.' You brought dishonor to the very idea of the human race's superiority! You shall die."

Xang Morrison stepped up to stand next to Janet.

"You attempted to provoke others to commit the crimes you needed. When that did not happen, you perpetrated the evil deed yourself, but tried to frame innocent people. You shall die."

C-the-Third did not come any closer. He simply said:

"You deprived me of my reason to exist. You destroyed a peaceful and prospering tourist agency. You reversed the very process of all races coming closer together. You shall die."

Puck Generalov was the last to approach the agent. His features were now obscured by a thick layer of cosmetics—red and black hues of mourning. His braid was loosened and a small black bow was woven into it.

"You're possessed by the idea of intellectual, physiological, and racial superiority," he pronounced quietly. "You've mocked the purest and the most sacred human emotions. You embody all the vices of the human race. You shall die."

The Zzygou stirred feebly in her capsule. A screen unfolded in the air, and across it ran the letters to form the merciless words:

You destroyed the genetic line of Zey-So, thus murdering numberless multitudes of females, drones, and working individuals. You shall die.

The detective walked up to the capsule and, lowering his hands through the reanimation fluid, carefully handed the control device to Sey-Zo.

"Do you remember how to operate this?"

The Zzygou nodded. Mental destructors had been created based on Zzygou technologies. Turning back towards the criminal, the detective said in a loud, solemn voice:

"Your evil deeds have overfilled the cup of patience of the people in the galaxy and the Emperor on Earth. If you know any prayers, pray, for your consciousness will now be reversed and reduced to zero. You will die as an individual, and your body will be handed over to the Zzygou for collective desecration."

The agent twitched as the Zzygou, lying in her capsule, pushed the three buttons one after the other.

A horrible scream was torn from his throat as the emitter of the mental destructor began working in the head ring, erasing his memory. Hour after hour, day after day, month after month . . . Every minute, two years of his life were destroyed . . . but the most terrible thing was that short-term memory was the last to be erased, and the criminal remained conscious till the very end.

Everyone spontaneously stepped back from the operating table. Dr. Watson covered her face with her hands, and even Kim O'Hara turned her head away.

"The first and the last time I conducted a mental destruction was six years ago," said Sherlock Holmes in a low voice. "The Case of the Dispersing Cloud . . . eight human casualties in less than a month. But we had determined the cause of the perpetrator's emotional dislocation, hidden among childhood complexes. We retained the maniac's consciousness at the level of a nine-year-old child. He went through a good psychotherapy course . . . and now he's a college graduate, atoning for his wrongdoing by honest work."

Nobody replied to Holmes's words—and the detective fell silent. All stood under the agent's hateful gaze, listening to his half-demented curses. Ten minutes later, he fell silent. Mental destructors had been invented only twenty years before, so by now the criminal didn't even understand what was happening to him.

When twenty minutes passed, the agent started weeping. Sobbing, like a child, looking around helplessly and trying to break free. Janet heaved a deep sigh—her maternal instincts were strong. And now a child was dying under the destructor ray . . . even if that child had long since grown up to become a ruthless killer.

She glanced at the Zzygou.

Sey-Zo was implacable.

She conducted the process for exactly twenty-five minutes, wiping the agent's mind clean, even his unconscious memories as an embryo. And only after that did she switch off the control device.

The person who had murdered her companion was now drooling on the operating table. His eyeballs were rolling aimlessly. His arms and legs twitched without any coordination. And it seemed as though his sphincter had loosened.

"Lady Sey-Zo, are you satisfied by the punishment of the criminal?" Holmes asked in an official tone of voice.

The screen lit up the word YES.

"What would you like to do with the body?"

Use it for something socially beneficial. Let it be known—I am carrying out Justice, not revenge.

"Do you agree to contact your race and inform them that justice has prevailed?"

Bring the transceiver.

C-the-Third went off to get the device.

It wasn't all that wise to be near the portable, poorly screened gluon transmitter, but they remained in the medical block till the end. They all watched the lines of the alien language flash on and disappear on the holographic screen—Sey-Zo couldn't use the neuro-terminal now. They watched some Zzygou faces flash by—of those who hadn't undergone anthropomorphosis and only partially resembled humans.

And only when the call was over and Sey-Zo's speech-screen showed the words The fleets have been recalled. Stop your warships did they all leave the medical module. C-the-Third and Janet stayed with Sey-Zo—the alien's condition was still very serious.

The recreation lounge had been straightened up. Only the broken table stood as a reminder of the recent fight.

First of all, Alex poured himself a glass full of ninety-proof bourbon and drained it in one gulp. Morrison, who entered the lounge right behind him, nodded in agreement and also applied himself to the fiery beverage. They refilled their glasses and silently sat down next to each other.

Even the modified metabolism of speshes had its limits. Now they had a chance to experience, for a while, a very real intoxication, the way their ancestors and the naturals felt it.

"He looked just like a regular guy . . . a youngster, fresh out of the academy." Xang shrugged. "I would never have thought he was more than twenty years old. . . ."

"Me neither. At first."

"What put you on guard, Alex?" Morrison looked at him demandingly.

"Does it make any difference?"

"It does. You're . . . you're a strange man, Captain Alex Romanov. I'd like to know how you found him out."

"I'm not a captain anymore, Xang. And I doubt that what has happened will look very good on my service record. I probably won't ever rise above a *Hamster* pilot, I'm afraid."

"Come on, Alex, stop it. For me . . . for all of us, you'll always be the captain. Tell me, how did you unmask the killer?"

Alex hesitated, but not for long. It didn't make any difference now.

"A few strange things in his behavior. On New Ukraine, for instance, Paul stayed at the bar, instead of going on a planetary tour. That's strange for a greenhorn who hasn't seen much of the galaxy, right? Of course, I've met youngsters who just loved being around astronauts and would sit in a bar day and night, sipping beer. But Paul Lourier was obviously not one of those. For instance, after getting hired onto the ship, he left the restaurant right away."

Morrison nodded uncertainly. Alex continued:

"And then there was the strange behavior of Generalov, who plotted the trek Quicksilver Pit-New Ukraine-Heraldica-Zodiac-Edem, even before we knew our route. The agent probably knew the route in advance. It would be logical to suppose that Puck was the actual killer. But . . . Generalov is a natural. Even becoming a navigator was already a leap above his head. To be an agent on top of that, and a professional assassin? Unthinkable. So there must have been some other reasons. Something had prompted him to think of that route. Remember, with whom did Generalov communicate most actively?"

"With Paul, of course."

"And during that conversation, Generalov, without realizing it himself, had received directions for that trek from Paul."

"But why?"

"Remember that tanker that tried to ram into us? Such a maneuver is really difficult to calculate. Our ship had to be entering the hyper-channel on a very precise route. And Generalov couldn't plot a course toward Zodiac through, say, Monica-3. He had to stop by New Ukraine."

"Puck said he was sure he had chosen that route all by himself," said Morrison meditatively.

"Of course he did. But who needs direct hints? All Paul had to do was to mention his fear of the Bronins, being scared he wouldn't be able to manage the engine in a combat situation . . . and Generalov would be set in his intent to avoid the Bronins' ritual fighting zone. A remark about ancestors who had lived in the place called Ukraine back on Earth—and there you have New Ukraine. Ask Generalov about his astrological sign—and there you have Zodiac."

"And that's precisely how it happened?"

"I don't know, Xang. We could ask Puck to remember everything, but why traumatize the guy any more than necessary? I'm sure it all happened more or less like that."

Alex got out a cigarette, lit up. Xang took a pensive gulp of bourbon.

"That's it?"

"Of course not. There were many such details. Well, like when we still didn't know that poor Zey-So was already dead, and I, not suspecting anything, asked the pseudo-Paul Lourier to call in the Zzygou . . . and approach Zey-So first, as the senior partner. Tell me, Xang, could you tell the little bees apart?"

"No."

"Did you know which cabin was Zey-So's and which was Sey-Zo's?"

"Of course not! Why would I?"

"But the agent did know, of course. And so he made a small mistake—he went off to the passenger cabins without asking how exactly to find Zey-So."

"Ah! That's more serious," admitted Xang.

"Yes . . . but still it doesn't really prove anything. Especially not to the Zzygou. That's why I had to . . . set up this difficult situation."

A strong, sinewy hand was lowered onto Alex's shoulder.

"Bravo," said Sherlock Holmes. "Bravo, Captain. If you ever want to make some clones of yourself and specialize them as detective-speshes, I will be for it in every way. And my word means a lot in our union, believe me!"

Alex turned around.

Holmes was not the only one there. Dr. Watson, looking at him with great admiration, was also in the recreation lounge, as were Kim and Generalov himself.

Alex smiled, a little embarrassed.

"I finally determined who the murderer was after I'd heard every crewmember's story," said Holmes. "My reasoning was based on the clues you've just enumerated . . . as well as a few other strange aspects of Paul Lourier's behavior. But he came very close to being an ideal murderer. All these little false steps . . . they could have been the basis of a court hearing, and of an in-depth investigation, but our time constraints were way too tight. Sey-Zo wouldn't have believed the circumstantial evidence. She knew very well that astronaut-speshes are capable of coordinating their actions and falsely accusing someone, or even forcing him or her to make a false confession. We had to have a complete confession. We needed a beautiful, demonstrative self-incrimination by the perpetrator. Therefore . . . we needed a provocation."

The detective took out his pipe. He pressed down the fragrant tobacco that filled it, then lifted his lighter.

"I had . . . two different plans . . . either one of which . . . should have led . . . to success . . ."

Holmes drew on his pipe, let out a stream of fragrant smoke.

"But I decided that your actions, Captain, would serve the same goal . . . so I resolved to give you a chance."

"Thank you, Mr. Holmes," said Alex.

"You can thank Dr. Watson," replied Holmes with a smile. "She was the one who insisted that you have a tenacious mind and the reasoning abilities of a natural detective. Your supposition about the killer's use of a gel spacesuit, for example, was really excellent. To my shame, I must admit I didn't pay any attention to that marvelous achievement of scientific thought."

Alex bowed gratefully to Dr. Watson. The woman smiled in reply. He asked:

"Mr. Holmes, was the game I played a bit too risky?"

"Yes, it was. Your force field trick scared me, but I took the chance of trusting you. By the way, how did you remove your own absolute order?"

Morrison laughed quietly.

"I got it, though not right away. A captain gives orders on two levels—the standard way, and the one with the captain's access, which allows absolutely everything. The first order did get executed, but it was given on the regular priority level. And when Alex decided to cancel his previous order, he simply used the magic words 'captain's access.' The ship removed the force field belts immediately."

Holmes nodded.

"Curious. And I supposed that our esteemed captain had ordered the ship in advance—to obey him for show, while actually still following his commands."

"Damn . . ." was all Alex could say. "That would've been just as effective, but even more secure . . . after all, the agent could've noticed that I was using the simple form of command!"

"Any investigation is a tug-and-pull of two sets of mistakes," said Dr. Watson thoughtfully. "The criminal makes his own mistakes, and the detective his. They're unavoidable, even if the detective is a spesh. The main thing is not to allow your own mistakes to become graver than the mistakes of the criminal."

Holmes nodded, and asked:

"And what was the basis of your faith in Kim? The girl . . ."—he

461

gently hugged Kim around the shoulders—"has practically no combat experience!"

"Kim and I have a mutual acquaintance," began Alex very cautiously. "And he has mentioned that the girl is well protected against sexual aggression. She has some undocumented and unusual fighter-spesh capabilities. The main risk was different—would the agent go for rape? But I made my bet on Kim's capabilities that lie more in the hetaera realm. The excitement of battle would inevitably lead to pheromone release, so the agent couldn't help himself. He was sick and tired of his role as a quiet, model cadet, and so . . ."—Alex smirked—"he bit and was snared."

Holmes shook his head in disapproval.

"What a monstrous genetic fantasy! Ancient myths, as I recall, frequently mention sly women with similar bodily features, but to make this terrible fairy tale a reality . . ."

Kim scoffed. "I don't see anything terrible about it. I control my body very well . . . and only a rapist has reason to fear. A tiny tooth that releases an extremely painful toxin . . . not a single woman, I think, would ever refuse such an ability."

Generalov cast a grim look upon her, but said nothing.

"Well," Holmes exhaled, as if drawing the line of finality, "I'm glad that most of you turned out not to have been involved in the crime. And what's more—that you were able to overcome your inhibitions, grudges, and ambitions, and work to be of great help to me. I think this tragic event will go down in the annals as 'The Case of the Nine Suspects.'"

"Nine?" asked Alex. "Are you sure, Mr. Holmes?"

"At first, I was not excluding C-the-Third, or Sey-Zo, not even the victim herself. Only after inspecting the crime scene did I become convinced that the extravagant suicide version should be dismissed."

"Ripping out your own guts and lying down to die?" Alex inquired.

"The Zzygou are very tenacious. But you're right, not even *they* are capable of that."

Holmes sighed, and his face lit up with the smallest and rarest of smiles—rare because it obviously came from the depths of his soul.

"Well, this investigation is over. Dr. Watson, is everything clear to you?"

"Yes." The woman nodded. Holmes looked rather startled—it seemed that Jenny's duties had always included asking a few more-or-less silly questions at the end. But his loyal companion added, looking at Alex, "I admire you, Pilot. And I'm also a little sorry . . . that you're a pilot-spesh."

For a moment, there was an uneasy silence.

"What's to become of us?" asked Generalov finally.

"You will now write detailed reports about the events that you witnessed. If I find them satisfactory, we will allow you to land on Zodiac, and after that, you will all be free to go. Your ship is, as I've already said, impounded, and you will have to look for other employment. But . . ." Holmes cocked his head, raising his eyebrows. "I can't help you there. Such is the will of the Emperor."

"Or, more exactly, of the Imperial Council, which probably includes a few of the agent's accomplices," added Morrison gloomily.

"I have no right to enter this discussion. And I advise you to restrain yourself from dubious comments about the ruling government!" said Holmes harshly.

"Mr. Holmes, what will be done with Paul Lourier's body?" asked Kim.

"The real Paul Lourier has probably found eternal rest in the soil of Quicksilver Pit," Holmes replied. "Or lies in some seedy bar, stuffed full of drugs. You mean, the agent's body?"

"Yes."

"It will be sold to a clinic on Zodiac. They will probably find a use for it . . . testing new drugs or teaching students to perform complex surgery."

"Can *I* buy the body?"

Holmes looked at Kim in surprise.

"I have money!" hastily added the girl. "We are entitled to sizable severance pay, right? Or will that not be enough?"

"I doubt that a body of a narrowly specialized fighter-specimen, devoid of all memory, will cost all that much," said Holmes pensively. "But, for goodness' sake, tell me, what do you need it for?"

"Maybe I'm sentimental," said Kim with a smile. "So maybe I want to care for the helpless human shell whose individuality has been destroyed with my help. Or maybe I'm a filthy sadist who wants to torture a soulless piece of organic material? No, wait . . . maybe I'm a crazy nymphomaniac who decided to get herself a super-submissive lover?"

"I think the real reason wasn't mentioned," Holmes replied. "In any case, I don't see any obstacles to it."

Alex caught Kim's triumphant glance and gave her a little

nod. Edward Garlitsky had gained a body. A strong and complex one . . . Oh, God . . . that was . . .

He shifted his gaze away.

That eerie impression of unity, of affinity between these two agent-speshes which had stung him for a moment during their fight—had it been just a coincidence? Garlitsky had created himself a bodyguard, a helper, a lover . . . but who said that he hadn't also started growing some bodies for himself a long, long time before that? Back when Eben wasn't yet part of the Empire, he had to have been a consultant for their geneticists. And Eben, ready to implement endless specifications for human bodies, could have served him as his best, most reliable testing ground!

"And now, ladies and gentlemen," said Holmes almost cheerfully, "I ask everyone to go back to his or her cabin and get started on compiling those reports."

Alex silently got up.

"And you, Mr. Romanov," said Holmes brusquely, "I will ask to stay!"

Dr. Watson seemed the most surprised. When Holmes asked her to leave for the second time, she gave up, but shook her head with a hurt expression.

Alex was not surprised by this demand to stay. What was much more surprising was that the detective preferred to speak with him one-on-one.

Before he said anything else, Holmes took a small black disk out of his pocket. He touched the control sensors and put it down on the floor. Their ears got a little stuffed up, and the room around them seemed to have gotten darker.

"Now we're insulated from your ship's internal surveillance devices," Holmes informed him. Alex was looking at him with growing astonishment. "I would like to get a few unofficial answers . . . unofficial for *now*," Holmes emphasized.

"Only an idiot lies to a detective-spesh," said Alex wearily.

"Yes, of course. Smart people just don't mention some details. Alex Romanov, what has happened to you and to your crew?"

"What are you referring to, Mr. Holmes?"

"To the strange behavior of the speshes, who were required to sacrifice themselves for humanity. You yourself, I believe, have said that a normal spesh has to readily perish for the good of the Empire?"

"Stress, perhaps?" ventured Alex. "We all found ourselves in such an alarming, ambiguous situation . . . besides, our common death wouldn't satisfy Sey-Zo anyway."

"This is the version I will express in the official report," said Holmes. "That is, I might express it. But now I would like to hear the truth."

Under the detective's intent stare, Alex lowered his hand into his pocket and took out the little vial.

"A while ago," he said, putting the vial next to the black disk, "I happened to get my hands on a rare drug."

"Yes," said Holmes, encouragingly.

"Its effect on the organism of a spesh . . . any spesh . . . leads to the blocking of all the emotional alterations."

"The emotional ones only?"

"Yes. Memory, professional characteristics, body modifications remain intact."

Holmes carefully lifted the vial, shook it. Pensively remarked:

"And you fed this drug to your crew."

"Yes. You saw the result."

"I'm baffled," Holmes confessed. "Was this drug obtained by you in an honest way?"

"Of course. The formula was given to me by its creator. As far as I understand, he had been working on the remedy for many years. The synthesis was performed in an ordinary automatic laboratory, and I paid for it the honest way . . . nothing shady here."

"Except that speshes start acting like naturals."

"This remedy doesn't force any extraneous emotions on anyone, Mr. Holmes. This isn't some narcotic. Even calling it a psychotropic drug would be a stretch. All it does is temporarily block the emotions distorted by specialization."

"You say that as if specialization were something evil."

"No, of course not. But . . . does the law forbid speshes to get rid of changes made to their own ethics?"

"Why forbid something that's impossible?" Holmes replied with a question. "There has not been a precedent."

"Maybe the fact that Imperial laws do allow a spesh to remove the physiological after-effects of specialization, if he so wishes, could serve as such a precedent?"

Holmes nodded. He dropped back in his armchair, still holding the vial in his hand.

"You can try the remedy, Mr. Holmes," Alex suggested. "Just a few drops will do it. An overdose isn't dangerous. And it works . . . um . . . for several days."

"Is this, by any chance, a bribe offer?" said Holmes with lively interest.

"No. It's an agreement to conduct an investigative experiment. You can estimate the consequences of the use of the drug and, if you find them dangerous, you can subject me to any punishment."

"You're quite a risk-taker, Alex Romanov!" Holmes frowned. "You're *that* sure of your decision, eh?"

"No. I'm not sure," Alex admitted frankly. "But I hope you will agree with me."

"Alex, my dear fellow." Holmes smiled. "Tell me, what would a detective-spesh be worth, if he were capable of falling in love? Afraid of a ray gun pointed at him? Overcome by sentiments?"

"I don't know what you'll be worth, Mr. Holmes." Alex leaned slightly toward him. "Honestly, I don't. But if specialization is the only thing that prevents you from taking bribes from criminals or hiding from murderers—you're not worth a dime, anyway. Neither you, nor your matrix, Peter Valke!"

"Don't you try to play on my curiosity, Alex!" replied Holmes harshly. "Don't! It's the only human trait I have left!"

"No, C-the-Forty-Fourth! It isn't! You also have your longing for truth. And truth is not something that is stuffed into your brain by peptide chains! Not at all! Truth is what you really, truly are!"

For a brief moment, Alex felt that Holmes would now take out a pair of handcuffs and utter the standard arrest formula.

But Holmes lowered his eyes.

And so he sat there for a few seconds, downcast, peering at the floor, turning the vial between his fingers. Then, with a brisk movement, he hid it in his pocket.

"I will take every precaution, Alex Romanov," he said quietly.

"Keep that in mind. And if you have lied . . . even unintention-ally . . . if the drug forces me to behave in ways unnatural to me . . ."

He didn't finish his warning. Just got up and left the recreation lounge.

Report writing was an activity speshes were quite accustomed to. At times Alex even wondered why it wasn't included in the spe-cialization. Or maybe it was included, but considered so insignifi-cant that it wasn't worth mentioning.

He decided not to use the neuro-terminal. Writing a text with "thoughts" demanded too much control over one's consciousness. Alex unfolded a virtual keyboard and, for almost an entire hour, sat drumming his fingers in the air, arranging words in the most grammatical, beautiful . . . and least dangerous order.

He even managed to mention the machination that had helped bring Kim O'Hara aboard the ship. No one could say that Alex had tampered with the truth in any way.

There was, of course, no mention whatsoever of the gel-crystal, of Edward Garlitsky, or of the emotions blocker.

His fingers were dancing in the air, lightly touching the holo-graphic letters. Blue sparks flashed with every tap on the invisible keys. An illusory sheet of paper slowly scrolled upwards, taking within it the whole story of the first and only tourist flight of the spaceship *Mirror* and its unusual crew.

Alex re-read what he had just written. Thought for a moment, shrugged.

It was hard to say what the outcome of it all would be. There was still a chance that the union would consider him liable for what had happened, and then a pilot's worst fate would befall Alex—he would be forbidden to fly.

But somehow, even that didn't really frighten him now.

He gave the computer the command to create a hard copy of the report, got up from behind the desk, and opened the processor panel. Carefully extracted the gel-crystal that contained the mind of Edward Garlitsky and his entire strange little world.

How weird. How absurd. A scientific genius, the person who had uncovered all the mysteries of genetic code—who had, for many years now, been dwelling in a chunk of crystallized liquid. Mad with rage, bored, lonesome . . . rearranging other people's genes over and over . . . constructing virtual worlds and fighting virtual wars . . . and the whole time, endlessly devising plan after plan after plan to break free.

Even if, in the meantime, he kept trampling over someone else's freedom over and over again . . .

Alex looked at the small hatch of the little microwave built into the cabin wall. An illusion of all the comforts of home. To warm up a sandwich, or fry up a steak on the infrared grill.

Or to incinerate a whole world with its only inhabitant . . .

Alex took out the neuro-shunt, inserted the crystal into the contact surface, and tied the headband around his head.

There were no rivers or forests, no castles or dragons. There were no guards with swords or seductive maidens in transparent garments.

There was a gray, sandy field and a low gray sky. On a simple wooden chair, half-buried in sand, sat a middle-aged man dressed in an old-fashioned suit with a tie around his neck—that archaic ritual noose, if you believed all the films about ancient life.

Alex walked up to the geneticist Edward Garlitsky, stopped, studying his face.

Strange.

He wasn't a copy of the spesh who had disguised himself as Paul Lourier. But the resemblance seemed undeniable. It wasn't in his features, or his gestures, or his age . . . It was an elusive likeness—as though you were ripping away everything false and trivial to reveal a common essence.

"Have you rendered the agent harmless?" the man asked. Alex nodded.

"Kim?" Garlitsky inquired.

"Yes. How did you ever get such an idea?"

He seemed not to notice the tone of the question.

"Too much time on my hands, Alex. You read old myths and can't help trying to fit the abilities of fairy-tale characters to real life. What can be created and what can't. What's useful, and what's not—"

Garlitsky stopped short.

"God will be your judge." Alex sat down nearby, right on the sand. Edward hadn't bothered creating another chair. "So you knew all about the plot?"

"It is impossible to know all, young man. Only in fairy tales does the hero gain omniscience and omnipotence." The geneticist smiled. "And there isn't anything good about that. For in much wisdom is much grief."

"I want to grieve."

Garlitsky sighed.

"Believe me, Alex Romanov, I had no part in that complexly planned provocation. But I did have some information about it. Not much . . ."

"Did Kim run into me by chance?"

"Of course."

"Did you know from the get-go that there was an agent aboard?"

"The thought did cross my mind. After the murder, I had no more doubts."

Alex shook his head.

"Still, it seems to me that you are lying."

"Why is that?" asked the geneticist with lively interest.

"Your reaction to the events was way too calm. You . . . it was like you knew everything in advance. Our every move."

"Young man, endure at least a couple of decades as an incorporeal but fully conscious shadow," said Garlitsky ironically. "You'll see how your idea of danger changes, and your reaction to it, as well. I got used to the thought that I might die at any moment—and that I wouldn't be able to do anything about it. These last few weeks, I've had the least worry ever about my survival."

"You are *that* sure of Kim's abilities?" Alex posed Sherlock Holmes's question.

"But of course I am!" Edward emphatically spread out his arms. "Is an architect-spesh sure of the house he built? Is a surgeon-spesh sure of his incision? Is a fighter-spesh sure of his marksmanship?"

"Kim isn't some brick in a wall. And you aren't a spesh. You're a spesh-creator."

"So what?" Garlitsky looked at him, uncomprehending. "There

have always, in any era, existed people who became speshes. Breaking their own bodies, reining in their spirit. Getting rid of one thing, adding another. Pity? Subtract pity. Intellect? Add intellect. Plus family—minus family. Plus friends—minus friends. Plus motherland—minus motherland! The entire life of a human is a continuous struggle for these pluses and minuses. People have spent decades of their short lives dashing this way and that, poisoning the existence of those around them, all to find their own combination of pluses and minuses. I removed these torments. From the cradle to the grave—all speshes are happy."

"Because you have forbidden them to add and subtract."

Edward laughed.

"Alex . . . Alex. I gave you an opportunity to decide everything anew. And? Are you happier?"

Alex was silent.

"You've lost the love, that wonderful love for your ship, that's given only to speshes. What did you get in return, Alex?"

No reply.

"Do you really think I am villainously withholding from humanity the remedy that returns their emotions to Old Testament norms? Come on! Humanity has always created everything for which there was a need. If there were a need, a blocker of altered emotions would have been created. And is it really all about the ethical factors that have been forced on them? You, for instance . . . you've taken the drug. Your artificially created kindness and sense of responsibility dissipated. So what prevented you, just a few minutes ago, from throwing my gel-crystal out into vacuum or frying it in a microwave?"

Alex looked him straight in the eye.

"I wasn't watching what was going on inside the ship," Edward added. "You've deprived me of the opportunity to do that. But I know people. You did want to put an end to me, right?"

"Yes. Because of what you've done to Kim. Because you took part in . . . I'm sure, one way or another, you took part in the conspiracy."

Garlitsky gave a few slow nods.

"Of course, of course. What I've done to Kim! Evil me! I've given her the gift of destiny—one of a great spy, provocateur, a lady of the demimonde, madly adored by both men and women. A person who will work for dozens of secret services. Books will be written about her, and movies made! People of power will order this kind of intriguing specialization for their children. Little girls will play, pretending to be Kim O'Hara. You can't even imagine what a fascinating life awaits this girl, Alex! Now she will help me gain a body, and then I will help her. We are both in for a most interesting life in this great and fascinating world! Although . . ." He raised his eyebrows. "You can change all that. Easily. I'd advise you to go the vacuum way—a fried gel-crystal reeks to high heaven, being organic after all. The stench will be too much like that of burnt human flesh. As for my participation in the conspiracy . . . you're also mistaken."

He got up, stretched, straightening his nonexistent body. Murmured:

"How I'd love to hear a creak in my sinews . . . hit a funny bone and feel the pain . . . or get a scratch . . . Well, what next, Alex? What will you do with me? Your murder blocks are off. You're fully in charge of your states of mind. Here it is—freedom!"

Alex got up from the sand, smiled bitterly, and nodded to Garlitsky before exiting the gel-crystal.

Forever.

Kim was sitting in the chair, flipping through the book he'd left on the table. When Alex took off the neuro-terminal, she smiled at him.

"Sorry to intrude—your door wasn't locked. Did you tell Edgar that everything was all right already?"

"No. I left it to you."

"Then let me . . ."

He silently handed her the crystal and the neuro-shunt. Kim winked at him, before putting her hand under her blouse to hide Edward Garlitsky's world in her own body. She said:

"I already turned in my report. Holmes said that in a couple of hours, when Janet finishes up the intensive treatment course for Sey-Zo, we'll go in for landing. And Xang wanted to know if you'd let him pilot the ship?"

"Everything's allowed now," Alex replied.

"Here, listen to this . . ." Kim threw a quick glance at the page, put the book aside. She really did have perfect photographic memory.

"No poems, please," said Alex.

"What?"

"I don't want poems now. Even if they're good."

"Are you mad at me for some reason?" asked Kim, after a pause.

"No, baby. Everything's all right."

"Really?"

"Tell me, are you still in love with me?"

She fell into thought.

"Don't worry, I won't get offended," said Alex. "You already know that pilot-speshes are incapable of love."

"Alex . . ." Kim did nevertheless jump off her armchair, sidle up to him, and hug him around the shoulders. "Alex, dearest. I'm so . . ."

She stopped, smiled apologetically, then finished the phrase she had started.

"I'm so grateful to you. You helped me through a very difficult and very painful time. When I was all alone against the whole world. It must be destiny—that we have met."

Alex hugged her. Kissed her hair, smelling of something warm, summery, floral. Gently, without any passion, to which he had no right anymore.

"I like to think that it really was destiny," he agreed.

"And I *so* wanted you to fall in love with me. The way I am. Inexperienced, stupid . . . I tried so very hard . . ."

"Forgive me."

Kim slid her hand along his cheek. A calm, assured gesture of a woman grown wise with experience.

"It's all right. I understand everything now! But you and I had fun, right?"

Alex smiled.

"Did we ever! 'Kitty scratch'—that was really something!"

Kim gave him a smacking little kiss on the cheek.

"Uh-huh. Well, I'll be going, okay, Alex? I need to talk to . . . and discuss all the details."

"Go ahead, baby."

He even walked her to the hallway door. Just seven steps—but a sign of respect, nevertheless. And slapped her on her behind so that she let out a happy little squeal.

"To hell with all of it . . ." said Alex, after the door had closed. He didn't finish his phrase. Rolled up the sleeve of his jersey, looked at the Demon.

The little devil was crouching, its head down on its knees, so that the face couldn't be seen.

Alex had no need for an emotion scanner now, but he was glad to see the Demon anyway. His old, trusted friend.

"We'll make it, buddy," he said. "Plenty of pretty girls in the galaxy, right?"

The little devil didn't stir. Alex walked up to the terminal.

"Connect to Janet Ruello's quarters."

"Blocked . . ." replied the service program in a regretful tone.

"Captain's access," said Alex, after a brief hesitation. "Unilateral surveillance."

A screen appeared.

Janet Ruello and Puck Generalov were sitting on the bed. Janet was naked. Puck was half-dressed.

"Still unpleasant?" asked Janet. She was holding Generalov's hand to her chest.

"I don't know . . . feels strange . . ." Puck heaved a deep sigh. "But why is it so big?"

"That's the way it's supposed to be," said Janet gently. "Relax."

"But you gotta understand, this is a perversion for me!" said Generalov piteously. "And then Kim . . . what she did . . . that was so . . ."

"My body is made much more simply," said Janet, soothingly

477

caressing his braid. "Trust me. You've been meaning to expand your life's experience? And now if we don't counter those negative impressions—all will be lost! I think we'd better start with something you're more accustomed to—"

Alex switched off the screen. Stood still for a second. And then burst out laughing. Said, to the Demon, or maybe to himself:

"So, the genetically altered emotions get blocked? Interesting..."

He lay down on the bed, yawned. Really wanted to take another look at the Demon—could it, too, appreciate the irony of the situation? Or was it still crouching there, hiding its tear-stained face?

But it made no difference, in the end.

AFTERWORD

This too was a sky.

From horizon to horizon stretched greenish-white oval leaves, drifting through the air at the height of about ten thousand feet.

Clouds, condensing to form a light mist under the giant lotuses, seemed to be fine pollen falling from the leaves. The city, sheltered from the deadly luminary by a living shield, was wrapped in mysterious shade. A glider gamboled high up, carefully avoiding the precious green cover. Sharp needles of skyscrapers seemed to bend, afraid to scratch the soft flesh of the plants. The slow drifting of the lotuses was almost imperceptible to the eye.

Alex gazed into the sky, and it was irregular.

Unprecedented.

"I never thought it would be beautiful," he said. "It looks as though an enormous dragon, with moss-covered scales, is hanging above the planet."

Only a vending machine near the hospital gates could hear these words. The bright little face of a holographic advertising screen frowned in puzzlement. Even if there were any moss or scales for sale, the electronic vendor prudently didn't offer them.

The quiet hospital lounge was as cozy and peaceful as any human hospital would be. The walls were painted in soft colors, the floors covered with a thick rug, the lights dimmed. Japanese or Japanese-style engravings depicted scenes from the life of the first planetary colonists.

Having approached an info-terminal, the pilot entered his identification and the goal of his visit.

"Alex Romanov, you are allowed a brief visit," politely reported the terminal. "Please wait to be escorted . . ."

"Jenny!" he cried, not listening to the rest of the robot's sentence. A woman, walking down the hall in an olive-colored robe, stopped, looked at the pilot in surprise.

A smile of astonishment lit up her face.

"We'll discuss this later, Yoko," she said to her companion, a very young girl with the features of a surgeon-spesh. The girl, not hiding her curiosity, looked the pilot over, lifted her eyebrows with a gentle, scoffing sound, and continued on her way.

"Alex? What . . ." The woman stopped short, then nodded, understanding. "She's quite all right. Our best doctors have been working on her."

"Maybe I've come to see you, rather than the Zzygou?"

"Very funny."

She shook her head, came closer to him.

"Honest."

"If you knew that I'd returned to the hospital. But I'll bet you didn't." Dr. Watson cocked her head. "Well, even if you did . . ."

A kind of awkward silence followed. The rainbow-colored streams of the fountain in the middle of the lounge sparkled. The water murmured softly. Two stern female nurse-speshes with expressions of deep concentration on their faces passed as quietly as ghosts in their soft shoes. A stretcher holding a moaning patient from the trauma ward rushed silently by. A young paramedic, sitting on a small collapsible side chair, was saying something soothing to the patient.

If this world had a less appropriate place for mutual teasing, it would surely be hard to find.

"Of course, I didn't know that. Forgive my bad joke." Alex bowed slightly and spread his arms in a gesture of apology. "Did you really get tired of being a detective's aide?"

Touching his hand, the woman softly prompted the pilot to follow her.

They had to submit to complete decontamination, even though human diseases were no threat to the patient. They were allowed to enter the ward only after a five-minute cycle and a thorough disinfection control. This patient was so special that the planetary government preferred to play it safe.

The naked body lying in the intensive care pod still resembled a human. Even the middle pair of limbs seemed to be some sort of practical joke, a trick of some unknown prankster. The wounded arms and legs looked normal already, though complete regeneration of the plasma-burnt sinews would, no doubt, take a while yet.

The Zzygou opened her eyes and looked at the visitors.

A barely noticeable semblance of a human smile appeared on her face. She probably was really pleased to see them. Or maybe the former companion of the princess just kept imitating human emotions?

"I've been trying to come see you for three days now. As soon as they let me out of the isolation room, I came to the hospital." Alex bowed apologetically.

"Fank you," said the representative of the alien race, perhaps the only one in the human territories now. Her tongue had already undergone a restoration course, but speaking remained difficult for her. "Zhe ozher appreciay you vizhi, shervan . . ."

Her smile turned the last word into bitter irony.

"We're always happy to serve you, Sey."

This was the name she was destined to go by, now that she had lost her senior companion. And probably for the rest of her life. She also would have to forsake the thought of an eventual return to the fold of her own civilization. The youthful "bees" always chose their life's direction and their companions once and for all. This was, perhaps, the very root of the strength, as well as the weakness, of their civilization.

Softly pushing the pilot aside, the former detective-spesh's aide silently walked up to the patient, checked a monitoring device, and nodded with satisfaction.

"Would you like me to tell you about what happened to the rest of the crew?" Alex somehow hoped that this would be an appropriate topic for conversation. "Are you interested? Well, the navigator, um, the male human with a braid and a painted face, has already got a job on another ship . . . and not alone, but with our female doctor."

Alex was glad to see a shadow of emotion on her weary, pain-wracked face.

"Shavage woma . . ."

Though barely able to move her tongue, she did, nonetheless, manage to express the strength of her feeling.

"Yes. That is, if we forget that she has saved your life."

"You're correkch, huma." Sey gave a feeble nod. "I harbor go anger. Zhe Ozherzh were her arch-foe. But she overpower her-shelf . . . Och everyong ish capabuh of zhach."

"O'Hara left in an unknown direction, having bought the crim-inal's body."

The alien wasn't interested in this fact, which meant so much to Alex. The young fighter-spesh, as well as the piece of meat into which the murderer had been turned, were already a past stage of Sey's life.

That is what always happens. Alex thought that between two individuals, even if they belong to the same race and culture, the names and words which are crucial to one person mean nothing to the other, and vice versa. It's such a peculiar thing—speech. After all, you can express anything orally, or on paper . . . But the prob-ability is high that you will be misunderstood.

Only a thin thread of words connects all intelligent beings into one whole, allowing them to understand each other. And what a shame it is when you try, over and over, to say something really important, but meet no understanding. The truth is always different for each person, so that a trifle of a joke might lead others to pay attention and take interest, while your pain and sorrow remain unaddressed. There are exceptions, of course, but they are monstrously rare.

"She became your firsh pashio, but way choo laich . . ." said Sey unexpectedly, half-closing her eyes. "We ofchen have zhach happeh, choo . . ."

"I don't know how you came to understand that, but thank you," the pilot replied. And then the former detective's aide bestowed a look upon him, the likes of which he had never known before. "The only person I don't know anything about . . ."

"Morrison went off to the sea. I've made my inquiries." Dr. Watson kept her surprised and intrigued eyes fixed upon him. "It may sound odd, but the pilot-spesh has decided to get into aquanautics. There is demand for dolphin herders, bathyscaphe drivers, and foresters to care for the lotuses. A very strange thing for a pilot to do . . . there was even a news report about it."

"Are you sure?"

"One hundred percent. That is, if his first name is Xang. Well, let's go, no need to tire out our guest—she's already dozing off . . ."

Quietly leaving the ward, they entered the hallway. Moved aside to let the same stretcher pass, carrying its patient.

"Eh-eh-eh . . ." mumbled the unconscious patient, and the paramedic was whispering into the walkie-talkie, "Yoko, please meet us in surgery room number seventeen, immediately. The patient's in serious condition . . ."

"The responsibility level must be as high here as it is in space," said Alex, glancing back at the patient. "It's nerve-wracking. Hard even on the doctors who are speshes—how do *you* handle it?"

"Are you considering becoming a doctor?" smiled his companion.

"Quite possibly . . . will they page you in to help?"

"Yoko'll manage. She's a capable girl, and a spesh, besides . . . Our hospital has hundreds of doctors. And I'm done with my shift for today."

"Are you free tonight?"

"Ah! Ten or so years ago, I would've been very flattered by such a question coming from an old space-wolf. Except my mom had warned me to never fall in love with pilots—they can't love back."

Alex answered, unruffled:

"But the thing is, I *can*."

"You're kidding?"

"Yes and no. Well, Yoko is a nice girl, too . . . but . . ." Stopping abruptly, the pilot embraced her. "She's not my type. It's you I like, and I'm rather afraid I'm falling in love."

Alex looked at her seriously, without a hint of a smile. The distrust in the woman's eyes began to fade.

"What's happened to you, Pilot? People like you should be shown off in a circus freak show! There'll be huge lines to get in. A spesh, a pilot-spesh, who is capable of love!"

"That's how it is. Of course, it didn't happen all at once." Alex was smiling, heartily enjoying her confusion. "Some thought that the sudden ability would fade away all by itself. If that had really happened, it would actually make my life easier. But alas, I'm still able to love."

Jenny mumbled in bewilderment:

"Alex, what you're saying is way too strange and serious . . ."

It must be difficult for a woman to continue arguing when a man she likes starts kissing her. Judging by Jenny's reaction, it was certainly so.

"Love is a strange thing—you feel it right away," said the pilot, taking his lips off hers for a moment.

"I sense that. But it's impossible!"

"If you doubt it, give me a trial period."

The hospital, as is customary, was located in the city's outskirts. From the gates, where some rental cars were parked, the two of them went on foot. Funny thing was—they didn't have to discuss this—they both felt like taking a stroll.

Alex gazed into the sky.

He may get to see perhaps hundreds of different planets, and he had seen quite a few already. Why, then, is each new sky so strange and wonderful? The fiery clouds of Omelia, the flying lotuses of Zodiac, the dust storms of Nangyala . . .

Alex said pensively:

"I think I'll remain a pilot, after all. So you'll have to master the work of a space doctor."

Dr. Watson laughed.

"Too bad my former boss can't hear you now. Of course, he would immediately start figuring out the causes of your weird behavior."

Alex shook his head.

"You know, I have a feeling he'll change jobs, too. Maybe he'll become a musician. If he hasn't already."

"What ever makes you say that?"

"Just a hunch."

An intrigue is an old weapon that never fails. Only now did the pilot realize what it really was to woo a woman—to entice, to attract, to seek her love . . . instead of abandoning himself to quick and carefree sex. If this was part of love—he liked it.

"Seems like you need help outside of my professional scope. My friend Olga is a great psychotherapist-spesh, and she won't charge much. Would you like me to write you a referral? By the end of the year, you'll be as good as new." Dr. Watson was smiling, but she was serious.

"This disorder she won't be able to cure."

Dr. Watson looked into his eyes for a long time before she realized that he was telling the truth.

How far away the sky seems, when you're lying on the grass . . .

The woman's naked body, her scent, her arms, her timid, wandering kisses . . .

The sky covered them with thousands of drifting lotuses—a living and tender blanket. If you pull it aside, there won't be only the scorching light of the white sun, there will also be stars.

A whole sky full of stars.

ABOUT THE AUTHOR

Sergei Lukyanenko was born in Kazakhstan, then a republic of the Soviet Union. In 1985 he entered the Alma-Ata Medical University, where he began to write science fiction and publish his first books. Though Lukyanenko completed his medical course, he realized that he would never be a doctor. In 1997 he moved to Moscow, and since then has published prolifically. Many of his works have become bestsellers and have won science fiction awards. Night Watch and Day Watch were released as films in 2004 and 2006, respectively. Lukyanenko's writing has been translated into more than twenty languages and continues to be hugely popular.

OPEN ROAD
INTEGRATED MEDIA

Open Road Integrated Media is a digital publisher and multimedia content company. Open Road creates connections between authors and their audiences by marketing its ebooks through a new proprietary online platform, which uses premium video content and social media.

Videos, Archival Documents, and New Releases

Sign up for the Open Road Media newsletter and get news delivered straight to your inbox.

Sign up now at
www.openroadmedia.com/newsletters

FIND OUT MORE AT
WWW.OPENROADMEDIA.COM

FOLLOW US:
@openroadmedia and
Facebook.com/OpenRoadMedia

CPSIA information can be obtained at www.ICGtesting.com
Printed in the USA
BVOW07s0059301014

372585BV00002B/1/P